Stories from MacKenzie Street

GOD'S AMAZING GRACE
UNFOLDS IN STORY

The Choosing

By
JIM AND TERRI KRAUS

BARBOUR
PUBLISHING

© 2004 by Jim and Terri Kraus

ISBN 1-59310-104-X

Cover Image © Corbis and Getty Images

Acquisitions and Editorial Director: Rebecca Germany
Editorial Consultant: Ramona Cramer Tucker
Art Director: Jason Rovenstine
Layout Design: Anita Cook

Published by Barbour Publishing, Inc., P.O. Box 719, Uhrichsville, OH 44683, www.barbourbooks.com

Our mission is to publish and distribute inspirational products offering exceptional value and biblical encouragement to the masses.

Member of the
Evangelical Christian
Publishers Association

Printed in the United States of America.
5 4 3 2 1

One

Chicago, Illinois

TUCKER ABBOTT SAT AT THE EDGE
of the couch in his suite of small rooms. With an indelible laundry pen, he carefully wrote his name and new address on the stiff canvas collar of his new green duffel. Then he filled the bag with his laundry, threaded the clasp through the holes, and buckled the bag shut. He lifted it once to test its weight.

Not too heavy—since it's only been a few days.

He checked to see if there might be something else he should gather. While the inventory didn't take long, he did decide, as he glanced around his bedroom, to take one of the books from his nightstand.

There were two books on the table, under the tiny lamp with the shade that wouldn't remain level no matter how many times Tucker attempted to straighten it. He hefted each of the books, as if testing for the weight of their words.

In his right hand, he held a recent biography—thick and massive—of Martin Luther. Tucker found the writing deep and nearly impenetrable. The work came highly recommended, with a full page of plaudits by well-known scholars glowing on the back cover. Each scholar's name was followed by an alphabet of degrees—many of them from seminaries Tucker had once considered attending.

The other book, a paperback, newly purchased only a week prior in the Minneapolis airport, displayed a metallic cover with a title so glossy it appeared to have been varnished. Thick red letters on the back cover shouted out: TERROR AT 40,000 FEET! There were no scholars on this book—just a flinty picture of the author in a worn jacket with dozens of pockets.

Tucker grimaced. After a second or two of internal debate, he slipped the biography of Luther into the duffel and resnapped the catch. He could almost hear the voice of his mother, clear and pleading.

"You need to be deliberate, young man. Maybe someone will see you reading a good book and they'll ask you about it. That might be an opening. . . . You have to plan for that and never leave an opportunity to share to chance."

Tucker offered a wry, nearly sad smile. It was a certainty no one would ask him about the Luther book—especially with the stern and very unsmiling portrait of the theologian on the cover.

Owatonna, Minnesota

Mrs. Abbott stood by the front door, almost as if she were expecting her son to return. She stepped out onto the small landing and

4

looked down the street. The elms had just begun to turn, and a scattering of yellow leaves rustled along the sidewalk, hastened by a short breeze.

Chicago is so far away, Mrs. Abbott thought. *Not like Northfield—or even Minneapolis.*

She patted at her hair, making sure the wind hadn't ruffled it from its proper place. She sighed at the sight of the empty street. She had been so certain when she and her husband sat Tucker down and explained the dangers of Chicago that their only son would be forced to reconsider.

But he didn't.

She waited outside for several more minutes, then stepped back inside the house and carefully locked the door behind her.

Chicago, Illinois

It was just September and still warm. Tucker left his light jacket in the closet and carefully locked the door to his apartment. He removed the key and jiggled the doorknob a few times, making sure it was secure. He pushed on the door to check if somehow the latch might slip open with a shoulder pressed against the jamb.

Habits observed for a lifetime were hard to escape.

The door and its lock held firm. Tucker slipped the duffel under his arm and adjusted the strap on his shoulder.

The short, swarthy fellow—the one with a narrow, pinched face and nearly black eyes—in the apartment across the hall had provided directions to the nearest Laundromat, or had at least attempted to. It had taken Tucker several minutes to convey that he needed to find a place to wash clothing. Afterward, he felt as if he were playing charades in a strange country where both English and the concept of doing one's laundry were completely foreign.

But Tucker had heard the name "MacKenzie Street" several times, and he thought he'd heard the word "north." He had proceeded to fetch his neatly folded map of the city of Chicago, and his neighbor had traced with his finger the route Tucker would need to take to find this Laundromat. Then the swarthy fellow had jabbed at an intersection several times with great enthusiasm, smiling and nodding and repeating a string of words that Tucker could make no sense of whatsoever.

To Tucker's relief, MacKenzie didn't appear to be a long street—only six blocks from the looks of it. He peered constantly at the street sign on the corner at the end of each block, worried that somehow the name would change as he traveled north. His parents' fussings and warnings, issued just a week prior to his departure, echoed loudly in Tucker's memory.

The two of them, knees pressed together, had perched on their green sofa in the front room of the compact house on the north side of Owatonna, Minnesota.

Tucker had thirty-four years of experience listening to such warnings. His parents had warned him of the dangers of attending college in Minneapolis. They had warned him, biannually for six years, of the dangers of living and working in that big city. Even when he finally listened to his mother and enrolled at a seminary twenty miles from home, they continued to issue monthly warnings.

After a time, Tucker stopped hearing them altogether.

The stoplight turned yellow as the images of those last few days in his hometown replayed themselves in Tucker's thoughts.

"You don't have to go to Chicago to serve God," his father had argued. *"He's right here in Minnesota, as well, Tucker. I'm sure He's here*

in Owatonna. You can change your mind. I'm sure they'll understand."

"*Chicago is dangerous,*" his mother had said. "*Ralph down at the Dollar General said that the North Side—where this church of yours is supposed to be—is the mugging capital of the upper Midwest.*" At these words, Tucker's mother had blanched white. She had practiced blanching for years.

Traffic stopped. Tucker looked both ways and hurried across the busy street. If his calculations were correct, MacKenzie Street lay three blocks farther east, toward the lake. He had seen Lake Michigan sparkle and glisten as his plane from Minnesota had banked and turned and rolled toward O'Hare.

The lake, at least what he could see of it, was bigger than he'd thought. And the water was colored a deeper blue than he had imagined.

MacKenzie Street did indeed lay three streets over. Tucker smiled and congratulated himself for having successfully navigated this simple journey in the complicated city of Chicago. In the four days he had lived here, his trips thus far had consisted of going to the church, the Aldi supermarket, and a small restaurant a block from the church.

He craned his neck to the south, then to the north. For some reason, he thought a Laundromat might be located more easily north than south, so he set off in that direction.

A block and a half farther north, he found himself looking up at a slowly flashing sign: WASH-DRY-FOLD.

He knew the wash and dry part but was unsure about the folding.

He found himself shaking his head as he talked to himself. *Of course I know what folding means—but does that mean* they *fold it? Do they have to fold? Does it cost extra? Do I want them to fold* everything?

Then he squared his shoulders. Without thinking further about implications, without thinking about the possibility of a stranger folding his clothes, without thinking about not having the right change, without thinking about feeling like an intruder, he opened the wooden screen door.

They have wooden screen doors in Chicago?

The door slapped closed behind him as he stepped inside. Though he didn't remind himself to smile, there was a smile, wide and comfortable, on his face.

Above the dryers, done with more artistry than graphic practicality, was a series of signs on painter's canvas. The signs listed, with curling flourishes, the cost of each machine, how to load, how long cycles lasted, what to do if clothes remained in machines with no one about, when to add soap, how to get change, what to do in case of malfunction.

One sign was in English. Tucker recognized Spanish on another, but the last two may have been Polish or Ukrainian or Russian or some language other than English or German—the only two languages Tucker had acquaintance with.

As he read through the rules, he lowered his duffel to the floor. It took only minutes to find empty machines, to sort his clothing according to color and shrink resistance. His mother had been such a stickler for never, ever mixing dirty clothes in inappropriate ways. And many of her ways had been ingrained in Tucker over the years.

He had set out that day with premeasured detergent in plastic bags and now emptied them precisely into each unit. He took quarters out of his pocket, counted them out, selected water temperatures, and started each machine.

Then he folded the duffel, took his book under his arm, and selected one of the plastic chairs arranged in a row by the front window, overlooking the street.

This is nice. Turning his chair parallel to the street and the bank of washers, Tucker laid the book in his lap and opened it, careful not to break the spine. He allowed himself a few seconds of feeling neatly smug with satisfaction—but not too long. At home he'd been taught that being prideful or smug was a sin but that humility about one's self was the closest thing to godliness.

By now Tucker had read for quite some time, yet had not finished an entire page. As pedestrians passed by the window, he would look up—not with obvious curiosity, since that would be rude, but with an intensity he hoped he kept hidden. Chicago was a big city—huge when compared to his hometown of Owatonna. And the city had so many people, almost all of them different than the people back home.

While he watched the street and the passersby, he listened to the rumblings and sloshings of his three washing machines. He knew that back home a full cycle took up to a half hour—the extra-dirty cycle added fifteen minutes for an additional wash and rinse. Perhaps commercial machines accomplished the same task more quickly.

Tucker glanced at his reflection in the round window of the washer. Not pleased or displeased with the image, he stared a moment. Scrutinizing his warbly reflection seemed less prideful than perusing his image in a mirror. His sandy brown hair had been cut short and was parted on the left. One couldn't tell the color of his eyes from the image in the window, but his driver's license listed them as brown. He saw them as green-brown, but that was not a color the state of Minnesota recognized.

Tucker wasn't tall, nor was he short. An inch and a half under six feet left him feeling average in most situations. He blinked at his reflection. His was not a face that was truly memorable—at least in his considerations. He would, when feeling charitable, describe himself as pleasant, even moderately attractive. His features were neither chiseled nor rounded, but pleasantly in between.

He smiled, thinking he would never be one who would be easily picked out in a police lineup—even though he could never imagine being in a police lineup.

The glassed-in room at the rear of the Laundromat was deserted when Tucker first looked. It appeared to be an office, but Tucker wasn't sure if a Laundromat required an office. As he read and reread the same paragraph at the bottom of page 105 concerning Luther's father's uncle's role in the town government in Eisleben, his eyes caught some movement—small, gray, indistinct—in the dark space that might have been an office.

Maybe it's a rat.

After all, this was a big city, and that was another story his parents had related in fearful urgency.

"The rats in Chicago are as big as cats," his father had claimed. *"They call them 'super rats' since even rat poison doesn't kill them—they can eat it all day and feel fit as a fiddle."*

But this particular gray furry object moved lazily and deliberately, with no rodentlike scurrying.

Tucker found his bookmark, slipped it between the open pages, placed the closed book on his chair, and covered it with the folded laundry bag. Then he walked toward the back of the room. He tapped at the glass, and presently a very furry, very weary-looking cat peered out at him through the panes. The animal stared at Tucker's finger, then smooched his nose against that point as if to rub against the indentation in the glass.

"How are you? You want to be scratched? Come here, boy," Tucker said softly. The cat fell to its side with a hollow *thump* on the cluttered desk under the window, as if Tucker might reach through the glass and rub the offered exposed belly.

The door at the rear of the office swung wider. Tucker stood up, embarrassed, as if he were intruding on some private moment, some private space. A young woman, blond and slight, perhaps midway through her twenties or a few years older than that, bounced into the room. "Petey! Where are you? You're wanted up-stairs for pictures," she called out.

The cat meowed reluctantly as the young woman scooped him up in her arms. Shaking her long bangs away from her eyes, she glanced up and smiled at Tucker. He was aware the woman held a red-and-white paper hat in one hand, but he noticed more her gently rounded face and full lips.

The young woman stared at him, evaluating his features and his form, as Tucker grew more and more uncomfortable. When she finally spoke, he nearly exhaled a huge sigh of relief.

"You're new here, aren't you? I haven't seen you in here before. And I think I know just about every customer."

Tucker wanted to turn around and make sure she wasn't talk-ing to someone else. A pretty woman conversing with him was rare—enough so that he found it intimidating.

"Uhhh. . .yes. It's the first time I've been in here." He took a deep breath, trying to look like he wasn't taking a deep breath. "I just moved to Chicago. I'm Tucker Abbott."

The young woman gave him an innocent yet knowing smile. "Well, Tucker Abbott, I'm Cass Fowler," she said as she hoisted the cat under her arm. "And this is Petey the Cat. We're both wanted upstairs. Petey here was bad and ran off without taking his birthday hat with him."

With a deft move, she slipped the red-and-white hat over the cat's head and snugged the elastic band under his chin. Never was a cat unhappier and more resigned to his fate than the gray fuzzy cat tucked under this young woman's arm, Tucker thought.

She half-turned, then stopped. "Would you like a piece of birthday cake, Mr. Abbott? We have plenty. Seeing how you're new here and all."

Tucker smiled. "That would be nice. I believe I would like a piece of cake."

A wail echoed down the steps. It was the wail of a young boy. "Petey!"

Cass pushed an errant hair behind her left ear. "That's our cue. I'll be back with your cake. Promise."

He tried not to stare as she hurried up the steps, but he did anyway, knowing no one was watching. He felt an odd rattling in his heart, as if somehow his future hinged on this one precise moment.

Tucker stood by the window for several minutes, not exactly sure if he was supposed to wait for his cake right there or if he was free to roam about the rest of the Laundromat while waiting for his promised dessert. He blinked toward the dim stairs leading up and away from where he now stood.

He listened for the sound of the washers and, not hearing them, wondered how long they had been silent. Hurrying his damp clothes to two dryers, he inserted his quarters and selected the medium-heat setting. His mother had given him enough warnings of the dangers of high heat, but he didn't consider any of his clothes to be at risk of shrinking. And he certainly didn't want to hang any clothing out to dry, except perhaps the blue denim shirt he'd purchased on his last trip to the Mall of America. That had been three weeks before he departed the state of Minnesota and "abandoned" his parents, to use their wording.

The warm tumblings started and he paused. *Should I go over by the window and wait? Did she really mean she would be right back? Maybe she was just being nice.*

He decided that waiting in the chair, even with an open book, would be acceptable. So he began to read. . .and surprised himself by getting through a score of pages. The dryers slowed, then groaned to a stop. Tucker busied himself with folding his clothes, patting them flat and according to crease. He was pleased that the Laundromat provided clean wide tables for the task. In short order everything was precisely folded and stacked, according to density and weight, then placed in the duffel.

Tucker wondered if he should wait for another minute or two now that he had finished. That young woman had said she'd return soon. And he wasn't averse to at least offering his thanks and a good-bye. Before he came to Chicago, had he not vowed to be more open to new experiences? He waited a moment longer, then stood. After all, he was done with his laundry, and if he was done, he should be on his way.

Just as he hoisted the bag to his shoulder, he saw a flurry of movement from the dark hallway and steps, moving into the office at the rear of the Laundromat.

"Oh, I'm so glad you're still here, Mr. Abbott. Things got a bit more hectic than I imagined."

Cass stood at the bottom of the stairs. She held a small paper plate with a ragged triangle of chocolate cake.

"I suspect a hat on a cat is not a good idea, despite what Dr. Seuss says—especially in a room filled with very loud four-year-olds. It took Daniel and me forever to pry Petey off the top of the curtains in the front room."

Tucker heard the name *Daniel* and, without cause, felt a stab of something akin to jealousy in his heart—then wondered with shame and amazement at those unexpected emotions. "That's okay," he replied, forgiving all for her smile. "I wasn't waiting for. . . I mean, I know. . .or imagined. . .that you had your hands full."

If asked, he would have described the young woman's expression as a pout—a happy, deliberate pout.

"But I promised, Mr. Abbott, and I keep my promises."

Tucker stepped to the open door and took the cake. She watched as he took his first forkful.

"This is delicious," he said.

"Thanks. We didn't really make it from scratch. It was a box cake. Our birthday boy specifically requested the flavor as well as the brand name."

Cass moved a stack of papers to the side and sat on the desk. Tucker felt as if she were observing him as he ate, so he did so carefully. He finished with a smile and deposited the plate in a nearby garbage can. "Thanks so much. I do like chocolate cake."

An energetic clumping sounded on the stairs, and both Cass and Tucker turned toward it. It was the sound of a man's footsteps. Tucker first noticed the shiny shoes. After all, Tucker's mother wouldn't let him out of the house in scuffed shoes. This fellow's shoes were shiny, almost patent-leather shiny. He was middling tall and perhaps, Tucker thought, in his late thirties. He had a brilliant smile.

"Well, Cass, gotta be going. Great party."

Cass smiled back. "Daniel, this is Tucker Abbott. He's new in the area. Tucker, this is Daniel Trevalli."

Tucker held out his hand, and Daniel grabbed it enthusiastically. Tucker decided this fellow had to be Italian; he had dark looks, dark hair, and dark eyes. Even though Tucker hadn't known any Italians personally, there had been one family who lived down the block when he was seven—and they'd had a similar odd-sounding name. But that had been a long time ago, and Tucker had no recollection if they had the same smoldering look.

"Tucker Abbott—now why is that name familiar?" Daniel mused.

Tucker reacted with a mystified look. "I. . .I don't know. I'm from Minnesota."

Daniel eyed him, then Cass. Suddenly he snapped his fingers and pointed his index finger at his own temple. "You're the new guy at the church, right? I heard they were going to get a new guy. When you said Minnesota, that did it. I mean, how many people from Minnesota move here every day? Not many, I bet. I remembered the name. That's what triggered it. The name was different somehow. Tucker Abbott. Yeah, that was it. That's right, isn't it? Am I right, or what? You *are* the new guy, right?"

Tucker waited until the words stopped pouring, then said, "You're talking about the Webster Avenue Church?"

Daniel nodded with vigor.

"Then I am that new guy. I start on Monday. I mean, officially on Monday. I have already stopped in a couple of times."

Cass brightened. "You're the new associate pastor? Pastor Yount has gone on and on about you. People have been talking all about it. Have your ears been burning?"

"I guess. . . ."

Daniel stepped out of the office. "I'm already late so I'm heading out, blondie. Tell Annie I'm taking off, would you? She was so busy with that pack of kids that she wasn't paying attention to me at all." He gestured to Tucker. "You need a ride? I'm heading up north. Or did you drive over here?"

Tucker shook his head. "No. I walked. It's only a few blocks south of here. And west, I guess—on Wells. Thanks for the offer, but I think I'll walk back. Get to know the area and all."

Daniel pointed his index finger at Tucker like a gun. "Gotcha." He waved to them both as he hurried out the front door.

Tucker waited a minute, then turned back to Cass. "Thank you for the cake. It was nice of you."

Cass beamed. She took hold of Tucker's forearm. "It was my pleasure. And I guess I'll see you Sunday." She lowered her voice to a pleasing whisper. "I go to your church, so please don't do anything bad—or I'll have to tell your boss. And if you do anything bad, don't let me see it, okay?"

Tucker smiled broadly in return. "There's not much chance of that happening. I mean—of me doing something bad. I'm not the type, I guess."

"One never knows, Mr. Tucker Abbott. One never knows." Cass tilted her head and giggled as if she heard the faint hint of regret in Tucker's voice.

Above the Laundromat, Annie Hamilton sat amid the wrapping paper and bows and napkins, tossed like autumn leaves in the wind. For the first time that day, the apartment was quiet. Chance, just turned four, was down for his nap. It had taken Annie nearly thirty minutes to get him settled. Cass had left a few minutes earlier, saying she was heading downtown. Even Petey the Cat was sleeping in a pile of red and white paper.

It had been a good party. A "Cat in the Hat" party. Chance loved it. His little friends seemed to love it. There had been a lot of screaming and shouting and only two episodes of angry tears. That was a significant accomplishment with a bunch of four-year-olds, Annie knew.

16

Annie was grateful for Cass's help. She'd been surprised when Danny had made an appearance. Earlier in the week, he had dropped off a gift for Chance, claiming that one child was fine, but a gaggle of them made him nervous. But something must have changed his mind. So Annie had become the party director, and Danny and Cass had done great work with the cake and refreshments.

She pursed her lips as she sat.

Midway through her son's party, Annie had hurried into the kitchen and found Danny and Cass in an animated conversation. Danny was standing much closer to Cass than Annie would have liked, both acting as friendly as could be. Annie had stopped short, and both Danny and Cass had taken an immediate guilty step apart. Danny had looked over at Annie, but his eyes had indicated nothing—as if there was no explanation needed.

That's ridiculous, she told herself after she replayed the scene several times in her mind. *Danny is much too old for Cass. I mean— he has to be at least fifteen years older than her.*

Annie picked up a loose bow that had been wedged between the seat cushions.

He is much too old.

And so she agreed with herself that their playful conversation hadn't amounted to anything. It was nothing to be concerned about.

They were just having a good time. It was a birthday party, after all.

Annie knew she had no claim over Danny, despite the fact that they had been "dating" for some time now—since Chance was two years old. Theirs was a casual relationship, though both knew that Annie would have preferred a more solid definition. Danny would stop by occasionally, and Annie would wish it were more often.

But she couldn't shake the niggling feeling that something had changed that day in their relationship.

Two

THE KEYS TO THE CHURCH WERE the heaviest and most numerous that Tucker had ever carried. He couldn't recall ever having more than three keys on his key ring at any one time. One, painted with a spot of red enamel, was for the front door of his family's home in Owatonna. The second had been the ignition key to his car—a 1992 Ford Escort with a badly rusted passenger side door, recently sold to his cousin over in Blooming Prairie. He carried a single key to his small apartment for the first six years he worked leasing cars in Northfield. The last key was an odd-shaped brass key to his dorm room at the Faribault Lake Seminary.

Pearl Hasse, the wiry mid-fifties office manager of Webster Avenue Church, rattled off the identity of each key in rapid succession. "The one with the blue tint—that's for the nursery—the north side doors. The one with the green tint—that's for the equipment storage in the multipurpose room." She went on for several minutes, holding up each key individually from the ring of dozens of keys.

"Why isn't there a master key?" Tucker asked.

Pearl shot him a look of incredulity. Instead of answering the question, she finished with a flourish. "This red key is to the front door of the church—the one on the south side. And the other red key is for your office."

My office. Tucker loved the sound of those words. He'd never had an office before. He had built a bunk bed above his desk in seminary that was as dark as it was cramped. He'd used a board across two filing cabinets for a desk in his bedroom at home.

He had reported to work at Webster Avenue Church early Monday morning. It was now Wednesday, and he was finally being given his official set of keys.

"You should probably have them with you all the time," Pearl advised. "Someone is always locked out of something around here. Especially on Sunday mornings."

Tucker only half-listened. He was anxious to get to his office and unlock his door by himself for the first time.

"And don't lose them," she said.

Tucker would have described it as a snarl, but rarely did anyone in Minnesota snarl—especially in a church.

"Four years ago we had an intern from. . .I forget. . .some school in Arkansas or Alabama. I never understood half of what he was saying, and when I did, he took so long to say it that it drove me nuts. Well, he went and *lost* his set of keys! Can you imagine that, Mr. Abbott? He lost them. And then he expected us to replace all the locks. Like that was a simple thing to do. Well, we didn't. But what I made him do. . .well, I didn't *make* him do it. . .I don't have that authority. But I strongly suggested that he make his bed here in church for the next few weeks in case somebody found the keys and tried using them in our locks and stealing everything that isn't nailed down. And that's what he did.

For the last month, he was here. Slept here and made sure one of those street people didn't slip and pretend this place was theirs for the asking."

Surprised, Tucker waited. He didn't think he had ever met anyone who talked as fast as Pearl. Pearl appeared too petite of a woman to maintain that sort of verbal velocity for a sustained period.

"So?" she asked.

Obviously Pearl isn't accustomed to silence in response, Tucker thought. "So?" he asked. Not sure why she chose that word, he decided to repeat it back to her.

"So. . .you're not going to lose them, are you?"

Tucker straightened up. He immediately shook his head in an emphatic no. "I will guard them with my life, Miss Hasse. I will seldom, if ever, allow them to leave my sight or my person. Do you think I should take them in the shower with me?" This somewhat adolescent response from his mouth came as a shock to Tucker. *Has my brain given up control?*

But Pearl Hasse appeared to be immune from such remarks. She did, however, narrow her eyes much as a mother might do with a precocious toddler. Then she softened. Perhaps she actually believed him, thinking he was sincere in guarding the keys with his life.

"Good," she harrumphed. "Now, I'm busy. Since Linda retired, I have more than my share of work to do, unlike some people around here."

Tucker didn't ask who those slackers on the church staff might be. Instead he watched, with as much awe as fear, as she hurried down the hall and took a sharp right, leaning hard into the turn, like a sprinter on a tight track.

Then he stepped into his office. There was a desk under the window that overlooked the alley and a small thicket of volunteer trees, each jostling for position in a patch of earth. All of the trees leaned to the east, their leaves and branches spread out in supplication toward the morning sun.

Tucker guessed his office might have been a storeroom once. Lurking beneath the odor of new paint was a disinfectant smell, perhaps from cartons of cleaning supplies stored there for decades.

He shrugged and set his new briefcase on the desk. He had bought the briefcase from a luggage store in the Mall of America. It was a gift from Tucker to himself. He had never carried a briefcase before. It had always been backpacks. But he was sure that a backpack was not the image Webster Avenue Church would want.

The walls of his office were painted a warm gray, and the window was covered with a new set of white horizontal blinds. The old wood desk was the color of thick honey. The desk had been used hard, with a profusion of nicks and scratches as ample evidence. The varnish was worn smooth in places. The church had purchased a new desk chair—a fancy model that adjusted in more ways than Tucker knew how to sit—and a brace of visitors' chairs.

The hardwood floor was badly in need of refinishing, but Tucker supposed covering it with an inexpensive area rug would suffice. His computer, promised during his final interview with the elder board, would be arriving at the end of the week.

The walls, save for a picture of Jesus, were clear of all ornamentation. Tucker wanted new pictures or posters but wasn't certain what kind. He hadn't made any demands when he'd been hired, and that included decorating allowances. Perhaps he could find a poster shop or a nearby Target. He'd find something to make this space his own.

He thumbed the snaps on his briefcase, and the latches barked open. After retrieving the two legal pads, two pens, and his personal-sized Bible, he shut the briefcase and set it to the side of his desk.

Placing the legal pads at a precise angle, he brushed off a scattering of imaginary dust and flattened his palms against the desk. He waited a long minute, then exhaled loudly, the sound of finality and achievement.

Tucker closed his eyes. He could see himself as a seven-year-old boy in an ill-fitting dark suit, purchased that summer at Allen's Clothery. The fabric had gathered loosely about his shoulders and arms and knees, for it would have to last at least two full seasons. His Sunday shoes were shiny, black, and uncomfortable. He could hear the gravelly sound they made as he made his way up the flagstone walkway and steep steps of the church. He could feel himself covered by the shadow of the steeple of the Settler's Ridge Bible Church. Then, once inside, in the damp, hushed silence, he'd sit on the cool, hard wood pews and peer up and over to the pulpit. It was lit in the mornings by a square ray of sunlight that passed through the stained-glass window's kaleidoscope of colors at the rear of the church. He recalled the soothing baritone of the pastor, a short man with intense dark eyes. Pastor Gilbert Ringhofer's words calmed and lifted, as if the sounds of heaven were filtered through that deep voice.

At a young age, Tucker had wanted to be that man. Even more, he was certain his mother wanted him to be that man—the one who stood in the raised pulpit, arms lifted up to the heavens. The person who could simply nod toward the organist to begin the throaty rumblings of the doxology, covering every soul with dulcet tones of tradition and history.

It had taken two decades of work and planning and nagging and nudging and dreaming to get to where he was now. Tucker blinked his eyes open and focused on the reproduction of the stern-faced Jesus, nailed too high on the wall, nearly two feet above the light switch.

And then he smiled.

He was where he wanted to be—finally.

Slowly, he slid his hands from the desk and placed them, folded, across his chest. As he leaned back into his chair, the new springs squealed gently.

A wide smile appeared on his face. It was almost a perfect world.

Tucker had carefully selected his suit and tie this particular morning, his first occasion to stand before the congregation of Webster Avenue Church. He had three suits to choose from, but he didn't agonize over this decision. He immediately picked the dark suit, the one with the fine gray lines—perfect for weddings, funerals, and job interviews. Instead of the suggestion made by the owner of Allen's Clothery—the dark red tie—he had chosen the light yellow one.

"You wear the red-striped or the blue-striped with the dark suit. More color than that and you'll look like one of those advertising people you see on your television," Mr. Allen had said.

Tucker hadn't been sure to whom Mr. Allen had been referring but figured that since the elderly man had more than fifty years in the clothing business, he must know something about style and color.

However, today the yellow tie with the small blue dots looked more cheerful to Tucker. So, after a short internal debate, he slipped it under the collar of his starched white shirt.

Now, during the first Sunday service, as he sat in one of the two large chairs off to the side of the platform, Tucker regretted his choices. He scanned the crowd and saw only the occasional sport coat. The ties were evidently worn by older men who believed that, while not technically a sin, not wearing a tie to church was close enough to make them nervous.

Tucker was overdressed in his somber suit and jaunty tie. Yet it was the outfit that best matched Pastor Yount's.

The music of the prelude echoed to silence. A sawing of coughs and the rustle of bulletin paper quickly filled the gap. Pastor Yount pushed himself up from his chair and strode to the pulpit. He grasped both sides and boomed out a "Welcome and good morning!"

A reply warbled back from the congregation.

"Well, we're glad that you're here today," Pastor Yount continued. "This is the first day in a long time that I could use the word *we* up here since our new associate pastor is on board with us this morning, after all these months."

Pastor Yount turned to face Tucker.

Tucker felt nervous. He worried that he might be near the brink of breaking a sweat.

"Tucker Abbott—meet the congregation," Pastor Yount said as he swept his arm in a circle, indicating the entire church seated out there in the pews. "Come on up here, son."

Tucker stood quickly, now closer to panic. This was not on the agenda! He was supposed to stand later and read the preprinted announcements. He had read through them so many times that he probably could have done it without notes. Pastor Yount had said nothing about an introduction before that time.

He glanced down at the bulletin in his hand.

It's not on the schedule!

"Come on," Pastor Yount cajoled. "We only have an hour up here. I understand there is some sort of football game on today at noon. We keep these fine people longer than that. . .and, well, you know what they say about Chicago sports fans."

No, I don't know what they say about Chicago sports fans. No one told me anything about this, Tucker thought to himself as his emotions rolled and pitched. Laughter rippled through the congregation. It sounded like honest laughter and not the forced, polite laughter that often occurs in church.

Somehow Tucker's legs were able to move, and he soon found himself beside Pastor Yount. The younger man put out a hand to the pulpit, almost as a gesture of steadying himself.

"This is Tucker Abbott," Pastor Yount continued. "Comes by way of the Faribault Lake Seminary. A fine school. . .they turned me down a number of years ago—so they must have pretty high standards."

The older pastor winked, and more polite laughter rippled through the church. Pastor Yount then placed his arm around the young man's shoulders. "So, Tucker, I know I said I was going to introduce you later. . .right after the collection, but let's do it now. Tell us about yourself."

Tucker's mind went blank.

Pastor Yount had Tucker's two-paragraph resume in his notes—the bare essentials about Tucker's life and schooling and family. He was supposed to read that. Tucker was to have nothing to do with his introduction.

Tucker looked at Pastor Yount and saw from the older man's expression he was certainly not treating this request as a joke. Obviously, he expected Tucker to speak.

Tucker gazed out over the congregation. A sea of expectant faces greeted him—smiles on some, frowns on a few, thinner noncommittal smiles on most. Those in the back rows were too far away to judge.

Tucker faced forward and cleared his throat. Something

released inside, like a snap being loosened. . .as if a gentle yet firm restraint were suddenly lifted. He'd never felt that sort of quick freedom before. It was not in Tucker's family to feel loose. But his family, with all its snaps and tighteners, was very, very far away, and the distance was freeing.

Amazingly, the pulpit began to feel most comfortable. Tucker smiled. "How many of you know where Wanamingo is?"

Silently, he counted to five. He knew it was an odd question—not the sort of question one begins an introduction with. He knew his mother and father would have winced and averted their eyes had they been there. They had been invited, but it was a long drive—over six hours—and "neither one of us is getting any younger, you know." That had been his father's response. He had never really said that they wouldn't be there, just that "it is a really, really long drive."

"No one? How many know where Owatonna is?"

A handful of people raised their hands.

"How many of you knew where Owatonna was before I applied for this job?"

All raised hands fell.

It was obvious to Tucker that geography was not this group's strong point. Tucker had made map-reading a favorite hobby. He could sit with a good *Rand-McNally Road Atlas* and spend hours with each individual state. His favorites were the Dakotas—huge stretches of open land with one- and two-lane roads winding through, connecting towns represented by the smallest black circle that the map legend allowed.

He wondered, as he traced the routes between Tuttle and Wing, if anyone lived on that tiny red road, if there were farms or gas stations, or did the prairie echo in its emptiness? He envisioned a single car, a single driver without a companion, rumbling down the road, the tires echoing off the rough macadam, cutting through the crisp, clean air.

Tucker scanned the church and grinned. "Well, then, that's good. There will be no preconceptions about me—since no one knows where I came from. Not like all of you here in Chicago. I was warned about you. In Owatonna we knew what you folks in Chicago were like."

The congregation responded with that polite laugh. For Tucker, it was enough for now.

"Owatonna is a small town in southeastern Minnesota—about an hour west of the Mayo Clinic in Rochester. You've all heard of the Mayo Clinic, right?"

Murmurs of assent followed.

"Well, I'm almost a Rochesterian then. That's the town you can think about when you think about me. Owatonna is much like Rochester—without the hospital. There are some factories and farms, and life is pretty much like it is here, I guess, but smaller. And I am a graduate of the University of Minnesota and the Faribault Lake Seminary. But I'm sure they made a mistake when they turned Pastor Yount down."

He ventured a glance at the senior pastor. Pastor Yount looked nearly happy.

"I'm an only child who has wanted to be a pastor since I was seven years old. My mother started wanting me to be a pastor a few years earlier than that. I have three suits and six ties—so don't expect much more fashion fireworks than you see right now."

Tucker took a breath. "I am very happy for this opportunity. I promise to get to know as many of you as quickly as I can. My office is down from Pastor Yount's—way down and around the hall. Please stop by and see me anytime."

He counted to five—the briefest, meaningful pause that he could employ. "But you have to tell me the truth. Was my office really a supply closet before I came here?"

The congregation waited only a moment until laughter broke out and filled the space. Tucker offered a short half wave and backed up until he felt the chair against his calves, then sat down.

Afterward, he couldn't recall a single word from Pastor Yount's sermon, or anything else that transpired during the service, so jangled were his thoughts. Part of him felt good and honest, but a bigger part regretted his flippancy and wondered if his words had been received with grace or hostility.

Back in Owatonna, in Tucker's home church, the senior pastor always offered the benediction at the end of the service, then made his solemn way down the center aisle and through the back doors. There he waited for everyone to exit, shaking hands and asking about details in the lives of his parishioners. In the summer and when the weather was pleasant, he would take position on the top of the front steps, his back almost against the white fluted column. In the winter he would retreat closer to the middle doors of the sanctuary.

No one had told Tucker where he should go after the service. Pastor Yount stayed up front. A smallish grouping of people stood about him, offering comments, shaking hands. There was no formal recessional.

Tucker didn't want to impose upon the pastor, so he decided to exit the sanctuary and head out toward the front doors. He would have to meet these people eventually. Having gone dozens of times through the church's pictorial directory—from two years prior—he was interested in seeing who was still in attendance at church and who looked remotely akin to the photos in the book.

A steady stream of people, couples mostly, stopped and greeted him. They extended dinner invitations, inquired about his living arrangements, offered to help him find a more suitable apartment, and promised to show him around the neighborhood and the city. Two very earnest invitations—almost to the point of demands— were made to join the church's bowling league, the Holy Rollers, or the softball team.

The crowd thinned some. Tucker would not have admitted it, but he was scanning the faces for the young woman he had met last week—the young woman from the Laundromat. He had looked, of course, through the pictorial directory and could not find her face among the pictures. He knew that was not unusual. Some people never have pictures taken for such a directory. The young woman also may have been a more recent arrival to the church. For a city church like this one, the transient population was most likely high.

Just then he felt a tug on his left arm.

"Pastor Abbott."

"Cass Fowler. I was hoping you would stop. It is nice to know at least one person in this church."

The young woman pushed a strand of hair from her forehead. "You were amusing up there. I bet a lot more people wanted to laugh but weren't sure if you were being funny or not." She put her hand on his forearm. "You *were* being funny, right?"

Tucker nodded.

"I hoped it was obvious. I'm not really a comedian. So I guess some people would be confused."

Cass leaned in closer. "It's just what this church needs. I mean, I really like Pastor Yount, but I also like to laugh, too. I'm glad you're here."

Cass shuffled her bag to her shoulder and appeared to begin her wave good-bye when a small child, perhaps four or five— Tucker was never good at guessing the ages of infants and small children—raced past him laughing and shouting nearly at the top of his lungs, "You'll never take me alive!"

A few seconds after that blur swept through the narthex, a woman, probably in her forties, came running, following the same twisting path. "Don't make me count," the woman called laughingly toward the child. "You don't want me to count!"

Tucker twisted about as he tried to follow both their routes. No one else remaining in the church seemed to pay much attention, so evidently this wasn't an unusual or isolated instance. In a far corner, the two runners collided in a happy intertwining of limbs, giggles, and "I gotcha." Their laughter—full, rich, inviting—sounded like music to Tucker.

Cass had remained at Tucker's side. She shook her head in bemused tolerance.

In Tucker's home church, such running and chasing would not be tolerated, so he couldn't be mute. "Who is that?"

"Which one?" Cass replied.

"Well. . .both."

"The little boy is Chance. You had a piece of his birthday cake the other day."

"And the woman?"

"That's Annie Hamilton. She's his mother," Cass said, her words edging to tartness.

"Really?" Tucker replied.

Cass nodded.

Annie Hamilton scooped the little boy into her arms and pretended to gnaw at his neck, as he gave a torrent of tickle-induced giggles.

"Really," Cass said in firm reply.

At that moment, Annie turned and looked at Tucker. He saw the slightest twitch in her smile, and she waved at him.

And then there was that odd something in his chest again, as if noting, or warning, of some future event—not cataclysmic or catastrophic—but something smaller and kinder and more puzzling. This something nestled just at the edge of the horizon, waiting for Tucker to recognize it as he marched forward into his new life.

"Pearl, do you know a woman named Annie Hamilton?"

Pearl stared hard at Tucker. It was obvious to Tucker that she was carefully preparing the story—most likely in an abridged form. What he couldn't figure out was why it would be abridged.

"I know her," Pearl replied. "Why do you ask?"

"No reason. I saw her at church. Does she work at the Laundromat on MacKenzie? I thought this woman named Cass owned it."

Pearl grimaced, her mental editing still obvious. "No. Annie owns it. Has for a number of years. She's a nice person. She really is. She started a crisis pregnancy group at church a few years back. The group moved to a storefront up north last year. She still works there, but they have a paid staff now. She's nice. A tireless worker."

Tucker smiled. He was glad his first positive assessment of Annie Hamilton—when he'd seen her tickling Chance—had been correct.

"Is Daniel Trevalli her husband?"

"No," Pearl replied curtly.

"Boyfriend?" Tucker asked in all innocence.

"I think so. But I'm not sure. I don't really know anything about that." Then Pearl became even more blunt. "Don't you have work to do, Pastor Abbott?"

It was clear to Tucker that he wouldn't find out any more details today.

Three

THE FOLLOWING WEDNESDAY, Tucker sat at his desk, working on next Sunday's bulletin. As he struggled over the wording for the Women's Prayer Society's annual kickoff luncheon, he was jangled alert by his phone.

"Tucker?"

"Yes, this is Tucker. How may I help you?"

He heard a most feminine giggle.

"Well, I can think of a few ways, but instead I'm going to help you. I'm offering something wonderful for you."

Tucker didn't know that many people in church yet and fewer by voice alone, but this time he had a good guess. "I hope this is Cass," he replied, not sure exactly what she was saying and less sure if his answer matched her playful attitude, "because if it's not, I'm going to be very disappointed."

"Of course it's Cass. I said I was going to call you someday. Remember? I told you last Sunday."

Tucker winced. Her words from a few days earlier had been

lost in a gale of conflicting conversations from a half dozen other church members, and he was not one who often asked people to repeat themselves. He thought that rude. So he'd simply smiled and nodded and wished her a good afternoon.

This is definitely a first—a woman calling Tucker Abbott.

"I have some great news for you."

"What sort of news?" he asked, again off balance. They had only chatted a few times, and nothing of a personal nature had developed.

"I found a place for you to live," she announced dramatically.

"But, Cass, I already have a place to live."

He heard her bright laughter.

"That place? On Wells? No. You can't live there. At least not now. Much too small. No character. And it's filled with Arabs and who knows what else. No. I have found something much better and probably a lot cheaper than you're paying now."

Tucker was going to defend his apartment—especially from the remark about the Arabs. There were *lots* of nationalities there—and not just Arabs. But the less-expensive part of her news caught his attention. While the Webster Avenue Church wasn't poor, neither was it noted for its largesse when it came to salaries. Tucker was earning more here—much more—than he would have in Owatonna, but the living expenses were much higher in Chicago.

Back home, he told himself on occasion, *I could rent a four-bedroom house for what I'm paying for a tiny, dark studio apartment here.*

At times like this, he gently reminded himself that he was no longer in Owatonna, that he made the right decision to move, that this was a good career opportunity, and that he was establishing himself.

"Really?" he asked. "How much cheaper? And how much worse?"

Cass laughed in reply. Tucker liked the fact that she laughed easily and that he could make her laugh.

"It's not worse, Tucker. It's much, much better. You'd have the third floor all to yourself—lots of windows and light. It doesn't have an elevator, so there's a few stairs, but you're young and strong, right?"

Tucker grinned. *She thinks I'm young and strong.* "Indeed," he replied. "So where is this apartment? And how much?"

Cass launched into a long, complicated explanation of how she found out about the apartment from a friend of a friend's uncle and that the building was just sold and they needed a tenant to make the mortgage. They wanted someone respectable who wouldn't have wild parties, because their grandmother or aunt or someone related to someone who was related to the owner lived on the second floor and was very sensitive and, by their own admission, somewhat on the nosy side.

Tucker always marveled at anyone who could carry on a long, coherent, one-sided conversation. When she finally took a breath, he said, "You haven't said where or how much."

And to this, Cass nearly bubbled over. "That's the best part. It's right on MacKenzie Street—just two buildings down from the Laundromat. Mr. Manos owns it—the guy who owns the deli. . . diner over on Fullerton. I used to waitress for him."

And Cass presented another long explanation of that relationship and all its details. "He doesn't really care about the money part. He's charging his relative or aunt or grandmother peanuts—a couple of hundred dollars a month—and doesn't want to charge the third-floor person any more. And when I told him that you were a pastor, he got all excited and said you would be perfect. He knows you wouldn't have any wild parties or play loud music."

Tucker felt so exhausted keeping up with Cass as she explained and cajoled and encouraged that *he* had to take a breath. "It does sound good."

"I thought of you right away, Tucker."

Tucker could almost hear Cass tapping her foot in anticipation. "Well? What do you think? Can you come over right now? Mr. Manos said if you wanted it, you'd better act fast. He said he had a cousin or there was a cousin of a brother-in-law who might want it. So. . .can you come right now? You could meet me at the Laundromat. Annie would let me take a few minutes off to go with you. Please say yes. It's a much better place than you're at now. And you'd be closer to the action."

Tucker wasn't sure what action she meant and was almost afraid to ask. But an apartment with windows would be so nice. And cheaper rent would be wonderful. It would also be two blocks closer to church.

He didn't hesitate. "Can you call Mr. Manos and tell him I'll take it?"

There was a surprised silence. "Without seeing it?"

"Have you seen it?"

"Yes—and it's wonderful. He showed it to Annie and asked if she knew of anyone who might be in the market. Then she told me and I ran right over there. It is a wonderful place. Sort of quirky and quaint—but big. Really big. And lots of light. So. . . sure. . .it's a really nice place."

"Then I trust you. Tell him I'll take it. Tell him I could meet him there at five thirty with a deposit—if that's all right with him."

She giggled. "I'll call you back in a minute."

Tucker actually looked at his watch. The phone rang three minutes later. He had timed it.

"He said sure," Cass said without a hello. "He'll meet you at the Laundromat at five thirty. You know where that's at, right?"

"I do. I'll see you then," Tucker replied, then added, "You'll be there, right?"

Cass giggled again. "I'll be there. You can be sure of that."

As Tucker replaced the phone on the cradle, he shook his head. He had never, ever done something like this—agreeing to move into a new apartment, sight unseen. Such a thing, at least in Minnesota, would simply not be done. He could almost imagine his mother's icy voice in response and his father's pained look.

However, when he stared out toward the small copse of trees in the alley behind the church, his parents' image faded. His heart began beating faster in anticipation.

But anticipation of what, he wasn't certain.

Tucker sat in a back booth at Peter Manos's restaurant, signing what he hoped was a standard one-year lease agreement. The two-page document was dense with small print and subclauses, none of which Tucker could easily understand.

Growing up in Minnesota, Tucker assumed that his fellow men were basically honest and trustworthy. He hoped that his trust carried into Illinois, as well.

"You stay for dinner, no?" Mr. Manos asked. "You sign the lease; I treat you to a first dinner. You like Greek food? I give you a Greek sampler plate. Okay?"

Tucker agreed, even though he couldn't recall ever having Greek food before.

The stuffed grape leaves were wonderful, as were the gyros and the rest of the items that Tucker couldn't pronounce. Sated, he sipped at his coffee and sat back. He looked toward the front door and was surprised to see someone he knew enter the restaurant. Danny Trevalli entered first, followed by Annie, who was holding hands with her son. Tucker felt an urge to go up and speak to them but did not move. He was sure they hadn't seen him, for his table was in the back, behind a divider and a grouping of plastic plants and flowers.

I don't know them all that well, he reasoned. *And maybe they want their privacy.*

Tucker wasn't a fellow given to glad-handing and table-hopping, so he simply watched as they sat down. Because of his shy nature—at least more shy than outgoing—Tucker was a keen observer of human interaction. He prided himself on learning a great deal about people by just watching them from a distance.

Tucker observed Annie watching Danny as Danny watched the waitress. The expression on Annie's face wasn't as much jealous as resigned. When the waitress did come to the table, Danny sat up straighter and became more animated, laughing, touching the waitress's arm, gesturing grandly with his other arm. Annie glanced first at the waitress, then at Chance, then at Danny. Finally she looked down at her menu.

She didn't even lift her eyes when Danny patted her hand in a fatherly fashion. When she gave her order to the waitress, she was pleasant and smiling, yet Tucker thought he saw in her eyes a feeling of lostness, betrayal. . .or was it an acceptance of something she wished could be different?

Tucker accepted his fourth cup of coffee. Annie, Danny, and Chance didn't speak much. Chance had some sort of toy with him, perhaps a video game, and Danny offered him a rather stern look when he tried to stand on the seat in the booth. Annie quickly pulled Chance back down. If she saw Danny's look, she gave no indication. Tucker couldn't hear anything she said, but it must have been soothing, for her son quieted and resumed his play.

Tucker stared at Annie. He was sure that everything about Annie and Danny's relationship was obvious but was just as sure that Annie chose not to see anything.

He was always surprised at what people chose to see. . .and not see.

Four

It took Tucker only part of an afternoon to move his possessions—with the help of Warren Hagland, a member of the church who owned a small city-battered pickup. Besides his clothing, which fit into two suitcases and a very stuffed duffel, Tucker had six boxes of books; a recently purchased AM/FM/CD boom box that had, so far, never been turned louder than halfway; two lamps; two small end tables; a coffee table; a clock radio; a coffeepot; dishes and silverware enough for three people; a starter set of pots and pans; six coffee mugs; and four boxes that Tucker had trouble classifying. Their contents were made up of ones or twos—the spatula (wrapped in a plastic bag) was placed in the same box that held his bathroom scale. Tucker wasn't certain why he wanted a bathroom scale, but it was one of his first purchases in Chicago. Perhaps it was because his mother and father back in Owatonna owned one scale that was in their bathroom, and Tucker could not recall the last time he stepped foot inside that room. He told himself that the room smelled too much of talc, Old Spice, and arthritis cream.

The books had been sent UPS from his parents in Owatonna. Nearly everything else had been purchased in Chicago at Target on North Avenue, the much less expensive Waldo's Discount City a few blocks farther west, or the resale shop south on MacKenzie.

Tucker spent merely an hour unpacking.

The apartment was indeed spacious—two bedrooms, a large living/dining room facing east, toward the lake, a kitchen with nearly new appliances, and a small balcony overlooking the alley with a very nice stretch of rear yards on the street to the west. There was a large oak tree that filled the sky to the south with green-leafed rustles. Tucker sat out on his balcony on a white plastic chair he had bought at the grocery store on North Avenue, thinking that for such a huge city, there were many quiet and peaceful places. The gentle whisper of the tree leaves calmed Tucker's soul.

And for a big city, with its reputation as a cold and heartless place, Chicago, or at least Mackenzie Street, was as far from unfriendly as Tucker could imagine.

Perhaps it was because he was a straight, single male or a member of the clergy. Perhaps it was due to Cass's enthusiastic promotion of his moving into the neighborhood. But during his first few days of occupancy, he was visited by no less than five older ladies from the neighborhood—each bearing some manner of foodstuff and an endless supply of advice, news, gossip, warnings, and welcome.

Tucker easily considered Mrs. Alvarez the unofficial "lady mayor" of the MacKenzie area neighborhood. She had been the first to call upon him, having taken Cass with her to do the formal introductions. Snuggled in her arms, wrapped in a clean but faded kitchen towel, was a steaming casserole with kidney beans, ground beef, tomatoes, and cheese—sort of a giant taco without the shell.

"It is good to have a man of God in the neighborhood," she exclaimed as she hoisted the dish into his arms. "Nothing better for a neighborhood than a priest living nearby."

Tucker took the dish, then explained he was a pastor, not a priest.

Mrs. Alvarez smiled and waved her hand in a gesture of benign dismissal. "I know, Pastor Abbott—but you are still a man of the cloth." She eyed him closely. "Do you wear one of those collars on Sunday?"

Tucker smiled and shook his head no. "I could get one," he added, "if you would promise to feed me."

Mrs. Alvarez reached up and pinched his cheek, harder than Tucker expected. She laughed. "A man of God who laughs. That is a good thing."

Tucker had hoped that Cass would stay around to share his food. But Mrs. Alvarez took charge, placed the young woman's arm firmly in her own, and escorted her out the front door and to the steps.

"A single young woman and a man of God alone in an apartment with my cooking—it is not good. Things have been known to happen. You enjoy it, Pastor Abbott. Bring the dish back when you're done."

Tucker did enjoy it—immensely.

The food that followed from other ladies in the neighborhood, while given graciously and accepted with enthusiasm, did not always match Mrs. Alvarez's for taste and palatability. Even though the food was not always outstanding, he thoroughly enjoyed his new minor celebrity role. As he walked down the street to work in the morning, people would stop and smile and offer greetings. The experience was so unlike what he had imagined it to be—and he totally delighted in it.

Tucker let himself relax in the soft leather chair. He had liked Pastor Yount's office the first time he had seen it in the interview process and now had grown to like it even more. It was nothing fancy. Bookcases—stacked and groaning with books—lined two walls. Two towers of magazines leaned against the wall under the window. Pastor Yount's desk was a near copy of Tucker's desk—but newer and less scarred and nicked. Tucker's desk was most likely Yount's hand-me-down.

Two vintage posters—one in French, and the other, probably in Polish—adorned the far wall opposite the desk. Both advertised some manner of food and drink. They were explosive with color and shape and emotions. Tucker couldn't help but grin when he saw them.

Three old leather chairs gathered together in the corner by another window, cordially circling around a small table. None of the chairs matched exactly, but all were worn handsomely, the leather smoothed to a dark shine on the arms and cushions. The chairs would creak and fuss when Tucker sat, as if the furniture were extending a welcome. The table proudly bore the stains of a hundred coffee cups. Every time he sat at one of the chairs for his daily meeting with the senior pastor, the older man would invariably apologize for the tattered condition of the table.

"We should get a new one—I know it looks a sight. But that would cost the church money. Freddie Kresbach keeps promising me he can refinish it, but I hate to call him on that promise. He has enough worries on his plate as it is."

Tucker knew that Mr. Kresbach—a kindhearted, overly generous man—worked two and sometimes three jobs to make ends meet.

"His heart is in the right place. . . ," Pastor Yount said and let the sentence hang there without finishing it. Presently, the older man shook his head slightly as if to clear the images in his eyes, turned to Tucker, slapped him on the knee, and asked, in his usual booming way, "So, Tucker, what's the crisis du jour? Or are we in a slow week?"

Since Tucker had joined the staff, they had weathered the resignation of a Sunday school chairman, the breakdown of the air-conditioning unit, and rumors circulating around the elders' discussion of a revamped morning worship schedule.

All but the air-conditioning problem were still active, ongoing concerns. Pastor Yount rarely referred to anything as a "problem." He would screw up his face and call it a "situation," drawing out each syllable, making the word sound three times as long and daunting as it actually was.

"The sit-u-a-ti-on with our morning worship schedule still on the front burner, Tucker?"

Tucker consulted his notes. "I had four phone calls yesterday, and all four wanted things left just as they are. One fellow said that since I was a newcomer, I had no business wanting to see things changed."

Pastor Yount chuckled. "You know my favorite cartoon about this? The cartoon is labeled 'Week Two of the Church Plant.' There's a table with ten people around it—and one man at the end is slamming his fist on the table. His face is all twisted. And the caption reads, *That's not the way we did it last week'!*"

Tucker had heard this before—twice actually—both times

from Pastor Yount. Once was during their daily meeting, and once was in a meeting with the elders. Tucker saw a few rolled eyes during the retelling, indicating that it was not the first time they'd heard it, either.

But Tucker laughed appropriately. *What else does one do in those situations?* he asked himself. *Not laugh? Tell the person you've already heard it?*

"Webster Avenue Church has been here awhile, Tucker. People get set in their ways very quickly. It's up to us to keep things changing—a little bit at a time. Otherwise we would still be singing Gregorian chants during the service and speaking in Latin. No one argues that that would be a good idea. But change a few songs and toss a guitar into the mix? People want to charge you with heresy."

When the older man ran out of steam, he settled back in the chair. Placing his palm against his cheek, he stared out the window overlooking Webster Street. The blinds were nearly closed, but if you squinted, you could make out the cars and pedestrians passing by.

Pastor Yount sighed deeply, then turned to face Tucker. "So. . ."

Tucker clicked his pen, ready to take notes.

Silence was loud in the room. Tucker could hear himself breathing; he hoped he wasn't doing it too loudly.

Pastor Yount leaned even farther back into the leather chair. "How are you getting along, Tucker? It has been, what—two months now?"

"One and a half. It will be two after next Sunday."

"A man who keeps track of such things means the experience has been so wonderful that he wants to savor every moment—or so terribly awful that he's counting the days like a convict. Which is it, Tucker? The good or the bad?"

44

Tucker felt as though his face may have blanched just a little, and as it did, he thought of his mother. He hoped his face wasn't a mirror image of hers. He hoped his surprise at the question wasn't overly dramatic.

If it was, Pastor Yount made no note of it. "Come now, Tucker, you've been here long enough to have some impressions. Are you feeling comfortable here? I know the elders said something about a six-month review—but that's too long to wait to find out if something isn't quite right." Pastor Yount inhaled loudly. "So. . .is everything fine? Dandy? Things not running amok?"

Tucker kept his pen in the air. He looked down at his tablet. It was blank. He half-expected there to be notes for him to review concerning the question. His thoughts shifted into a higher gear, running past him too fast for any to become lodged in his awareness. It was the same giddy, almost sick feeling he'd had months and months ago whenever a seminary professor sprang an unannounced quiz.

Tucker stared at the back of his hands and wondered, strangely, if his knuckles had always been that large and bony. Then he addressed the senior pastor. "Well. . .yes," he managed to stammer. "Things are going well, I think. I mean, I don't have anything to compare it to. But I am enjoying the work. I feel overwhelmed at times. But I like being here. I like Chicago. A lot. I didn't think I would. I mean, growing up in a small town and all that. People back there talk about Chicago like it's some wicked, dangerous place. It's not. People are friendly. I already have as many friends here as I had back home, and I lived there for nearly twenty years. And MacKenzie Street is a great place to live. People are so nice. The older women there—widows mostly—keep bringing me food. Like if they don't feed me, I'll starve to death or something. And I can walk to the lake in under ten minutes. I think things are going very, very well." Tucker studied his knuckles once again.

"And how are things here at the church?" the older pastor pressed. "Are you enjoying the job?"

Tucker cleared his throat to buy a few more seconds to compose himself. "I like the work, Pastor Yount. Like I said when I first came, I've dreamed about being a pastor, and now I am one."

"The disagreements and little battles—they're not bothering you, are they?"

Tucker shook his head. "I grew up in a small church. So far I haven't heard anything new or seen anything that I haven't seen at my home church—at least once. We're all human but are trying to do a good job of serving the church."

The older man entwined his hands over his small but definitely rounded belly. "I'm glad. You seem to fit in well here. And from the gossip—I mean, the discussions—people like you. You're doing a good job. You seem to have found a place here."

Tucker resisted swelling a bit and straightening his shoulders in response. Instead he mumbled a soft, "That's good to hear, sir."

Pastor Yount sat up straight and eyed Tucker. "But I need to talk to you about something. Maybe you know all about it. Maybe it's something they teach in seminary now. I wouldn't know about Faribault—since I wasn't good enough for them."

It was the standing joke between them. Pastor Yount was a very intelligent man and one who knew more about the Scriptures than Tucker might ever hope to know.

Pastor Yount's smile slipped away, and a most somber expression appeared on his face. "You're a single fellow, Tucker."

Tucker waited a second or two, then nodded.

"A single fellow. We've never had a single fellow on our church staff before. At least not while I've been here."

Tucker waited. He examined Pastor Yount's face for any type

of clue, but the older man's features gave little evidence of his thoughts.

"When we hired you—before we extended the offer to you— there was discussion about your status. I mean, being unmarried and all."

Tucker recalled a few questions during the interview process about his dating activities. Pastor Yount had asked if Tucker was leaving a girl behind at home. There was no girl, Tucker had replied. At one time there had been someone named Elizabeth, but he was pretty sure she was not waiting for his return.

"I just want to make sure that you understand all about the. . . well, the temptations involved. . .in girls. . .I mean, women."

Tucker felt a hint of redness in his cheeks. And he could see that Pastor Yount was growing more uncomfortable by the minute.

"Good grief!" Pastor Yount suddenly exclaimed, obviously irritated with himself. "I counsel people all the time about these matters, and here I am, embarrassed to be talking about sex with you."

Tucker didn't move. He tried not to reveal any expression.

"Tucker, you seem like an upstanding young man. I've watched you work since you arrived. Never a hint of impropriety. Not even a little tiny one. That's good. A man of the church. . .well, we are judged by a higher standard."

Tucker nodded.

"And I know that you're starting to get invitations for dinner and lunch and whatnot from the church people. . .and your neighbors. A fair number of these invitations will have some sort of hidden agenda. There'll be a daughter or a cousin or a friend there, and she'll just *happen* to sit next to you."

Tucker nodded again. He had accepted a few invitations already. And Pastor Yount was correct. There had been single women involved.

"A handsome young man with a decent profession and normal proclivities—it's probably more uncommon in this part of the city than you realize. So your company will be at a premium. Some of these young women may not have the. . .backbone of the women you have known. Do you know what I mean, Tucker?"

"Backbone, sir?" Tucker replied, not totally sure what Pastor Yount was referring to.

"Backbone. Morality. Virtue. Call it any one of those things. Now do you understand?"

"Morality, sir?" Then Tucker had a dawning realization. "Oh, you mean that they may not be well schooled in resisting temptations? I mean, as well schooled as a graduate of Faribault Lake Seminary?"

Pastor Yount replied with a relieved smile. "Exactly. You know, I see the way our young women dress. I see what they wear even in church. I wonder what their life is like outside these walls. I'm distressed for them. And those are the types of women that you're going to be meeting, Tucker."

The senior pastor leaned forward and placed his hand on Tucker's shoulder. "I just don't want to see you make a mistake. It could happen, Tucker," the older man said, his voice trembling. "I know how tempting it all can be. You're young and handsome. You would be a prize—in more ways than one."

"Yes, sir," Tucker replied, realizing that Pastor Yount was warning him. Yet inside he felt a tiny thrilling pride that there were indeed women who would consider *him* as a prize.

"I'm not saying don't go to these dinners. I'm not saying you shouldn't have fun or meet any single women your age. But you need to be vigilant, Tucker. You need to be on guard, son. Your life is out in front of you. You need to choose the right path every day. You need to choose the way the Lord would have you walk.

It's hard. I know it will be hard. But you need to do it, Tucker. You need to resist."

"I understand, sir. I really do. And you don't need to worry about me. I know what can happen, and I won't let you down."

The brass clock on Pastor Yount's desk sounded out eleven o'clock.

"It's good for a pastor to be married, Tucker. You know that, don't you?" Pastor Yount asked.

"I do, sir. And someday I probably will get married."

"That's good you think that way. A pastor isn't nearly as effective alone. I've nothing against celibacy and all that—but a woman brings something to a man."

"Yes, sir," Tucker added.

"And, Tucker, well, Mrs. Yount wanted me to bring this up. She likes you, too, you know. Thinks you're quite the young man."

Pastor Yount's wife always sat near the back of the church and hurried out after the service. Tucker had only spoken to the brown-haired woman on a few occasions.

"I have a niece, Tucker," Pastor Yount began, appearing to pick his words carefully. "She's going to Moody nearby. You know—Moody Bible Institute."

"Yes, sir. I know it well. I applied there."

"Anyhow, Susan—that's her name—is my wife's brother's daughter. She lives with us since it's too dangerous to live in the city by yourself. I don't think she wanted to stay in a dorm—not with her aunt and uncle just a few blocks away. It's no trouble, really. She has a room on the third floor. Comes and goes as she pleases."

Tucker waited.

"Well, the thinking at our house is that maybe you two should meet. That's what Mrs. Yount thinks anyway. She wants you to come to dinner. I told her that I had to tell you that we have an ulterior motive, so you wouldn't be surprised. That okay with you, Tucker? Dinner? Meet my niece? What do you think?"

"Sir, I'd be delighted to have dinner with you. You name the time."

"Well, good. You're sure I'm not coercing you or anything like that? Hate to get reported to whatever government agency that deals with this sort of matter."

Tucker laughed. "No, sir. I'd like to meet your niece."

"Then Mrs. Yount will call you with a time. If I were to pick out a date, she would want to know why it had to be that date instead of this one and why at six thirty instead of seven. I find that it's easier to have her do all the arranging."

"I'll wait for her call, then," Tucker said.

"Good. And now I have a counseling session. Nothing to do with sex or dating or any of that sort of thing, thank heavens. I must be getting old."

Tucker stood.

"There wasn't anything important on your list today, was there, Tucker?"

"No, sir. Nothing that I can't try and handle myself."

"That's good. You make my job so much easier."

Tucker sat at his desk most of the afternoon, answering mail, making a few calls concerning the upcoming tryouts for the children's Christmas pageant. Being Wednesday, the bulletin was due. It was no one's favorite task, but Tucker enjoyed the mechanical nature of putting it together—like the jigsaw puzzles he so enjoyed as a child. Since he began at the church, he had only missed the Wednesday deadline once.

And he vowed never to let it happen again. There was no wrath like the wrath of a church secretary who had to rush proofing the product, then fight rush-hour traffic to get the material to the printer by 5:00 p.m.

They could have e-mailed it, but no one other than Tucker trusted the process.

"I want to hand it to the printer," Pearl said emphatically. "Otherwise it won't get done, and he'll claim that his computer never got it. No, thanks. I'm happy to drive it over there."

Tucker glanced at his watch. He had a full twenty minutes to finish the final details. His phone warbled, and without looking at the caller ID, he reached over and grabbed it.

"Tucker Abbott here. How may I help you?"

A heartbeat of a pause was followed by a short giggle.

"Well, Tucker, that depends. Are you in the mood to grant a parishioner a favor?"

Tucker hurriedly glanced at the caller ID on the phone.

Caller Unknown.

Then he realized the caller had to be Cass. Tucker smiled. "I may be in the mood. . .depending on the favor. That's the pastoral answer. And the safest answer."

"Well, Tucker, it's not really a favor for me. It's a wonderful opportunity for you. A very wonderful opportunity."

"An opportunity? Of the wonderful variety? Those opportunities are usually followed by a pitch for something that needs a wonderful donation. Is this one of those? Is there a catch?"

"Well, Tucker, I am in possession of two tickets to the Chicago Bulls game. Courtside seats. And I need someone to escort me there—and maybe take me to dinner afterward."

"Cass, that is a wonderful opportunity. I would love to go. I know the Bulls aren't what they used to be, but sure—I'd love to go with you. When is it?"

"This Friday night. That way we don't have to worry about getting you home early for church."

"Friday night is clear," Tucker said, not even glancing at his calendar. He knew all too well that he had nothing planned. "But I can't let you pay for the tickets. We'll split the cost, okay?"

Cass giggled. "I could have made money on this deal, but I'm too honest. Danny gave them to me. He got them from a customer, and he's going to Wisconsin with his friends and couldn't make it. Annie doesn't really like basketball, and Chance is a bit too young, so I'm the lucky one."

"And now I am, too," Tucker added.

Cass giggled again, her laughter a bit deeper than before. "Yes, you are, Tucker. You are the lucky one."

Tucker blinked but didn't think about her comments too long. For if he did, he knew he would get flustered. Instead he merely asked, "What time should we meet?"

"The game is at seven. I'll come by your place at six. It's fun to get to the game early and watch the team warm up. We can take a cab to the United Center, okay? I don't like riding buses."

"Sure," Tucker said.

"Do you want me to pick a nice restaurant afterward? Since you're new here and all."

Tucker felt almost giddy. "That would be great. Just don't pick a sushi place. I've never eaten that before, and I don't think I want to start now."

"Don't worry," Cass answered. "I'll pick a nice spot. With regular food that's open late."

"Well, then, I guess I'll see you Friday night."

"I'm sure you will," Cass replied.

In his mind he could see her slowly and gently lowering the phone back into its receiver.

⤬

Friday night brought Tucker to the edge of near-fatal amazement several times.

The tickets that Cass offered were not just good, they were fantastic—on the court in folding chairs no more than an arm's length from the action. Tucker had gone to high school basketball games and several times saw the Golden Gophers' games in Minneapolis, but those players paled in comparison. Professional basketball players were huge—monumental in size—and the game was violent and edgy up close.

"On television it looks so polite," Tucker shouted to Cass during the third quarter. "But here it looks like they're trying to kill each other with their elbows and knees."

Cass nodded, grinning widely. "I know. Isn't this the coolest thing ever?"

After the game, Tucker felt as if his entire being had been charged with an electrical current. He found it hard to sit still in the cab on the way to the restaurant.

Tucker again was amazed at the restaurant Cass picked. He'd never heard of Topolobampo, but Cass assured him it was one of the trendiest spots in town.

Tucker knew his way around Faribault and had dined out more often in his short life than his parents had their entire lives. But he had never tasted Mexican food so refined, so complex, so delicious from the very first bite.

All during dinner, Cass kept the conversation flowing. Tucker knew his mother would have said that Cass prattled on and on and told stories that verged on the embarrassing—or worse, revealed too many intimate details. However, Tucker did not press for any information. And, as he reviewed the evening later, he couldn't remember asking Cass any specific question. Her words simply flowed like a brook.

Perhaps a brook after a heavy rain, he thought and grinned.

He found himself laughing easily and often—and sometimes at stories that he didn't fully understand. It was all part of being a gentleman and a pastor. He had learned to listen well.

Tucker had never been out with a woman as striking as Cass. She wasn't a traditional beauty, but she would have turned heads in Owatonna—and Faribault, as well—had she traveled there. While Tucker knew beauty diminished criticism, he had never felt as expansive and joyful as he did that evening. He didn't even wince when presented with the bill, even when he could hear the echo of his mother's shrill money voice: *"I could feed us for a month on what you just spent on two dinners! And she had wine! What sort of woman drinks wine?"*

The cab dropped them off at the far end of the block. It was late—very late for Tucker—and the air was as cold as early winter air gets in Chicago. Cass took his arm, drew him tightly next to her as if seeking warmth, and they walked together toward his apartment and hers, as well, two doors down.

Cass had her keys in her hand. But she stopped in front of Tucker's door first. "I had a really wonderful time, Tucker. You're an easy man to talk to."

"Thanks. I had a great time, too."

She put her hand on his forearm. "And for a pastor, you're a whole lot of fun."

"Thanks."

She gazed into his eyes and drew a bit closer. Tucker wanted to gulp but didn't.

"I could come up," she whispered. "It's not that late."

Tucker was at a loss to know how to respond. He knew what he *should* say, but how could he say it and keep his feelings in check and hers from being hurt? "Uhhh. . .but. . ."

Cass put her palm against his chest. "Tucker, you're not one of those men, are you?" She edged her shoulder at him. "You know, one of those men who would kiss and tell. . .or gay."

Tucker's entire body was charged by her nearness. But he managed to respond quietly, "No, I'm not either of those."

Cass leaned forward, obviously not content with a firm handshake, and didn't close her eyes until her lips found his.

Tucker was dumbfounded, hardly responding, but then responding. He remained mute as Cass waved good-bye and hurried the two buildings north toward her apartment, keys jangling in her hand.

Tucker simply stood there, as if in a momentary paralysis.

It was later, much later that he realized his head was in such a spin that he could have stood there in the cold for much longer than a moment. And it was later than that when he finally managed to still his thoughts enough to fall into a twisting, embracing sleep.

Five

TUCKER'S DREAM—OR AT LEAST
a part of his and his mother's dream—finally became a reality. He
stepped into the pulpit of the Webster Avenue Church, carefully
laid his sermon notes on the lectern, and greeted the congregation with an earnest but faint smile.

Pastor Yount had circled the first week of November on his
calendar back in late August when Tucker first arrived in Chicago.
A pastors' conference was scheduled in Phoenix that weekend.
The elders may have grumbled secretly about the added—and to
some—unnecessary expense, but they approved the trip for both
Pastor Yount and his wife. The Younts had left Wednesday and
would not return until the following Tuesday.

"This ship is in your hands," Pastor Yount had declared with
some solemnity as he picked up his briefcase and headed toward
the taxi.

If Tucker were any judge of people's expressions, he was certain Mrs. Yount was the more anxious of the two to get away,

since she was already inside the taxi.

"Do a good job," Pastor Yount concluded.

Tucker nodded, shook the pastor's hand, and stood on the sidewalk until the cab had slipped from view. He could see his breath in the air.

He turned back toward the church steps. Pearl Hasse stood at the top, arms folded across her chest, her face marked with a Norwegian sternness that Tucker had seen before and often, back home in Owatonna.

"No funny business, mister. Just remember—Pastor Yount is *still* the senior pastor."

Tucker couldn't help himself. He burst out laughing. What did she think he would try to do? Stage some sort of church coup, taking over the pastor's office, barricading himself inside, refusing to leave until crowned the new pastor?

He bounced up the steps. "Pearl, I'll only do something funny if *you* say it's okay."

Pearl possessed the world's least-developed sense of humor—or at least the world's worst understanding of gentle sarcasm. The tight lines on her lips moved nary an inch. "That's good. Just stick to the basics. And remember that I'm watching you."

Tucker promised to be good and hurried back into the steamy warmth of the church.

His message that Sunday focused on a passage in 1 Corinthians. As much as Tucker was energized by just being in the pulpit, he had hedged his bet somewhat. The sermon that day was not a brand-new missive. He had preached it before, to his homiletics class. Old Man Mangusen, one of the patriarchs of the Faribault Seminary, had given Tucker's message one of the few *A* grades he'd issued that last semester.

Tucker was sure of the message. While it wasn't a complicated passage, he was sure of the interpretation. He was almost as sure of the three half jokes he scattered throughout the sermon. Pastor Yount always included a joke or two.

Afterward, Tucker stood at the main door outside, even though there was a hint of snowflakes in the air, and happily accepted the handshakes and congratulations over his first sermon from the pulpit of the Webster Avenue Church. He enjoyed greeting people as they exited the church and asking them as to their health and plans for the upcoming Thanksgiving holiday. It felt as right as it could be.

But later Tucker could recall little of that first experience in the pulpit, save that it scared him. He had fantasized for years about this first time in the pulpit—how compelling and fulfilling it would be. And yet, for some reason, he was a little disappointed. It wasn't that the experience was bad—far from that, Tucker assured himself. It simply hadn't enveloped him in the joyous, celebrative bubble he'd expected.

If Tucker had dared to be entirely truthful with himself, he would have said outright that his first real sermon was smaller than he thought, and much smaller than his mother had always promised.

The weekend after Pastor and Mrs. Yount returned was the weekend of Tucker's "dinner with Susan." He had taken to calling it that in his thoughts. After all, he'd accepted the engagement under some duress. How could he have said no to his boss, the senior pastor? So he'd decided to make the best of the evening. After all, it was a free meal.

The Younts lived a short walk north of the church on a quiet tree-lined street, filled with a mix of refurbished and glittering brownstones. Alongside were some worn two-story and three-story flats, waiting in great anticipation of being restored to their former glory. The Younts' three-story brick home was somewhere between those extremes. Built originally to house three families, it had been reconverted to single-family living two decades earlier. Shaded by two large poplar trees, it had a friendly little porch across the front and a pleasant garden encircling it that was Mrs. Yount's pride and joy.

Tucker rang the bell. It seemed to echo for a second; then Mrs. Yount came to the door. Wiping her hands on her apron, an industrial-looking apron—white, with thick straps and large pockets—she said, "Tucker, how nice to see you again. We hardly ever get a chance to chat after church. Do come in."

Beyond the foyer and its somewhat ornate staircase was the spacious living room with floor-to-ceiling windows, high ceilings, inlaid wood floors, and thick ornate moldings. The walls had been painted, surprisingly, a scarlet color. Tucker never would have guessed that either Mr. or Mrs. Yount would have lived in a home with scarlet walls. The furnishings were minimal and tasteful—at least by Tucker's Minnesota standards. In the corner, at an angle to the room, an impressive fireplace glowed with a crackling blaze. It wasn't quite chilly enough for a fire, but the effect was pleasing.

Tucker stepped into the room.

"Tucker, I would like you to meet my niece, Susan."

Tucker extended his hand as Susan rose from one of the love seats that flanked the fireplace.

"Pleased to meet you, Tucker," she said, her bold brown eyes meeting his. "My uncle goes on and on about how wonderful you are. I do hope you'll be able to do your reputation justice."

Tucker said hello.

Susan, he was sure, didn't represent the typical Bible college student. She was tall, with blond hair cut in an aggressive, chunky style. She wore a good bit of makeup—more than most women at Tucker's home church would ever wear, unless they were heading to homecoming or the prom. But on Susan, it worked. Her red lips set off her high cheekbones. She wore a fashionable white shirt and well-fitting black slacks.

Pastor Yount entered the room, carrying three logs in his arms. "Not cold enough for a fire, I say, but does anyone listen? No, they don't. I'll have to turn on the air-conditioning in a minute if the blaze gets any hotter."

During dinner, Tucker learned a great deal about Susan. She was originally from Idaho, but her family, including three younger sisters, had moved to Tulsa when she was in junior high. Her father worked for Delson, a company that made surveying equipment. Her mother was a stay-at-home mom and organist for their church. Susan was valedictorian of her high school and spent two years at the University of Texas. But then she'd decided to come to Moody. She now had two years of schooling left.

As Mrs. Yount extolled Susan's virtues, Pastor Yount did much the same about Tucker. *As if both of us are being auctioned off,* Tucker thought wryly.

Dessert was homemade brownies, homemade hot fudge, and expensive ice cream with lots of whipped cream. Tucker watched Susan attack her full portion; she didn't stop until it was entirely consumed. He was impressed, since he had to struggle to finish all of his.

After coffee, Pastor Yount suggested, "Why don't you two go for a walk while the missus and I clean up? We wash in a certain way, so you two would just be in the way." He winked at Tucker.

Susan was already getting her coat from the hall closet. "Tucker, you'd best do what they say. I've lived with them for over a year, and I haven't been allowed to wash a single dish. I don't know the secret, and they won't tell me."

"Are you sure?" he asked.

Mrs. Yount already had Tucker's coat in her arms. "We're sure."

Once outside, Susan and Tucker walked in silence for a few blocks toward the lake.

"Tucker," she finally said, "how uncomfortable do you feel right now?"

Tucker patted his stomach. "Well, I did eat a lot, but I think I'm okay."

Susan eyed him for an instant, then laughed.

Tucker pretended to be surprised. "Oh, you must have meant if I felt uncomfortable being with you at dinner."

"Bingo. But you had me going there for a minute." Susan slipped her hands in her black leather coat pockets.

"I have to admit I was a little nervous at first. I mean, the boss's niece and all that. But I'm relieved to find out you're normal."

Susan turned to him. "Thanks. And you are, too. The way Uncle Richard described you, I thought you were a cross between Billy Graham, Martin Luther, and a Boy Scout."

Tucker replied, "That's not a cross. That would be more like a mutation. A cross is a breeding between *two* plants, and you've got *three* elements going there."

Susan slapped him playfully on the arm. "I know Uncle Richard means well. But I'm glad you're normal."

"Me, too."

Tucker hadn't put in enough time at church to warrant a vacation, but Pastor Yount had been in an expansive, generous mood ever since his return from Arizona.

"I know you aren't planning to head back home to Minnesota so soon, but I'll take the Thanksgiving Eve service. There has never been a crowd in the twelve years I've preached. Most people in this church go someplace else for the holiday. So why don't you head home on Tuesday morning and come back Saturday evening? Have Thanksgiving with your family. No one wants to eat alone on Thanksgiving—and eating with strangers, no matter how well meaning they are, just doesn't feel right."

To date, Tucker hadn't received any invitations for Thanksgiving dinner. He'd noted one difference between Chicagoans and Owatonners: People in Owatonna liked to have their calendar tidy and dates and events confirmed months and months in advance. But Chicagoans left things tentative—often until the very last moment and then some, before agreeing to some event or commitment.

"But I'll never get a flight out on short notice," Tucker protested weakly. "Everyone says that the airlines are booked solid for the holiday."

Pastor Yount smiled as if he had anticipated the problem. "Take my car—our second car. It's nothing fancy, but it runs and is more dependable than the new one."

It didn't seem proper to let the older man be so generous. "Sir, I couldn't ask you for such a favor," Tucker began.

"Nonsense. You haven't asked. I've offered. And no need to be overly polite. Sometimes all you wind up doing is forcing the other person to withdraw their offer in order to match your level of properness. One thing I've learned over the years is to allow people to be gracious. Don't make them engage in some sort of etiquette-mandated back-and-forth battle. You should be glad that I'm not weary this morning, or else I would have stopped and agreed with you that you don't deserve the car. Think about the

Good Book. Grace is grace, my boy. None of us deserves it, but unlike our Lord, there are people out there who will quickly withdraw their offer. Please take the car."

Tucker knew the pastor's observations were on target. Tucker's mother would have argued for at least another three declinations before reluctantly accepting—and only accepting after both parties were almost worn out by the haggling.

"All right then. I'll borrow your car."

"That's my boy."

"Just be prepared for me to return with some awkwardly large thank-you gift from home. I don't know if there are any traditional folk crafts back in Owatonna, so it may not be an indigenous product—but I'll find something."

Pastor Yount chuckled as he stepped back into his office, dismissing Tucker with a gentle wave of his hand.

On the way to Owatonna, Minnesota

On Tuesday morning, Tucker set out west, away from Chicago and back toward Owatonna, Minnesota. Since his arrival in late August, he had not ventured far from his new home. He had traveled down to the Loop on a few occasions, been as far south as the Museum of Science and Industry, as far north as the Bahai Temple on the lakefront, as far west as the United Center to watch the Bulls play, and as far east as the lake. Now he had to find his way out of his new neighborhood.

The directions he got from the computer were explicit. "Five point seven miles west on North Avenue. Take 90/94 West toward O'Hare and Rockford." The directions all but memorized,

Tucker still held them on his lap until he was well inside the Wisconsin state line.

Everyone claimed the trip took no more than seven hours. But in seminary, no one had ever accused Tucker of being too speedy of a driver. Easily tricked by modern freeways, he navigated slowly and surely. Besides, it was not his car, so his trepidations increased.

Once in Wisconsin, the roadway seemed to shake itself like a dog and spread out expansively, following a wide path through the shorn brown fields. Tucker carried a thermos filled with coffee. He hadn't actually considered the fact that there were rest stops all along the way, as well as restaurants and gas station/convenience stores.

He recalled as a child that the gaps between available stops appeared to be longer. Then again, the only trips his family had made were to Montevideo, in the western part of Minnesota, to visit his father's sister and family on their farm. It was a yearly pilgrimage and made only after intense preparations. Any of his family's trips were seen as arduous journeys and were seldom done in a spirit of joyful exploration.

Tucker soon realized that he could not easily drive and pour coffee from his thermos. He would have to hold the cup between his legs or place it on the gently curved seat—risking a full cup tilting onto someone else's upholstery. And if he held it in his lap, he risked something worse altogether.

He had left the Webster Avenue Church parking lot at 9:00 a.m. on Tuesday morning. By noon he was through Madison,

Wisconsin, and that was nearly halfway home. Maybe the trip *was* no more than seven hours.

But he had told his mother he'd be arriving sometime in early evening. If he kept at his current pace, he'd be there before five, and he feared an early arrival would be a disruption.

He decided to stop for lunch. And perhaps he could drive more slowly. He spotted the sign, BLACK RIVER FALLS—NEXT TWO EXITS. He glanced at the atlas spread out on the seat next to him. He could only look for a second or two until he became nervous and returned his eyes to the freeway in front of him. He couldn't tell which exit would offer the most promise of a restaurant and a gas station.

"I can get off at the first exit," he said aloud to himself. "If I don't find anything, I'll get back on the freeway and head to the second exit. Good grief—I don't have to be a nervous traveler like my parents."

By Tucker's simple incantation of the obvious, a hulking presence was removed from the front seat. For the first time ever, Tucker was driving without a firm plan, with no list of gas stations at certain exits. He was driving on pure faith, and the freedom tasted delicious. That refreshing sweetness surprised Tucker as much as anything had surprised him over the last four months.

Tucker let up on the gas, turned the wheel, and glided off the freeway, then down to the stop sign on the two-lane county road. He nudged the car farther past the sign and looked both ways. To his right, the road disappeared into the distance, barren fields fading into nothingness. To the left, down a quarter mile, was a miniscule gas station. He could tell by the multicolored pennants fluttering in the chilly November air. A neon sign facing him blinked the word EAT in pale purple.

Tucker smiled. His guess had worked out all right.

He had not driven in nearly six months, so if the gas prices were high, he had no way to make a recent comparison. He filled the car with gas, then pulled into an empty parking place, locked the door, checked the trunk and the tires, then walked into the station to pay.

He was hit by the fragrance of cinnamon and coffee. The scattering of tables in the dining room were deserted. A row of stools by the counter appeared more inviting. Tucker slipped the change from the gas into his wallet.

"Is the restaurant open?"

The man behind the counter looked up, his eyes rheumy. "It's open. Let me yell for Marie. She may be out back with her dogs. Have a seat. Be right back."

Tucker took a seat at the bar on one of the stools. As a child, he always wanted to sit on a stool at Ev's Kitchen in Owatonna on his family's very infrequent visits there but was told firmly by his parents that only transients and migrant workers ate at the counter.

A chalkboard held the menu—burgers, brats, Wisconsin cheese curds, fresh-cut fries, coffee, soda, pie.

Still jangly from the road, Tucker only wanted coffee and maybe pie, if it was homemade and fresh. He turned on his stool, resisting the urge to spin around in circles, and stared out the window at the deserted road.

"Coffee?"

Tucker spun back to the counter. A woman, well past fifty, stood there. Her drab blond hair was cut shorter than most rural haircuts, and lines were deep-set about her eyes, as if she had spent too many hours squinting into the sun.

"Sure. Regular would be fine." A fresh-roasted smell steamed from the pot. "What kind of pie do you have?"

"Cherry is fresh today. The apple is from yesterday—but it was a good day yesterday. And we have coconut cream and chocolate cream, but I didn't make those. They're from a place in Madison but still pretty good."

Tucker sighed. He wasn't sure why. Perhaps it was the unexpected honesty.

"Cherry?"

Marie slapped the counter softly. "That's your best choice. Ice cream? Pie warmed?"

"Neither."

In a flash, the largest slice of restaurant pie that Tucker had ever seen appeared on the counter. The crust was flaky, the abundant fruit both sweet and biting at the same time. If any pie could be perfect, this slice came close.

"This is good," Tucker exclaimed, pointing at the remaining pie with his fork.

"Thanks."

"I expected the road to be more crowded," Tucker said as he swallowed the last bite. "I expected everything to be more crowded."

Marie leaned against the counter as she made out his bill. "The rush starts tomorrow. Though here. . .well, we don't usually see much of a rush. Most people get gas and food in Madison. And if they didn't, they usually head one more exit north if they're going north because there's a McDonald's that way. We used to be busier, but then McDonald's put up a billboard just a mile down the road. So people who miss their stops at Madison keep going. They sort of pass us by." Marie's words were edged with regret.

"Well, they shouldn't," Tucker said determinedly. "This pie is really something."

"Yeah, people pass by what's good and get what's quick and filling instead. That happens a lot these days. I mean, I eat fast food sometimes, but it doesn't really satisfy. I like things that people actually thought about before they cooked it—not something that came out of a machine. But that's the modern way, right?"

"I suspect you're right."

Marie turned the check facedown and slid it along the counter as if to conceal the total from prying eyes. Tucker was disarmed by the sweet gesture.

"Where you heading? Home for Thanksgiving?" she asked.

"Is it that obvious?"

She took the ten-dollar bill from him. "You're young and obviously single. No ring. No companions. You're heading north—probably from Chicago."

"Wow."

"I cheated. I can see your license plates—and there's a sticker on the windshield. Only cities make people buy them. You don't have a family with you. You're probably heading back to your folks'. If you didn't have folks to go to, why would you head north when it's cold? Too early for skiing and you don't have any skis."

"You have a good eye. You're right. I'm going back to Owatonna to see my folks."

"I know Owatonna. My parents grew up in Mankato. So what do you do in Chicago?" Marie asked as she counted out his change.

Tucker didn't know why he hesitated. He was proud of what he had chosen to do with his life. He was not ashamed of the gospel. He witnessed to others on a regular basis.

But yet he hesitated.

"I'm. . .I'm an associate pastor at a church near Lincoln Park in Chicago."

Marie pursed her lips. Tucker could see a complexity of lines under her soft red lipstick.

"You know," she said slowly, "if I had to guess at what you did before you told me, I might have guessed that you were in some sort of ministry. I guess there's something in your eyes that gives it away. Or maybe in the gentle way you talk."

"Really?"

"My first husband was in the ministry. An independent church over in Abbotsford—an hour north of here."

Tucker was stymied. He wanted to be friendly and continue the conversation, but how could he, as a pastor, ask about a woman's first husband without sounding judgmental?

Marie waited a full thirty seconds until she continued. "I left him. There were too many times he chose the church over me. Well, that's not exactly true. It was *always* the church over me."

A shudder grazed Tucker's spine as if the words from the waitress had been some sort of warning he must heed. He took another sip of his coffee and, thankfully, the shudder passed.

"But that's water over the dam, you know? Ancient history and all." Marie reached into the pocket of her apron and pulled out a pack of Chesterfields. Then she took out a disposable lighter, lit the end of one cigarette, and inhaled deeply. "You drive carefully now. I hear the winds are picking up. Marley said there might even be a house trailer ban on the freeway. If they do that, maybe we'll get a few more customers who might try and wait out the wind."

Tucker agreed to be careful.

And he left her a five-dollar tip—as if atoning for the shortcomings of a fellow man of the church.

Chicago, Illinois

Annie sat back in the couch in the front room and sighed. It had been one of those mornings. Chance was fussy and ill tempered. Cass almost seemed to egg him on. Annie was greatly relieved when Cass grabbed her coat and said she was headed downtown.

Chance had gone down for a nap, and Annie wondered if she had the time to spare to join him. But the mound of dirty dishes would rob her of any slumber.

She stood by the sink and let the warm water run over the stack of breakfast plates. Annie was not the type of person to grumble, but she wondered why she always seemed to be in charge of cleaning up.

Cass had entered Annie's life in a similar serendipitous fashion as Chance had. Cass was almost a runaway, leaving her family back in North Dakota with hardly more than could be packed in a compact suitcase. Cass had spent an entire afternoon washing a tiny load of laundry. Annie had watched her. It was obvious the young woman had no place else to go.

They had struck up a conversation. Annie had quickly found out that Cass was nearing her last few dollars. Annie had taken pity on the young woman and invited her to share the empty bedroom. Cass had jumped at the chance. Annie wanted help with her son and thought a roommate would be great. But sometimes she wasn't so sure.

She stacked the last plate on the drying rack and stared out the window. It was at times like these that Annie felt the loneliness of being a single parent the most acutely.

She dried her hands, stood by Chance's bedroom door, and listened to him breathe deeply as he slept. It was both an anchor to her life and a weight.

Owatonna, Minnesota

Tucker lay in the narrow bed of his boyhood bedroom. Little had been changed. He had never been one for posters or pennants—nor had his parents. So besides the curtains and a picture of praying hands, the room contained no ornamentation.

It was his final night in Owatonna. He planned on leaving very early on Saturday. WCCO had predicted snow flurries for the past three days. A scudding of slate-colored clouds hung over southern Minnesota like a shawl on a snowman. He did not want to risk being trapped in Owatonna and disappointing Pastor Yount. He had promised to return on Saturday, and he would do his best to fulfill that promise.

Tucker had no problem sleeping in Chicago. But once he passed the Wisconsin/Minnesota state line, sleep became an elusive target. He stared out the same window he had stared out as a child. The pine tree had grown taller and denser over the years. All that remained of the sky was a few needling glimpses of the dark clouds, untouched by moonlight or streetlight.

A slice of orange from the Penskes' porch light across the street pooled on the ceiling in Tucker's bedroom. But at ten thirty, after the early news, Mr. Penske turned the light off, and Tucker's room went dark and still.

Save for Tucker's racing thoughts.

The visit had gone well, all things considered. His mother's widowed brother, Neil, an insurance man from New Ulm, had come for turkey dinner. His two teenaged daughters, who alternated between giddy and sullen, accompanied him. Neil, nothing like his sister, talked nonstop from the minute he arrived until they left at almost ten.

Tucker tried once to defend Chicago from everyone's misconceptions but gave up after he realized no one believed a word he said. Once Cindy and Martha, the two teenagers, found out that Tucker didn't venture into Chicago's club and concert scene, they stopped feigning any interest in the debate.

The day after Thanksgiving, he was on his own. His mother had promised to go with friends to the Mall of America, an hour north of Owatonna. That was a shock to Tucker.

"I don't want to go, but I promised," his mother stated flatly. "Hazel Allen said they have good sales on right now up there. Not that I need anything, mind you. But your father has to work, and there was no sense being alone all day. Of course, that was before we knew you were coming. I could call and cancel if you'd like."

Tucker said he would be fine on his own.

He walked to downtown Owatonna to enjoy a late breakfast at Ev's Kitchen. He sat at the counter and ordered the "Farmer's Special." Come winter, many of the area's farmers, who had little to do because of the fallow fields, came into town in their overalls and flannel shirts. They spent hours over endless cups of coffee and grunting conversations concerning the Vikings, the weather, and the price of soybeans and corn.

Halfway through Tucker's breakfast of three eggs, fried ham, and hash browns, Wayne Klinkhammer sidled up to the counter, extending a much firmer and more sincere handshake than he normally did following services at Tucker's boyhood church. "Chicago has been treating you well, my boy. I can tell that. You look fuller and smarter. If that's possible."

Wayne sold real estate and was everyone's best friend—at times. And he was one of seven church elders at Settler's Ridge Bible Church. He sat with Tucker only a minute while Tucker consumed a quarter slice of wheat toast. But what he said was most intriguing.

When Tucker graduated from seminary, the Settler's Ridge elder board had made it most clear—while not issuing a formal statement—that Tucker had the education, but not the experience, to be considered for the church's open assistant-pastor position.

"You know the ropes, don't you, Tucker? I mean, how long does it take to figure things out? Right? Am I right?"

It seemed that the fellow they hired, a short young man with a goatee who was from Anoka and a graduate of the St. Paul Standard Seminary and Bible College with two years' experience at a Lutheran parish in Minnetonka, hadn't exactly worked out as planned. Wayne offered no details other than a whispered, "No one saw it coming—you know what I mean?"

Since Tucker's parents had never commented on this via letter, he had no idea what Wayne meant. At once Tucker was curious. But he also realized that, as a pastor now, he had to deny the temptation of gossip, especially when it sounded so delicious.

Wayne continued, "I know you're doing great in Chicago. And we know the salaries that they pay there—whew—I mean, what church around here could match those salaries? But keep us in mind, Tucker. Keep us in mind. You know the territory here. Nothing to learn. No learning curve, right? We're a small church, but we're a good church."

Tucker agreed to keep everything in mind.

"Call us—I mean, Chairman Thompson. After Christmas. No one will do anything until then. Call him. Promise?"

Tucker promised.

"And you just missed Elizabeth. She took her aunt back to North Dakota. The poor woman is old and won't fly, and Elizabeth—bless her heart—volunteered to drive her both ways. She asked about you, Tucker. She did. She didn't know that you were going to be home over the holidays. She said if I saw you to say hello for her. And that's what I'm doing. Saying hello. You should call her. She's a real nice girl—and still available. Don't wait on this one. She'll be snapped up before too long. Like a house that's underpriced. A bargain, so to speak. Promise me you'll call her if you come back over the Christmas holidays. Don't make a liar out of me. Promise?"

Tucker promised a second time.

He watched Wayne bustle out of Ev's, then calmly returned to his eggs and hash browns, ham and toast, coffee and large fresh-squeezed orange juice.

It certainly didn't look like much had changed in Owatonna.

Six

Chicago, Illinois

TUCKER DIDN'T THINK PREPARATIONS for Christmas could be so involved. At home, ever since he'd learned to drive, he had been put in charge of selecting the family Christmas tree. He had to make sure it was not too tall or too spindly and that its needles were firmly attached, not dry. In the weeks leading up to Christmas, Tucker had to find and buy only two presents—one each for his parents. But what does one buy, he had wondered to himself each December, for people who have elevated self-denial into an art form?

It was different at the Webster Avenue Church. *Pearl may not smile much,* he thought, *but she's crazy over decorations.* Box after box was dragged from the attic storage as the offices transformed into a tinselly, red-green, flocked wonderland of wreaths, trees with quilted skirts, lights, ornaments, candles, ribbons, and pine roping with holly berries. To Tucker, the church offices reminded him more of the Christmas windows in Dayton's Department Store in downtown Minneapolis than they did of a church.

But he didn't question the church's priorities, as some members in his family would have done. Especially since everyone was in such a good mood.

The only decoration that graced Tucker's office was a foot-tall Christmas tree that glowed and rotated when plugged in. As it revolved, it hummed, and every half turn it would chink. Tucker seldom plugged it in since he already had as many distractions as he could handle without the whirring and chinking and blinking lights.

His walls remained relatively bare. He did hang his seminary diploma, just under the stern picture of Jesus. But at times it seemed too boastful. Tucker still hadn't found any artwork. He was unable to decide what poster to buy, despite repeated trips to the nearby Target. And he had few other comforts. There wasn't even a coffeepot in his office. In truth, he preferred it that way. When the urge for caffeine and stimulation struck, he traveled down the hall to the twenty-four-cup, stainless steel, industrial model, ensconced in an alcove adjacent to Pearl's desk. If Tucker had a coffeepot nearby, he knew he'd drink all twelve cups by himself—most likely before lunch. But the steely atmosphere around Pearl's desk, as well as her steely glint, helped reduce his caffeine intake by 50 percent.

It was nearing ten thirty, time for his third cup. He did not time it exactly, but Pearl did, remarking if he arrived a few minutes early or a few minutes late. She had actually walked down the hall on a few occasions to check on him when he missed his regular coffee times by more than fifteen minutes.

He poured his coffee, made small talk with Pearl and Sharon, the part-time bookkeeper and computer expert for the church.

Nodding to both, he took his leave, explaining that the bulletin awaited him.

But once out in the hall, he heard the front door riffle twice, as if someone were trying to open it unsuccessfully.

Tucker hurried to the door and pushed it open. Out in the cold stood Annie Hamilton, her arms heaped with a mound of garments and cloth. The tip of the pile nestled just under her chin. She bustled in, took a few steps, and dumped the pile onto a cleaner section of carpet.

"Next time, I'll have someone come and get them. I don't know what I was thinking—that I could walk all of this over in the wind without dropping anything. I walked the last block backward, making sure I didn't drop a sash or turban."

Annie did not sound angry, Tucker thought. It just seemed she needed to explain this to someone.

Tucker liked Annie, although he had only talked to her a few times and then not for long. Their circles, even at church, didn't intersect often. He didn't know why he found talking with her so pleasant. Perhaps it was something about her calm yet joyful tone, her consistent smiles, her natural friendliness.

She was obviously not from Minnesota.

"Well, I know how you feel. Backward, I mean," Tucker said in a gesture of sympathy. "Not that you're backward. Or me, either. But I get confused easily—and often. And maybe try to do too much without thinking about the consequences."

Annie smiled broadly and knelt, sorting through the jumble. "It's endemic to modern culture."

Tucker walked to the other side of the pile and knelt down to help, even though he wasn't really sure what he was helping with.

Annie began folding. "Back a hundred years ago, you might get lost in the woods. But you knew where you were in the big picture.

And you knew what you were: a farmer, a trapper, a hunter. Now we get lost all the time because we can no longer see the big picture. It's too big. And we're really not sure who we are—at least not in context."

Tucker nodded. Although he didn't understand exactly what she meant, he thought it might be rude to ask for an explanation. This sort of thing happened a lot to Tucker. People assumed he was aware of their thoughts preceding the conversation, and they just started talking. So Tucker had become well versed in the sage nod and affirming grunt.

After a few seconds, Tucker looked up at Annie, noticing the unusual shade of green in her eyes. "What am I supposed to be doing with this?" he asked as he held up a robe with gaudy patches sewn on it like a quilt.

Annie laughed out loud. It was a hearty, full-force laugh, with nothing held in reserve. It was a healthy laugh.

"I'm sorry, Pastor Abbott. . . ."

"Tucker."

"Tucker, then. These are costumes. For the children's Christmas pageant. Most of this was abandoned at my Laundromat. You would think something as big as a robe would be hard to overlook if you lost it—but I have twelve of them here. I mean, how do you misplace a robe? You wear it from the bathroom to the bedroom. If it's gone, where do you think it went? It's not like socks. You're not missing a robe, are you?"

"No," Tucker said and grinned.

"I added some details and buttons and hemmed and trimmed, and now we have robes for the Magi and shepherds and assorted villagers. With turbans and sashes and all sorts of colorful accessories."

Tucker tried to fold one of the robes like a shirt, but it was longer and more awkward with a belt that got tangled. Somehow he managed to squeeze it into a neat shape.

"Although I'm pretty certain that the shepherds weren't all that keen on color-coordinated accessories," Annie added.

"Can I help you put these somewhere?" Tucker asked.

Annie gathered up most of them and headed to the stairs. "I promised Mrs. Englehart that I'd put them in the Sunday school storage closet."

They hung the robes and placed the turbans and scarves in a cardboard box that Annie marked *Christmas Hats*.

"Is Chance in the pageant?" Tucker asked.

Annie shook her head. "He's only four. Much too unpredictable. Without a tether on him, he's apt to lurch off in some uncharted direction. No. No pageant this year, though he will be up on stage with his class to sing a song. At least the first verse of the song. He'll just mumble verses two and three. But his teacher has a good voice."

Tucker chuckled. "But they always sing twisting or facing away from the audience, don't they?"

Annie smiled. She put her hand on the church door but didn't make any effort to push it open. "How are you getting along in your new apartment? Do you like living on MacKenzie Street? Is Mrs. Alvarez keeping you full of food. . .and gossip?"

Tucker was glad for the chance to talk. He glanced at Annie's hand on the door and willed it to stay shut for a minute or two. He was not certain as to why, but with some people—and Annie was one of those people—conversation came easily. With someone like Cass, Tucker listened well. With Annie, at least the few times he'd conversed with her, Tucker felt that he talked well. That he was wittier, and possibly even more charming, than he was with anyone else.

"The apartment is wonderful. More room than I know what to do with. If it wasn't so inexpensive, I might consider a roommate."

"Roommates are fine," Annie said, "but they can present complications."

"And MacKenzie Street is great. Everything I need is within walking distance. And you're right—Mrs. Alvarez is a great source of both food and. . .neighborhood news. Gossip sounds so. . . malevolent. And I don't think she ever means it that way."

"You're right," Annie agreed. "She doesn't have a malevolent bone in her body."

"But I do know more about Mrs. Erstwur's kidney stones than I care to."

Annie laughed loudly, then looked embarrassed. "The poor woman would die if she knew we were talking about her plumbing," Annie said in an exaggerated whisper, as if she were imitating Mrs. Alvarez's whispered news reports.

"I keep wanting to turn up her volume," Tucker replied. "She forces me to pay closer attention than I should. It just means that I have to remember it all because I'm concentrating so hard to hear."

The laughter his words generated made him bolder. "I think she does it so I have to lean in close. Then she can reach up and grab my cheek. I have a permanent bruise here." He pointed to his cheek. "People are asking me if it's a birthmark—one that showed up a few decades late."

By now Annie was laughing so hard that she gasped, "Stop, please stop. I'll have an accident if you don't."

Her gaze caught his and, suddenly, Tucker wondered just how old Annie was. Older than he was, to be sure, but the laughter made her look younger. Maybe she wasn't that much older than he.

"Pastor Abbott—"

Tucker held up a finger as if offering a warning.

"Tucker, I mean," Annie corrected herself. "Would you like to come over for dinner sometime? After all, we are neighbors, almost next-door neighbors. I know you come to the Laundromat, so you know where I live."

"Why, that would be very nice."

Tucker surprised himself. Usually he let most invitations hang, unanswered for a moment, unspecified and undesignated. If the folks doing the inviting really wanted him to come, they would offer a date.

But this time he didn't follow his own protocol. "How about this weekend? Friday or Saturday is good," he said, hoping he didn't sound too eager.

Annie pursed her lips. "Friday would be better. Saturday would give me too much time to obsess about the food and cleaning the apartment. And Cass will be gone Friday night. That means Chance can have you all to himself."

"I love kids," Tucker said, though he wasn't really sure it was true. He was an only child who had grown up with no relatives nearby. It wasn't that he liked or disliked small children—he simply didn't know anything about them. But he had wanted, and liked, new experiences.

"Chance acts differently when there's a man at the table. Maybe it's because he gets a little jealous. Maybe it's something else. But he really likes it. He gets to tussle. Little boys are like puppies. They like to tussle. You don't mind tussling, do you?"

"No, not at all. I'll wear my tussling clothes, if that's okay."

Annie giggled again. Tucker liked the sound of her giggle.

"Anything like they wear in WWF? You know—professional wrestling?"

Tucker, with a straight face, replied, "Of course I know. The sport was born in Minnesota. But as to my outfit—more spandex, out of necessity, and fewer sequins. Because, after all, I am a man of the cloth."

Annie exited laughing. Tucker stood by the door and watched her walk away. As she reached the corner, she turned and waved back to Tucker as if she knew he would be waiting at the top of the steps, watching her walk and waiting for her wave.

And he was.

Tucker stopped at Pearl's desk. She glanced up, distracted.

"Annie Hamilton—" Tucker said without finishing the sentence.

"What about her, Pastor Abbott?" Pearl replied. "I have a million things to do and can't be wasting my time."

"Is she still dating that fellow. . .Danny Trevalli?"

"Why?" All of a sudden, Pearl's voice actually sounded concerned.

"She asked me to dinner. I'm just curious."

Pearl spread her hands on the desk. "You're a pastor. Lots of people ask their pastor to dinner. It's not a date. She hasn't asked you for a date. It's just dinner. Okay?"

"Okay," Tucker said, holding his hands up in mock surrender. "I was just asking, that's all."

On Friday night, Tucker zipped his coat up and set out for a long walk around the block. If he didn't walk tonight, he wouldn't sleep.

Annie's apartment had contained the most fascinating artwork Tucker had ever seen—intricate boxes filled with tiny, detailed paintings, objects, and layers of texture and cloth and mirrors and tile. Each told a story, and each small section told a chapter of that story.

He was dumbfounded when Annie had said they were hers. At first Tucker had thought she meant that she owned them.

"No, I mean I made them," she clarified. "That's the sort of stuff I do. Although with Chance around, I've done less this year. When he goes to kindergarten next year, though, I'll have more time."

Tucker had never known a real artist. Mrs. Helman back home painted, but every face looked only vaguely familiar, and all of her trees appeared to have some sort of wooden arthritis.

Chance had not come out of his bedroom for the first few minutes. They both could see him eyeing Tucker from a narrow opening in the door. Annie had laughed out loud, and that seemed to draw him out.

Chance had stared hard at Tucker while Annie made introductions and they shook hands.

"You want to wrestle?" Chance had asked.

Annie had arched her eyebrows. "I warned you."

Halfway through their match—a best out of three takedowns—Annie had cautioned Chance about playing rough.

"Tucker, tell him when to stop. Honestly, I don't know where he gets this. I never let him watch wrestling on TV. Are little boys born with this knowledge?"

Tucker had simply nodded. "It's his peer group in Sunday school. I've heard them talking about it. They pass it on from older brother to younger brother."

For the next half hour, Chance and Tucker had rolled about the living room with Chance leaping from the couch on occasion, screaming out, "Flying scissors!"

When dinner was announced, Chance had obeyed without a second request. After washing his hands and drying them on his shirt, he sat politely at his spot. And when asked to say grace, the little boy did so with enthusiasm. He even included "this pastor here" in his prayer.

Tucker's favorite part of the evening was watching Annie and Chance dance about the living room as Chance got ready for bed. Annie sang a good-night sort of melody, and the two danced as if they were in a grand ballroom. Tucker was certain this was a tradition between them.

Tucker had stayed until nine thirty—only forty-five minutes after Chance went to bed. He and Annie had talked about their childhoods, their schooling, Chance, the church, Chicago, MacKenzie Street, Mrs. Alvarez, Annie's hopes for Chance, planning for the Christmas pageant, going home for the holidays, food, high school, parents, favorite movies, hopes, best cheap restaurants, and a few dozen other subjects.

Now, an hour later, Tucker inhaled the cold December air. The residual heat from Lake Michigan moderated the temperatures in the city—at least the neighborhoods that were close to shore. The weatherman had called for temperatures in the twenties inland, but this evening the flashing sign over First Bank at the end of the next block read *37 degrees*.

Tucker rounded the block for the second time, finding himself smiling again.

Annie Hamilton could be a very good friend.

He stopped at the door to his apartment.

This was a very, very good evening.

Seven

TUCKER HEARD THE SLIGHTEST
tapping at his office door. He usually kept it half-closed, owing
more to the drafts than a desire for privacy.

It was a female hand.

"Come in," he called.

Susan stuck only her head inside the doorway. "I was visiting
my uncle. He made me come and say hello. I said you were too
busy, at least from the way he described your day. I didn't want to
interrupt."

Tucker rose from his chair and stepped around his desk.
"Nonsense. I'm never too busy to say hello."

Susan appeared much different this day than she had at the
recent dinner at the Younts'. Although Tucker was adrift in the
sea of hairstyles, he knew her hair was more rolled and curled
somehow. How she wore it this day would match perfectly with
the majority of women in any church pictorial directory. She carried a light coat and wore a modest blue dress with a turtleneck

that may have been a half size small on her, but a deceiving half size. She really did look pretty.

Susan appeared to be absolutely comfortable in a church setting. Tucker knew that to attend Moody, one had to be more than just familiar with faith. One had to possess it and understand it. But even people who knew and understood faith often seemed ill at ease within the walls of a church, as if their attendance were troubling them. But Susan settled easily into one of Tucker's armchairs. She adjusted the hem of her skirt and smiled sweetly, as if there were nothing else in the world that she would rather be doing than sitting in Tucker's office.

"I had a break," she said. "They canceled my afternoon class. I stopped by to take my uncle to lunch, but he had a Rotary meeting to go to. I think he may have mentioned it at breakfast, but it must have slipped my mind."

When she paused, Tucker got the feeling it was intentional.

"Susan, I'm. . .I'm free for lunch," Tucker heard himself say, trying to fill the silence. "And I don't mind being your second choice."

Susan brightened. "Why, Tucker, that would be so nice. I would love to have lunch with you."

Tucker selected a Greek restaurant a few blocks west of the church.

"I've never been here before," Susan said as she slid into the booth. "I didn't even know it was here, and I know most of the restaurants in the neighborhood."

She opened the menu and carefully considered her choices, then leaned heavily on Tucker's recommendations, ordering exactly what he suggested.

"This is so good," she exclaimed when tasting the pasticcio, the Greek version of lasagna made with a hint of nutmeg. "I kept seeing this dish on menus but was afraid to order it. You know so much about food."

"I don't really," he answered. "But I do like to try new things."

Susan slipped a forkful in her mouth, chewed slowly, then looked up at him and added with a husky, innocent voice, "So do I, Tucker. So do I."

Then she batted her eyes. He couldn't be sure if she had a piece of dust in them or if what she did was intentional.

Whatever the reason for the blinking, it diverted his attention, and he dropped his spoon onto his lap.

One of Tucker's least favorite tasks was serving as the unofficial mail room of the Webster Avenue Church. Ever since Pearl had discarded a check for a wedding service seven years ago, she'd refused to deal with the incoming mail.

"It looked just like a piece of junk mail," she explained to Tucker. Tucker wanted to say that it was only fifty dollars and it was seven years ago. Wasn't it about time that she and the church forgave and forgot and started over?

But Pearl would not hear of it, claiming that it was much too dangerous to allow her to handle the responsibility. So it became Tucker's job, and he muddled through the large stack of mail every morning, sorting the wheat from the chaff and stacking it into different piles: magazines, bills, personal Pastor Yount mail, not-personal Pastor Yount mail, junk mail, and whatever else was left.

Tucker seldom received any mail—other than solicitations to join the Christian Singles Network.

Most of the mail he discarded without opening. Sometimes he

would read through the offer, and sometimes he would recommend a purchase based on the pitch.

But today's mail, inflated in amount by Christmas cards sent in wild profusion—most from businesses that did work for the church—included a letter addressed to Tucker. He knew who it was from without looking at the return address. His mother had nearly perfect cursive writing, the kind of writing that one would find in a schoolbook from 1947, done exactly correct with equal spacing on the loops and curls.

He marveled at her consistency and the ability of teachers back then to ingrain such long-standing habits. Tucker's handwriting began to fail as early as sixth grade. Since becoming computer literate, he now only wrote his name—and that was scrawling and loopy.

Pushing all the other detritus aside, he slit open the envelope. He extracted a two-page letter, written on thick vellum stationery. That was not his mother's style at all. Nor did the paper fit the envelope. He turned the pages over and saw that a small sticky note was attached, bearing the Federal Insurance Company logo—where his father worked—and bearing his mother's neat writing.

Dear Son,

I am glad to hear that you will be coming back for the holidays. We will wait to open our gifts until you arrive. Please call if you will be late. I am enclosing a letter that I opened by mistake. It is from that lovely Elizabeth Thompson. She has included her picture. Your father wants you to call her father when you get in—and you should talk to Elizabeth, as well.

Mother

Tucker wondered how his mother could mistake his name for hers or his father's on the envelope. He wondered why she had read the letter after realizing her mistake. And he wondered why she was encouraging him to contact Elizabeth—and her father, as well.

He unfolded Elizabeth's letter. Her handwriting was nearly as neat as his mother's but not quite so dated.

Dear Tucker,

I hear about you all the time from my father. You know he's now the chairman of the elder board at church, and I guess he gets the news from your parents.

I am glad that you are doing well in Chicago. I was there once for a teachers' seminar and convention. I liked it, but it seemed awfully large. I would be afraid of getting lost all the time.

Do you remember Hank MacAulis? He dated Margarie Dutters, my friend from college. Did you know they got married—and now they are expecting their first baby? Isn't that exciting? They bought the old Crandall home on Larch Street. He seems to be doing very well with his insurance agency.

And Bruce Benidt is engaged to Julia Horner—that just happened last week.

My father said that you are planning to come home over Christmas. He said that if I write you I should ask you to stop by his office and see him. He said he had something important to discuss with you. And I would like it if you stopped by to see me, too. We could catch up on the news, and you could tell me all about Chicago.

I look forward to seeing you again. Promise me that
you'll call!

Warmly,
Elizabeth

P.S. I am including my picture from this year's yearbook.
They give teachers a free pack, and I don't know what to do
with them all.

A picture slipped out of the envelope and fluttered to the desk. Her hair was longer and a little blonder than Tucker remembered. She smiled comfortably at the camera. She had filled out a little, and the few additional pounds gave her a healthier glow. Tucker knew that these commercial pictures never did justice to anyone's appearance, but Elizabeth looked very nice, much nicer than he remembered.

He slid the letter into the top drawer of his desk. He wasn't sure what to do with it. He received so few personal letters that starting a file would be odd. And he wasn't sure if this was the sort of letter one saved. It was just chatty—not discussing any serious matters.

He figured he would throw it away after Christmas vacation. Then there would be less guilt.

But the picture was another matter altogether. *You don't throw pictures away,* he reasoned. Tucker pondered what to do with it.

If I had a bulletin board, maybe I would pin it up there. But then people would ask about it. And what would I tell them? That she was a girl I knew back home? That she teaches civics classes at the Owatonna Senior High School? That we almost got engaged while I was at seminary?

Tucker shook his head and slipped the picture into the desk drawer.

He would decide what to do after the holidays. There would be plenty of time after the holidays.

❦

"It's my treat," Pearl insisted. "I have always taken the senior pastor out to a Christmas lunch."

"But I'm not senior pastor," Tucker insisted. "You should be taking Pastor Yount to lunch. You don't want me to be getting the wrong idea, do you?"

For once Pearl's serious façade broke and she smiled. Then Tucker knew it was indeed Christmas. The smile didn't last long, but it was a generous smile nonetheless.

"Pastor Yount is busy every lunchtime right through Christmas. I have a gift certificate for this great place that expires at the end of the year. He won't be here after Christmas. You'll be gone. I'm not about to let this money go to waste."

"But you could take your friends out—or your family."

Pearl stared at him as if his suggestions made no sense or were spoken in a foreign language. "No. I said I'm taking a pastor out to lunch with this—and I am taking a pastor out to lunch. You're a pastor. It's lunchtime," she said firmly as she waved the card in the air. "That's all there is to it. Now get your coat. . .please."

And then Tucker saw her smile again. He sighed, stood up, and made a great show of being coerced to abandon his desk and retrieve his heavy coat.

"But I get to pay for the cab ride," Tucker insisted

"Cab ride? It's only six blocks," Pearl replied.

"But it's twenty degrees out there—with a twenty-mile-an-hour wind."

Pearl offered a perturbed scowl in return. "Well, if you really don't want to walk, go ahead and waste your money on a cab."

Tucker stared at her, trying to decide if her gruff exterior was all a charade—a wonderfully acted, twenty-four-hours-a-day charade. He couldn't tell for certain.

As the cab pulled over to the curb, Tucker thought he glimpsed another smile on Pearl's face. But it disappeared when she got inside.

Zuma's was an elegant place, full of the lacy promise of nouvelle cuisine. Tucker was not sure what nouvelle cuisine was, but if any place had it, it would be Zuma's. The walls were eggplant and turquoise, with misshapen chandeliers, and a gaggle of waiters in bow ties with attitudes and polished, condescending manners.

"This is nice," Tucker said as they sat in a quiet corner of the restaurant.

"The waiters are snotty here—so you have to give as good as they give—but the food is wonderful."

She's been here before?

"If it's on the menu today, the lamb risotto is fabulous. Their goat cheese pizza sounds bizarre but is really good."

She's been here often enough to have favorites?

Tucker could only manage a wry, bemused grin. *I have to stop prejudging people. Really. I have to stop.* He smoothed his napkin to his lap. "So, do you come here often?"

Pearl shrugged, nonchalant. "Often enough. It's not my favorite place—but I like it."

A gentle whir of conversation lulled through the restaurant, mixed with a light dusting of soft jazz. Tucker took a piece of crusty bread, carefully tore off a smaller piece and buttered just that, according to his mother's etiquette instructions.

"It was a nice Christmas pageant, wasn't it?" Tucker asked, rebreaking the ice.

"It was one of the nicer I've seen. Annie did such a good job on those costumes. I think they made the show."

Tucker agreed, then asked, "Pearl, what do you know about Annie? I've talked to her at church a few times and had dinner with her and Chance once, but I never got up the nerve to ask her about her personal life."

Pearl leaned in close. "You're not asking me to gossip, are you?"

Tucker knew she knew she had him. He had rehearsed his answer. "No, not at all. I just would like to minister more effectively—and the more I understand about people, the more effective I can be."

Pearl twisted her lips into a smile. "That's what Pastor Yount says, too, and I don't believe him for a groundhog's second."

Tucker feigned great hurt until Pearl offered him a grace-filled smile.

"It's okay. I understand. Knowing does help avoid making stupidly awkward statements," Pearl said. "Annie's a very good person. She's been to college. I think she graduated. She's more or less estranged from her father. Pastor Yount said that her mother committed suicide a long time ago. She moved into the area—ten years ago? Maybe more. She bought the Laundromat on MacKenzie and made a go of it. I don't know where the money came from. Are Laundromats expensive? Anyhow, she does that artwork stuff of hers, as well. I like it, but I can't afford it."

"Really? Is it that expensive? The shadow boxes that I saw in her apartment?"

"They are. She calls them her 'unfoldings.' I heard she charges upwards of a thousand dollars for a big piece. But since Chance, she doesn't do it as much."

A waiter glided over with two iced teas, each with a ring of delicately sliced lemon and a sprig of mint, dusted with blue sugar.

Tucker had never experienced blue sugar before. And if more sugar was needed, there were skewers of rock candy on a silver platter.

Impressed as Tucker was, it did not break his train of thought. "So was she with someone? Married or whatever? Is Chance's father around?"

Pearl stirred her iced tea with a rock-candy stirrer and grew serious. "No. I mean, I don't know who the father is. And Annie is not his birth mother. Before Cass Fowler, Annie had picked up another stray—Taylor Evans. She came from Wisconsin with a bellyful and stayed with Annie. A few months after Taylor had the baby, she left. Just took off and left the child with Annie, who was nearly a total stranger at that time."

"What? How could. . . ?"

"That's not the worst. After almost a year and a half, Taylor, the birth mother, came back and took the child away. It was a mess—lawyers and trials and DCFS agents. Annie lost the boy after raising him for so long by herself. She was heartbroken. But after eight or nine months, the birth mother came back again and gave the child back to Annie. Said she had made a huge mistake. Said she couldn't raise him and the birth father was a bum and a drug addict and offered no help. I understand that she drew up some legal papers. Annie is not his official parent, but she's close enough. Even her Greek lawyer said it was safe to relax."

Tucker was amazed. After the one dinner he'd had with them and watching Annie and Chance further at the Christmas pageant, he could tell how much they loved each other. He would have never guessed—never in a million years—that Chance was not Annie's natural offspring.

"And Cass?"

"Another stray. Some people keep finding stray dogs or cats.

Some people, like Annie, find stray people. Cass was alone and scared. I don't think she ran away from home, exactly—especially since I hear she's going back to North Dakota for Christmas—but I don't think it's a totally healthy situation. She was at the Laundromat, Annie struck up a conversation, and the next thing you know, Cass moves into the back bedroom upstairs and begins helping out at the Laundromat."

"Cass seems nice," Tucker said, wondering how much information to volunteer.

A different waiter than the iced tea waiter sidled up to the table and deposited two steaming cups of mushroom and lobster bisque. Tucker tasted it. It was delicious, and the strange-looking mushrooms were intriguing.

Breaking some expensive crackers into the soup, Pearl eyed Tucker closely. "You don't have to be shy with me, Pastor Abbott, or embarrassed. I know you and Cass have been out a few times. Webster Avenue is small enough that word gets around—but it usually stops at my desk first."

"We're just friends, Pearl. Honestly."

Pearl reached over and gripped his wrist with surprising strength. "And that is all it had better be, Pastor Abbott. I like you, and I will not have some woman ruin things for you."

Alarm must have registered on Tucker's face.

"I know that Cass is very pretty," Pearl continued. "And while I don't know her all that well, I'm a good judge of people. No, I take that back. I am an *expert* judge of people."

"But, Pearl—"

"I would bet a thousand dollars she kissed you before you even thought about kissing her."

"Pearl, really. We shouldn't be—"

"I win my thousand dollars, right? You don't have to say a

thing. She's a gorgeous girl. You're a healthy young man. I can understand it." She squeezed his hand again so tightly that Tucker almost winced. "Just be careful. She's not the girl for you. Girls like that see a pastor as some sort of almost unattainable goal. I bet she thinks that if she gets you, there's a prize involved. But once she gets you, she probably won't want you. Not because you're not a wonderful person and a potentially wonderful husband, but the attraction of the forbidden will be gone."

Tucker nodded, hoping that Pearl would release his wrist without his having to ask her to let him go. She did so a second later.

"Pearl, I understand. I really do. And she *is* just a friend," he insisted.

"That's not what I see in her eyes, but I believe you. You keep telling yourself that, okay? Stay away from dangerous situations."

"I will."

"A solemn promise?"

"A promise."

"Anyhow," Pearl continued, "Susan would be a much better match for you."

Tucker sipped on his tea.

"You think it was a secret that you had lunch with Pastor Yount's niece? And dinner with the family? You think Pearl is blind?"

Tucker felt embarrassed.

"I don't know her all that well," Pearl continued, "since she doesn't come to her uncle's church and all. But she's nice. Maybe a bit on the beige side. But beige is good, Tucker. Beige is a nice comfortable color. You don't get tired of beige."

"I do like beige," Tucker replied.

"It's a safe color," Pearl said, then smiled broadly. Tucker wasn't sure if it was because of his choice in colors or because yet another waiter delivered the bowls of hot lamb risotto with mint. A comfortable silence settled about the table, save for the scraping of forks and spoons on very elegant square china.

"Pearl, I have never tasted risotto before, but it has become my new favorite dish. I will come back every day."

Pearl snorted pleasantly. "You won't be able to afford it."

Later Pearl didn't ask but simply ordered cappuccino for both of them and a plate of profiteroles.

"Yum, cream puffs with chocolate sauce," Tucker exclaimed when the fifth waiter of the evening delivered the dessert. After a few bites, Tucker added, "Oh, I'm sorry. They are nothing like cream puffs. Pearl, you have spoiled me forever."

A self-satisfied grin appeared on her face. Her steel gray eyes sparkled, betraying her usual harsh demeanor. Perhaps it was the light or the season, but even Pearl's short salt-and-pepper hair seemed softer around her face, as if all her features had taken a pleasant holiday turn.

Tucker sipped the creamy coffee and sighed happily. "Pearl," he said softly, "about Annie. . ."

Pearl signaled for another cup and turned to him.

"What about Annie and that fellow Danny Trevalli? Cass said they were an item, but Annie didn't mention him at all during dinner. I asked you before and you never really answered me. Are they an item?"

Pearl shook her head. "An item? That's what Cass called Annie and Daniel? Well, maybe. In some sense of the word."

"So are they dating, or what?" Tucker asked, confused.

Tucker could tell that Pearl wanted to ask him why he cared, but she had already opened the gates of information. It wasn't as if she could claim some sort of immunity from the knowledge of a person's dating habits.

"They've dated. They're still dating, I think. I've known Danny all his life. His mother and I went to school together over on Kedzie. That big brick building used to be a high school."

"Really? Does he go to our church? I don't think I've ever seen him."

"Sometimes," Pearl said slowly. "For a special event. I expected him to be at the Christmas pageant. I know it would have meant a lot to Annie. But he wasn't there. So, no, he doesn't come very often."

"And the two of them? Are they an item, as Cass said?"

"No. Like I said, I'm an expert judge of people. Danny will never marry Annie—and I think marriage is what Annie wants."

"Why? What's the matter?"

Pearl bent closer over the frothy topping of her cappuccino. "Danny's too handsome to marry Annie."

Tucker couldn't help it. He knew dismay was written all over his face.

Pearl responded with an odd, tilted stare. "It's not because Annie isn't pretty. That's not it at all. Annie *is* pretty. Pretty in a plain sort of way. But Danny is handsome. Real handsome. Movie-star handsome—and he knows it. And when the man knows he's handsome, he looks for a real pretty woman. Like a matched set. Real handsome men go for the real pretty women. Regular men—like you, Tucker—go for the just-pretty women."

Tucker wasn't sure if he should be insulted or not. "I'm a regular sort of man? Really?"

Pearl eyed him critically. "Yes, you're a regular sort of man. Just the type that Annie would go for, if you were ten or fifteen years older."

"Really?"

Pearl nodded; then she gazed at Tucker for the longest time without saying a word.

Had she unleashed some manner of thought that would have been best left unthought and unspoken? Suddenly he wondered.

Then Pearl grabbed his wrist again—right at the sore part. "Fifteen years, Tucker. Fifteen. You remember that, as well."

"Okay, Pearl. I promise to remember."

It was the day before Christmas Eve, and the streets were dusted with snow, shoppers, tourists, and holiday greetings. There had been snow—a few inches the day before. Just enough to add a sugar-thin layer of white to the trees and façades of buildings.

Even though Tucker was a native of the North and had spent virtually all of his life within ten miles of Owatonna, he was no fan of snow. He didn't like shoveling it or scraping it off cars. He didn't frolic in the snow. The Abbotts did not frolic.

Tucker had a week's vacation between the holidays. And once again Pastor Yount all but mandated his car's use for Tucker to head back home. "We're not going to use it. Save yourself the airfare. Avoid the crowds. Take it with my blessings."

Tucker remembered their first discussion about the subject and accepted the gift graciously and with profuse thanks.

Webster Avenue Church had not held a Christmas Eve service for several years. The services, most people agreed, were seen more as an obligation than inspirational. The Sunday before Christmas, the choir had presented a short program; Pastor Yount had preached a short message and wished everyone traveling mercies and a blessed holiday.

Christmas was on Friday, and Tucker planned to leave on Wednesday morning. On Tuesday, he made several stops.

It was the first Christmas in memory that he so enjoyed

planning, shopping, buying, and wrapping the seven gifts he wanted to give his new friends in Chicago. He gave Pearl a large gift certificate to Zuma's, secretly hoping that she might take him with her when she cashed it in. He bought Pastor Yount an old, nearly first edition of Oswald Chambers's classic devotional, *My Utmost for His Highest*, redone in buttery calfskin, from a second-hand bookstore for only ten dollars. For Mrs. Alvarez, he bought a hand-painted casserole dish, with roosters and chickens. He was not sure if it was oven safe, but the dish was as colorful as she was. He bought Cass a long plush scarf from Marshall Fields. Cass claimed to be delighted with it—insisting that she be allowed to open it in his presence. She rewarded him with a very vocal and long kiss. . .in the middle of the day. . .in the middle of the Laundromat.

He bought Susan a leather organizer that the woman in the luggage store said she was guaranteed to love. He dropped it off at the Younts' home. Susan met him at the door in a demure Christmas sweater and pulled him inside while she opened his gift. She claimed over and over that it was perfect and that she could use it in school every day. As he gathered his coat to leave, she went to give him a quick peck on the cheek but turned at the last minute. Was it intentional, he wondered, that she landed much closer to his lips than just a polite air kiss? He didn't think he would have liked it as much as he did, but he did.

Chance presented Tucker with a thornier dilemma. He had no idea what a four-year-old might like, so he took the recommendation of a clerk, who appeared to be no more than fourteen, at the Toys R Us store on Clark. Tucker purchased some sort of animal-robot construction toy in a plastic tube. He was assured that any child could assemble it in minutes. After reading the back of the package, he wasn't sure he himself could put it together successfully.

But he figured the children of today had to be more adept than he had been as a child.

Chance seemed delighted with the gift, even before he opened it. It was almost enough just to be given a present. Chance rewarded Tucker by launching himself in a flying hug, fierce enough to cause tissue damage, had Tucker let him continue.

Annie was Tucker's problem gift recipient. He had no idea what she might want. He had wandered through several department stores on Michigan Avenue, finding nothing appropriate. He ventured into a series of antique stores on Lincoln Avenue and, quite by happenstance, found what he considered to be a perfect gift. It was a small handmade mahogany box, obviously built with great care and skill. The box glowed with a gentle, worn patina. He imagined it was something that could be found in one of her constructions—or "unfoldings." She rewarded Tucker with a hug as well, although less fierce than her son's.

And now, on Wednesday morning, with all his gifts delivered, he was about to head back to Owatonna for a five-day stay, arriving just before Christmas and leaving a few days before the New Year's holiday. The car was packed with his suitcase, gifts for his parents, and several books he hoped to read during his time off.

The streets were bustling, even at the early hour, and Tucker felt fortunate to have found a parking place just in front of his apartment. With the window cleaner he'd brought with him, he proceeded to clean every window in the car. Tucker didn't like smudged windows when he drove. He wasn't sure what Pastor Yount did, but the few times Tucker used this car, the windows were smeared with some sort of film to the point of being opaque. As he finished the last window, he looked up, and through the clear glass, he saw Annie. She hurried out of the Laundromat carrying a wrapped present.

"This is wonderful!" she cried when she saw Tucker standing by the car. "I thought I had missed you, and I wanted to give this to you before you left."

Tucker took the present, surprisingly heavy for its size. "Thank you," he said, "but you didn't have to do this."

"But you got me a gift," she said, smiling.

"I know. But I wanted to. I didn't do it to get something in return."

"I know. But I like giving things. That's what Christmas is all about, right?"

Tucker nodded. "It is. But it wasn't that I was giving presents to get presents or anything like that."

"I know. If I thought that, you wouldn't have gotten anything," Annie answered. She grasped his hand. "Thanks for being a friend. I have to tell you that Chance couldn't wait to open your present. He opened it up right after you left—even though I insisted he wait until Christmas Day."

"I hope he can put it together. They said it was perfect for him at the toy store."

"It's already together. It took him five minutes, max. I'm amazed at what kids these days can do. And now he carries it around the apartment making growling noises."

The two of them stood in silence for a minute, the noise of the street swirling about them.

"You drive safely. Have a good time," Annie said softly, as if she had more to say but could not find the right words. Tucker hoped that his observation was true. All he knew was that he wanted more than anything to lock the car and go have coffee somewhere with Annie. He held the keys lightly in his hand. But if he hesitated, the traffic would build and it would take him longer. Then he'd have to call his mother and try to explain why he was late and listen to how complicated it would be to hold dinner for him.

No, he knew he had to leave within the next few minutes.

Tucker offered a wan smile. "I'll try my best. I'm a safe driver." He paused, then continued. "It's different back home than it is here. I would almost rather have stayed."

"But your parents are looking forward to you being at home. I'm sure they are."

Tucker nodded. "I'm sure they are."

He then did something that he had not planned or prepared to do. He stood up on the curb and gave Annie a long hug of farewell. If she was taken by surprise, her return hug gave no evidence.

"You have a good Christmas, too," he said as he climbed into the car.

"I will," Annie replied cheerfully.

But on her face was a hint of sadness.

Pearl's words came back to him in a torrent. *Just the type that Annie would go for, if you were ten or fifteen years older.*

Danny banged on the back door to the office and shouted up the stairs. "Annie! Are you up there? I've only got a few minutes."

Annie peered down from the top of the steps. "Danny, I didn't think you would be by today," she said as she hurried down to meet him.

He gave her a one-armed hug and a kiss on the top of her head. "Here, this is for Chance," he said as he fished a gift out of his pocket. He tossed it to her and she caught it. It felt light. "I didn't know what to get him."

"I'm sure he'll love it." Annie brightened. "Wait here. I'll be right back."

She raced up the steps and returned carrying a thin box, wrapped in Burberry paper. It was a long Burberry scarf. Annie had paid more for it than she intended but wanted to get Danny something nice. She hoped he wore scarves.

"Hey, thanks," he said and slipped the box under his arm. He extracted a small envelope from his breast pocket. "And this is for you. You don't have to open it now. Wait till Christmas. That's the best time to open presents, I always say."

Annie nodded politely. The envelope was not big enough for more than a card and perhaps a gift certificate. Annie would never admit it, but she had hoped for something more—not more expensive, but a gift that took at least a little time and consideration.

"Well," Danny said, sneaking a look at his reflection in the office window, "I should get going. I have a couple of calls to make this afternoon."

"Okay, Danny," Annie said. "It was nice of you to stop by— with the presents and all."

"Sure."

He stopped at the door. "You know I'll be with family over Christmas, right?"

He hadn't said anything about his plans, but Annie allowed him this oversight.

"You know how families can be. My mother has been cooking up a storm for the last week. 'All that Italian fish stuff nobody eats anymore, but you gotta do it,' she says. 'What would they think if I didn't do it?' she says. It's always crazy at our house over Christmas—relatives and friends and who knows what else."

"It sounds like a lot of fun," Annie said in a soft voice. For the briefest moment, a question flashed through her mind: *Why aren't you inviting me and Chance? Aren't we friends?* But as soon as the question formed, she dismissed it as petty and mean-spirited.

"So I'll give you a call. After Christmas, okay?" Danny said.

How soon after Christmas? Again she wondered, but she kept the question silent.

As Danny waved to her and headed up the street, she wondered why she so easily let him off the hook. Then she realized that this was the first time she had even allowed such a thought to remain in her mind for more than a second before she tried to force it away.

And then she wondered why she had waited so long to realize that.

Annie was a forgiving person. But sometimes she disliked herself for being that forgiving. When Chance had first entered her life, Danny had made himself scarce, and Annie had allowed him that, explaining the absence to herself by saying that Danny was just uncomfortable around small children. Later, as Chance grew older, Danny came around more often but never as much as she would have liked. Although everyone assumed they were dating, Annie often wondered.

It was an odd state of limbo in which she never truly felt settled.

Eight

On the way to Owatonna, Minnesota

THE SKIES HAD GONE TO SLATE, and the clouds hung lower and lower. Tucker would have sworn they were ready to unleash a major snowstorm. But the threat never materialized into a single snowflake. He noticed the winds had picked up; and the air, when he stopped for gas in Madison, seemed colder, with a humid, icy chill. He stopped just to fill the tank as he headed straight through Wisconsin—Tucker didn't like to travel with it less than half full—and crossed the Minnesota state line by midafternoon.

During these drives, his thoughts would usually scurry about, and he would fret, growing more and more restless. But not so this trip. In fact, he surprised himself when he reached La Crosse. He had not one single, cogent thought in his head from the preceding hours.

And then, in a rush, when he thought about that sweet

nothingness, an image of Annie sprang into his mind. . .her hair tousled by the lake breeze, standing on the curb, wearing a deep blue denim coat with fleece lining. He saw the tentative smile on her lips, her hand raised over her head, offering an energetic good-bye wave to Tucker as he drove away. As the image came closer into view, his throat tightened. And his hands tightened around the steering wheel as if he were in pain.

But to Tucker's surprise, it was not pain; it was not pain at all.

It was something he could not identify or quantify. Something he had never felt before.

And then the feeling passed. Once again air flowed back into his lungs, and a different set of emotions—familiar and tight and fully expected—gripped him.

His mother was waiting for him by the front door as he pulled close to the curb in front of the house. They had a one-car garage and a one-car driveway, and Tucker would not think of blocking his father's car in.

As he switched off the engine, he wondered if he should bring his bags in now or wait. When his family visited relatives in Montevideo, his mother always nervously insisted that they not bring their bags when they first went to the door.

"We will look like we're expecting them to put us up," she would whisper harshly. "Like we're gypsies or migrants. Like we're taking over."

And Tucker wanted to shout every time, "But they *are* putting us up! They know it and we know it!" But he never did.

Now he went to the door and shuffled in through the half opening. Since it was winter, no one with an ounce of sense let the front door go wide open. "After all," his mother would remind him, "we're not going to pay for heating the outside, too."

His mother gave him a hug—not a long hug but enough close

contact to be considered a hug. That was unusual.

"You've lost weight since Thanksgiving," she said. "And you cut your hair too short. And that shirt—you can tell that is a Chicago shirt, for sure."

Tucker had learned late, but he had learned, that some comments did not require an answer—ever.

He knew he was the same weight he was in seminary. His hair may now be a touch shorter, but it was easier to keep combed and styled. And he had no idea of what made a shirt a "Chicago" shirt.

"You're not going to wear that to church, are you? You do have a nice white shirt, right? Or maybe a plain blue one?"

Instead of a response to her comments, Tucker nodded, then replied, "Shall I bring my bag in now? And the presents?"

She touched his shoulder and held her hand there. It was a small gesture but filled with import and meaning.

"Yes, you could bring them in now," she said slowly. "But, Tucker, you know what I have always told you about presents."

It was Christmas Day. Tucker received a check from his parents— quite large by their standards—as well as a very nice white polo shirt and a charcoal gray sweater from Hudson's. The polo shirt was in a plain white box, so it probably had come from the outlet mall in Mankato. The sweater was in a Hudson's box.

He had given his father an adjustable walking stick with a padded handle and both a rubber bottom and a metal pointed end. His father walked almost every day, even in winter, and a walking stick would be a help on the icy, slippery sidewalks.

To Tucker's surprise, his father seemed touched by the gift and, for once, made no comment about returning it. He went on for some time about the versatility of the walking stick. "Summer and winter! How about that?" and had Tucker show him how to adjust the height—twice—"just in case I shrink an inch or two."

Tucker was more fretful over the gift he had brought for his mother. It was one of Annie Hamilton's "unfoldings." He had found a gallery in the River North area that represented Annie's works. They had only two pieces. One was large and expensive. The other one, a small piece tucked away near the back of the gallery, was more than he had spent on three Christmas presents, Mother's Day presents, and birthday gifts to his mother combined. It was a small shadow box, the size of a shoe box, but shallower. In it were sprigs of delicate dried flowers, a child's teacup and saucer, a series of buttons, and a tattered piece of fabric with the embroidered words, "God sees us, and He understands." There were two postcards—from the 1930s, Tucker imagined— and the sepia images reminded him of what he imagined the town of Albert Lea, his mother's hometown, looked like back then. And in one corner, behind a scrap of flowered wallpaper, was a gold glinting—just the edge of a heart-shaped locket, as if it were buried behind the history.

Tucker thought it was amazing but knew his mother was not one to appreciate the impractical.

Again Tucker was surprised. His mother claimed she loved it and held it in her hands for the longest time, staring at the objects hidden behind the glass, frosted by age at the edges. If Tucker had to write about that moment, he would have said his mother was reliving some of her childhood as she held that box. Annie's work had that effect on people.

His mother made no comment as to the cost or impracticality. In fact, she fussed for half an hour over the best place to hang or display her gift.

For once, Tucker came to a Christmas Day evening feeling self-satisfaction and something akin to complete happiness at home.

Chicago, Illinois

Chance lay at the end of the couch, on his back, holding the toy that Tucker had given him a few days earlier. He raised his arm, then swooped down in a long curve, flying the toy through the air, alternating between animal noises, airplane noises, and explosions.

Annie reached over and tousled his hair. "You have a good Christmas, sport?"

Chance nodded. "It was the best, Mom. I like this. Tucker gave it to me. It's cool."

Annie wondered where he'd learned the word *cool*. "That's nice. You have to write him a thank-you card tomorrow, okay?"

Chance twisted so he could see his mother's face. "But, Mom, I don't know how to write yet."

Annie grinned at him. "How about you tell me what to write—and then you can sign it, okay?"

"Okay."

Chance had been ecstatic with every gift he opened. There were not many gifts, but Chance did not know that. The women's group at church was generous, as well as the widow ladies in the neighborhood.

Annie's brightest spot, her best gift, was a short note and a small check from her father. They had not spoken in several years, ever since she had tried to introduce him to Chance. But Annie had dutifully remembered his birthdays and holidays. In a few lines, he said he would be in California over Christmas and New

Year's, that he was still at the same job, and that his health was good. It was not much, but Annie treasured the reconnection.

Her worst gift was from Danny. It was a fifty-dollar gift certificate from Jewel—the sort of card you buy at the grocery store register at the same time you're buying a nondescript Christmas card.

Annie sighed as Chance continued to zoom his toy through the air. Christmas had been so very, very good and so very, very disappointing.

Owatonna, Minnesota

Later that evening, Tucker sat on his bed in his childhood bedroom, wearing slippers and staring at the package in his hand. He held Annie's gift. Unsure of the reason, he knew he did not want to open it in front of his parents. He heard the click of the furnace and the fan drumming softly. Turning the package over, he slipped his finger under the tape and carefully pulled the paper apart.

Silently, he turned it back over and removed the paper, letting it tumble to the floor. He held one of Annie's "unfoldings." A card taped to the glass read:

> *To Tucker—*
> *This felt like you.*
> *All the best, Annie*
> *Hope your Christmas is full of blessings.*

He slipped the card off and angled the box toward the lamp on the nightstand. A foot square, it was filled with doors. It appeared that they had been lifted from a score of different dollhouses. Each door was a different style; each was a different color; some were faded and nicked; others looked new. The doors, in their frames, filled the box and snuggled together in a seamless jigsaw puzzle. Only a few were open. A larger door, placed in the middle, was sprung to an open position, and behind the door were the torn fragments of a watercolor scene of a park. It may have been a painting, or perhaps Annie painted it herself. She had pasted the pieces back together carefully, yet the painting was slightly akimbo—askew but inviting.

Another door opened into a child's oval mirror, the kind that would come in a kiddie cosmetics bag. There was one that opened up to a garishly colored photograph of a nameless couple from the fifties. Another opened, but barely, and Tucker tilted the box farther to make out the image behind it. It may have been the photo of a woman, but he was not certain. Yet another door opened into darkness, bringing to mind the word *evocative*.

Tucker held the piece for a very long time, staring at it, tilting it this way and that, peering behind the partial scenes. He picked up her note again. Her pen strokes were bold and definite, as fitting an artist who knew what to say and how to get it said effectively.

This felt like you. . . .

He put his hand on the glass and held it there, gently, as if he could feel vibrations emanating from the object. Many minutes later, he carefully rewrapped the gift, using the original piece of tape, and replaced it in the bottom of his suitcase.

There were some things, he told himself, that needed to remain private.

The kitchen was nearly dark, save the tiny glow of the illuminated clock above the stove. Mrs. Abbott silently slipped into the room and switched on the small lamp on the desk tucked beside the refrigerator. She picked up the gift from her son that she had left there. Tilting the blue lampshade, she leaned close to what he had called an "unfolding."

She smoothed her hand across the glass as if to clear the haze from the past that the work evoked. She was all but certain that the scraps of wallpaper under the glass were exactly the same as she remembered as a little girl.

She remembered spending hours and hours alone in that room, hiding but not hiding from the shouts and banging that swirled around the house on Moulder Street in Albert Lea. She remembered slipping into her cramped closet, closing the door tightly, barely breathing, her dresses brushing against her head like spirits, and wishing that the loud voices and acrid smells would stop, even if only for an evening.

She stopped and rested her hand on the glass, just above the glinting of a nearly hidden locket. Her breath came tight in her throat and unexpected tears formed, unbidden, at the corners of her eyes.

Setting the unfolding down, she grabbed at the tissue in the pocket of her robe and dabbed at her cheeks. She blinked several times. Then gently, almost reverently, she patted the glass of the unfolding, righted the lampshade, switched off the light, and silently padded out of the kitchen and into the dark.

Tucker awoke the following morning to the scents of bacon and toasting bread. His mother was not much on elaborate breakfasts, but Tucker realized that his being home was cause for celebration.

Tucker didn't like wearing pajamas or robes in front of other people, so he washed and dressed quickly and hurried downstairs. He wore khakis and a University of Minnesota sweatshirt.

His father was at the table, hidden behind the morning *Minneapolis Star*. All Tucker could see was his father's thinning hair and the temples of the reading glasses he'd bought at the drugstore.

His mother, her makeup already perfectly applied, placed a full plate of eggs, toast, and bacon in front of him. "I thought since we're all home and no one has to be anywhere early, that we could have breakfast together."

As they ate, Tucker's mother asked, "So, Son, I know that you're an associate pastor, but what is it exactly that you do there? Your letters have been a bit vague."

Tucker knew that being an associate pastor can mean many different things in different churches. So, between bites, he tried to explain. "Well, for one, I do all the announcements and Scripture reading from the pulpit. I've preached twice now, and Pastor Yount goes on vacation for all of March, so there's another four weeks."

"Four weeks' vacation?" his father asked, then whistled. "How long has he been there?"

Tucker wasn't sure, but he said, "I think four weeks goes with the job, regardless."

His father nodded, obviously impressed.

"And I'm in charge of the adult education—Sunday school—picking curriculum and all that. I teach one of the classes. I've been organizing an effort to develop small groups in the church. I'm leading a prayer and study group for men on Friday mornings. Pastor Yount has asked me to investigate an adult missions trip for the summer. I've done some counseling, and there's always visitations and hospital calls."

His mother nodded as he ticked off his list. Her carefully

coiffured hair was much less gray and browner than Tucker remembered, but it still moved as a single unit. "And since the senior pastor really doesn't like administrative matters, he has me running the weekly staff meeting. I handle most of the service and maintenance needs. Oh, and I almost forgot. The youth group. Not that it's all that large—about forty or so. We have a lot of young couples without kids. And a lot of older people whose kids are grown and not around. There are a fewer middle-aged families with children. So I handle the youth group outings and teaching, as well."

"Wow," his father said. "Those folks in Chicago really keep you busy."

"I like being busy. And most of it doesn't feel like work."

His mother was beaming. "See, Nathan, I told you he was already doing all this. He has the experience. He would be perfect."

"Perfect for what?" asked Tucker.

Embarrassed a little, his mother stood up from the table, wiped her hands on her apron, and cheerfully called out, "I have donuts from Hart's. Anyone want a donut?"

Later that morning, Tucker put the phone down.

"Who was that, dear?" his mother asked.

"Tommy Thompson."

"Elizabeth's father?"

"Yep," Tucker replied. "He wants me to come over to talk."

His mother edged closer. "And you *are* going, aren't you? I would wear a nice shirt, though. Or maybe that sweater we bought you for Christmas. That would be nice. And nicer shoes."

Tucker offered a great sigh. Mr. Thompson was the chairman of the church elder board. Tucker knew, from his trip home at

Thanksgiving, that their associate pastor had been terminated a few months earlier. It was not hard for Tucker to "do the math."

Robert Bergen, the current senior pastor with six years' tenure, was nearing sixty-five. He refused to handle any administration for the church. He had never been good at details, so the burden often fell to the elder board. The church had grown, and now, with an attendance nearing five hundred each Sunday, Settler's Ridge desperately needed a second-in-command.

I have four months' experience under my belt—and now they're interested in me?

To make his mother less nervous, he did as he was told and changed into a nicer shirt. It was still a "Chicago" shirt, but he had taken off the sweatshirt and replaced it with an actual sport coat. He would not put on a tie, though, no matter how much pleading he saw in his mother's eyes.

Tucker settled into the plush upholstered chair opposite Mr. Thompson's desk.

"You look good," Mr. Thompson said as he smoothed the blotter on his desktop. Tucker noticed immediately that there was no computer in his office, unless he had a laptop tucked away in a drawer. The office seemed naked without some sort of electronic device and a snaking of wires tumbling out the back.

"Thank you, sir. I feel good."

"Nice shirt, son. Looks like you've gained a few pounds, right? Good Chicago cooking, eh?" the older man said, then appeared puzzled. "What is Chicago cooking? Brats? No, that's Wisconsin. Hot dogs? But they're everywhere, aren't they? Oh, well, doesn't matter. Wait—pizza—that's it. Deep-dish pizza. That's it. Right?"

Tucker sat quietly, his hands folded in his lap. He adjusted his sport coat so it didn't blouse open. He tugged his cuffs down so that an inch showed beyond the herringbone pattern of the coat.

"And that church in Chicago—that going well?"

"It is, sir. The Webster Avenue Church. It is going very well. The work is rewarding."

"Good to hear, good to hear," Mr. Thompson replied, clearing his throat loudly. "But then, Tucker, that's not why I asked you to drop by, is it?"

"I don't imagine it is, sir."

"No, it isn't," Mr. Thompson said, peering out the front window of his office.

Mr. Thompson's office occupied a small storefront in downtown Owatonna. Some of the downtown retail presence had migrated to the mall, now twenty years old, built just outside of town. But a core remained. In fact, there were only two empty storefronts, and both were under option. Thomas "Tommy" Thompson sold financial services—mutual funds, IRAs, Roth accounts—all the sort of thing that caused Tucker's eyes to glaze over when being discussed. Behind Mr. Thompson were stacked piles of annual reports and flip charts in three-ring binders. The walls were decorated with various brass and oak plaques, naming him as the top performer for a number of companies and products.

Now Mr. Thompson stared at Tucker. His glasses, Tucker thought, were too big for his face, and his sideburns called out to be trimmed upward.

"No, Tucker, it isn't," he repeated. "I won't beat around the bush. No sense in that. When it comes time for asking for the order—then you ask for the order." He pulled out a single sheet of paper from a drawer. "You graduated from the University of Minnesota."

"Right," Tucker said.

"You worked up in St. Paul for a while, right?"

"Yes, sir. For a car leasing company. It took me six years to figure out that I didn't like leasing cars."

"A job, not a career, right, Tucker?"

"Yes, sir," Tucker replied.

"Then you attended that seminary in Faribault."

"Yes, sir. It was always my mother's dream to see me become a pastor. And mine, too, I guess."

"And you graduated third in your class."

Tucker felt embarrassed. "It was a small class, sir."

"That's nonsense. Third out of five hundred is quite an accomplishment."

"Thank you, sir."

"And you never applied for the open position at our church. Why is that?"

Tucker cleared his throat. "My father made it clear that you were looking for a man with experience. I didn't have any. And maybe it was time to try something else—go somewhere else."

Mr. Thompson shrugged expansively as if he understood anyone's reason for leaving southern Minnesota. "Well, you got me there. We *were* looking for experience. That's what that fancy church consultant said: Hire experience. We shouldn't have cared. When I got this job, I didn't know beans about investments. Hiring that St. Paul Standard Seminary and Bible College fellow— well, all it meant is that we got an experienced man—who was experienced in fouling things up and making messes. Biggest mistake I made as church chairman. . .so far, anyways," he said, laughing hard at his own humor.

Tucker remained silent. He could think of nothing pertinent to add.

"So. . .Tucker. . .we want you to work for us. For the church.

Back where you belong. What do you say?"

Mr. Thompson's invitation filled the room with its bulk. Tucker felt crowded.

"Now I know this is sudden," Mr. Thompson added. "We all know that. And we know you church guys have to think about things for a while—pray about them and all that. Take your time, Tucker. I don't expect an answer right away. I mean, I don't expect one now. But if you had one, I would sure listen to it. That is, unless you say no or think you're going to say no. Then I don't want to hear a word right now. I'm in too good a mood from Christmas."

Tucker remained silent, his mouth all but dry.

"So. . .think about it for a few days. Remember, if it's no, I'm not listening. Not until you say yes." Mr. Thompson leaned back, looking satisfied. "You know what my wife got me for Christmas? You'll never guess."

He used his thumb to point at a few pictures of himself standing on various golf courses with various men Tucker didn't know.

"You know I'm a golfer? Well, the missus bought me a round of golf with Lee Trevino. Next June when he's here for some tournament. I didn't know you could do that. And I sure as shooting didn't know that Trevino was up for sale like that. I don't know what she paid and I don't want to know. Don't that beat all—you can rent somebody famous for an afternoon."

Tucker, uncertain how to process this information, wondered if this marked the end of the meeting. Mr. Thompson became distracted.

"Well, I'll consider it," Tucker replied. "The job offer, that is."

"And you know what I said about not being able to match Chicago pay? It isn't the truth. I know all about big-city salaries— and I'm sure we'll be able to do a little bit better than them. Economy around here is good, and giving is up some this year."

Tucker stood. "I'll think about it."

As he approached the door, Mr. Thompson called out. "Wait. One more thing. She would kill me if I forgot. You have to call Elizabeth. I said you were coming and she said to tell you to call. So call her, okay? She made me promise that you would."

Tucker nodded and replied, "Yes, sir, I will call her."

"Better yet, let me call her now. She's at home. No school and all that. I'll tell her you're coming over. She lives downtown now; did you know that?" he said as he punched in her phone number.

She was not on his speed dial—if he had speed dial.

There were too many thoughts in Tucker's mind to raise the wherewithal to find a way to politely decline.

Elizabeth had moved out of her parents' home when she was twenty-seven and had four years of experience teaching at Owatonna High. And now, on this cold day, with a biting wind hissing from the north, Tucker turned on Main Street, bundled his coat about his neck, and marched the two blocks to the door of Elizabeth's apartment.

He rubbed his hands together. His gloves had been fine for Chicago—so far—but seemed nearly useless in Minnesota cold. He breathed into them with little effect. There was only one name written on the brass nameplate to the side of the solid door: *E. Thompson.*

He pressed the buzzer. He heard it echo above him, like the cry of a saw biting into plywood.

Stairs creaked loudly.

Tucker stood back and tried his best to offer a genuine, un-affected smile to the peephole. The door swung open, and Elizabeth all but launched herself into his arms, embracing him in a long-lost-relationship-rejoined sort of hug, full and intense. Tucker felt swamped. The embrace was too passionate and lengthy for being outdoors, on the sidewalk, in front of passersby.

After the long uncomfortable hug, with Elizabeth's head buried into the crook of Tucker's neck, she leaned back.

Her hair was longer—and blonder. Tucker wasn't sure if blonder was a word, but that was what her hair was. Before, it had been sort of blond and brown; now it was blond with a capital *B*. She had gained weight, too. . .perhaps fifteen to twenty pounds. It rounded her cheeks some. The narrow pinched look was gone.

"Tucker," she said, finally breaking their silence. "I am so glad that you stopped."

And then the unexpected happened.

When they had dissolved their relationship, Tucker figured she'd never voluntarily speak with him again, since he was the one who had initiated their separation. So what happened next was more than unexpected—it was shocking.

She reached around the back of his head, stood on tiptoe, and firmly kissed him hard on the lips.

"I'm so glad to see you," she said as she lowered her heels to the ground. "Now let's get out of the cold. I have coffee on. I know you like coffee."

Chicago, Illinois

The apartment was quiet. There was no one in the Laundromat; the holidays kept customers at home with their families. Annie had checked twice that morning. Cass was busy with friends and had hardly been home in recent days.

Chance had fallen asleep on the couch watching television. Annie quietly sat in the dining room with a cup of tea. On the table in front of her was the wonderful antique box that Tucker had bought her as a gift. She kept his note inside the box.

> *To Annie—*
> *You're a special friend. Have a wonderful Christmas. I hope we'll have a chance to get together when I get back from Minnesota.*
>
> *Tucker*

She ran her hands across the note, as if trying to feel the pressure of his pen on the paper.

I wish Tucker were here, she thought, then stopped. "Now that's a first," she said aloud. "Where did that thought come from?"

Nine

Owatonna, Minnesota

"I'm sorry I was so bold," Elizabeth said. "But it's been so long and I'm so glad to see you again. I talk to your mother when I see her. Mostly at church. She keeps me posted on your activities. I hope you don't mind."

"No. Owatonna is a small town. How could you help but know?"

Elizabeth took Tucker by the arm and led him into a large living room—larger than his by half.

"This is very nice," Tucker said, still reeling from the uncomfortable kiss. "Your furniture is nice."

"A present from my parents. They said I might be a high school teacher, but I don't have to live like one. And Daddy is good friends with Walter Armburst—the fellow with the furniture store out by the freeway. He was very generous with his discount. And everything in the room matches. I like that. Even the

123

pictures sort of match, don't they?"

Three views of the same stream and forest location showed the seasons of spring, fall, and winter. Spring and winter hung over the couch. Autumn hung over the dining room table.

"I have the summer painting in the bedroom," Elizabeth explained. "Those colors go better with my bedspread."

"Very nice," Tucker said. "I like it. Nothing quite matches back at my place in Chicago. I'm the second or third—or maybe fourth—owner of everything. It's all clean and nice and comfortable, but nothing really goes together. Beggars can't be choosers, I guess."

Elizabeth wrinkled her nose. "I don't think I would like that at all. I like things to go together. I don't think I'd like to sit on somebody else's couch." She motioned for Tucker to sit down. "I'll get the coffee. And I have some cookies. You still like cookies, don't you?"

Even though breakfast had been less than two hours earlier, Tucker smiled in acceptance. "That would be great."

Elizabeth hurried off to the kitchen as Tucker perched on the edge of the couch. Everything was too neat and predictable, appearing to be at right angles to something else. Tucker found the precision unnerving. He nudged the stack of *Martha Stewart Living* magazines on the coffee table, canting them to a 105-degree angle.

It felt much better. Tucker took a deep breath.

Elizabeth returned with a silver tray, two cups of coffee, and a dainty plate, complete with paper doily, stacked with cookies. Tucker recognized them as Girl Scout Trefoils. They weren't his favorite.

"It's decaf," Elizabeth explained. "That's all I drink when I drink coffee. Otherwise I'm up all night. And I only have skim milk. I hope that's okay with you."

Tucker never drank decaf and if he ran out of half-and-half, he would drop whatever he was doing, get dressed, and head out to a store, no matter what the time or weather.

"Sure, that's fine," he said.

"That's good," Elizabeth said softly. "I remember you being funny about your coffee. Good to see that you're past that now."

An uncomfortable silence followed. It may have lasted only ten seconds, but each second was amplified for Tucker as it ticked past.

"So. . .your classes going well?" he finally asked. "You enjoying teaching? My mom said you were doing very well."

"You've been keeping tabs on me, too. I like that, Tucker. Checking up on me and all." She smiled slyly.

Tucker wanted to explain that he hadn't, really. His mother faithfully reported the news on scores of his former classmates and friends—often in excruciating detail. Elizabeth was in the pool of former friends that his mother reported on.

Elizabeth took a sip from the cup, then carefully placed it down on a coaster. "I do like teaching. I'm enjoying myself. It's almost like being back in high school." She laughed. "Well, I *am* back in high school, really. Just not as a student. I like teaching civics. We get to use current events and bring in newspapers and not just get stuck working from one old textbook. And I'm cosponsor of the pep squad, and I travel to most of the games— football and basketball. None of the other sports really need a pep squad. So I keep pretty busy."

Tucker sipped at his coffee. He did his best not to wince. "I followed them over the Internet. The football team did well this year."

"The Internet? Really? You can do that with high school teams?" Elizabeth chirped. "I guess I knew that. After all, the

Owatonna Press is online, right?"

Tucker nodded. He was at a loss of what to say next. He came to the sudden and complete revelation that Elizabeth was not the easiest person to talk with. She was always polite and generous and pleasant and never became shrewish or demanding. But Tucker recalled never knowing what subject to bring up next. With Elizabeth, selecting the conversation and the topic was always a conscious decision.

"So," she said, breaking his reverie, "you talked to my father."

"I did."

Elizabeth beamed. "Then. . .you're moving back?"

"Moving back?"

Elizabeth buckled her lips in confused concentration. "Back to Owatonna."

"I. . .I. . ." Tucker's answer would not come.

"Daddy did offer you the job, right? He said he was going to offer you more money than they did in Chicago. Tucker, that's a big salary. More than I make. He did offer the job, didn't he? He didn't lie to me, did he? Did he change his mind at the last minute? Please tell me he didn't do that."

"No, he didn't. He made the offer."

Elizabeth relaxed into the couch—slowly, so she wouldn't spill any coffee. "Thank goodness. I thought for a minute that something had gone wrong."

Tucker took a cookie and chewed on it.

"So?" Elizabeth said, not sharply but close to sharply.

"So. . . ?" Mr. Thompson had made the offer less than thirty minutes prior to this very moment. Could she think that Tucker would have come to a decision so quickly?

"So you have decided, right?"

Evidently she could. And she did.

"You *are* going to take the offer, right? You talked about how great it would be to work in your home church. You said that. I remember that distinctly. We were in my parents' living room watching the Twins or the Vikings—some sports thing. You said it would be great to stay in Owatonna. You said that was one of your goals."

Tucker kept his words even and low. "Elizabeth, that was years ago. I was still in seminary. We were still. . .you know. . . together."

Elizabeth turned to face Tucker head-on. "Well, we were together because you were still here. If you come back to Owatonna, we can still be together."

A headache rapidly began to develop. Tucker never thought clearly with a headache. He wished he had some aspirin. He wished he were outdoors. He wished that this day might start over.

"Elizabeth," he began, then stopped to examine her eager features.

Tucker would never use the word *corn-fed* to describe Elizabeth, but that's the image that first came to his mind. She was wholesome, robust, and as pretty as a cornfield in July. She was fuller now than when they had dated—her skin seemed to fit her better. Her blond hair was as bright as sunlight, and she wore it longer, to her shoulders. There was a looseness about her movements, as if she had become more comfortable in who she was.

Tucker had to admit that Elizabeth was a very attractive woman. More attractive than Cass—much more attractive—in that sweet-corn-and-fresh-milk sort of way. When they first began to date, he had wondered why she would be interested in him—a mild-mannered, not terribly attractive seminary student who never would make as much money as a tenured high school teacher. Elizabeth had confided to him once that she liked him because he was smart and polite and dressed neater than most of his friends. Tucker now remembered the conversation. . .and how fortunate he had felt.

The two of them had dated for nearly three years. He had been the one who broke off the relationship. He clearly remembered why.

It had come to him as an epiphany one evening. The two of them were in his car in her driveway, saying good-bye. He had his arm around her shoulder. She was talking about marriage—not theirs, exactly—but marriage in general. A thought had flashed through his mind: *We could get married, and if it doesn't work out, well, there is always divorce.*

The thought scared Tucker so badly that, within two weeks, he broke off their relationship. He would not allow himself to stumble into marriage while holding onto a "get-out-of-marriage" card. It wasn't fair to Elizabeth. Tucker considered himself more honorable than that.

"Elizabeth," he repeated, "I don't know if I'm going to accept this job. I like Chicago. I like my work there. The people are nice. Webster Avenue is a wonderful church. I have to think about this."

"You're going to have to *think* about it?" she said, astonished. "But, Tucker, you *always* said you wanted to work here. Back at our church. Back home. I'm here. In Owatonna. We never really broke up. You just said that you had to take a job in another church to get some experience. That you would have to leave the area for a while. And that, in order to be fair to me, we should go our separate ways. But I never thought you meant it to be permanent. I tried to do what you said. I even dated once or twice. But land sakes, it was nothing serious. In fact, I haven't even kissed a boy since last Thanksgiving. That is, until I saw you standing outside my door. And I couldn't help myself. I thought, 'Elizabeth, here is Tucker. He's come back for you.' Now you have some experience. More than enough experience. You've got what you needed. You can come home now."

Tucker could not hold back his exhale. "But, Elizabeth, we *did* break up. Maybe we never made any announcements. But don't you remember? We were really, really close to getting engaged. Then we stopped seeing each other. Don't you think that meant we broke up?"

Elizabeth smiled patiently. "No." As an older sibling might gently explain the rules of a new game to a younger sibling, she continued. "You needed time. I gave you time. And space. You said something about space. So you had both. Then you moved to Chicago. I don't know anyone who's moved to Chicago—or even Minneapolis—who's really happy with their life there. They come home. . .or at least they want to come home. We're small-town people, Tucker. We belong here. I do. You do, too."

Tucker wanted to challenge her observation but did not.

"This may come as a shock to you, but I still love you, Tucker. I do. Sure, for a few years, we didn't talk. It's just like when people go off to war or something and they don't talk for years, and when they come home, they pick up exactly where they left off. It happens all the time. My mother said it happens all the time. Tucker, you're a nice person—a very nice person. You dress well. You're funny. You make me laugh. I may not understand everything you say, but I think your jokes are funny."

"But, Elizabeth," Tucker stammered, "it's been years."

She folded her hands in her lap. "Tucker, this is a small town. There aren't that many options. You know a lot of our friends got married right out of high school. And the rest of them got married right after college. I'm done with college. And so are you."

Tucker waited. The day had become more bizarre by the minute.

"You come back home, Tucker," she instructed, her words firm. "You come back and we can start over again. It's time. We have spent enough time apart. It's time now."

Tucker drank the rest of his coffee, now cold. "Elizabeth. . ."

"You don't have to answer right now, Tucker. You told my father you would think about it, right?"

He nodded.

"Then think about it. I know you'll make the right decision."

Tucker did not stagger down the street in utter confusion, clutching at the brick walls and façades for support, but he felt like it.

All smiles and nods and touches on his arm, Elizabeth had finally let him leave her apartment. She gave him a short hug and a chaste peck on the cheek, as if she had been issuing him soft hugs and gentle pecks on the cheek for years, and no silence had ever existed between them.

It's like a Fellini movie, Tucker thought. Then he realized he had never really seen a Fellini movie—only read about them. *But it's how I would imagine a Fellini movie to be. Odd characters, bizarre settings, absurdist dialogue. Just like today.*

Three blocks north of Elizabeth's apartment stood Ev's Kitchen. Ev Brooten, the original owner, had passed away years ago, but it still remained Ev's Kitchen, even though there was no longer an Ev.

Tucker slipped his coat on a brass hook on the wall, sat down at the counter, then shifted his gaze to take in the street out front.

"Coffee?"

"Real, with cream."

"Anything to eat?"

Tucker was far from hungry but thought it might be impolite to only order coffee. "Pie?"

"What kind? I bet if you name your favorite, we have it."

"Chocolate cream?"

The waitress set the coffeepot down on the counter. "That's not your favorite."

"It isn't? It used to be. It was when I came in."

"No," the waitress replied, chuckling. "It's either pecan or cherry. That's your favorite. One of them is. Always has been."

"Pecan, please," Tucker replied brightly. "Is it homemade?"

The waitress stopped. "If it wasn't, would you still order it?"

Tucker shrugged. "I don't know."

"Well, it is homemade. Or at least restaurant made. It's really good. We should charge more for it. Ice cream?"

"No. It gets in the way of the pecans."

"Warmed?"

"Only if it's real cold."

"Room temperature," she replied.

"I'll take it like that."

"That's the right way to eat pie." She smiled.

There were only a few people in the diner. The after-Christmas sale participants must have headed en masse to the malls. The downtown streets, while not empty, were no busier than a normal weekday. The lunch hour had since passed, so the only people left inside were those with lots of time on their hands, content to linger in pools of soft conversation.

Tucker's waitress stayed at the end of the counter, not hovering about her customers—a habit he disliked greatly. Her arms were folded across her chest as she rested her back against the stainless steel refrigerator/cooler. She looked down at her feet, then back up at Tucker. She stared hard for a moment, then smiled.

She took a few steps forward. "I thought I knew you. You're Tucker Abbott, aren't you?"

By now Tucker had finished his pie and was stirring a second and third sugar packet into his coffee. "I am."

"You looked so familiar when you came in. But lots of people look like other people. Half the time, I'm afraid of being recognized; the other half, I wonder if that customer is who I think it is."

Tucker narrowed his eyes, trying to think who she was.

"It's okay if you don't get the name—or even the face. It seems like a long time ago. Bonnie Howell. It used to be Howell. It's Middlestadt now."

Tucker's expression remained unchanged.

"From tenth-grade English class. With Mrs. Rosenberg."

Tucker tilted his head to the other side, thinking that maybe it was the light or shadow or some odd refraction. "I remember Mrs. Rosenberg," he said slowly.

The waitress offered an overly dramatic sigh. "I sat two or three desks behind you. We were in the same group for the Shakespeare plays."

"Was your hair different?"

The young woman laughed. "It was longer. And more. . .red. I was twenty, maybe thirty, pounds lighter. I was younger. And much shyer than I am now."

Tucker's mind was still drawing a blank.

"I played Ophelia when we did our little skits for the combined classes."

Tucker slapped his head. "Now I know you. Sure. When you said Ophelia. I remember that. You were good at that, right? Acting and all that?"

"It was one of the shining moments in my small box of high school memories. One of a very few."

Tucker nodded. "High school isn't as pleasant as most people think it is. It's a hard time."

"Not for you. You were smart. And funny. I remember you as being funny."

Tucker shrugged. "I guess. Funny, maybe. But I don't know about smart."

Bonnie stepped closer. "So what are you doing now? Did you go to college?"

"University of Minnesota. I worked for several years. Then three years at Faribault Seminary. Three and a half, actually."

"Wow. Seminary. So you're a preacher, then?"

"Associate pastor."

"Around here?"

"Chicago."

"Chicago? No kidding. I was in Chicago for a long weekend quite a few years ago. My boyfriend—husband now—took me there. He wanted to go to a Cubs game. Said he's trying to go to every major-league park."

"How many has he been to?"

"He's watched the Twins—and the Cubs. Maybe it's a life-long project or something. I don't ask all that often."

"So you're married?"

She nodded and refilled his coffee cup without asking. "Ten years now. Two kids. A girl and another girl."

"That's great."

She waved her hand in a gentle sort of dismissal and headed off to take an order from a newly arrived customer. When she returned, she came around the counter and sat down two stools away from Tucker.

"You like Chicago? When I was there, it seemed big and busy—and expensive."

"It is all of that," Tucker said. "But I like it. All kinds of people and all sorts of wonderful restaurants and things to do."

Bonnie's eyes focused on the street beyond, almost as if she weren't really listening.

"The fellow you married—is he from Owatonna, too? Would I have known him?"

"No. He's from Blooming Prairie. He was going to take over his dad's farm but didn't. Long story there, none of it worth repeating. I guess if it isn't your fate to do something, there's no power on earth that can make it happen. Eric was not fated to be a farmer. He works over at the grain elevator in Medford."

"So married life is good?"

It appeared as if Bonnie was about to shrug but thought about it first and didn't. She focused on the counter instead. "Sure. It's good. The kids are great. Most of the time. Eric is there when I get home. He pays the bills, cuts the grass, fixes things. We go to the movies once in a while. We got a satellite dish six months ago, and we just wait a month or two, and we see the same movies at home for free. Or almost free. The dish costs some, I guess."

Tucker drank his coffee silently.

"And then there's the other benefits of being married. . .you know, wink, wink, nudge, nudge?"

Tucker felt his cheeks redden at her brazenness. Suddenly bold himself, he said, "Bonnie, can I ask you a question?"

"Sure. I'm not going anywhere in particular."

"My question is: Why would a woman you broke up with years ago want to get married all of a sudden?"

It was the waitress's turn to look surprised. "Married? Someone asked you to *marry* them? Today?"

"No, not today, nothing like that. But sort of. All I had to do was step aboard. Like getting on a train."

Tucker saw an older man in a table by the window raise his hand and point at his coffee cup. Bonnie saw it, too. She slowly rose and walked to the coffee warmer. Returning with the pot, she set it on the counter.

"Maybe it's just the right time. Settling-down time. I guess everyone feels it differently. But there is a clock. . .or a calendar involved. A season-of-life sort of thing."

Tucker nodded at the information.

"I don't want to be nosy," she asked, "but since we're being stupidly honest this afternoon—probably something to do with the weather—do I know this woman? Is she from around here?"

Tucker had come too far in this unexpected intimacy with an almost-total stranger to worry about being considered foolish. "Elizabeth Thompson," he stated evenly.

"Really? I know her. Well, I don't really *know* her. But I know who she is. She comes in here sometimes. She's really pretty. She teaches at Owatonna High, doesn't she?"

Tucker again felt that sense of disconnection—as if he didn't belong where he was, and he was only observing his life, not living it.

"She is pretty," he agreed. "And she does teach at the high school."

"Hmmm," she said, examining Tucker as if he were a used car. "Well, I can see you together. Sure. You would make a cute couple."

Tucker sighed. He couldn't help it.

Bonnie touched his shoulder as she headed to the cash register. "Well, Tucker, you could do worse. You could do much worse, you know."

Tucker paid his tab at Ev's, left a five-dollar tip, and promised to stop in and see Bonnie again when he came back to Owatonna to visit. Then he buttoned up his coat, adjusted his knit cap low across his forehead, and started toward home.

He had not forgotten how biting the wind could be, how damp and humid the cold could be. Taking deep, cleansing breaths, he marched down Main Street, walked down Third toward the park, then cut over, heading up Western and toward home.

This is all ridiculous, he thought. *I haven't seen or talked to Elizabeth in so long, yet she thinks nothing has changed and wants to get married. That's ridiculous.*

He stamped his feet on the pavement while he waited for the light at the power plant to change.

I should have worn my winter boots. This is cold out here.

A car slowed and beeped. Tucker looked up, realized the light must have changed, and hurried across the street.

No. This is crazy. She may be ready, but I'm certainly not. The relationship didn't really work back then, so why would it work now? She might think it can work, but she also thinks it's time to settle down. I don't. I like Chicago. I want to stay there, at least for a time. A year, anyhow. Two years, maybe.

He turned at Cross and headed east. Three more blocks.

Not enough time to think it through, but I'm too cold to go farther.

Tucker wasn't used to these types of dilemmas. He was absolutely inexperienced in dealing with them. His roommate had said during one of their last conversations at Faribault, "There comes a time when both men and women decide to settle down. It may not happen at the same time for both, but when it does, it doesn't really matter who they're with—that's who they marry. Not because of love," he expounded, "but because of expediency—and that person happened to be in the line of fire."

Tucker had scoffed at him then. But his roommate went on

to get married that fall to a woman he had met at the beginning of the summer. The two of them were involved in a church plant in Oregon.

Tucker stopped walking, closed his eyes, and lowered his chin to his chest. He inhaled deeply and lifted his eyes. Then, as weary as he had ever felt before in his life, he began to trudge the final block to home.

He couldn't recall the color of Elizabeth's eyes but remembered, in agonizing detail, every facet and emotion of Annie's farewell hug, standing in the early gray chill of a Chicago morning.

But Annie is too old. Pearl said that Annie is too old.

And Pearl is right. . .right?

Tucker began to wonder if the twinges he felt were what lying to your own heart felt like.

"So, do you think Tucker will hold out for more money?" Mr. Abbott asked his wife as they sat in the quiet of the living room.

"More money?" Mrs. Abbott replied.

"From the church," he answered. "Thompson said that they were willing to go higher."

Mrs. Abbott folded her hands in her lap. "I don't think he's going to say yes."

Mr. Abbott rustled his evening paper together and gently slapped it on the table beside his chair. "What do you mean? Did he say something to you? He didn't say anything to me about it. Just that the interview went well."

Mrs. Abbott stood, walked to the front door, and switched on the outside lamps. "No, he didn't say anything. But I saw something in his eyes."

"Saw what?"

She made sure that the door was locked, checking the deadbolt and the doorknob. "I'm not sure. Something unsettled. I know we talked about him coming back to our home church, but I don't think he's going to choose this path."

Mr. Abbott harrumphed, picked up his paper again, and carefully folded the pages back. "I think he will. He's a smart boy. He knows how to make the right decisions. He'll say yes. He just needs time to think about it, that's all."

Mrs. Abbott offered her husband a short smile, hoping that he was correct but knowing, somehow, that he wasn't.

Ten

Chicago, Illinois

TUCKER SILENTLY SLIPPED INTO the narthex, stone dark save for the weak warbling exit light at the far side.

Just enough, Tucker thought, for him to navigate slowly to his office, his arm stretched out in front of him, his steps shuffling.

He turned the corner in the hall. The hallway glowed with the light from the street corner lamp, and Tucker hurried his steps to his office. He unlocked the door. He did not lock it for any other reason than that Pearl had insisted on it.

"Your office is out here in the hall. You have a computer in plain view. How hard would it be to steal that?" she had said.

Locking internal doors seemed to denote a certain lack of trust, Tucker thought, but he admitted that Pearl might be right.

No sense tempting the weak to make bad choices, he told himself, providing a reason for the extra vigilance.

He tossed his briefcase onto one of the two matching upholstered chairs that he had found for twenty-five dollars each at a
sidewalk sale. The chairs were covered in blue denim, faded to
light on the arms. A couple of new pillows from Target spruced
the pair up enough so they appeared to be an intentional design
statement. He had positioned them close enough to his desk that
they doubled as visitor chairs.

He snapped on his desk light and switched on his computer.

It was the beginning of the third week of January, and he had
three letters to write—letters he had put off for too long. On Friday,
while in the office, he had dodged phone calls, afraid of who might
be on the line. All because he hadn't written the letters. Over the
weekend, he stayed out of his apartment for as long as he could.
He didn't have an answering machine, so a missed call was truly a
missed call.

Monday morning, very early Monday morning, he awoke,
startled. The clock blinked 3:02 a.m. He knew he'd be unable to
return to sleep after that. He showered as quickly as possible, not
wanting to disturb Mrs. Carswell on the second floor. Water rattled and hissed loud in the old pipes. He dressed quietly, bundled
up against the January cold, and nearly jogged to the church.

He did not bother making coffee. There was a twenty-four-
hour convenience store on his way. He bought a large coffee with
a heavy dose of real cream and real sugar. Once at the church, he
sat down, edged off the plastic lid, and took a sip. He liked the
way the warmth spread from his throat and fingered out along his
chest and stomach. It was only the first few sips that felt so good,
and Tucker tried his best to savor them.

The screen on his computer blinked once and issued a tiny
whirring buzz as it geared into action.

He took another long sip. He placed the cup to the side,

moved the keyboard closer, flexed his fingers several times—just like a cartoon concert pianist did before beginning banging on the keys—then proceeded to type rapidly, staring at the letters as they popped onto the screen.

He did the easiest one first. It was also the shortest.

Dear Mr. Thompson,

I apologize for not responding in a timely manner. The decision was more difficult than I at first thought.

I must, with great regret, turn down your generous offer of the associate pastor position at Settler's Ridge Bible Church. I understand that it is a good opportunity for me and that it would mean serving at the church where I grew up. But I have made a commitment to the people here at Webster Avenue Church, and I intend to honor that commitment. If your offer presented itself a year or two from now, my decision may have been different.

I have prayed about this—a great deal—and I sense that God is directing me to stay the course and remain where I am.

Thank you again. I am honored that you considered me for the position. May God lead you to the right candidate.

Yours truly,
Tucker Abbott

He read over the letter several times, making a slight correction here, adding a word there, deleting a few others. It had not been an easy decision. Deciding about his future with Elizabeth was easier, in some ways, than the job offer. He was surprised at the amount of money they had offered him—more than he was making now. And in Owatonna, that extra income would go a long way. It would go a long way anywhere, but it would go much farther in southern Minnesota. *Maybe,* he thought, *as far as a new car and a small but nice house.*

It would be, he admitted, a thrill to serve in his old church. The culmination of an old dream.

But there was a problem, maybe several problems. The first was a severe case of being too familiar. He couldn't bring himself to fully embrace the picture of himself standing in that very familiar pulpit, speaking to a group of very familiar people. Those people would be people who knew all of his history and his weaknesses and his family and their weaknesses. How could you witness to anyone who knew that you had once, in a moment of reckless teenaged abandon, climbed the town water tower on a dare and painted some unflattering epithets concerning the high school principal in large, block purple letters? How could you even think that you could be a credible witness?

Tucker also worried about the looming avalanche of unspoken expectations—expectations from his parents, from the church, from Mr. Thompson, from Elizabeth. Fear of being ground to pieces in that avalanche was the most haunting and scary factor in his considerations.

He tapped at the keyboard and sent the document to the printer down by Pearl's office. Not having a printer of his own was another reason for his early morning arrival.

He waited, saved the document into a file marked *Abbott/ Private*, then started on the second letter.

Dear Mom and Dad,

I know this letter will disappoint you, and for that I am sorry in advance—but I am not going to take the position at the church. . . .

Tucker went on for three pages—probably two pages too long—as to his reasons for wanting to stay in Chicago. He stressed that he had made a commitment at this new church.

The reasons he gave were not entirely true. Yes, he had made a commitment, but he had given no verbal or written promise that spoke to a specific length of employment. Pastor Yount had not asked for any—and none of the elders attempted to elicit such a promise from Tucker. During one interview, Tucker recalled one of the elders saying that if they got more than two years out of a young associate pastor, they would consider they got their money's worth.

Tucker had made friends. Good friends. And he imagined, or hoped, that certain people trusted him and expected him to be there and remain there—both in the youth group and in his adult class. He would not turn his back in a cavalier way on those unspoken expectations.

And I have signed a lease, Tucker typed. *If I leave now, I would be liable for the rest of the rent. Finding anyone to sublet the place—given the economy and all—would be nearly impossible. So I would be out over four thousand dollars.*

The truth be told, Tucker knew he could find a replacement to sublet the apartment within hours, owing to how affordable and spacious the place was. He hoped it wasn't too much of a lie—but it would help his mother take the news.

He read over the letter a couple of times, made only a change or two, and hit PRINT.

He was left with the letter he owed Elizabeth. He was not anxious, nor did he have second thoughts. No, he was certain there was no possibility of resuming their relationship. True, Elizabeth was pretty, maybe edging to beautiful. She was pleasant with a kind heart. But there was no—and he hated to use this word, for its trendiness distracted him—*chemistry* between them.

Tucker told himself that she was prettier than most. But that was not the driving force behind a relationship—at least not to Tucker, and at least not now.

As he looked back, he realized that during the time they had dated, he was never totally "take-your-shoes-off" comfortable with Elizabeth. He knew it was terrible of him to describe her that way now, after all these months and months had passed, but it was true. They had some good times and pleasant memories, but mostly Tucker recalled an uneasy sense of. . .of always being slightly uncomfortable. He could have grown to accept it; that's what he told himself. But he didn't want to.

Whatever the reason, he knew for sure that Elizabeth had no future in his life.

He opened his drawer and took out a single sheet of paper and began to write—carefully, with small letters and even spaces. It would grow loopier and disjointed when he got to pages two and three, but by then the momentum carried him past spelling mistakes and oddly placed grammar.

When he was finished, he reread it. It said what he wanted to say. That the two of them shared no future together. He was careful to add several times that he cared for her as a person and that they had good memories. But he was clear—he was not coming back to Owatonna. Not to the church. Not to her. He wrote that she was a beautiful woman and that she should move on with her life.

Then he signed the letter, *With affection, Tucker*.

He folded it, slipped the pages into an envelope, addressed it, sealed it, and placed it at the corner of his desk.

The coffee had gone cold, but he drank the rest of it anyhow, grimacing. Then he stood up and went out into the hall to retrieve his first two letters.

That's odd. I don't think that office light was on when I came in.

He glanced at his watch. It was a dozen minutes past six. No one came in this early. He was sure of that.

Perhaps one of the lights is on a timer.

He opened the office door, and if he had done what he had felt, he would have clutched his hand to his chest, pretending he was having a heart attack.

Pearl sat at her desk, a cup of coffee in her hands. She did not appear surprised or disturbed in the least.

"I always come in early. It's quieter here than at home," she said. Then she slid a short stack of papers across her desk. They were facedown. She offered a wry smile and said softly, "We should talk."

Pearl, calmly and evenly, took another sip of her coffee. "I would have thought you would have waited a bit longer."

Tucker's breath came back. He found his voice. "You shouldn't be reading my personal letters." He hoped he sounded hard and edgy and almost angry.

Pearl narrowed her eyes. Tucker tried not to cringe but was afraid he did, at least a little.

"And, you, young man, should not be using a communal printer for personal letters. You should not be turning other jobs down using our church's supplies. You should not be looking for another job just yet. And you should not be lying to your parents." She took a huffy breath. "I'm finished."

Tucker felt his hand move, as if he were going to say something. But he could find no words to convey the conflicting, complex emotions that exploded inside him. So his hand dropped to his side again.

"Is. . .is that fresh coffee?" he asked meekly instead.

In an accommodating and gentle gesture, Pearl smiled. "It is. That's why it's always so strong when you get in."

Tucker grabbed one of the thick paper cups reserved for visitors and guests. He returned and sat in one of Pearl's visitor chairs, slumping down farther than usual. "Do I need to tell Pastor Yount?"

Pearl shook her head. "No. Unless these letters aren't true. You aren't going to take the job after these letters, are you? They're not some sort of bargaining ploy, are they?"

"No. It's the wrong place. It's the wrong time. And I'm the wrong person."

Pearl leaned back, her chair creaking softly. "I expect you to get other offers. Pastor Yount gets offers. No reason you shouldn't get them. You're a good man. You do good work. Word spreads. It will happen again. Another church will try. It's the way of the world."

Tucker shrugged. "I feel terrible about it."

"You think you let your parents down?"

"I did. Especially my mother. It's always been her dream, I think, to see me in a pulpit."

"But you are in a pulpit," Pearl answered.

"But not the hometown pulpit. To her there's a big difference."

Pearl tilted her head. "There was an old girlfriend there, too, right?"

Tucker guessed his face didn't hide his astonishment.

Pearl waved him off. "There is always an old girlfriend." Her words became almost motherly, comforting. "She expected you to come back, too?"

Tucker just nodded. The story was too curious to attempt to describe neatly in a sentence or two.

"Breaking hearts left and right, aren't you, Tucker?"

He shrugged, making a helpless gesture with his free hand.

"And you never thought you would be one of those men— men who break women's hearts. You considered yourself one of the good guys, who are kind and considerate and nice."

"I *am* that sort of guy."

Pearl snorted. "No. You're not. You are a nice fellow. But you can't make everyone happy. You need to wake up and see what sort of world you really live in—and what sort of world everyone else lives in these days. I bet you seriously considered moving back just so your mother and old girlfriend wouldn't be mad at you."

"No. It wasn't that bad."

"Malarkey. It was. You just don't want to admit it."

Tucker slumped farther, to an almost prone position. "Maybe. Maybe a little of that is true."

Pearl folded her newspaper and tapped it back together. "It's almost seven thirty. Pastor Yount will be here any minute. Last year he made a New Year's resolution to jog before work three times a week. That lasted two weeks. This year he resolved to get here early before the phone calls start." She slid the paper under her desk. "I sure hope he stops soon. He's wrecking my schedule, for sure."

Tucker stood and straightened his shirt. "Thanks, Pearl. You're a good person, too."

Her smile vanished as soon as it started. "Wait. There's not a woman here in Chicago, is there? Is that why you turned it down?"

"No. There's no one here."

Tucker hoped his answer sounded convincing.

Tucker skipped lunch. That was unusual. Instead of eating, he walked back to his apartment and stared out the window. The phone rang on two occasions, and he ignored them both.

When he returned to the church, the small light on his phone was blinking impatiently.

He punched in his code.

"Tucker? Where are you? I've been looking all over for you!"

It was Cass. Since New Year's, he had seen her at church and had coffee with her twice, in the afternoon both times, nothing more than a few minutes over a latte.

"Well, since I can't find you, I'm just going to tell your tape machine the good news. I hope that it doesn't cut me off like you said it did the last time. The news is that I got a new job, a really good job, in the juniors department at—get this—Saks Fifth Avenue. Can you believe it! Me at Saks! Me, a farm girl from North Dakota, working at Saks. I keep pinching myself."

Tucker didn't exactly know what a juniors department at Sak's was, but it sounded trendy and expensive. He had never shopped at a Saks Fifth Avenue but knew from reputation alone that the store had nothing he could afford or feel comfortable in.

"I start next Wednesday. I'm so excited. And that's not all. You remember my friend—Molly Amerson? She and I are going to be living together! She found this great place over on Hubbard. It's on the fifth floor and there's no elevator, but it's huge. We get to move in next weekend. You can help, can't you? We need all the strong backs we can get. You will help, right?"

Tucker closed his eyes.

"I told Annie and she was excited for me," the message continued. "She really was. I loved living with her, but having a four-year-old around all the time can really cramp your style."

Tucker heard a soft, maybe suggestive giggle.

"You know what I mean, Tucker? I'm sure you do."

There was a beep, and an automated voice came on the line. "You have fifteen seconds left."

Cass growled. "Anyhow, Tucker, call me. Use my cell number. You call me. Once we're all moved in, we'll have a big party to

christen the place. How's that sound? Maybe just you and me could
have a more private party before that. How does that sound?"

Tucker blushed, knowing that Cass liked to make him squirm.
"You call me. Okay? Bye."

Then he heard the sound of the disconnect.

Tucker waited several minutes, then dialed her number with
an odd combination of weariness and fear.

Eleven

AS TUCKER LISTENED TO CASS'S cell phone ring, myriad images and thoughts flooded his mind.

Of all the people he knew, of all the people he'd ever known, Tucker would have placed himself at the top of the list of men who never, ever would have had a problem with too many choices—especially when it came to women. He was just not that sort of fellow. He had never been that sort of fellow and never imagined becoming that sort of fellow.

But yet here he was, a man with too many possibilities.

If he was looking for a spark or chemistry to identify the "right" woman in his life, then he had already turned down several leading candidates.

He kept thinking about his old roommate from seminary, now married and apparently wonderfully happy, according to his latest e-mails. Was his contention correct—that when it's time, it's time, and no matter what, the person nearest that realization might just be the person you marry?

Was it time?

Tucker looked at his watch. It was eleven thirty.

He let the phone continue to ring.

Should he wait for that "right" woman? Would God purposefully select just the perfect person and lead the two of them to meet and fall in love? Was that sort of micromanagement the way God worked? What happened if Tucker met the "right" woman and didn't recognize her? Could he miss her? Could he be confused by the choices and let her get away?

Tucker also wondered: What if he stumbled across the "almost-right" woman? What would happen then? In the process of making the relationship work, he would learn about love and sacrifice and obedience. Wouldn't that be a good thing?

Tucker rubbed the bridge of his nose.

And then the ringing stopped.

"Hello?" he said into the phone.

It was Cass, and as the seconds ticked by, Tucker had no idea what to say.

Annie sighed deeply and watched Cass hurry down the steps with another box full of clothes and shoes and cosmetics. She had not lived with Annie all that long but had accumulated, to Annie's standards, a vast store of stuff.

Annie was happy for Cass—that she was making her own way in the city, that she had found friends and work she enjoyed and a new life. But she was also a little sad. Having Cass live with her was at times inconvenient, yet it was company. Even though Annie had Chance, conversing with a four-year-old was just not the same. By evening, Annie yearned for an adult conversation.

Chance was playing with Joshua across the street, and Annie was alone. She had not recalled her life being quite this quiet before.

Danny—the first and only man she had known and dated since Chance had been born—had offered his resignation, as it were, a few days earlier. It wasn't exactly a resignation, but to Annie it had the same impact, the same pain.

"We're friends, Annie," he had said while leaning against a dryer in the Laundromat. "You are my friend, right?"

Annie had to agree. She knew they were friends but had always considered Danny to be more than just a friend.

"I like you being my friend," Danny had continued, not looking directly at her. "We had some good times together, and I don't see why we can't have some good times in the future."

Annie had spoken up. "Then why are you bringing this up? What's the problem, Danny?"

He had dismissed her questions with a wave of his hand. "It's not a problem with you, Annie. It's me."

When she was silent, he went on, "You need more than I can give you. . .I mean, with Chance and all. I don't think I'm ready for all that. Kids complicate life. I don't think I can handle that, Annie."

Annie had wanted to scream but didn't. She had wanted to argue and debate with him, but she didn't. What she did do was let him leave. She didn't want to let him leave, but what choice did she have? She had no control over him. She had no claim. She could not—and would not—offer him any other intimate inducements to stay. Besides being wrong in God's eyes, she knew that such inducements, such liberties allowed, would smack of desperation and that they would not work. A man like Danny had options—lots of options. She would be offering nothing that he couldn't find in many other places.

"Danny, if that's how you feel, then that's how you feel," she had said to him, her words even and calm. "If you want to be friends, I would like that, too. We did have some good times."

Danny had looked at her for the first time during his visit. "Thatta girl." He grinned. "We can still be friends. That's right; we can be. We can still go out sometimes."

Annie couldn't recall if Danny had hugged her good-bye or not. It wouldn't make any difference. A friend gone was still gone.

As Danny climbed into his service truck and drove away without so much as a backward glance, two short prayers popped into Annie's mind.

The first was: *Lord, don't let Chance be hurt by this.*

And the second was: *Lord, send a man into Chance's life. He so desperately needs a father.*

Tucker had decided he couldn't help Cass move. But he was sending, as his proxies, a trio of the biggest, strongest teenagers from his youth group to lend a hand. They were more than happy with the pay of unlimited donuts, Coke, and pizza.

One of the things Tucker had decided, especially after sending his firm letter to Elizabeth, was that it was damaging to everyone to be strung along or to be the one who did the stringing. He liked Cass and was sure she found him pleasant to be around and somewhat amusing. But Tucker knew that Cass was not the "right" woman for him, even if she was more than a little tempting. He also knew he would feel regret when he told her they should "just be friends." Yet he knew it was the right thing to do.

Cass went from happy to cutting and snippy in seconds. "What do you mean 'just friends,' Tucker?"

Tucker had hoped this would not turn confrontational. "I mean that. . .we should just be friends. Nothing more."

"Oh, I see. So up to now, it was just fun and games for you. And now you want to walk away?"

Tucker tried to relieve the tension in his neck by twisting one way, then the other, to crack the bones. Nothing worked.

It was clear that Cass did not like silence in any form. "Fine, Tucker, go on your merry way. You just beat me to it, that's all. After I moved, I would have done the same, I bet. Actually, I'm looking for someone with a lot more pizzazz than you have—you know, like walking on the wild side. That's not you, is it, Tucker?"

Tucker sighed. "No, I guess that's not me."

He could almost hear Cass tapping her foot, impatient.

"Tucker," she said, her voice softer, "I can't say it hasn't been fun. At least most of it."

"Thanks," he replied.

"And be sure to tell those guys to get to my place at eight. I have a lot of stuff to move."

"I will."

"Thanks, Tucker. I guess I'll see you around."

When the silence returned to his office, he tilted back in his chair, exhaled, and closed his eyes.

After that talk with Cass, Tucker pitched himself into his work with a doubling of his energy and enthusiasm. The programs he assisted or led benefited greatly from his additional time. Pastor Yount complimented and congratulated Tucker early and often.

"Tucker, you're doing wonderful work. Have I told you that? Recently?"

Tucker looked up from his desk. Pastor Yount did not often walk the halls, preferring people to come to him.

"Thank you, sir."

"How many in the combined youth groups this year? I have your status report on my desk, but the numbers escape me."

"Between fifty-five and sixty."

"Wonderful," the older man added. "That's the most we have ever had. Impressive. They must like what you do."

Tucker didn't know what to do with praise; he had trouble knowing where to look.

The senior pastor rapped his knuckles on the doorframe as a sort of coda. "Well, son, keep up the good work. People are noticing it. *I'm* noticing it."

Despite the praise for the youth group success, the resurgence of attendance at adult Sunday school classes, the beginnings of a small-group ministry, and an almost error-free bulletin, Tucker wasn't sure how to feel. He had some pride in his accomplishments but tried not to think about that since his mother insisted that all forms of pride were sinful. Tucker hoped he felt fulfilled, but he didn't feel full. Despite the successes, despite the high praise, there was always a little bit of an ache just under the surface. It was a longing, a yearning he didn't understand. But it was at the edge of his awareness all the time.

No life is free from doubts, Tucker reminded himself. His mother had said that the strongest Christian faced them sometimes.

But what Tucker felt was not doubt. He was sure of that. It was close to doubt, perhaps, but it was not doubt.

"Susan wanted me to tell you that she enjoyed having you over for dinner the other night. I know it was just a thrown-together meal, what with Mrs. Yount being out of town and all," Pastor Yount was saying.

"Nonsense, sir. She did a wonderful job. Everything was delicious."

"Tucker, you pay attention now. She's a good cook; she's pretty. . .although I am a bit biased. And she can play the piano. Did you know that?"

"Yes, sir. She told me she's taken lessons since first grade."

"Wonderful piano player," Pastor Yount said again, almost to himself. "A find, that one. A real find." Then he snapped back to reality and looked at his watch. "Well, I have a lunch appointment. I'll see you later this afternoon."

The minute after Pastor Yount left, Tucker could hear the big bells in the big church two blocks over sound out the noon tolling. It was a huge, Gothic, Presbyterian masterpiece of a church, and Tucker envied the sterling punctuality of its clarion call.

He had no lunch meeting scheduled. Instead he looked forward to heading home to cook up a package of ramen noodles and to grab a twenty-minute nap.

Tucker stopped at the corner of MacKenzie and Phillips, waiting for the light to change. From behind him came a muffled rapping sound, then something sharper, like a ring or a coin on glass. And he could have sworn he heard his name being called out—but from a faraway place.

He looked about him and didn't see anyone. He didn't want to do a complete 360 degree turn with that puzzled, "where is that sound coming from" look on his face. But whatever the source, it grew louder and more insistent.

"Abbott! Pastor Abbott!" followed a sharp series of raps.

The sound was coming from the front window of the coffee shop directly behind him, occupying the southwestern corner of the intersection.

Tucker turned and was greeted with the sun glaring off the window. He could see an arm and an outline of someone. He walked closer, shielding his eyes. He grinned when he found the source of the sound.

It was Annie Hamilton, tapping at the window with her coffee spoon. She gestured expansively. "Come join me," she called. It must have been very loud inside, for it was almost loud out on the street.

How could Tucker refuse?

He had talked only sparingly to Annie since the holidays. In church once, in the Laundromat once, both very briefly; and he had waved to her across the street once. But nothing more than that. Pearl's warning kept buzzing about him like a swarm of invisible flies.

"Pastor Abbott!" Annie cried when he stepped inside the almost-steamy shop, thick with coffee fumes. "I was going on and on trying to get your attention, shouting like a banshee, and almost broke the window."

"I kept hearing this small voice calling out to me." He smiled. "I was expecting it would turn out to be a voice from the heavens. You know, you could have just come out and got me."

Annie shook her head quickly. "No. If you give up the window table for any reason, the jackals will steal it from you in an instant. It's a coveted position. You can eat and watch people passing by. Like you saw—the sun makes you invisible so you can observe at your leisure with no guilty stares back from the street."

She wedged herself farther into the corner and pulled the

table closer. "You have to join me. I could tell that you were heading home for lunch, and I know you're not going to eat right. Get a sprout-and-turkey sandwich—or a toasted Gouda and ham. They make the best sandwiches here. They really do. They even bake their own whole-grain bread."

Tucker had walked past this coffee and sandwich bar hundreds of times, it seemed, and had never once stopped. "I do like sandwiches. And coffee. And all of a sudden, that sounds very tasty."

Annie grinned again. "Then I will save this chair for your return. But hurry. I see a lot of envious stares from the rest of the jackals. . .I mean, customers."

Tucker thought she was kidding, but when he looked around, he admitted to himself that she was right. A dozen people crowded at counters, eating standing up. Tucker hurried to get his order in. In addition to the Gouda and ham on a toasted onion roll, he ordered a tall latte and a cream soda with a small bag of organic, sweet potato chips. The food, in a little wicker basket with a patterned wax tissue, looked healthy. Tucker's stomach growled in anticipation.

All the while, Annie, with legs wrapped underneath her torso, remained perched on the small stool. Tucker wondered how she did that. Even though he was younger, he knew for a fact that it would take three people to get him into the same position. Annie simply slid into it effortlessly.

"We haven't talked for ages," she said. "The holidays are always so busy, and then. . .I don't know, time just slips away, doesn't it?"

Tucker nodded through a mouthful of warm, toasty Gouda, slippery with German mustard. "This is delicious," he mumbled through the crumbs.

"I know," Annie agreed. "I'm afraid it will get more popular, and then I'll never get a seat here."

Tucker chewed on another bite, hesitant to eat quickly, for he didn't want the meal to end too soon.

Annie looked down at her hands. "I heard you called Cass."

Tucker gulped.

"She told me just about everything. Even the things I didn't want to know."

"I hope I didn't hurt her feelings too badly," he said contritely.

Annie snorted out a loud laugh. "I'm sorry, Tucker, I didn't mean that. . . Well, I guess I did."

"What?" Tucker asked. "Did she think it was funny?"

Annie tapped at his hand with hers. "No. It's just that I don't think anybody is ever going to get to Cass. She is one very tough girl. She plays men better than anyone I have ever seen."

"Plays?"

"Not like that, Tucker. She's not mean-spirited, really. But she had a tough childhood. She didn't tell me a lot about that but enough. I think she's getting back at men for some things that happened to her a long time ago. You may have been one of the few men who said good-bye before she did."

"Really?" Tucker replied, not knowing whether to sound glad or sad or concerned.

"Cass is really pretty. I see other men around her. I think that's why your high school guys were so eager to help. She's a very attractive single woman with her own place."

"Oh, my," Tucker replied, now worried.

"Don't be concerned," Annie answered. "She would never go for a younger man. I'm sure she liked the attention, though."

Tucker chewed thoughtfully. "I wish you would have said something earlier."

Annie shrugged. "I couldn't. I wouldn't. Maybe I would have stepped in if I thought either of you were about to make any big mistakes. You weren't about to make any big mistakes, were you?"

Tucker shook his head no. He waited a minute, then said, "Pearl says you started the crisis pregnancy center—the one on Walton Street. I didn't know that before."

Annie appeared almost embarrassed. "I didn't really start it. I just happened to see a need—with Chance and all—and I called some people and they all thought it was a good idea, and we raised some money, etcetera, etcetera. It snowballed without much work on my part."

"That's not what Pearl said," Tucker replied. "She said you were tireless."

"Pearl is too kind," Annie said. "I'm glad I had a part in it. But seriously, other people run it now. I just volunteer occasionally."

A couple of minutes of silence passed as Tucker ate and Annie sipped at her coffee.

"Chance asks about you," Annie said, her voice suddenly softer. "He sees you in church and asks when you're coming back to wrestle more."

"Anytime, Annie. I can come any time you'd like," Tucker said. And he really meant it.

A studied look came on Annie's face, as if she was carefully measuring her words. "Tonight? I have soup in the Crock-Pot. Do you like soup?"

"I love soup," Tucker said enthusiastically. "Soup. . .soup is good food." He shook his head wryly. "I've come to repeating ad slogans as if they were original thought. How impoverished."

"I do that all the time, too." She grinned. "I get something in my head, then forget where it came from. Those advertising people are truly pernicious."

Tucker had talked to no one recently who could use the word *pernicious* both correctly and effortlessly. He smiled. "You're right.

We are corrupted so slowly that we cannot count the progress."

"So tonight is good? I didn't mean to put you on the spot," Annie said.

Tucker tried to talk while chewing. "No. Tonight is great. I would have said no if I had something planned."

Annie scowled in a friendly way. It was as if something suddenly troubled her. "You know, Pastor Abbott, it's not that I doubt you—"

He held up his hand. She remembered.

"Tucker," she continued, "I want you to come to dinner. That would be nice. But I don't want you to think that I'm using Chance to manipulate you into doing something you would rather not do."

"No, Annie," he protested. "I would *love* to come for dinner."

"It's just that I don't want to ever use him as a pry bar to get people to do things for me because they feel sorry for me because. . .you know. . .being a single mother and all that. People do feel that way. I see it when I volunteer at the center. I know they do."

Tucker picked up the second half of his sandwich. He knew the conversation had taken a quick turn to the serious, and if he stopped eating, that would make the moment seem even more serious. From what he knew of Annie, she wouldn't want that to happen.

He stuffed a bite of sandwich into his cheek. "Annie, I deserve a rematch with Chance. Give me an opportunity to get even."

Annie tilted her head back and laughed with abandon. Her gesture was both disarming and most vulnerable. "You're funny, Tucker. You're even funnier, considering you're a pastor and all."

And at this Tucker himself laughed, holding his hand to his mouth to prevent any food from tumbling out.

Annie turned her coffee cup a half circle. Tucker grabbed a

potato chip and tried to chew softly. He was surprised at the sweet, salty taste and wondered how anything deep-fried could be organic and good for you.

"I just want to make sure, that's all," she said, growing serious. "I have experienced a bit too much pity recently, and I want to make sure that's not why people do things for me. Pity works for a while, but most people tire of giving it after a bit. Then they just get angry. Angry that you haven't gotten any better or the situation hasn't improved any. And some situations aren't ever going to change enough to suit some people."

Tucker kept on eating, wanting her to continue. Over his months at Webster Avenue Church, he'd found that if he just shut up and kept his mouth closed, people opened up. As a trained pastor and as a man, he was geared to fix things. Fix things in a hurry. *Boom*—do this. *Bam*—do that. Just follow my instructions and the problem will go away. It was remarkable how simple problems became when he used his analytical mind on them. Thirty seconds was all he really required. Sometimes less—even before the other person finished talking.

His flippant attitude had changed when a member of his youth group came to him in tears, pregnant and scared. She was the child of kindly yet overprotective parents—at least that's what Tucker had thought until that night. She bore the black eye and bruises of a beating and had a bag packed, ready to leave. Tucker listened that night for what seemed like hours. It was not a situation that lent itself to easy fixes and quick platitudes. It was complicated, brutish, and thorny—and it involved people who claimed to understand forgiveness and salvation.

So instead of presenting Annie with a quick Scripture, he waited. He listened. He attempted to soften his face into saying without words that he was a mirror of acceptance. He tried to encourage Annie with his eyes alone to talk more.

"You know about Chance, don't you, Tucker? You know how he came into my life?"

Tucker nodded. "I asked Pastor Yount about you. I hope you don't mind. It's an amazing story. God doesn't always use the usual methods to get things done, does He?"

Annie's smile was tight. "No. No, He doesn't. I wish He had. There was so much. . .so much has happened to me since Chance was born. It would have been easier to have the lessons I needed to learn all written down neatly in a book rather than having to live through them—but everyone must feel that way."

"I suppose you're right. But that doesn't ever happen. You have to go through it."

"I know. And Pastor Yount, even though he was sort of prickly at first, came around. Anyhow, it's me and Chance—and that's all. I thought at first that. . .well, people sometimes see us as a project that needs to be rescued or fixed or something. Men do that a lot."

Tucker twisted the cap off his cream soda. "Are you talking about Danny?"

"Danny?" Annie replied.

"Danny Trevalli?" Tucker responded, knowing Annie had heard him the first time and knew very well who he was talking about.

"Yes," she murmured.

Tucker smoothed some crumbs off the table, brushing them absentmindedly into his lap. "You two are. . .seeing each other, aren't you? That's what Cass said."

Annie shook her head, then focused her eyes on Tucker. "We had been. For a long time, it seemed. That's the reason I want you to be sure that you're not doing anything for us because you feel sorry for us. Because when people stop feeling sorry, they just leave. Or what's worse than just leaving is getting angry before they leave and telling you how much you have messed up their life as well as your own. I guess people use up whatever compassion they have pretty quickly. Tucker, I don't care if people lose interest in me. I've been around the block a time or two. I know what failed relationships look like and feel like. So for me, I don't care. But Chance cares. He cares a lot. And I don't want someone spending time with him—or us—because they simply feel sorry for him or me or both of us."

Tucker wasn't surprised by the level of emotion that Annie had reached in the span of a few moments. Disappointment and regret make fertile ground for anger and bitterness.

"So don't come to dinner if you feel sorry for me or Chance or both of us," she insisted. "You know, I must sound like a crazed harpy who presents a list of demands the first time she says hello to a man. Please forgive me if I sound loony. I guess I'm just sensitive—at having people feel pity. And I need to protect Chance."

Tucker did not have to pretend to be concerned. "No, Annie, I don't feel sorry for you. You made a choice. From what I was told and what I can see, it was the right choice. How can I feel pity for someone who followed her heart? Maybe your road isn't as easy as others, but it seems like you're doing okay."

Annie sat up straight. "I *am* doing okay. Chance is doing okay, too. He really is."

"So I'm not going to eat your soup because I feel sorry for you. I like playing with Chance. I like talking to you."

Annie grinned, seeming relieved.

"And besides, I can't cook for beans. Anything would be better than undercooked ramen noodles."

Annie reached over and put her hand on top of his. It surprised Tucker, but he liked the feeling.

"Thank you. I'll tell Chance when he gets back from school. He will be so excited. But I need to make it early. He goes to bed at eight on school nights. So if you want time to recuperate from any wrestling injuries, dinner will have to be early. Can you come at five thirty or six?"

"Five thirty is fine," Tucker said.

Only then did Annie slowly remove her hand from atop his.

Once Chance was put to bed, Tucker felt a wash of total calm in his chest—caused, he thought, by the total absence of the unusual or the totality of the ordinary. When he was with other people, a part of him was always on guard for what they might do un-expectedly or what he might be asked to do reluctantly. It was an edge that Tucker never grew acquainted or at ease with.

He helped Annie clear the coffee cups and dessert plates from the table, stacking them neatly in the kitchen. She rinsed them just like his mother used to rinse plates before washing them. When he was by himself, he never rinsed—he just washed. *Rinsing must be a female sort of nicety,* he thought.

Annie hummed as she puttered about, filling the sink with hot water and soap, wiping countertops, wrapping leftover carrot cake with plastic wrap and placing it in a very organized refrigerator.

The evening felt so typical, so normal, so expected, so easy. Tucker could not recall being more comfortable. Even by himself, he would often be pricked by a sliver of nervousness, anticipation, anxiety. The feeling never overwhelmed him, never caused him to lose sleep, but he could imagine himself doing just that if he let the sliver expand.

But here, in Annie's warm apartment, he didn't feel the

festering of that sliver at all. The humming, the soft lights, the good food, the easy laughter, the wrestling marathon with Chance before dinner—all of it was a soothing balm. Tucker finally relaxed, as if emitting a great body-width sigh.

"Go into the living room," she said. "Relax for a minute. I'll finish here. You must be exhausted after your workout with Chance."

Tucker rubbed his shoulder, wincing dramatically. "He is one tough little guy. And I will take you up on that offer."

Tucker took the one end of the sofa unoccupied by the cushion-long, gray Petey the Cat.

A minute or two later, Annie stepped out of the kitchen, holding an empty mug. "More coffee?"

Tucker wanted to say yes but did not. "I'd better not. It's late, and you have to be up earlier than I do."

Annie set the cup down. "Are you sure? It's no bother."

Tucker repeated himself by standing up. "Thanks so much for dinner. The soup was delicious. And the bread—thanks for telling me about that bakery. I'll be sure to stop there."

"I'm glad you came. Chance was sure excited, as well."

"He's a good boy."

"He is," Annie confirmed proudly. She stopped, then added, almost under her breath, "Danny never played with him like you do. Danny always said he was too old and that Chance would mess up his hair. He was so proud of his hair, even if it was thinning."

Annie had a faraway look in her eyes as she spoke. Then, as if to clear those painful images, she shook her head. "Let me walk you down to the street."

Tucker played at being offended. "I can find my way home, Annie."

"I was pretty sure that you could, but I have to check in on the Laundromat. Two birds with one stone, you know."

Once on the sidewalk, Tucker took a step toward his apartment, only a few doors away. The air was still cold enough to chill him quickly. "You have such a nice place, Annie. It seems so. . .so pleasant. Peaceful."

Annie's broad smile was genuine. "Why, thank you, Tucker."

"Can I ask you a question, Annie? Probably a question you get often."

"Sure."

"Why a Laundromat? And why here?"

"Oh. . .one of those easy-to-answer in twenty-five words or less sort of questions?"

Tucker retreated. "Annie, if it's too personal a question, feel free to tell me to buzz off. I just like to know about. . ."

Annie took a step closer to him. Tucker knew she wanted to put her hand on his arm, but she didn't.

"You know, Tucker, you aren't the first to ask me that question. I've given a lot of different answers. I'll be the first to admit that there was—or is—an element of serendipity about my life, yet most of it was a conscious, deliberate decision. I was in college, doing what my father wanted me to do. My mother was dead, and I didn't have much of a peer group to mislead me, so I did as I was told. I was on my way to being a teacher and getting married, and all of a sudden I felt stuffed. Like I was a bear that climbed halfway into an old log to get at a huge hive filled with sweet clover honey, and who ate and ate and finally ate so much that he couldn't get out. And then the bear started to get very nervous because he could hear the bees coming back. And he knew if he stayed there, it would get very painful in little doses. But he ate too much and now he was stuck."

She inhaled deeply. A UPS truck rumbled past in the street, and she followed it with her eyes. "Do you know what I mean?"

Tucker did, indeed. "I think so."

"I more or less threw everything away—the honey, the college, the engagement, my father. I left with only a few dollars in the bank and headed to the city. I wasn't running away, because I grew up just north of the city. The money I had was the money that I made selling my art in college. Anyhow, I was in Lincoln Park, walking. It was a nice spring day, the sky was blue, and I just wandered about the neighborhood. I walked past this place," she said, gesturing with her arm toward the Laundromat. "And I stopped, dumbfounded about the wooden screen door—in Chicago. Like a fish out of water. Like the odd object where it shouldn't be."

She folded her arms over her chest. "Taped to the window, on three corners with masking tape, was a handwritten FOR SALE sign. I opened the screen door, and in less time than it takes to get coffee at Starbucks, I had bought a Laundromat. Well, me and the bank."

"And you knew then that was what you wanted to do with your life?"

Annie snorted a laugh. "No. But I knew what I didn't want to do with my life. And this place oozed with pleasantness and sweetness and calm. I knew right then, and right away, that I could take my time with the next step in my life—without getting stuck in that dead log, eating honey, getting fat, and waiting for the pain of a thousand bee stings." A smile drifted to her lips, and her eyes crinkled at the corners. "It felt so right. Do you know what I mean?"

"I do. I think I do," Tucker said. "And you're happy here. You're satisfied with what happened? Not getting the honey, you know?"

Annie's shrug told more than words. "Who dreams of a Laundromat? But without it, my life never would have intersected with Chance. And without Chance, what would life be?"

Tucker smiled. He had never wanted to give anyone a hug as much as he wanted to hug Annie—and she saw it, too, he was sure. But he didn't hug her, though after a minute he regretted it. Tucker figured that if one hesitated on a hug, it was not a hug meant to be given.

However, they did stare at each other for a long, quiet, deep moment.

"Annie, thanks again for dinner. Tell Chance I'll see him Saturday. I was serious about the zoo. I love the zoo."

Annie waited to reply. "I know you were serious. I could tell. And so could Chance."

In that instant, Tucker wished he lived farther away so he could savor the satisfying serenity of the walk home.

Twelve

FROM HIS FRONT WINDOW, overlooking MacKenzie Street, Tucker could see Annie's bay window, barely, through the tree branches. He could see the street and sidewalk below his apartment. His building, too many years old, did not have a buzzer system. If his bell rang, he faced three flights of steps. So instead of automatically running down the thirty-nine steps, he would push his forehead against the window, trying to discern who might be calling on him from the view of the top of his or her head.

He could ignore door-to-door missionaries and solicitations for Greenpeace and other innumerable requesters of charity. And for Tucker, this was good. He found it hard to say no, and it was much easier and less costly to hide, never answering the uninvited calls.

Saturday morning often brought out solicitors in flocks, and Tucker reluctantly made his way over to the window for the third time that day. He had to kneel on the couch and push his head almost sideways to get the best view.

The buzzer shouted again, and Tucker tore down the steps to greet his visitor.

"Mrs. Alvarez," he announced with a grin, "how did you know I was hungry?"

She laughed and would have offered a wave of dismissal if her hands had not been filled—her left with a reused shopping bag and her right hugging a covered dish to her chest.

"Young men are always hungry," she scolded. "And I have not visited my almost-the-priest neighbor for weeks. I have felt guilty—almost enough for penance. Instead of asking forgiveness, I have cooked you a meal."

"Please come up, Mrs. Alvarez. I can make you coffee. I may have some cookies."

"My doctor, the teenager, says I am no longer allowed to have cookies. Sugar in the blood."

"But coffee? You can have coffee?"

Mrs. Alvarez squinted. "Yes. But what kind of cookies do you have? Are they small? Walking up three flights will burn off the sugar, right?"

Tucker gladly grabbed the dish and bag from her and led the way, slowly, up the steps. He was surprised that she kept up with his much-younger knees.

"It is a pill he gives me," she explained. "The knees are the first to go. The pill makes me forget about them for a while. For a teenager, he is a good doctor."

Tucker set the bag and dish on the counter. "He's not really a teenager, is he? Your doctor, I mean."

Mrs. Alvarez lowered herself into a kitchen chair. "He is as old as you—and you are a teenager, too. All of a sudden the whole world is being run by teenagers. No one asked me about this. It simply happened. It's not fair, Pastor Abbott. It is not fair."

Tucker busied himself with the coffee—grinding the beans and measuring the water. He took pride in making coffee well. It was one of the only things he did in the kitchen that could generate pride. No matter the guest, they all complimented him on the robust flavor of his coffee.

"Did you hear what happened to poor Mr. Dravogivitch?"

Tucker admitted that he hadn't, and that allowed Mrs. Alvarez an opening for a ten-minute recap of the neighborhood news. Tucker knew more about MacKenzie Street and its inhabitants than he knew about his neighbors back home in Owatonna. Mrs. Alvarez made his mother look like a slouch when it came to the local news.

He poured the coffee into the two matching mugs he owned and took the half-and-half from the refrigerator.

"Ahh, this is good coffee, Pastor Abbott. All the clergy at my church make coffee like a poor person—so weak that you can mistake it for tea. No sense in drinking something like that."

"I have only a few vices, Mrs. Alvarez, and coffee is one of them."

"Better than most, I admit. I mean vices. If you have to select a vice, I would agree that coffee is a good one to pick. Something you can enjoy every day for the rest of your life. What other vice can make that claim?"

She sipped in silence. She used silence, Tucker figured, like he used it, to get people to talk. When they had the chance to chat, dueling silences often occurred.

Mrs. Alvarez spoke first, and Tucker congratulated himself—until he heard her whole question.

"So have you seen Annie again?"

"Annie?"

Mrs. Alvarez gave him a withering, incredulous look, while still affectionate.

"Pastor Abbott, unless you do not wish anyone to know, I suggest you wear a disguise or use the back entrance of places. I was out sweeping my stoop when you rang her bell. And I just happened to be at my window when I saw you leave. It was too long for a pastoral call—so dinner must have been involved. And no one else visited after you entered."

Tucker couldn't help but admire her detective work. "But it wasn't a date. She asked me to dinner, and I played with Chance. She's a member of the church. There's no law against having dinner with a church member, is there?"

With a sly turn of her eyes, she replied, "That depends on which church you attend."

Even though amused, Tucker could not let the assumption go unchallenged. "It really wasn't a date, Mrs. Alvarez. Besides, Annie is a lot older than I am. I'm sure she didn't consider me a date."

Mrs. Alvarez shrugged. "Just asking, Pastor Abbott."

They retreated to their respective silences.

"More coffee?"

She nodded, and a miffed look suddenly crossed her face. "You said something about cookies. I don't see any cookies. Have you lied to me about cookies?"

Tucker nearly stumbled out of his chair to retrieve the three boxes of assorted Girl Scout cookies he had purchased last week. He hadn't been able to see who was camped outside his door, and the girl's innocent smile had trapped him.

As Mrs. Alvarez picked up her third chocolate-mint cookie, Tucker softly said, "I thought Dr. Teenager said to be careful with sweets."

She held the cookie midway between her mouth and the

plate. Very evenly she replied, "He did." And then she popped the entire cookie in her mouth and chewed it with great happiness.

"I don't want to get you in trouble with your doctor, Mrs. Alvarez. I don't want you to say a man of the church tempted you and led you astray."

She shook her head. "Pastor Abbott, I am nearly seventy-six years old."

Tucker was amazed. He would have guessed sixty-five at the high end.

"For an old lady, I'm in good health—up to a point. I have no real reason to complain. Everything hurts when I wake up, but at least I'm still waking up. And because of that teenager, I do watch sweets. I walk. I walked up these three flights of steps to get here, right? That counts for something."

"I am sure it all helps," Tucker replied.

"When you get to my age, you start getting smart. The good Lord could have another twenty years for me, but I'm thinking He won't give me that long. And if I can't have a cookie now and again, then another twenty years won't count for much. It has taken me seventy-six years to realize that life is really short, after all. When I was your age, I thought to live another fifty years would be like an eternity—and then some. But let me tell you: The last fifty years have come and gone in the blink of an eye. Life is too short to waste it on anger or disappointment or bitterness. Or not having the occasional cookie."

Tucker found himself nodding in complete agreement.

"Annie is older than you. Danny is her age. You are not. She knows more about life than you. It is the curse of getting old. Only when you are old do you get true wisdom. So it is wise of you to get to know her—she can teach you a great deal about life. You can see that she knows about life because of her art. Artists understand life more deeply than most people, like you and me."

She sighed, then brightened. "And I want two more cookies. Then I will leave you alone, Pastor Abbott. And I want the chocolate ones. If you are going to wander from the straight and narrow, you should make sure it's for something that you really, really want." She giggled, sounding much younger. "And I really want the chocolate cookies."

Tucker pulled mail from the slot by his name. Circulars, offers for credit cards, bills, and a single letter with his name handwritten.

He held it up to the light.

It was from his mother.

He unlocked the door and hurried upstairs. He splashed water in the kettle and set the flame to high. He assembled the instant coffee and sugar and cream. Even though he was particular about his coffee, at times he preferred the metallic taste of instant coffee. Instant offered a more brittle, harder flavor, and he knew that it would be perfect for this evening.

He placed the bills in the drawer by the toaster. The first of every month, he removed them all and spent an evening writing checks and wondering how a family of four or five could make ends meet on a salary half as large as his.

He tossed the circulars and promotions and advertisements in the trash can by the sink. The water began to boil, and he measured and scooped and poured and brought the mug to the table. He slit the envelope with a butter knife. Turning his back on the overhead light, he let it illuminate the letter he held in his hands.

Dear Son,

I hope you are doing well. Dad and I are fine. He has had some trouble with his headaches this week. I claim it's because of the furnace and the dry heat. He refuses to consider a humidifier, claiming that they are a big source of mold. He may be right. There is nothing worse than the smell of a moldy house.

I am still very hurt and most confused by your turning Mr. Thompson's and the church's offer down. Mr. Thompson told your father that the church offered three thousand dollars more than you make now. To me and to your father, there seems as if there would be no question in the matter—more money and a chance to come home. I'm trying to understand. You say you have to follow your heart. But you always talked of preaching from behind the old pulpit at our church. Even as a little boy, I imagined you standing in the pulpit. I know that it was your dream as well as mine. It was your choice, Tucker. But nothing makes sense these days, and everyone does just what they want with no regard to tradition. Following one's heart takes precedence. I'm not sure your father or I will ever truly understand. But I suspect that everything is fine as long as you do, right?

You do, don't you?

Just so you know, the position at church remains open and probably will for a while longer. Mr. Thompson said he interviewed one young man who had studied at a seminary north of Chicago. Deerfield? He said that the money this one wanted was more than our senior pastor makes.

Coming from a big city, people have inflated opinions of themselves and their worth.

I ran into Elizabeth Thompson last week. She was very

pleasant to me, despite what happened.

She is getting very serious with a fellow she just met from Eden Center. He may have been divorced. That's what Mr. Bainbridge said, but he wasn't sure if it was him or a cousin. Elizabeth has only known him for a few months, and people are beginning to think of them as a couple.

Remember Louise Guthry? She lived on Pelly Street by the fairgrounds? She died—and was only fifty-three. She taught your Sunday school class when you were in fourth grade. She never married, and they didn't find her until she hadn't shown up for work for four or five days. They say that the stench was horrible—a life wasted like that.

I hope you're well and that you truly understand what you're doing. Dad says hello.

Your mother

Tucker refolded the letter and slipped it back into the envelope. He placed it on the table before him. Picking up his coffee, he took a long sip, waiting for the clutching warmth to fill his chest, hoping it would dissipate the growing sense of dislocation and emptiness that nestled in his heart.

Susan sat down and smiled up at Tucker. "I like it when a man pulls out my chair like this. It's such a gentlemanly thing to do."

Tucker sat down and took the linen napkin. "I guess it's a dying art—good manners. At least that's what I see if I use my youth group as a model."

"Discouraging," Susan said, "but with you as their role model, maybe there's still hope for the next generation."

Tucker shook his head. "Susan, I'm not sure how big an impact I'm going to make in the world."

Susan opened her menu. "Tucker, this place is really expensive. Are you sure you can afford this? Maybe I could pitch in for my share?"

"No, this is my treat, Susan. I've been here before, and as long as you don't order the surf and turf, I'll be fine. I'm a man of simple consumptions, remember? No car, an inexpensive apartment, and I'm not a clothes horse. I think a good meal every now and then is in order."

Susan looked around the restaurant. "It must be the bow ties on the waiters that intimidate me. A man in a bow tie seems out of place in a restaurant."

"It's just their statement. You have to give it back to them as good as they give it out. And if they're offering the risotto tonight, you have to try it. It's wonderful." Tucker chuckled to himself at how much he was sounding like Pearl.

He held the menu in his hands as a choir member holds their music. He peered over the top and watched Susan go through her deliberations. He imagined that she was calculating prices, not wanting to order the most expensive item, nor the cheapest—instead looking at the middle of the range. She could not order the "roasted chicken platter" because there wasn't one on the menu.

She was not adventuresome with food choices. She asked first about the lasagna, as Tucker had bet with himself that she would, then declined when learning that there were mushrooms included. She moved on to the baked manicotti but worried for at least a minute that the tomato gravy might be too spicy—it did, after all, have Italian sausage in it. Spicy was to be avoided, if possible.

Tucker watched as she touched her hair, toyed with the thin gold chain of her necklace, pursed her lips in deep concentration.

She was pretty, he told himself, and most pleasant to be with.

He dropped his eyes to his watch. It was early. On Saturday nights, Tucker never felt loose or carefree, knowing he had to rise early for work.

"I'm think I'm ready, Tucker. I know you can't stay out late tonight, and I don't want to be the cause of you falling asleep in the service."

He recalled Pearl's observation a few days earlier. "*She's pretty, can play the piano, and has hips made for having a lot of kids. A perfect pastor's wife, isn't she?*"

When Tucker had stared into Pearl's eyes, he couldn't tell if she was serious. . .or mocking Pastor Yount's more blatant sales attempts on behalf of his comely niece.

❦

That evening, after arriving back at his apartment, Tucker sat in the darkness of his living room and stared out to the eastern sky. He missed seeing the stars. The city lights drowned out all but the brightest stars.

He knew he should go to bed, but he also knew he wouldn't sleep well.

The uneasy yearning in his heart had grown louder. His dinner with Susan had only increased its volume. As he had interacted with her, in his mind had flashed an image of his mother, sitting in the darkened front parlor of their home, wringing her hands on a handkerchief, the family Bible in her lap, trying her best to understand a wayward son.

He enjoyed Susan's company—but somehow, somewhere— there was a hollowness, as if they were both actors in a pre-ordained play, going through a complex bit of maneuvering on a stage not to either of their choosing.

Tucker knew he was a worrier by nature but wasn't sure if the root cause was nature or nurture. The Abbotts, his mother said on one occasion, are not a family to leave any detail unconsidered.

Tucker's thoughts rolled and tumbled. He knew his uneasiness with Susan was as minor as the width of a hair. And he knew his worries about his mother were melodramatic at best.

But what worried Tucker the most was a fear that first appeared only a week ago. He remembered walking with confident steps toward the pulpit to give a brief set of announcements and a plea for workers in the children's department, when his heart started clenching like a prizefighter's fist. In the space of climbing the five podium steps, sweat began to bubble across his shoulders and chest.

A heart attack was his first thought, but then he realized there was no accompanying pain—only sheer terror. His mind flashed to the symptoms of a panic attack, but a fellow down the hall at Faribault had had them, and what Tucker was feeling was nothing like the other student had described.

That left Tucker with only one conclusion—that it was his subconscious telling him that he was not where he was supposed to be.

Even as Tucker gave the announcements that day, he continued to argue with himself.

And in the end, he was further from the truth than when he started. And a lot more confused than he had ever been in his life.

The following Tuesday, he tapped at the door to Pastor Yount's office. Tucker often worked Mondays, even though it was his official day off. Pastor Yount had never worked a Monday in all the time Tucker had been at the church.

"Come in."

"Good morning, sir," Tucker said, his voice more formal than usual.

"And good morning to you. Have a good day off?"

Tucker had spent most of the day in the office. "I did."

"Good. What can I do for you?"

"I want to take a few days off. And if it's not asking too much, could I borrow your car? Just for a few days?"

Pastor Yount folded the book he had been reading. He focused on Tucker. "That would be fine—and you can borrow my car anytime you need it."

"Thank you, sir." Tucker took a step to leave as the older man held up a finger, bidding him to pause.

"May I ask where you're going? Back home for a quick visit?"

"No, sir. Not this time. I. . .I was planning on visiting my former pastor—he ministered at my home church for years and years. He's been retired, and I haven't seen him since before I graduated. He lives up in Wisconsin, and I'd like a day or two in the country."

Pastor Yount nodded as if he understood the urgency to Tucker's request.

"And I'll be back by Thursday evening for youth group. I can get there in six hours or so."

"Son, you could miss your youth group if you needed to. You have a core of good adult volunteers to take over."

Just as certainly as Tucker knew Pastor Yount would offer the extra time, he knew he'd decline it. "No, sir. A couple of days is all I need. I just wanted to see him. He's getting up there and all."

Pastor Yount added, laughing, "Aren't we all?" And then he coughed.

"Sir, are you feeling okay? I don't have to go this week. Next week would be just as good."

Pastor Yount waved his offer away. "No. I'm fine. I'm recycling an old sermon this week, anyhow. I'm fine. Just a little tired today."

"I could be ready with a sermon for Sunday if you need me."

"Nonsense. You go." He fumbled in his drawer and tossed Tucker a key ring with three keys. "Close the garage when you leave. And don't bother washing it like you did the last time. It doesn't know how to act when it's clean."

Tucker offered him a mock salute. "I'll let Pearl know where to find me."

"And take your cell phone. After all, the church is paying for it."

After telling Pearl about his plans and leaving before she had a chance to question him about the trip, Tucker headed home quickly. He threw a few pairs of jeans and some sweatshirts into an oversized gym bag. He tossed his toothbrush and a few other items in, zipped it up, and hurried down the steps, taking two at a time, until he reached the street.

He did not look north along the sidewalk, north to where Annie lived and where the Laundromat lay.

He did not want to see her just now. He did not want any more confusion in his thoughts than he already possessed.

He opened the car door, tossed the bag onto the passenger seat, and pulled away from the curb, not even caring that the windows were streaked and gray with city dust.

I'll stop in Wisconsin to wash them. Plenty of time to wash them in Wisconsin.

Thirteen

On the way to Spooner Lake, Wisconsin

WINTER HELD ON TIGHTER IN Wisconsin, Tucker decided, as he edged the car farther and farther north. Patches of snow lay huddled in shadowy places. Prairie grasses slumped over, bruised from the heavy snows, just now melting. A thick residue of salt covered much of the roadways. And the bright orange drift fences at the side of the road appeared tired and stretched after a winter's work.

The sunlight seeped away as Tucker checked the speedometer. He was at 336 miles from departure. His computer had provided a one-way distance to Spooner Lake of 351 miles. A few miles back, he had seen a sign advertising a bait shop and boat rental agency on Spooner Lake. He had a few more miles to go— a few more miles to Pastor Ringhofer's retirement cottage.

Gilbert Ringhofer had been pastor of the Settler's Ridge Bible Church during the years of Tucker's childhood through young adulthood. The man had confirmed Tucker, baptized him, and welcomed him into the official membership of the church. It was Ringhofer who was his mentor when Tucker came of age.

Tucker recalled him as a dynamic leader. He was short in stature, with intense dark eyes. Ringhofer's dark hair often seemed to have a mind of its own. . .the wind catching it or his forearm, since he gestured wildly when he spoke.

As Tucker drove deeper into the north woods, he tried to remember what Pastor Ringhofer had said or done to lead a young boy to consider the ministry as a vocation. Tucker recalled being impressed with the man and his sermons, with the way he remained unruffled in any setting. But the pastor's specific words—the ones that had made such an impact—eluded Tucker.

Pastor Ringhofer's wife had died when Tucker was in high school. The pastor had held on to the pulpit for another year, then announced his retirement after two decades of service to the church. Everyone was taken by surprise. It would have been easy enough for Pastor Ringhofer to stay on, become the pastor emeritus, enjoy an easier life, coasting on his twenty-year reputation. But he did not.

Within two months of his retirement, he sold his house, bought a cottage on Spooner Lake, and intended to spend his golden years "fishing, writing, and reading—all with a little solitude—to have some time for meditating."

The church had purchased a new bass boat for Pastor Ringhofer as a farewell gift. Donny Davidson, a member of the church for years, owned a small marina and offered the church elders a deal that was almost below his wholesale cost.

Pastor Ringhofer had lived on the shores of Spooner Lake for nearly seven years now. Tucker had seen him once since he had retired—at the hundredth anniversary for the church. Tucker thought he looked thin but hale enough. There was still the hint of intensity in his eyes, but the two of them had not found time to talk much that day. Tucker wrote an occasional letter, but, for the past year, he hadn't received any correspondence in return. Tucker was not totally surprised—the last letter he'd received had revealed the retired pastor was becoming more solitary and a bit gruffer during his years in Wisconsin.

Tucker drove on, past the bait shop, past the two-block downtown of Spooner, past the new mini-mart and Burger King, down to Spooner Lake Road. He slowed the car and read his handwritten directions one more time.

"Turn left on Spooner Lk. Rd. Go 1.5 mile. Big white house on right/lake. Two houses past. Blue siding. Boat in front."

He had called Pastor Ringhofer for directions, and while Tucker had been certain he surprised him, Pastor Ringhofer sounded cordial and inviting.

"You spending the night?"

Tucker replied that he wasn't sure.

"There's a new motel five miles north. I'll call for you. It's off-season and real cheap. You don't want to sleep on my couch."

The last mile and a half seemed to take as long as the previous 350 miles. Tucker was scared. He hadn't come for a social visit or to check if the muskies or northern pike were biting. He had come to ask a question he could not ask anyone else—not Pastor Yount, not Annie, certainly not his parents, or any of his new friends in Chicago.

He wanted to know what a crisis in confidence felt like—and if that was what he was experiencing.

Chicago, Illinois

Annie slipped out of her son's bedroom. She left him reading a teetering stack of books—some picture books, some word books. She insisted that he spend part of his day reading by himself.

Petey the Cat stared up at her as she snicked the door closed. The cat looked perturbed.

"Oh, my goodness, Petey. I haven't fed you this afternoon, have I?"

The cat cried plaintively and circled about her legs as she walked to the kitchen. Then, elbows on the counter, her chin cupped in her hand, she watched Petey attack his food.

She debated if she should cook something. Chance had eaten a bowl of mac-and-cheese an hour earlier. Annie couldn't bear to join him. Mac-and-cheese, to Annie, was an acquired taste. Only if she were completely desperate would she join her son in such a meal.

And she did not feel that desperate.

She opened the refrigerator and stared in, hoping that something new might develop as she gazed on the jars and containers and milk and cream and twelve-pack of diet soda.

Nothing did. She considered, for a second, running down to the end of the block to get an Italian beef sandwich at Al's. But she would not leave Chance alone. She would travel only as far as downstairs, into the Laundromat, while he was upstairs by himself.

She could call for delivery of something, but no matter how far or close, it would take a half hour to be delivered, and everyone these days tacked on a delivery charge. Annie's frugal, practical nature would seldom allow her to do so.

She reached in and moved a plastic carton—a pork chop from three days ago. She wouldn't eat it. Chance viewed pork chops as "yucky" food. She returned it to the shelf. The chop certainly would not age well and become a more attractive meal tomorrow, yet Annie could not summon up the strength to toss it into the garbage. *Besides,* she told herself, *I would have to take it to the Dumpster. If it's in the trash up here, Petey will howl over the smell all night.*

She pulled out a diet soda. She seldom drank soda. But somehow Chance had decided that sodas were the most perfect drink on the planet—this after more than four years of a steady diet of organic milk, natural juices, and water. She doled the cans out as an infrequent reward for doing chores or modeling good behavior.

This past week, Chance had only managed to get two cans of soda. He had become whiny and petulant and downright disobedient.

Mrs. Alvarez said it was a phase. When Annie asked what she might do, the older woman smiled as only a grandmother can smile and said, "By the time you get this phase figured out, he will have moved on to another, and that one will drive you even crazier. I remember my youngest—he liked to throw things. Anything he could pick up he threw. You couldn't turn your back for a minute. Something would sail past your ear if you did."

Annie asked what Mrs. Alvarez had done to stop it.

"I just waited him out, Annie," the older woman replied. "I didn't do anything different. I just waited him out. Just do your best, Annie, and keep loving him. He'll come around."

At times like that, Annie really missed her mother. So it was nice to have an older, more experienced woman she could ask for advice.

Annie took a long sip of the soda. She didn't even like the taste but drank from the can anyway, as if she were on autopilot. She wandered back into the living room and fell into her couch by the bay window. If she leaned just so, she could see the corner of the one window of Tucker's apartment—not into it, actually, but shadows and light coming from within. She had phoned him earlier and got his recorded message that he was heading out of town until late Thursday. She made a mental note to tell him not to give out such details on a phone message.

Tucker, you don't know who is going to be calling. What happens if somebody calls, and you don't know who they are? They might get ideas. You need to be careful.

Annie took another sip.

I'm beginning to sound like Mrs. Alvarez.

She settled back into the sofa. Petey, smelling of tuna, jumped up and flopped against her legs, licking his paws. It was the part of cat ownership that she most disliked—the after-dinner baths that Petey felt obliged to share.

As the cat groomed, Annie stared out the window, down the block. She found herself thinking about Tucker. She wondered why he'd left town so suddenly. Had he gone home for a visit? Cass once mentioned something about an old girlfriend of Tucker's teaching high school in his hometown. That image alone was enough to make Annie want to stop thinking about Tucker. And the almost-jealous feeling that soon followed surprised her. It made her want to stop thinking about Tucker even more.

She sipped on her diet soda.

The images did not stop.

She scratched the cat under his chin. Petey began to purr deep in his chest.

Besides, he's so much younger than I am.

And then she wondered where that thought had sprung from. It wasn't like her to obsess about anyone.

I'm not obsessing. I'm just thinking.

She stood up so suddenly that Petey almost tumbled from the couch.

"I'm *not* obsessing. Not at all," she said out loud to herself. "Thinking about someone is not obsessing."

She heard a stirring from Chance's room and placed her ear close to his door. The sound of a book's pages being turned was all she heard.

This time she whispered, "I am not obsessing."

And as if to prove it to herself, she made her way back to the third bedroom, the one she had reclaimed from Cass. It was now her studio again. On the table in the center of the room lay a small pine box, the box Tucker had given her for Christmas. She looked at the assembly of materials she had gathered about the box in preparation. When she selected materials, she gave no conscious thought to what would be included and why. She let her instinct take over. This time she had gathered a packet of black-and-white snapshots from an old book, a clutching of pages from a Bible she discovered on the street in front of the Laundromat, an old token for the Chicago elevated train system, the dried blossoms of both wildflowers and weeds, and a tie tack from the Minneapolis Good Fellows club.

Without pondering, without deliberation, she picked up the photos first and began to work.

"I am not obsessing," she heard herself whisper again.

Spooner Lake, Wisconsin

Tucker pulled the car into the rutted driveway. He usually found the sound of car tires on gravel to be a comforting, welcoming sound; but this afternoon, in the Wisconsin chill, he imagined it to be a lonelier sound. A sound of departure, not welcome.

The cottage, covered in blue aluminum siding, faced the lake. The shore was a hundred steps or so to the west. There was a small porch in front, its screening bulged and bowed. Under a tall pine, a boat covered with a faded blue tarp rested on a trailer. The tarp held a season's worth of leaves. Water filled the dips in the tarp. A rope on one side of the tarp had come loose. Water from the rain or snow had pushed the tarp down inside the boat, and a thickness of water, darkened by the tannin from the pine needles and leaves, pooled in the discolored fiberglass.

On the shore of the lake lay a grouping of dock pilings and planks. Weeds had grown up through the wood.

Tucker opened the car door and stepped out. Despite the quiet of the chilled air, he noted the scents of moss, still water, leaves, and fish. The smells were rural and timeless.

Tucker had made this impromptu, totally unplanned trip to settle the roiling in his heart. If any member of the clergy could answer Tucker's questions, it would be this man.

Since Christmas, Tucker had felt at odds within himself. At first he attributed it to having said no to his home church, his parents, and, of course, to Elizabeth. He wondered if he was simply feeling guilty. He figured he may indeed be the sort of man Pearl had described—a man who wanted so badly to please others that he would deny himself and deny his needs. He had dismissed Pearl's explanation, but as the weeks wore on his uneasiness grew, as did his questioning.

Tucker had been told at the end of his seminary years that many pastors, especially young pastors, would endure an early season of doubt and a period of questioning their calling. It was to be expected and would no doubt pass, as all phases do. The two professors issuing the warning had gone through the same process. "Anyone who takes a new job faces it," they explained.

"Until you fully settle in, which may take a year or longer, you will wonder if you have what it takes to do God's work. But we want to assure you all that you *do* have what it takes, especially since you've shown so much promise during your years at Faribault."

For Tucker, the expected phase was not subsiding but lingering and growing more intense. Tucker began to wonder if his worry was moving from expected and benign to something more malignant.

Tucker shrugged on his jacket, his shirt no match for the snaky breeze that hissed up from the lake. The dried flowers in front of the porch bent to the breeze. There was no bell by the porch door, so Tucker squeaked the wooden frame open and stepped to the real front door. A couple of lawn chairs leaned against the side of the house.

He knocked and waited. Then he knocked again. The door swung open.

"Tucker? Is that you making all the racket? I thought so."

Gilbert Ringhofer stepped out into the late sunshine. The old man must have shrunk some over the past seven years, for he was much shorter than Tucker remembered. He was wearing a faded Wisconsin Dells sweatshirt, and his whiskery cheeks were drawn. His hair was no longer dark but white.

"Let me take you on a tour before I bring you inside. While there's still some light in the day. I really hate daylight savings time."

The two of them walked down the lakeshore nearly a half mile till they came to a wide stream.

"In the summer, you can just wade it. The main road is a half mile that way," Pastor Ringhofer said, pointing. "But you get the idea. Let me show you what's north of me."

And they trundled back, past the cottage, and walked for nearly half an hour over the uneven terrain. The lake appeared gray and somber, much like Tucker's mood. The cottages, with the exception of one or two, were summer residences only, dark and wrapped tight.

"I'm ready to head back," Pastor Ringhofer said, his voice a bit raspy. "I've seen this before and not much changes as you walk around the lake. Prettier in summer, for sure. But you get a sense of the land."

The two of them made it back to the cottage as the sun slipped to the tree line at the western horizon. Pastor Ringhofer escorted Tucker inside.

"Sit down, son, over there on that couch under the window. The other one is the one the dog uses and it's full of dog hair. No one wants to sit in a big pile of dog hair, right? You want some coffee? You always liked coffee, right? I've got some instant. Or would you rather have some percolated coffee? I stashed my old percolator way up on the top shelf of the pantry. But I could get it down if you'd prefer that."

"No, don't bother. The instant is fine. I drink it all the time," Tucker said.

"Make yourself at home. I'll have it in a jiff."

Tucker sat at the end of the couch. The tiny house was not dirty, but it was far from tidy. There was a teetering stack of newspapers by the door. A few books lay open on the small table that must also have functioned as his dining room. The windows could have used a cleaning. The couch Tucker sat on was covered in some sort of green-fringed throw—the kind they sell at discount stores as an alternative to re-covering a piece of furniture. From the other couch an old Irish setter lifted his head and stared at Tucker, having made no effort to investigate when Tucker first arrived. Presently the dog rose stiffly, hobbled off the cushion, and walked slowly over to Tucker, snuffling loudly. He planted his nose against Tucker's leg and inhaled noisily. Tucker patted his head, and the dog looked up, a lopsided grin on his face, one eye having turned milky.

Tucker peered toward the kitchen, lit by a strong fluorescent. The cabinets looked metallic. He heard water gargling from the pipes, then a sharp, acrid smell of gas, but only for a moment.

A couple of minutes later, Pastor Ringhofer stepped out of the kitchen holding two mugs. "I put milk in 'em both. Don't have any sugar left in the house, so we'll have to drink it hard. That okay, Tucker?"

Tucker nodded and took the mug. It hardly felt warm at all.

"Well, we did the grand tour. Not that there's that much to see this time of year. Worst time, I say, before spring returns. If you're down, this gray makes it worse, that's for sure."

Tucker watched as the old man's expression fell nearly to blankness. Then Pastor Ringhofer blinked once and asked, "So, tell me. How you been? How's that fancy church in Chicago treating you?"

Tucker knew he'd tell his old pastor everything in due time, but now he answered, "Fine. Things are going fine."

"I heard that Chairman Thompson made you an offer for the associate position at Settler's Ridge. That true, son? Or are my sources going bad?"

"No, he offered. I turned him down. I feel obligated to stay in Chicago at least a year or two."

Pastor Ringhofer took a long swallow and grimaced. "That's noble of you, Tucker. You were always a noble sort of fellow."

Silence descended. The dog circled twice and thumped to the floor.

"I like your place. It sure is quiet," Tucker said. "A lot different than Chicago, that's for sure. You're really out in the woods."

Pastor Ringhofer looked around. From his expression, it

seemed he was seeing the place afresh. "It's not much, that's for sure. When you're alone, your standards slip a little. I guess I could have done a bit more tidying up. Being by myself, well, I know where everything is at, let's just say."

"It looks fine," Tucker reassured him. He took another sip of the lukewarm coffee. His stomach, now a bit queasy, lurched. "So how have you been, Pastor Ringhofer? We haven't talked in a long time. Are you still writing?"

The old man put his coffee cup on the dining room table and snorted. "No. Not anymore. When I first came here, I started writing one of those 'I remember when' books. I was going to write about my life and times. I got a couple of hundred pages written, and then I just stopped. I liked what I wrote, but truth be told, I don't think I ever want anyone else to know that much about my life. When I was younger, maybe I did. But now that I'm a cranky old man, I just don't want to share everything. And besides, who's going to publish a book about a pastor from a small town who winds up alone on a lake in Wisconsin? Not a sexy proposition. And it seems to me, from what I see on television, only the sexy stuff gets published."

Tucker put his coffee cup on the end table. He looked for a coaster but realized he didn't have to worry about staining the furniture.

"Put it anywhere, son. Nothing here is antique, except me, and I don't see well enough to spot a coffee ring these days."

Tucker wiped the bottom of his cup with his other hand, just to be polite, and set the cup down. He knew now why he insisted on half-and-half for his coffee, especially for his instant coffee.

"You still reading a lot? I remember you always had three or four books going at one time."

"I read some. Not as much as I used to. I read a lot slower

now. Maybe it's because I have more time to appreciate it. There's not as many people up here to trade ideas with. I go down to the library in Rice Lake once in a while, but I think they're near to their limit on bored, crotchety seniors these days."

The old man barked a laugh. He wiped at his mouth with the back of his hand. The stubble scratched along his skin, loud as a saw blade in wet pine.

Tucker pointed out the window to the lake. "How's the fishing? Use the boat a lot, I bet."

The former pastor shrugged. "Fishing is pretty good. I don't do so much anymore. Those bandits from the marina want five hundred dollars to put in my pier. Five hundred bucks—can you believe that? I didn't put it up last summer. I can launch the boat from the city dock for free, seeing as how I'm a senior citizen and all." He peered out at the lake, too. "But the trailer throws off my driving some. Backing up, I never know which way to turn the wheel. A dozen times a season is all I can manage. Sometimes I drive down to the dam and fish a bit. But you know, a couple of years ago, I finally figured out that I really didn't like the taste of fish. So why spend all day getting sunburned on the lake to yank fish out of the water—like you're some sort of fish god—and then throw them back in with a big hole torn in their lips. That realization took the edge off the sport for me."

"Spooner seems like a nice little town, though," Tucker said.

"Yeah, maybe. I don't find myself in town all that often. Groceries. Gas. Dog food. A better meal than I can manage to cook myself once or twice a week. I guess it's okay. I could be stuck on one of those lakes north of here where the closest town is fifty miles away. That's when you feel isolated. Takes a special sort of person to live up there."

The old man stood up and walked to the front door. He

stared out the square window. "Tucker, you know what?" he said, still facing the door. "I realize that I'm an old, old man. And a little bit bitter. A lifetime of small regrets, you know." Then he turned toward his guest. "I'm sorry, Tucker. I'm dumping all this on you. I don't get that many visitors. And the dog already heard this story a few times. So I'm just venting—isn't that what they call it nowadays—venting? Does the soul good, right?"

"Pastor Ringhofer, it just sounds like you're lonely," Tucker said, hoping to regain his own emotional equilibrium. "That's all. Being out here all by yourself."

Pastor Ringhofer shook his head. "No. I was just as lonely when Martha was alive. It's just that the house was a whole lot neater and that I ate better. Hollow is hollow; you know what I mean?"

"What do you mean? You and Martha. . .you always seemed so happy."

"There were some good times, Tucker. I'd be lying if I said there weren't," the old man said as he walked to the chair facing the television. He picked up the remote that was on the seat and carefully set it on the table next to the chair. "I married the right woman."

Tucker nodded. "That's what it looked like to me."

The old man wearily shook his head. "Not that sort of right—it's the sort of right that gets put in quotation marks. She was the perfect woman. She was mostly pretty and from a preacher's family. She could sing and she could play the piano. She wasn't one to stir up any trouble. My dad said she'd be the perfect preacher's wife. And she was. It's just that I knew it was a mistake from the first day. Not a big mistake. Not enough to say, 'I'm leaving,' or anything horrible like that. Just that I don't think I was ever fully settled. Even with the kids. I love each one of them, but I never stopped wondering."

Tucker didn't know what to say.

Pastor Ringhofer apologized again. "Tucker, you live up here alone and you get used to carrying on long conversations between yourself or between yourself and the dog. No matter, really. Both of them are more or less one-sided. I forget that I've had a few years to mull all this over and get settled into the truths of it. I must have shocked you. But don't be. I bet there are a whole lot of widows and widowers who have come to the same conclusion. What was the right choice so many years ago doesn't always seem to stay the right choice."

"But you were a great pastor," Tucker claimed. He was compelled to say something to right this downward spiral. "Back in Owatonna, you were the best. I'm in the ministry because of your example. That couldn't have happened if you really believe what you're saying now."

"Well, Tucker, the pool was pretty shallow in Owatonna," he said with a thin, forced smile. "But I'm perceptive. I do take some pride in that. No one just stops up in the north woods for a social call. Not in gray weather like this. You came here to ask me some questions, but I've already burst your balloon. Now you think I'm not the one to reassure you."

Tucker blinked.

"I'm right, aren't I?"

Tucker could only manage a nod.

"Tell you what. I've already flummoxed your plans. Let's forget about all this, and I'll let you take me to dinner. There's a supper club a few miles north of here that puts on a decent meal. And it's not Friday, so the place won't stink from their fish fry. You up for an old Wisconsin roadhouse meal?"

Tucker hoped that a full stomach would help his nausea. "Sure. I guess I'm hungry."

"Then let's go. But you're driving. I don't see all that well after dark."

Chicago, Illinois

An unfolding often took Annie weeks to complete. She would build up in layers, as it were, sort of a reverse archaeology, putting down a history, then layering more and more on top, until the genesis was all but obscured by the current reality.

Her latest had been completed in an evening.

She had used a picture of Tucker, clipped from the church newsletter. She hid it behind layers of tattered Bible pages and photos and tokens and book covers and old church bulletins and poster fragments from a youth group fund-raiser and detergent box tops. Standing to one side, peering in at one specific angle, you could see his picture. Tucker was near to being buried under all the rest of the contents.

Annie did not smile as she worked. This unfolding had not made her happy, as they usually did, but driven and determined.

Once it was finished, she placed the glass back on top. She wiped the haze off the glass and looked hard. She was done.

And then she wondered aloud, "What am I going to do with this one? Sell it? I can't do that. But I can't hang it here, either."

After a few moments of thought, she picked the piece up and carefully placed it on the top shelf in the closet of the third bedroom. Tomorrow would be soon enough to decide.

She was well aware that she had never made an unfolding that contained Danny's picture and had seldom, if ever, chosen and used a picture of someone whom she knew.

She wondered, but only for a minute, if some sort of sign was hidden in that choosing.

Spooner Lake, Wisconsin

Tucker wasn't a large fan of country music, especially the real twangy variety. When Pastor Ringhofer opened the door, they were washed by a storm of guitars and nasal singing.

"It's only loud when they play the jukebox," Pastor Ringhofer shouted. "And most people are too cheap to run it all night."

The hostess greeted Pastor Ringhofer with a familiar smile. "Well, honey, I haven't seen you here at dinnertime for a month of Sundays. Taking a chance on driving to come see me again?"

"No," he said with a laugh. "I brought a chauffeur with me. He's my designated driver."

The hostess stuck out her hand. "I'm Hazel—like the nut. If you're a friend of his, you have my sympathies."

Pastor Ringhofer dismissed her with a cheerful wave, and he and Tucker settled into a dark booth, far away from the bar and the music.

"Everything is good here," he explained. "At least it is for lunch. Like I said, darkness and me don't mix. In the summer I can make it here for dinner—but not now."

Tucker wasn't hungry at all. His mentor's revelations had unsettled him. He wanted to order just toast and coffee but didn't.

Midway through the meal, Pastor Ringhofer stopped, his fork midway from plate to mouth. "Tucker, you came here to ask me something. I've been prattling on and on because I think I know your question, and maybe I don't want to answer. But I can't dodge you all night and I'm plumb out of secrets. So go ahead. Go ahead and ask your questions."

Tucker chewed his meat loaf carefully.

"I am right about the question thing, aren't I?" Pastor Ringhofer asked before Tucker began.

"Yes," Tucker replied.

"And you want to know if you really have been called. If what you're doing is the real deal, right?"

Tucker nodded. "They told us in seminary that a lot of us would start questioning our call within the first year."

"You know, the one big thing they didn't tell you then was that the doubts don't really stop. They ebb and flow, but they never stop." Pastor Ringhofer took another large swallow. "And there I go again, talking about me. I'm supposed to be talking about you, right?"

Tucker shrugged.

The older man put down his fork and knife. "You want to know if I would do it all over again?"

Tucker hesitated, fearing how he might feel if the answer was no.

"Well, I'm going to tell you anyhow. I would do it again in a heartbeat. I would. The call was there. I was sure of it. Maybe my life was a little bit crippled—not by a bad choice but by a careless choice. I should have thought about things more. I should have waited longer to decide certain things. I was young and in a hurry. I made mistakes and never let myself grow into them. I trusted that God's call made up for my mistakes. I'm not sure it did. I think we knew it—both me and my wife. We knew that we had settled. So that's the big reason I stay up here in the woods all alone. Doing penance. There's not enough fishing in the world to take care of an empty old man. I love God. I will always love God, but. . .I don't know. Choices. Choices are the sticking point."

Tucker remained silent.

"But that doesn't help you, does it?"

Tucker shook his head. "I like what I'm doing and I think I'm good at it, but these last few weeks I keep getting this overwhelming feeling of. . .something that's not right."

Someone must have found some loose change, for the jukebox began blaring again. It might have been the flip side of the record they heard when they first arrived.

"Pastor Ringhofer, if you heard about the offer from the church, did you also hear about Elizabeth?"

The old man suddenly appeared weary. "I heard. Not many secrets in a small town. Not like Chicago, I bet. My conduit for the news is Bess Arters. She's still church secretary, and she still calls me once or twice a month. When you turned them down, it was a couple of calls a week. Of course she told me about Elizabeth."

"She's a really nice girl."

Pastor Ringhofer slapped his palm hard on the table. The saltshaker nearly danced off the edge. "You almost made the same mistake I did. She would have been perfect. She probably played the piano, too. But she was transparent—like there was nothing inside. I know. I had dinner at the Thompson house more times than I care to recall. She was waiting for a husband to make everything complete. You need to find someone who is already complete."

Tucker was no longer sure what he needed to ask. There had been too many revelations, too much advice, and too many obvious problems apparent in the retired pastor's face.

The old man thrust his torso forward suddenly, creasing his plaid shirt hard on the edge of the table. "If all you remember is one thing about this day, Tucker, let it be this. God called you. He called all of us. You're a special young man, and I think God does have something special in store for you. You're called, but everything in life is a calling. You can serve God anywhere. It doesn't have to be in a church, you know." He ran his fingers through his thin white hair. "I wish someone had told me that a long time ago. Maybe I would have stayed in the church. Maybe I would have done something different."

The music suddenly stopped.

"Like what?"

The old man sighed. "I don't know. But when I look back—maybe I'm trying to punish myself for all those years of not telling the truth to myself. I served God as best I could, but I missed something. Don't make the wrong choice, Tucker. Pay attention. You'll know what is right if you wait for the right sign, for doors to open. You'll know. I never waited. I didn't."

"A sign?"

They were both startled when they heard the familiar strains of a Bach concerto warbling from underneath Tucker's coat.

"It's my cell phone," Tucker said as he realized the source of the music.

Tucker extracted the phone from his pocket and flipped it open.

"Tucker, is that you? This is Pearl."

He heard her gasp, as if she had been crying.

"You have to come home. Pastor Yount is dead. You have to come home now."

Fourteen

On the way to Chicago, Ilinois

TUCKER DIDN'T STOP, EXCEPT for gas, until he reached MacKenzie Street. He didn't stop for food and he didn't cry. Instead of grief, Tucker became aware of an urgency, a bubbling, near-panicked urgency—the sort of overwhelming urgency he had not felt since grade school when the teacher announced a surprise test. The anxious, jangled feeling wrapped about him tightly. Even stopping for a hamburger would have been too complex an activity.

So he drove on, alone and in silence.

His old pastor understood his leaving and saw him off with a chorus of "Drive safely" and "I understand" and "Next time you can stay longer."

As Tucker drove into the darkness, the winds increased and rain dogged him the entire trip. He arrived home a few hours past midnight, when the streets were quiet. He managed to find a legal parking place a few doors down from his apartment. After turning off the car, he waited a moment, listening to the engine *ping* and *tick* as it cooled.

He was tired. Very tired. He forced himself out of the car, grabbed his overnight bag, and climbed the stairs to his apartment. He dropped the bag as he entered, walked to the couch, and lowered himself to it. But as he stared into the dark, he knew that, though exhausted, he wouldn't be able to sleep.

Tucker could string together no more than a few brief coherent memories of the funeral and the weeks following.

Pastor Yount had died in his office. The paramedics claimed a heart attack had killed him—and quickly. Even had they been stationed next door, they claimed, there would have been little they could have done to save him. No one requested an autopsy, no foul play was suspected, and no one wanted to delay his funeral services. His wife told Tucker that her husband had not felt totally well for several months and, despite her urging, had never once consulted with a doctor. Pearl blamed herself, claiming she should have seen the pain in his face and forced him to be examined. Both women consoled each other, absolving each other of their assumed guilt.

Somber crowds filled the church on the Saturday of his funeral. Chairs had to be set up in the lobby for the overflow, and even at that, large groups of people stood. Tucker had never officiated at a funeral before, and in the months that he had been at the church, there had been no funerals and thus no model for Tucker to use.

Sam Bawrenski, one of the elders, explained the typical funeral. "This is what he always used," Sam said patiently, holding an old hymnal of the church. In the back were outlines and responsive readings for various services, with funerals being listed first.

"Are you sure?" Tucker asked. He could not imagine Pastor Yount leading a responsive reading at a funeral.

"Well, I don't go to all that many funerals," Sam admitted. "Gives me the creeps. But I'm pretty sure he used this book at the last funeral. Or maybe it was just for the song. No, you got me wondering. Maybe he didn't." He appeared puzzled, then brightened. "I guess you don't have to use this old book. You pastors must have a book somewhere that spells out what you do and what you say for all sorts of occasions, don't you? You don't write new stuff for every wedding, do you? So there must be a book on funerals. You need to go look in the pastor's office," Sam insisted. "I bet he had a book like that. I mean, every wedding that I went to at this church sounded the same to me. Pastor Yount must have had a book."

It was not the time, Tucker soon realized, to be composing new funeral rites. Sam was most likely correct. There would be that sort of book in the old pastor's office.

Tucker made a point of announcing himself and his intentions to Pearl. She had taken the pastor's death hard and had been sniffling and crying for two full days.

"Go ahead," she said, a wadded tissue in her hand. "It's unlocked. Just don't touch anything, okay? His wife will need to come in later and clean things up."

Tucker left the door open. He felt an ominous silence in the room, a sort of chill. He shook his head, ridding himself of all the bad horror-movie images that had crowded into his thoughts. Death had not often touched Tucker or his family. His grandparents were gone, having died when Tucker was still young, and he had not been allowed at their funerals.

Pastor Yount's chair was lying on the floor. It must have been tipped over when the paramedics came and had been left that way. Tucker picked it up and slid it back under the desk, then wondered, with a start, if that meant that he had tampered with some sort of evidence.

He faced the bookcases and began to run his finger along the spines of the books. Pastor Yount must have had some sort of filing system, but the logic of it was not readily discernible to Tucker. He traveled the length of one wall and started on the other when a series of books on death stopped him. He slowed down and soon found a slim booklet, *Funerals with Meaning*, which had been printed by the Essex Funeral Home on Clark Street in Chicago. The booklet had been well used, the corners frayed and bent. Tucker flipped through the pages. On some pages penciled notes of names and odd fragments were scrawled in the margin. The handwriting was Pastor Yount's—the tilt and angle of the writing was distinctive, Tucker thought. He smiled, realizing he had stumbled on one of the old man's secrets. In the back of the book were a dozen short homilies, with death the common subject of all.

Tucker was certainly glad he wasn't expected to deliver the eulogy. That responsibility went to an old friend in the clergy.

Tucker knew from seminary that he could use the booklet to draft an order of service.

He was about to leave when the yellow legal pad on Pastor Yount's desk caught his eye. Tucker stepped closer. He could see Pastor Yount had been making a list. He peered over his shoulder to make sure no one was spying on him. Then he leaned closer. *It isn't wrong to look,* Tucker told himself, *but it doesn't feel exactly right, either.*

It was a to-do list. The words *TO DO* were printed in harsh capitals and underlined several times. He had penned the date— the date of his death—in the upper right-hand corner of the page.

Finish message
P/U suit dry cleaners
Call/visit Eliz. Check with hospital.
Elder meeting Tuesday—agenda?
Travel Agent/Orbitz—Belize? Aruba?

Tucker stared at the list for a long time.

Of course it was number five on the pastor's list that most puzzled and dismayed Tucker. Pastor Yount had never once talked about Belize or Aruba. Tucker knew the pastor and his wife were headed to upper Michigan over summer vacation. His wife's family lived there, and they gathered every summer for an extended reunion. He had said that he enjoyed the get-togethers.

So why Belize and Aruba?

Tucker stood there, like a dog seeing a horse for the first time, unsure of what to do but a little frightened. However, he wasn't frightened enough to call out or run.

Maybe he just wanted to plan a trip for next year. Or a winter getaway?

Tucker snapped out of his reverie when he heard the phone ring in the outside office. He hurried out, told Pearl he had found the book he needed, and went back to his office to prepare an order of service.

And he tried not to think of Aruba or Belize the rest of the day.

Two weeks after the funeral, Tucker received a short note from Mrs. Yount.

Dear Tucker,

Thank you so much for your help during this difficult time. My husband would have been so proud of the way you handled the ceremony. I can see your calling evident in your work.

My husband left a will, but he made no mention of his books. I would not surmise that you would want any of them or all of them, but please feel free to take what you need. I have no desire to keep them, and at some time in the future I will no doubt consider relocating to a smaller residence.

Again, Tucker, thank you for being there for me. You have been a godsend. I don't know what the church would have done without you.

All the best,
Mrs. Richard Yount

"So did you get your questions answered up in Wisconsin?" Pearl asked one quiet afternoon, four weeks to the day after Pastor Yount died.

"Yes," Tucker said, then squinted at her. "But I never said why I was going."

Pearl offered him an incredulous look. "Like you're good at keeping your emotions hidden? You were moping around for weeks like a dog who lost its favorite toy. Why else would a young pastor seek out an old pastor deep in the woods? To compare notes on Scripture? No, Tucker—to make sure that what he was doing was right. That's why you went."

Tucker opened his palms to her. "That's why I went, Pearl. And you missed your calling. You should have been a policeman or a detective."

She laughed. "No, this is more fun."

He took a seat in the visitor's chair opposite her desk and slumped down. "He told me secrets that I never expected to hear, Pearl. About his marriage. About his calling. *Shocked* is a mild word to describe it. *Dumbfounded* would be better. He spent his whole life with regrets. I don't want that to happen. I don't."

Pearl folded her hands on top of her desk and simply listened.

"It was funny. . .in a macabre sort of way. He said I would know if my calling was true and that I should expect to see some sort of sign. It was precisely then that you called my cell phone with the news. If that wasn't a sign, I don't know what would be."

Pearl waited a few seconds, then asked, "What about Susan?"

"Susan?"

"You know what Susan I mean. Pastor Yount's niece."

Tucker had no energy to be coy. "I've only seen her once since the funeral. I keep hearing my old pastor's words about his mistake of marrying the 'right' woman. How he regretted it all his life. Susan is one of those 'right' women. I just don't know. . . ."

Pearl came around her desk and sat in the chair next to Tucker. She reached around him, and he almost flinched but instead let her hug him in a most motherly way.

"Tucker, when it's right, you'll know it. Just don't force it—especially now. Just don't force it."

Tucker stood at the back of the church at the open door, smiling and shaking hands. It was not yet springlike, so the cool air felt healthy and refreshing after breathing the air that never seemed to circulate around the pulpit.

"Pastor Abbott, I really appreciated your message today. I never thought about forgiveness like that. You've given me something to think about."

"Pastor Abbott, have the elders said when you're going to be senior pastor? I don't like them waiting like this. A church needs a senior pastor."

"Pastor Abbott, are you supposed to be doing hospital calls now? It's been over a month since Pastor Yount. . .you know. . . and no one told me who's supposed to be doing them. I got an aunt over in Rockford who's going in for some sort of female work, and she needs someone to visit her. Are you going to handle that or what?"

"Pastor Abbott, there was a horrible draft on my neck the whole service. I think those kids in the balcony opened a window or something. Can you see to fixing that?"

"Pastor Abbott, great sermon, really great. I really liked that joke you told at the beginning. I like it when you tell jokes up there."

"Pastor Abbott, can you promise me we're going to start using the hymnal more? My late husband, God rest his soul, paid for most of them; and we haven't sung more than two hymns in the last two weeks."

Tucker kept smiling and nodding and offering small murmurs, as if that were answer enough to the questions. As long as there were people still in line waiting to greet him, the questioning never became intense. He would never ignore a member of the congregation on purpose, but some of their requests were so odd or inappropriate that he knew he couldn't—or shouldn't—answer.

As he stood there, right hand extended, a thought came to him. *Is this how You answer my crisis of confidence, God? I ask if my calling is authentic, and You put me in the pulpit? Is that how it works?*

Tucker was not angry or upset—just overwhelmed. He had wanted to be a senior pastor, to be the shepherd of a church, but this was never the way he had envisioned it happening.

"Pastor Abbott, you're doing a bang-up job there in the sermon department. You're every bit as good as Pastor Yount was—and maybe a little better. You're funnier than he was. Keep up the good work."

The bells from the Presbyterian church sounded out the quarter hour. A handful of the congregation was left, talking in clusters. Tucker was exhausted. Preaching was not physical work, he knew, but perhaps more draining. All he wanted to do now was go home, put on a pair of jeans and a sweatshirt, and fall asleep watching whatever sports event was on television. He wouldn't even mind if it were a golf tournament.

But then he heard a familiar laugh. It was Annie's laugh. She held a piece of white construction paper as Chance gestured at it, miming a bear or some other wild animal slashing with his claws. Annie, engrossed in the story, laughed and followed every action.

When they got to the door, Chance stuck out his hand as firmly as a boxer's right hook. Tucker took it, and the little boy pumped as if priming a hand-drawn well.

"How are you, Chance?"

"I'm fine."

"What was the story in Sunday school? Something about a bear or lion?"

"It was about some guy named Daniel and a whole bunch of lions. How did you know? Were you in my class?"

Annie was behind her son, buttoning her coat.

"I'm sure Pastor Abbott knows what the Sunday school lesson is."

"You do? You must be real busy," said Chance.

Tucker smiled. Chance's face was streaked with sweat, and his shirttails were flapping about. They had long ago pulled out of his trousers.

"I am. Or at least I feel like I am," Tucker said.

Annie bent to zip up Chance's coat. As she did, she looked up at Tucker. "You look tired. Are you getting enough rest?" There was tenderness in her words.

Tucker nodded. "I think so. There's just a lot to do."

"I know. It's been such a shock to everyone. Sometimes I just feel like crying all over again. He was such a wonderful man."

"I know. I feel the same way," Tucker replied.

Annie straightened up and pushed her hair behind her ear, then cocked her head. "Listen, I have stew in the Crock-Pot. Why don't you come over for lunch? I know you don't have any food back at your apartment, and I don't want to think of you eating all alone in a restaurant."

Chance nearly jumped up and down. "Can you? Can you come? Please, please?"

Annie gripped Chance's shoulder. "You're not going to be there, young man. You have a birthday party to go to. Remember? Joshua is having a party."

"Oh, yeah, I 'member now. Maybe we can wrestle when we get back, okay?"

At first Tucker was set to decline the invitation. He really felt that tired. But since the invitation now no longer included wrestling, he quickly changed his mind. "Sure, I can come. I'd love to. But I have to finish up a few things here and then change. Is one o'clock too late?"

"No, that will be just perfect."

"The stew was delicious, Annie. I don't think I've enjoyed a meal more than today."

"Didn't your mother make stew?" Annie asked. "I thought every mom in the Midwest made stew."

Tucker picked up his plate and carried it into the kitchen. "You know, I don't ever recall having stew. I don't think my mother had all that many signature dishes."

"Is she a good cook?"

The lines on Tucker's forehead deepened. "I don't know. I guess she's all right as a cook. I just. . .don't remember anything special coming from her kitchen."

Annie turned on the water and added soap. "What about birthdays?"

Tucker paused. "We went out. I think. To a restaurant. I usually asked to go to the McDonald's in Faribault. They never tried to talk me out of it. It was a pretty inexpensive birthday meal."

Annie laughed as she slipped the plates into the soapy water. "What is it about little boys and McDonald's? Chance would go there every night if I let him."

Tucker leaned against the kitchen counter. "Lots of grease and lots of sugar—two of nature's perfect foods."

Annie sighed and returned to the sink. "With Chance, well, there seems to be a new test every minute."

"Really? I wouldn't have guessed it. Chance seems like a very well-behaved little boy."

Annie lifted a glass to the light, then returned it to the soapy water. "He is, for the most part. It's when he's so deliberate in his disobedience. Testing to see if I keep the same rules from day to day."

"Do you?"

"Sometimes I get so tired. And then he swipes a soda and winds up watching too much television."

Tucker picked up a dish towel, ready to begin drying the dishes. It felt so absolutely normal.

"You don't have to, Tucker. You're my guest."

"I know. But I never do this at home. It's kind of fun."

Annie offered a bemused smile. "You don't wash dishes?"

Tucker grinned. "No, I wash them. But I'm a firm believer in 'air-drying.' And also, there's never anyone to talk to while I do the dishes. This is nicer."

Annie looked away, almost quickly, and Tucker wondered if he had said something that might be misinterpreted. He reviewed the conversation and did not recall any sensitive issues.

"Anything left to clean up—or dry? I'm getting good at drying," Tucker said.

Annie checked around. "No, I don't think so. Why don't you go out and sit down? There's probably some sort of game on television—maybe even golf. Relax a minute. I'll make coffee, okay?"

Annie carried a metal tray with an insulated carafe, two cups, and a cream and sugar service. There was also a plate of cookies.

"I'm not big on desserts," she explained as she set the tray on the chest that doubled as a coffee table.

Tucker added his cream and sugar and sipped. "Good coffee."

"As good as you make? Pearl says you make the best coffee." Annie sat down on the floor and tucked her legs up underneath her.

"Just about as good. You have to use more coffee, that's all. People are too stingy with the coffee."

He leaned back into the soft cushion. He could hear the gentle passing of the traffic on the street below. Sunday brought fewer cars. Someone must have brought a boom box into the Laundromat; soft bass chords threaded through the floor.

"This is very nice, Annie. I do want to thank you for the invitation. If you hadn't, I would have been asleep on my sofa by now, with an empty potato-chip bag on the floor."

Annie smiled. "It was my pleasure."

Tucker let the silence linger awhile. It was a very pleasant sound.

"You look tired, Tucker."

"I am. It's been a hard few weeks."

Annie turned to him, concerned. "You do have enough help, don't you? You're not trying to do everything yourself?"

Tucker drank his coffee. "I have a pretty good group of volunteers helping. I just never figured on taking so much responsibility all at once. Most pastors get to grow into the position."

"Are the elders talking about offering you the senior pastor job? I mean, officially and permanently?"

Tucker slumped down. "They're talking about it, I guess. But I've looked at the constitution. To hire a senior pastor, the church has to form a search committee. The elders said they are taking nominations. It will take a couple of months at least, most likely more, before anyone could legally talk to me about it. Maybe they will offer me the position. And maybe they won't."

"Do you want to be senior pastor?"

Tucker gazed out the window, toward the lake. He lay his head back on the sofa pillow. "I don't know. I'm sure I'm not prepared for it. My mother wouldn't agree with that, but it's the truth. You know what I was doing up in Wisconsin?"

Annie held her cup with both hands. "Pearl said you were visiting an old pastor friend."

"That's part of it. I haven't shared this with anyone, but all of a sudden I started being. . .uncertain. Annie, it may not sound serious to you, but I've always been very certain of everything. And all of a sudden, that certainty disappears in a flash, and I'm lost and floundering. Seriously. It was more than I could deal with on my own. I wanted to talk to somebody about this, and I knew my old pastor would be the perfect man to give me godly counsel. I just had to see him. I had to ask if he had faced the same insecurities."

"Did he give you some answers?" Annie asked.

"A few. But he actually raised more questions than he gave answers for. He's been alone for enough years now, since his wife died and he left the church, that he's been considering what his life was for—and I don't think he liked the answers he came up with all that much. But we didn't get a chance to really talk it all out. I had just asked him how I would know if my calling was truly from God. He said I would have a sign. And at that moment Pearl called. Talk about your signs."

He slouched farther into the couch. "I'm pretty sure I like what I do. I like serving God. But my old pastor kept saying that you can serve God anywhere. It doesn't have to be in a church."

Annie sat up straighter. "I know what you're saying. When Chance was born, I had no idea what being a parent meant. And all of a sudden, I was one. I never thought I asked God for that, but He gave Chance to me. And even when he was gone for that year, God didn't forget. He gave Chance back again. I guess He thought I'd be a good parent. He must have, or else why would all this have worked out like it did? He chose me for the job. I didn't pick it, that's for sure."

Tucker heard her words, but they became more and more faint. Comfort settled over him like an old rug. . . .

❧

Annie stared at her hands, then said softly to Tucker, "You'll make a wonderful senior pastor, Tucker. You're good at what you do. Everybody likes you. I know they do. Your preaching is so good. I really want the elders to offer you the job. It would be so nice to have you with us. It really would be. I think you're called. I think God chose you to be right here—right now—for a very specific reason. And I believe you are on the cusp of something with your life that no one could have imagined. I don't know why I feel that way, but I do. You have been chosen, Tucker."

She glanced up at Tucker to see if he believed her. His eyes were closed. His breathing had become softly regular.

Annie smiled, shook her head, and stood up. When she lifted his legs onto the couch, he did not stir. Taking a quilt from the chair, she laid it across him, tucking it close around his neck. And then she slid down onto her knees by the couch and watched as he slept, his chest rising and falling in rhythm. She stared at his right hand, which had slumped away from the quilt and toward the floor.

Her thoughts buzzed about like so many honeybees, looking for nectar and sweetness, dancing in the air. She brushed a lock of his hair from his forehead and smoothed it back into place. She traced her fingers down his cheek and let her open palm rest against it for a minute.

Then she quickly stood up.

Tucker slept, peaceful, a shaft of afternoon sun spilling about his face, lighting him like an angel.

She watched for only a heartbeat more, then hurried downstairs, seeking refuge amid the tumbling heat of the dryers. Suddenly she was very afraid of the images that rushed like a torrent into her thoughts.

Fifteen

Mrs. Alvarez caught Tucker as he exited his apartment on Monday. He was dressed in jeans and a sweatshirt, obviously not heading to the church.

"Pastor Abbott," she called out from across the street. "You go to work looking like a bum?"

Tucker glanced down at himself, then spread his arms. "I do not look like a bum. These are new jeans. And for your information, even pastors get a day off. I'm on my way to have coffee and read the paper for an hour or two."

She ambled across the street. Traffic was light, and she hardly looked in either direction. "Yes, pastors deserve some time off, but in my day, they still looked like pastors."

She reached up, grabbed his cheek, and tugged on it. "And you have not shaved, either. Such sloth."

Tucker laughed. "I have only one day. I don't have enough hours to find the pool of the seven deadly sins, let alone go swimming."

Mrs. Alvarez tightened her gaze. She wrapped her knobby,

yet powerful fingers around his upper arm and pulled him down, closer to her face. He felt certain her fingers would leave a bruise on his arm.

"An afternoon is enough time," she insisted. "Many things can happen in an afternoon."

As her eyes bored in on him, he realized what she was talking about. "I fell asleep on her couch, Mrs. Alvarez. I fell asleep and didn't wake up until Chance got back from his birthday party."

The old woman waited. A bus rumbled past. Tucker could almost taste the diesel fumes.

"Mrs. Alvarez, all I did was have lunch and fall asleep."

Slowly she appeared to soften. The barest hint of a smile released on her face. "I know. Annie told me all about it yesterday as you slept on upstairs. I was doing laundry."

Tucker gave a sigh of relief. The old woman continued, her voice now whispering. "You must be careful, Pastor Abbott. You have a reputation as well as she. You must be careful."

"Mrs. Alvarez, we are just friends. Annie is a nice person. She's easy to talk to. And I like Chance."

She clucked softly as he spoke. "I know all this, Pastor Abbott, but you must be careful. What we may not see, God sees. God watches."

But he may not be as vigilant as you, Mrs. Alvarez, Tucker couldn't help thinking.

"I'll be careful, Mrs. Alvarez. I don't want to do anything to hurt Annie. She is too nice to put in jeopardy."

Mrs. Alvarez patted his cheek, a gesture born from years of being the matriarch and grandmother to many. "I know. I know, Pastor Abbott. And I will do what I can to make both your choices proper."

Spring and summer passed so quickly that Tucker had to check the newspaper twice in September just to make sure it was truly September. He'd looked forward to summer and swimming in Lake Michigan but had only made it to the beach a handful of times.

Tucker had remained in the pulpit since Pastor Yount passed away, save two Sundays in June, when his duties were relieved by visiting missionaries. But even on those two Sundays, he attended the service.

To Tucker, the church appeared healthy. Donations had actually increased. Perhaps the increase was guilt-motivated, but it was an increase, nonetheless. Attendance ebbed and flowed as always, but the average attendance had held steady and actually ticked upward as summer ended.

The elders praised Tucker for his work, his willingness to pitch in, his gentle assumption of the role of leader. The members of a search committee had just been finalized and voted upon by the congregation. From what the bylaws indicated, it would be at least another two months, maybe three, before the first application would be solicited. They had to conduct a churchwide survey, draft a senior pastor profile, rewrite the job description, and vote as a congregation on the changes needed to the constitution, among others. A myriad of details would consume their time.

Tucker was, if nothing else, a realist. Churches moved at glacial speed. Even when pressed in an emergency, they would only speed up to molasses-in-January velocity.

As the days passed, Tucker slowly became more confident that God had answered his questions about his calling. Every Sunday Tucker could count on one or two people coming to him after the message with traces of tears on their faces, telling him that a weight had been lifted from their shoulders, or a splinter taken from their eyes, or that a relationship was now on the way to being mended.

Even Pearl felt it. "You have a gift, Tucker," she said one Tuesday morning. "I can't figure it out, but people respond. People understand. People are moved. That didn't happen all that often before. You keep surprising me."

His music leader, Noah Quince, a young graduate student from Northwestern, began adding a contemporary spin to the worship service. Tucker had been braced for a deluge of complaints about the volume and the repetitions and not always using the hymnals—and only a handful came. Perhaps it was Noah's infectious smile and bubbly personality that did it, but even the older pillars of the church began to clap their hands in time to the changing musical tastes.

Pastor Yount's office remained vacant. Tucker said that it was the office of the senior pastor, and he was only filling the void until the church made a decision.

Now that it was September, Tucker's one-year anniversary arrived. The elders made him promise to take the middle two weeks of September off—a real vacation.

"You get burned up by the work," Sam said, slapping him on the back during an elder meeting. "Then the church loses. You got to take care of yourself. A couple of weeks—you go home or something. Rest. Relax."

And Tucker did not argue. He was looking forward to not thinking about the church for several days. In fact, he was looking forward to thinking about nothing at all.

Tucker jerked awake. He was in his office and had closed his eyes, just for a minute or two, after making a final note on his sermon for Sunday.

"Tucker," came a sweet voice from the other side of the door, "are you in there?"

He stood and called out, "Yes, please come in."

He had so seldom shut his door that he had forgotten it was closed.

"Susan," he called out and quickly stepped around the desk.

She gave him a quick hug. "You look so good," she said in her singsong voice. "Pearl said I could come back and disturb you. I hope it's okay."

"Sure, it's fine. Sit down. When did you get back to Chicago?"

Over the summer, when she was home with her parents, Susan had sent Tucker a score of short notes—nothing long, nothing personal—and Tucker had responded with a handful of notes of his own. Neither of them had committed affection to paper.

"Just today. On an early flight. I'm staying with my aunt for a few days. The house is so big and quiet these days."

"Is she still planning to move?" Tucker asked.

"Yes, but she needs to decide whether to stay in Chicago or move closer to her sisters in Oklahoma."

"Your aunt mentioned your missions trip. That starts in a week or two, doesn't it?"

"It does. I'm heading to Belize," Susan said. When Tucker had found out, he'd been so relieved. The mystery on Pastor Yount's notebook the day he died had been neatly resolved. She had contemplated both locations—Belize and Aruba.

"You should make plans to visit me there," Susan said. "It's not really the jungle or anything, but I bet you would love the experience."

Tucker folded his hands. "I'd love to, but I don't think the church is going to send their temporary senior pastor on a long trip."

Susan was as pretty as Tucker remembered. She reached up and tucked her hair behind her ear. It was longer than it had been, and she had picked up the hint of a tan over the summer. She had used a lipstick in a lighter red shade than before.

"I would love it if you could visit," Susan said. Then, without flinching or looking away, she continued, "Barry is going to be there for part of the time, as well."

Tucker knew who Barry was—a young man in her class at Moody who had asked Susan out a few times at the end of the last semester. She had told Tucker that they were simply friends and had gone out as a group.

Tucker didn't think Susan expected an angry or jealous response. But it was most revealing that she'd brought Barry's name up again now, the very first time they had seen each other after her absence.

All at once Tucker felt weary. . .weary and absolutely ready for his short vacation to begin.

"I would love to visit," he heard himself saying. "But you'll have friends there, I'm sure. It's not like you'll be alone, right?"

"No," Susan replied. "Two other girls from Moody are going. We're helping with the boarding school. I'm the only one truly fluent in Spanish, so I guess I'll be busy."

"Well, I couldn't help there. My Spanish never progressed beyond the high school level."

"That's what Barry said, too," Susan quickly added. "But we've done some practicing, and he has picked a lot up over the last few months."

Tucker might have asked how the two of them could have practiced. But he did not ask. He could see in her eyes an excitement he'd have no part of. She was ready and anxious to leave

Chicago. And it was clear she was anxious to see Barry again.

A few minutes later, when he hugged Susan good-bye, Tucker found it curious that he felt no pang of regret or loss. He simply wished her well. She smiled and waved back to him over her shoulder, never fully looking back as she walked down the hall and toward the door.

Some choices were much easier to make than others, Tucker realized.

⁂

Tucker leaned against the dryer. The warmth felt good against his back; the gentle rumbling made him want to close his eyes and sleep. Tucker was midway through his laundry. He disliked the thought of leaving town with dirty clothes in his hamper. In five days he would leave Chicago for his vacation, and he wanted to settle every loose end that he could.

Annie stepped into her office. Tucker saw the movement from the corner of his eye. She smiled broadly and waved to him through the glass. Several seconds later, she had come around and now stood leaning against the washer opposite him.

During the spring and summer, Annie had invited Tucker to dinner several times. He had managed to accept only a few times. Senior pastors—even "interim" senior pastors—had evenings filled with meetings and appointments. Tucker would have preferred to dismiss other obligations in favor of spending time with Annie and Chance but simply could not.

"You getting ready to leave?" she asked.

Tucker noted that she had taken a thickness of her hair and twisted it around her fingers. He had read somewhere about that gesture—that it communicated something important. But for the life of him, he couldn't remember what it was. He hoped the action was positive but had the nagging feeling it wasn't.

"I like leaving the place neat and tidy with clean clothes."

"That's what I do, as well. The few times we've gone anywhere, I'm like a maniac before we go—leaving everything spotless."

"It probably means we really don't want to leave and that we don't like giving up control."

"Exactly," Annie replied. "Pearl said you were going home?"

"I am. I haven't been there in a while. I guess I'm due. And just in time for the big harvest festival."

"That sounds like fun. I should get Chance out in the country. He needs to see what the country looks like."

The dryer buzzed and shuddered to a stop. Tucker swung the door and reached in. He hefted a few items, then shut the door again, reached into his pocket, and pulled out another two quarters.

"Not quite. A few more minutes," he said.

Besides Tucker, three other patrons busied about the Laundromat. Two older women folded sheets while chattering to each other in animated Spanish. An older man sat by the front window and dozed lightly.

"I bet Chance would love our fall festival," Tucker said. "They used to hold it in October, but October in Minnesota can be really cold. So they shifted it to September. There are hayrides and a petting zoo and pony rides, and they close off one block downtown for a carnival. Too bad he has school this week."

Suddenly Annie looked puzzled, surprised, even apprehensive. "Actually, he doesn't."

"He doesn't? But city schools started at the end of August. Chance is in kindergarten now, right?"

Annie twisted her hair again. "He is. But there was a problem with the plumbing in his school. The boiler blew up or sprung a leak or something, and it left a foot of water in the basement. It was a real mess. So instead of trying to do the work at night, they closed school all next week."

"Really?"

Annie nodded, apparently mortified that she had put Tucker on the spot. It was obvious she hadn't planned on calling his bluff.

"Well, then. . . ," Tucker began.

Annie jumped in, "Tucker, I know you weren't serious—"

"But I was," Tucker replied, perhaps too quickly.

"I know you were being nice, but—"

Tucker turned to face Annie. "Why don't you two come with me? It would be great to show you around. Chance would have a ball. He could visit a real farm and explore a real barn—not like the one at the zoo."

"No, Tucker," Annie demurred. "That would be going too far. I mean, it would be a total imposition. And you're visiting family. We would be in the way. No. We couldn't."

Tucker brightened. "No, it would be great. I would have something to do rather than sit in my parents' living room and watch *The Price Is Right* with my mother. No, this isn't just an invitation. This is a command. You *have* to come with me. Chance won't miss any school. Can you get someone to watch the Laundromat? We could pretend we're tourists. It would be great. Really. You have to come."

The two Spanish women stopped talking and watched intently as Tucker became louder and more animated.

Annie made a vague gesture with both hands.

"Does that thing with your hands mean yes?" Tucker asked.

"I don't know. What would people think?"

Tucker opened his hands, palms up. "Listen, it's not that long of a drive. No overnight stops. And we're staying with my parents, for heaven's sake."

Annie glanced around the Laundromat as if she were searching for some celestial input.

Tucker knew at that instant that she and Chance had to come with him. He wasn't sure why, but he knew they did. He and Annie were not dating. They were not a couple. They were not even on their way to being a couple. Tucker knew that; he was sure Annie knew that. Pearl knew it. Everyone knew it. They were friends, and Chance needed a male role model and a chance to explore America a little bit. Tucker wanted something to do back home besides visiting with his parents. Steele County wasn't abuzz with tourist attractions, but there were some. Annie was too often homebound, tied to her business, not wealthy enough to take trips like this on her own, not to mention the fact that she didn't own a car. She and Chance had remained in town all summer, venturing no farther than the lake a few blocks east and the museums in downtown Chicago. Chance deserved more than that, and so did Annie. To Tucker, it was the most perfect opportunity. The more he considered the situation, the more excited he became and the more certain he was that it was the right thing to invite them both.

"Well, I don't know. . . ."

"Annie, what's not to know? You have an opportunity here— for you and Chance. I was planning to leave on Monday and come back that Sunday, but that's not set in stone. We could make it longer or shorter."

Tucker feared for Annie's hair, so hard was her twisting.

"Don't think about it anymore," he begged. "Just say yes. Chance will be thrilled."

She inhaled deeply, held her breath as she considered, then exhaled. "Okay."

"Okay? You'll go?"

Annie nodded. "But only if I can get Carl to watch the Laundromat. He said to call him if I ever needed him, but maybe he only meant a day or two. This is like a whole week."

"Carl? Carl Zietz from church?"

"Yes. He used to repair washing machines."

"He'll do it. If he says no, I'll talk to him."

"Tucker, don't you dare. I'll call him. If he says he can do it, then we can go. And you're right, Chance would be thrilled—absolutely thrilled to go on a trip."

Tucker agreed.

Annie headed upstairs to call Carl, and Tucker went back to his laundry with a smile. He kept smiling until sobered by a single thought: *What do I tell my mother if Annie does come with me?*

He stopped folding and stared blankly out the front window. His chest tightened.

What exactly do *I tell her?*

Owatonna, Minnesota

Mrs. Abbott stood in the hall and stared at the phone. She had just hung up after a brief conversation with her son.

Mr. Abbott lowered his newspaper. "Was that Tucker? Is anything wrong?"

It was very unlike his wife to remain mute after talking with her only son.

"Tucker is bringing some woman with him." Her words were as flat as the prairie.

"Some woman?"

"She has a young son. He didn't say anything about the boy's father."

"A son? Why? Why a woman with a son?"

"I didn't think in time to ask. He said something about showing the boy what the country was all about. Why does Tucker feel the need to show some stranger that? It doesn't make any sense."

Mr. Abbott folded the paper. "Maybe he feels sorry for her. There's a lot of single mothers in Chicago from what I read. Maybe it's some sort of outreach or something," he said quietly.

But his words were wasted on his wife.

"I suggested that she and her son might be more comfortable out at the new Best Western on Highway 35," she said firmly. "I told him they have an indoor pool. It's heated."

"What did he say to that?" Mr. Abbott asked.

"Nothing. Like he didn't even hear me."

Mr. Abbott sighed deeply, as if reaching a conclusion. "Maybe that's all it is. He's being nice to this poor woman and her son. Maybe he means what he said—that it will be a special treat for them. Maybe that's what their church does."

Mrs. Abbott huffed softly. "Our church doesn't do things like that. Can you imagine Pastor Bergen taking some strange woman with him to Chicago? It just isn't done."

The only sound from the living room was Mr. Abbott shuffling the afternoon paper.

Mrs. Abbott walked to the front door and glared out the side window, as if expecting to see Tucker and his guests parking at the curb at any minute. She spoke without caring if her husband heard or not.

"I don't think this is normal at all. Now I'm really worried about our son."

Chicago, Illinois

Tucker stood in the dark street-level alcove that led to his apartment steps. It was not yet 6:00 a.m., but he could easily tell who was on the other side of the front door by one glance at the squat shadow hulking there.

Tucker opened the door. "Mrs. Alvarez," he called out as cheerily as he could manage at this early hour.

"You have coffee?"

He nodded.

"Then we will have coffee and talk."

Tucker was well aware that this was a serious matter—too serious for a standing conversation. And Tucker knew that just a glance at the old woman's face told the story: In less than two or three minutes, he'd be defending himself against her accusations.

It took Mrs. Alvarez a few minutes to climb all three flights, but she wouldn't tolerate any consideration of heading to a public coffee shop at street level. "Private conversations are to be private. Like I would want some teenager in Starbucks to know my business. I will climb the steps. If my knees hurt later, I have a whole drawer filled with pills."

Tucker knew he couldn't dissuade her, regardless of the reason, so he didn't try.

She held onto the nicked railing the whole way and pulled herself up and forward with her right arm. Once inside, she walked purposely to the kitchen, pulled up a chair, and folded her arms on the table.

"Cream, sugar, and cookies. I know you have all three."

It took Tucker no more than a minute to assemble her demands. The night before, he'd purchased a dozen biscotti, thinking he might take them home to Owatonna. Few Italians took up residence in southern Minnesota, and he thought the different cookies might be appreciated. Since Tucker also knew he could get more, he placed the entire dozen on a serving plate and slipped it close to Mrs. Alvarez.

Tucker searched her face for a sign. He anticipated anger or indignation but saw nothing. He wondered if she ever played poker and concluded that if she did, she'd be good at it.

Neither of them spoke for a couple of minutes. Tucker sat across from her and drank his second cup of coffee. He ate one of the Italian cookies to her three. When she had finished, she folded her arms over her chest and appeared to scowl. Tucker thought she might be doing it for effect.

"So you think no one cares about reputations anymore?"

Tucker had been right about the subject of the discussion. "I think people care."

"And so you think people are stupid?"

"No, I don't."

Mrs. Alvarez all but glared at him. "You are not a married man. Annie is not a married woman. And yet you go on vacation with her? You think no one sees this?"

Tucker ran his fingers through his hair. "Mrs. Alvarez, I'm doing this for Chance."

She slapped the table with the palm of her hand. The sugar cubes danced in their bowl, one escaping to the table, then onto the floor. Tucker would pick it up later. This was no time for distractions.

"It's not Chance I'm concerned about."

Tucker sat up straight. He would take some level of chastising, but there was a limit. He didn't know exactly what that limit was but felt it near.

"Annie and I are friends," he said evenly. "I am driving to see my parents. Chance could visit a farm and a carnival and see what small-town life is like. If you think something untoward could happen in my parents' house, Mrs. Alvarez, you have too low an opinion of my mother."

The anger smoldering on Mrs. Alvarez's face began to abate. She didn't yet smile, but the scowl disappeared. "Your mother knows you are bringing Annie and her son?"

"Of course she does. So does my father."

"And she has accepted this? A man of the cloth traveling with an unmarried woman?"

"And with the woman's son. . .in a car. . .for a few hours. It's like driving to Rockford and back. She may not have said a lot about it, Mrs. Alvarez, but she didn't say no."

Mrs. Alvarez pressed her compact bulk against the table. "You know this situation is more than just a long drive in the country. But if your mother says your visit with Annie and her son is acceptable, then I accept it. Have you told the church?"

Tucker was taken aback. "You mean from the pulpit?"

His tone was harder than he intended, and he could see that he'd hurt Mrs. Alvarez's feelings a little. So he continued more softly, "No. I have not. I told Pearl."

"And she has said it was fine?"

Tucker shrugged. "She didn't say I couldn't go." He spread his palms flat on the table. "Really, Mrs. Alvarez, Annie and I are just friends, and I want to do something nice for Chance. He's a good little boy, and he could use something special in his life, too. Annie can't afford a lot of luxuries."

The old woman picked up both her coffee cup and Tucker's and took them to the sink. She began running water to wash them.

"I'll do that," Tucker protested.

"No. It's fine."

As the water splashed, Mrs. Alvarez turned to Tucker. "Just do nothing to hurt either of them, Pastor Abbott. I have asked God to protect them; and if you do wrong, you answer to Him, not me."

Tucker lowered his head and laughed.

"It's not funny, Pastor Abbott."

"I know, I know. It's just that I think I'd rather face God's wrath than yours."

At this, Mrs. Alvarez smiled. "And that is the way it should be, Pastor Abbott. Remember that my wrath is one that lives across the street. God may have to travel here from heaven. I live closer to you than He does."

Tucker carried the cookies back to the counter. "Of that I am fully aware, Mrs. Alvarez. I know you know where I live. It is a most sobering knowledge. And you have my word that I will do *nothing* to hurt either Annie or Chance. My solemn promise."

With those words of his, she reached up a wet, soapy hand and pinched his cheek hard enough to bring a tear to his eye.

Monday morning brought a pellucid sky of incredible blue. There was a certain crispness, as if the very air was telling everyone that fall was soon to follow. A tree, here and there, began to hint at its fall colors.

Pastor's Yount's widow had given their old car to Tucker—permanently. "I have no use for it, and selling it won't make me rich. It would probably cost more to run the ads than I would sell it for. You take it. Keep it in our garage if you want. Until I move, whenever that might be."

Tucker had checked and rechecked all the car's levels and pressures and mechanical operations. If any car could be described as trustworthy, it would be this one. Unpretentious and trustworthy.

He loaded their three suitcases into the trunk and a cooler full of drinks and sandwiches and chips and fruit and a full thermos of coffee. He wanted to tell Annie that the roadside abounded with restaurants the entire way to Minnesota and Steele County, but she had been so excited about planning and executing the menu that he didn't have the heart to dissuade her.

She had already forced him to accept forty dollars—her share of the gas and wear and tear on the car. He didn't argue with her. He knew it would be useless, just as it was with Mrs. Alvarez.

As Tucker started the car, Chance yelled "Stop!" so loud that both Tucker and Annie jumped in their seat and twisted themselves to see if he had somehow slammed a door on his finger.

"We have to pray before we leave," Chance insisted. "That's what Mrs. Schmidt told us to do when we go on trips. So Jesus knows to follow you where you're going."

Tucker, smiling, replied, "That's good, Chance. We almost forgot. Do you want to pray?"

"Sure, but you got to shut your eyes."

All three did.

"Dear Jesus," Chance began, "we're going to Minnesota. I don't know where that is, but they have a farm there. And a carnival. Protect us and keep us safe. Thanks for choosing us. Amen."

There was a two-voice chorus of amens from the front seat as Tucker put the car in gear and pointed it west.

Sixteen

On the way to Owatonna, Minnesota

CHANCE ASKED WHAT SEEMED like several thousand questions between Chicago and the Wisconsin/Minnesota border—not all of which Tucker could answer or even pretend that he could answer.

If the little boy had been driving, he would have stopped dozens of times. Fifteen minutes out of the city, they passed O'Hare Airport just as a jumbo jetliner rumbled in for a landing. It passed overhead in a distance measured in feet, not miles. Chance's face pressed hard against the glass long after the jet touched down on the runway that lay a mile south of the freeway.

Tucker told Chance everything he knew about airports, aerodynamics, jet engines, emergency landings, parachutes, ultralights, gliders, the Wright Brothers, and Stealth bombers. The entire journey to Madison and beyond was filled with questions and explanations.

The second barrage of questions began as they passed the Wisconsin Dells and saw, from the roadway, several huge hotels and water-park complexes. Chance actually undid his seat belt at that point so he could watch them fade into the distance as they motored on.

So Tucker, who had visited several water parks as a child, mostly on a youth group outing, had to explain to Chance the detailed workings of waterslides, chutes, indoor rivers, and what a dell was.

All the while Tucker and Chance talked, Annie sat quietly, her hands folded in her lap, staring out the window. As they moved farther north, some of the red maples had begun turning into crimson flames amid the yellows and greens. They stopped once for gas and once at a roadside rest area to eat their sandwiches.

"Look, Chance—there's the river I told you about."

Annie turned around and whispered, "He's asleep."

"Sorry," Tucker whispered back.

"No, he won't wake up, I'm sure. He's a pretty deep sleeper. The car and road noise can be pretty hypnotic."

Tucker agreed.

"It's so pretty out here," Annie said. "I've traveled this before, but it seems like such a long time ago. It's easy to forget how big America is—and this is only a little sliver."

Tucker consulted the map on the seat between them, then squinted at a roadside sign. "I'm getting off at Route 14. It's a good road. After a while, the interstate all looks the same. This one goes through some small towns on the way to Owatonna."

Annie nodded. From Rochester to Dodge Center, she had remained silent. Tucker explained that this was soybean and wheat and corn and cow and pig country. Large family farms still dominated the landscape.

"That's the Petersen spread. They're one of the biggest pork producers around here," Tucker explained. "Their grandparents live a few blocks from us back home."

Annie continued to stare out the window.

Tucker slowed down as they rolled through Dodge Center, a spattering of old buildings crowded about the crossroads. A few local merchants struggled on.

"Down there—see that big brick building—that's the high school. They've been talking about consolidating it with the younger grades and closing it down. But everybody's afraid if they do that, what's left of the town will just wither away."

Annie stared straight ahead.

As Tucker gradually sped up, he glanced over at his passenger. Annie appeared to be nibbling at her lower lip. Her hands were clasped together more tightly than Tucker thought normal.

"Annie, is something wrong? Should I pull over? I never get carsick, so I don't know if that's a problem. . . ."

Annie shook her head. "No, I'm fine. I feel fine."

"Then what. . .is there something wrong?"

Tucker could hear her gulp for breath. Then she exhaled loudly.

"Tucker, I'm scared."

"Scared? Of what?"

"Meeting your parents."

"My parents? Why?" he asked.

"I don't know."

She adjusted the seat belt so she could turn directly to face him. Chance slept on in the backseat.

"Tucker, I know we're friends. I like being your friend. But this trip—meeting your parents and all that—makes it feel like we're something else altogether."

"But we aren't," Tucker replied. "You're right. We *are* friends. And a friend should be able to meet parents without getting scared."

She twisted her hands together. "I'm scared about what she'll think about me. Everybody back in Chicago knows the story. But here, no one does. They'll ask questions. Maybe they won't believe everything. I don't know if I want to tell the story again. I'm just worried. I want this to be a nice trip for Chance. I don't want anybody saying something. . .something mean without meaning to be mean." She looked away. "I'm not explaining myself very well, am I?"

"I think I understand. But I'm sure everything will be fine. And you'll be there with me. I'm the local boy who is a big-city preacher now. They'll be talking too much about me to even notice you."

Annie smiled. "Are you sure?"

"Sure, I'm sure," he replied. "You have nothing to worry about. I'm sure my mother will like you. And she will love Chance."

Annie reached over and patted Tucker's arm. "Thanks. I just get nervous sometimes. I'm glad you understand."

Tucker hoped his smile would reassure her. He glanced at her for as long as he could without risking an accident. The afternoon sun poured into the car and lit her face. Tucker could see the few lines spidering about her eyes and etched on her forehead. But he also saw her intense green eyes and the mass of auburn curls that framed her face in a halo.

At that moment he felt a sudden thump in his heart, as if he were seeing Annie Hamilton anew. She was so pretty, and he found himself staring longer than was safe.

Maybe the age thing doesn't matter.

Tucker's parents were precisely correct and exactly polite. They greeted Tucker and Annie and Chance with such a warm welcome that Tucker was certain the words, if not the actions, had been rehearsed.

Tucker, Chance, and Tucker's father each grabbed a piece of luggage.

Tucker's mother listed the arrangements. "Annie, I think you'll be most comfortable in the room at the end of the hall. The bath is right next to it, and there is a little more privacy there—being around the corner and all. We have a rollaway bed for your son. He can stay with you in that room or down in the basement with Tucker."

"Downstairs!" Chance called out, then quickly put his hand over his mouth. Annie's last-minute instructions to him in the car had been to only speak when spoken to.

Annie's smile now became a bit more forced. "Downstairs? Are you sure, Chance?"

Chance grabbed the opportunity to redeem himself. "If Tucker and Tucker's mom says it's okay, I mean. I've never slept in a basement before."

Tucker's mother laughed. "The basement it is, which is good, because that's where the bed is. Would you like me to show you where it's at, Chance?"

Chance nodded vigorously. "Are there any toys down there?" he asked as they descended the steps.

"There's a whole box of Tucker's old toys," she replied.

Tucker's father took Annie's bag upstairs.

"Better get the cooler. We don't want to waste any of the food," Annie said to Tucker, who had remained stationed in the tiny entryway.

"Was it as bad as you thought?" he whispered to her.

"Not quite so bad," she replied to him, her voice small. "But I could tell they were both pretty nervous. It's you and another woman."

Tucker opened the front door and walked down the steps to retrieve their cooler.

Another woman? Is that what Annie is?

He hefted the cooler from the backseat.

Maybe she is. . .sort of, anyhow.

When the luggage had been placed and partially unpacked and when bathrooms had been visited, the five of them gathered in the kitchen, bathed in a forced silence.

"I like your home, Mrs. Abbott," Annie said. "It's so cozy."

"Thank you," Tucker's mother replied.

"And I like the basement a lot," Chance piped up. "It's the best basement I've ever been in."

"Why, thank you, young man," Tucker's mother said, and Tucker actually believed she was touched by the boy's expansiveness.

Annie pointed to the wall in the kitchen by the desk. It was obvious she didn't know what to say. Tucker turned, as they all did. Annie's unfolding was hung there, the unfolding that Tucker had given his mother for Christmas.

"Tucker. . .is that. . .is that mine?" Annie asked.

"It is. I found it in a gallery in River North," he said.

Tucker's mother looked at Annie, at Tucker, then back to Annie. "You made that? Tucker said he knew the artist. . .but I had no idea."

Chance ran over to it and peered at it closely. "I remember this one. It's kind of girly."

Tucker's mother walked over and put her arm around the

young boy's shoulder. "It is kind of girly, isn't it? I think that's why I love it so much. I don't have many girly things around. It makes me remember my childhood—back when I was your age—every time I look at it. I just love this. . .box, Miss Hamilton."

"Annie, please. Just Annie."

"Well, Annie," Tucker's mother continued, "I can't say how much this means to me. Like you knew about my childhood. I believe I had this same wallpaper in my bedroom. You did a perfect job with this. I would. . .well, I would like to have another one someday."

"My mom is making them all the time now," Chance said politely. "She has a bunch of them."

Tucker took advantage of the pleasant moment and grabbed his coat. He tried to herd Annie and Chance together. "We're going to have to hurry. They stop selling the one-price ticket at the carnival at three."

Tucker's father checked his watch. "You're right. You pay for individual rides, and you'll spend a fortune. I heard Stan talking about it at church. He said he heard that someone spent fifty dollars on rides without the discount. You'd better hurry."

Tucker knew that his parents were standing on the porch as he, Annie, and Chance hurried to the car. As he put the car into gear and drove away, he risked a glance in his parents' direction. Both were waving, and his mother was actually smiling—at least a little.

Tucker felt as if he'd been given yet another sign.

The town of Owatonna began celebrating the fall harvest in earnest ten years prior, when they realized that an autumn festival could boost the local economy. The Chamber of Commerce got into the act and promoted the event heavily in the Twin Cities newspapers and on WCCO radio. If the weather was good, as it promised to be this year, hundreds and hundreds of city folk would take the hour's drive and see what small-town Minnesota was all about.

Bridge Street was blocked to traffic, and food booths lined the streets. The Rotarians offered roasted sweet corn, dripping in butter; the Elks had mulled cider. The Chamber of Commerce was roasting chestnuts, and a score of local restaurants offered a sampling of their wares. The park in the center of town was taken over by artisans and craftspeople, offering a range of objects from true folk-art treasures to mass-produced weathered signs. A carnival occupied the municipal parking lot by the police station, and Chance was drawn to the lights and the noise with the burning intensity of a moth to a flame.

He rode the small roller coaster five times by himself. Chance and Annie went with him on the Ferris wheel, with Tucker pointing out geographical points of interest as they hung at the top of the wheel for an uncomfortable minute or two. Tucker accompanied a reluctant Chance on the tilt-a-whirl. After one short ride, Tucker became a most reluctant passenger.

"I used to love that ride," he explained as he rested on a bench. "Another few minutes and I would have been green."

Annie laughed and replied, "You're already a bit green."

Chance went on every child's ride in the carnival, some of them three times.

Within a few hours, all three of them were tired and hungry and a little bit dirty.

"Let's go home for dinner," Tucker announced. "Mom will have the meal on the table at six thirty sharp. We have a half hour to get back and wash up."

Conversation flowed easily at dinner, and for that Tucker was as grateful as Annie appeared relieved. Tucker's mother prepared a most typical Midwestern meal—meat loaf, mashed potatoes, creamed corn (which Tucker could tell Chance hated but politely gagged down two spoonfuls without complaint), tossed green salad, iced tea, and coffee.

"Mrs. Abbott, everything was delightful," Annie said with great manufactured cheer. She nudged Chance under the table with her foot.

"Yeah," Chance called out. "I liked everything but that corn stuff. The rest of it was real good."

Tucker held his breath.

Then his father laughed. The kind of laugh that meant he'd forgotten the odd, disjointed pacing that a child brings into a home. "Son, I imagine it's an acquired taste. Like olives."

His mother stood, lifting her plate and taking her husband's. "Who wants coffee?"

Tucker stood, too, as did Chance and Annie, each taking their plate in hand.

"Not right now, thanks," Tucker told his mother. "Chance has to get to bed."

After setting their plates carefully on the kitchen counter, Annie and Chance headed downstairs.

"And after that," Tucker told his parents, "I thought I might take Annie on a walk around the neighborhood."

Tucker was glad that Annie wasn't there to see his mother's expression. The glance was fleeting but unmistakable. There was pain, anxiety, and an acceptance of the inevitable, no matter how distasteful the whole affair might be.

"Are you sure?" his mother pressed. "It would be no problem. Your father and I don't drink coffee after lunch, but I could get a pot going in no time."

"Not now, anyhow," Tucker said, stacking the dishes on the green Formica countertop.

His mother glanced at his father, as if trying to decipher the hidden code.

Maybe there isn't a hidden code, Tucker thought with a start. *Maybe all these years it has just been an odd glance from her to him. And maybe my father has no idea what she means, either.*

His father took the morning paper from the kitchen table and headed out to the living room. The water sputtered on, and the *chink* of plates and silverware filled the quiet kitchen. Tucker knew where the dish towels were stored. He took one that looked worn—there was no sense in using a new one when there were old ones that worked just as well.

Silently, Tucker accepted the wet plates and carefully dried each one. He stacked them on the counter, not really remembering his mother's filing system in the kitchen. Growing up, Tucker's list of chores seldom included anything related to food.

Five minutes later, Annie came up from the basement. "He's already asleep. He's had a busy day."

Tucker carefully folded the towel and hung it on the thin silver rack by the stove. "We'll only be a short while."

Annie appeared confused.

"I told my mother I should take you on a quick walking tour of the neighborhood. Get some good country air."

For a second Annie looked scared. "Tucker," she said quietly, "we can't just go out and expect your mother and father to stay here. Chance is sleeping, but. . ."

"You don't mind, do you, Mother?" Tucker asked, more

cheerful than usual. "It will only be a few minutes. Annie says that Chance could sleep through an earthquake."

Tucker was sure that if he gave his mother enough time, she would figure out a way not only to decline the request but to make him feel guilty about making it in the first place. So he grabbed his jacket and Annie's and hurried toward the front door.

"I have my cell phone with me—just in case," Tucker said as he helped Annie on with her coat.

"Wait a minute," his mother said nervously. "We don't have a cell phone. How would we call you?"

Tucker unclipped the phone from his belt. "You dial my number from your phone; you'll get through. The number is on the pad in the kitchen."

"Ohh. . .I thought. . .oh, never mind." His mother smiled again. It was enough to throw Tucker off rhythm. Before anyone could say another word, Tucker all but shoved Annie through the front door, down the steps, and onto the sidewalk that pointed to town, ten blocks away.

Mrs. Abbott stood by the front door, her hand on the worn brass doorknob. She stared for several minutes out through the prism-cut glass that angled and edged the view into multiple refractions. Then she sighed and switched on the overhead porch light. She locked the door, then unlocked it, not being able to recall if Tucker still carried a key.

Mr. Abbott turned the page of his newspaper. The rustling noise was like a leaf brushing against a leaf. He flapped the page again and folded it in half. Lifting his glasses to his forehead, he brought the page close to his face.

His wife padded down the front hall. After cleaning and dusting all that morning, she was mortified to see a cluster of dust lurking in the corner by the closet, where everyone could see it. She bent and picked it up, balling it between her fingers, before she walked past the dining room. She listened at the top of the basement stairs but heard nothing. Slowly and with care, she stepped down one step; it creaked loudly. She stepped once again. There was another creak, but this one was gentle. She kept each creak gentle as she made her way down.

Chance was sprawled across the foldaway bed, the comforter already askew and off his shoulders.

She bent down and readjusted the blue ticking over his small body. His lips were full, like his mother's, but his hair was straight and corn-colored blond—unlike her curly red hair.

With deliberate steps, she returned to the living room. She consulted the clock. They had already been gone for forty-five minutes. She wondered how long a tour of the neighborhood might take. Stepping to the drapes, she parted the thick fabric sections. The street and sidewalk outside remained empty. The moon, a golden harvest moon, had risen over the open field opposite their house, spilling a buttery silver light over the neighborhood.

Without turning back to the room, she spoke. "Annie is nice."

Her husband responded with a grunt of affirmation.

"And that Chance is a real charmer."

"Umm."

She paused.

"She's older than Tucker, you know."

Silence followed.

"I don't know. A few years," he said.

"More than that. Ten or twelve at least," she replied.

"Hmmm. Didn't he say they were just friends?"

Mrs. Abbott now turned to face her husband. "That's what he said. I don't think I. . .maybe she doesn't see it."

"See what?" he asked.

"How he looks at her. That's not the way a friend looks at a friend," she said.

Her husband lowered the newspaper. "I didn't see anything like that."

She glanced at him with a mix of sorrow and anger and understanding and disbelief. "You wouldn't. You never do. You never have. You're a man." And with that, she quickly pivoted back to the window.

Mr. Abbott waited a moment, as if waiting to see if she might say something else. Then when silence reigned, he raised the newspaper, covering his face, drawing it close to his eyes.

"How much farther?" Annie asked.

"Two blocks. You can see the lights from here," Tucker replied.

He walked Annie by the stream that meandered through his neighborhood and pointed out the locations of some of his favorite childhood memories: the site where he and Rod dammed the stream and flooded out the intersection of Larch and Broadway; the oak tree that used to support a large, roofed tree house until the city deemed it a dangerous eyesore and pulled it down; the spot where Tucker wrecked his first bike and suffered his first stitches yielding his first scar—a jagged two-inch tear across his right kneecap.

"I don't want to impose on your parents," Annie said firmly. "They didn't really offer to babysit, you know. You sort of volunteered them."

Tucker picked up a chestnut from the sidewalk. "I know. But they're not going anywhere. And you said yourself, Chance will sleep through anything. If he wakes up, my mother knows what to do."

Annie stuck her hands into the pockets of her coat. "I don't want to take advantage of them, that's all."

"We're only going to be here for a few nights. It will be hard to really take advantage of them."

They turned the corner.

"Here it is," Tucker said. "The world-famous Ev's Kitchen. I know it doesn't look like much."

Tucker examined the restaurant through Annie's eyes. He saw the posters in the front window for the high school football team, a poster announcing the harvest festival, a pancake breakfast at St. Bartholomew's sponsored by Boy Scout Troop #106 and a scattering of taped ends and scraps from numerous prior posters. The glass door was a vision of scratches and handprints. At least six different hues were represented in the plastic seat coverings on the chairs. The fluorescent lights cast a uniform pallor on the few patrons.

Annie took Tucker's arm and squeezed. "I *love* this. It looks exactly like it's supposed to look. Not a single premeditation or presumption in the entire restaurant. It's wonderful."

Tucker liked the fact that she grabbed his arm in excitement. "Counter or booth?"

Annie spun around, eyeing every seating opportunity with care. "Counter. Because you never got to sit there as a little boy, right?"

Tucker took a stool and spun around several times.

"I was right," Annie said and clapped her hands together in happiness. "And your mother won't mind that we have coffee here and not home?"

"We can have coffee here—at home it will be tinted water."

Annie giggled again.

Tucker liked the fact that he could make her laugh. He opened the sewed plastic menu. The offerings appeared to have been typed on a very old typewriter.

Annie ran her fingers down the list and whispered, "I love this place. Please promise me that they'll never let it change. Don't let them buy a computer or fix the chairs or change the sign behind the counter. You have to promise me that, Tucker. I've been here for two minutes, and already this is my most favorite restaurant in the whole world."

Tucker ordered apple pie; Annie selected cherry, with ice cream, and of course, coffee.

Annie pronounced her choice as the most delicious she had ever tasted.

From where they sat, they could sip at their coffee—coffee cups at Ev's never ran dry—and watch the traffic on the street, both cars and people. Every once in a while Tucker would nod toward the window. "That fellow with the ball cap—I went to school with him. Rob something or other."

And as he did, Annie would guess at their occupations and what they were like back in high school.

When the waitress sidled over again, Annie held her hand over her cup, indicating that she was surrendering. Tucker eyed his cup, shrugged, and said, "Last call. You can top it off."

Tucker poured sugar into the cup from a tall glass dispenser and stirred it twice. He knew this wasn't a date, but he was having fun. He knew they weren't a boyfriend and girlfriend, but he was enjoying her company more than he had ever enjoyed the company of a female friend.

She glanced around. "The restrooms?"

Tucker pointed.

"Tell me they're not labeled something like Heifers and Bovines—something only a farm girl might know."

"No, I think they keep things simple here. You should be able to figure it out."

As he sat there at the counter alone, in the cool bluish glow of the fluorescent lights, sipping coffee from a nicked and battered cup, he found himself grinning. He had never been quite this happy and at ease. Even by himself, he was never this at ease. There was something about Annie, about her quick and honest smile, about her exuberant laughter, about her warmth and openness, that made Tucker feel better about himself and more complete than he had in years. When he was with her, his worries scurried well into the background of his thoughts. Without her, he would never have considered bringing home a single mother and child, regardless of his noble rationalizations.

He sighed. It was a pity, he thought, that they were just friends and that there was such an age difference between them. And with Chance in her life, well. . . Tucker had read the studies. An older woman with a child had a better chance of winning the lottery than finding a mate.

Annie came bouncing back to her seat. "Do you smell anything wonderful?" She giggled.

Tucker dutifully sniffed at the air.

"No, you silly—here," she said, as if that explained it all, then leaned into Tucker and presented to him the right side of the nape of her neck. For a moment he was perplexed; then he haltingly lowered his head and sniffed. There was visceral pungency, a flood of the scent of. . . "Lilacs?"

She clapped her hands. "Yes! They had a perfume dispenser in the ladies' room. For a quarter, I get to smell like lilacs. Don't you just love this?" She twirled around on her stool.

Tucker had not seen Annie quite so animated before this evening. Perhaps it was because she was out without Chance, and the Laundromat was being cared for by someone else. But to Tucker, Annie appeared ten years younger this evening—if not in actual physical characteristics, then in outlook and attitude.

Tucker left a more-than-healthy tip for the waitress; then he and Annie set off for his boyhood home.

"I like it here," Annie said.

"But you like everywhere," Tucker replied. "I remember you saying that if your happiness depends on a place, then you'll never really be happy."

"I said that?"

"You did."

"Sounds awfully smart of me, don't you think?"

He gave her a playful nudge on her shoulder and, laughing, she returned the nudge, a little harder than his had been. Then, giggling, she tried it again. Tucker caught her arm and held it. It was the most natural movement in the world, Tucker thought to himself, to let her hand fall into his own. He could tell that she had tensed for a brief second, then let her fingers relax and fold into his own.

As they crossed Broadway and made their way to Maple, they also crossed another unstated and unsurveyed boundary. The city had never gotten around to placing streetlamps on Maple past Broadway, but the moon lit their path well. Tucker felt Annie soften a bit with each step they took while holding hands, and he felt her slowly slide closer to him. Or perhaps he was sliding closer to her, and she no longer moved away. He could not tell who moved and who stayed.

But after a block, their hands were caught between the two of them.

"What's that over there?" Annie asked, pointing with her free hand.

"Veterans' Park."

"Is that a swing set?"

"Come on," he said. "You want a push?"

She laughed and said yes. Soon she was settled in the seat, and he began to push her in the swing, in the golden moonlight, in the crisp Minnesota night.

After a few seconds, she dragged her heels and stopped. "I think swings are in the same category as that tilt-a-whirl."

"That's why I like pushing," he replied, "instead of swinging."

He came around in front of her and extended his hand. She took it. The skin on her palm was chilled from holding the metal chain. He took her other hand and held them both tight.

"It's colder than it looks," he said.

She gazed up at him. The moonlight lit her cheekbones. Tucker could feel his heart, usually silent in his chest. He had not planned on any of this. It was just a trip home to show Chance a small town and a carnival and a farm. It was just going to be a trip with a friend.

He heard, for a brief instant, the voices of Pearl first, then Mrs. Alvarez, and he chose to shut them out. He leaned forward and realized that Annie had leaned forward, as well. Bending slightly, he turned his head. She offered the mirror image to his actions. He slowed down, wondering if, at some point, either he or she might pull back and murmur a reluctant "no."

But neither of them stopped. In a heartbeat, perhaps two, their lips met. Annie let go of his hands and placed her palms against his face and pulled him close to her. And in the distance a pair of doves called to each other.

Seventeen

TUCKER WAS UP BEFORE ANYONE else that next morning. He dressed in the dark, not wanting to wake Chance, and padded silently up to the kitchen. He had to open three drawers until he found the coffee filters, then blankly stared at the old Mr. Coffee as it slowly whooshed hot water through the grounds.

Awhile later his mother entered. She didn't seem surprised to see him sitting by himself in the kitchen, the small television offering a bluish glow, the sound muted.

"Did you sleep well? I'm not sure anyone has ever really slept on the fold-out bed before. I keep asking your father if we should replace it, and he always says the same thing: 'Why? We don't ever have overnight company.' I guess he's right, but still. . ."

"No, Mom, it was fine. I don't think I would want to make it my permanent bed, but for a few days, it's just fine."

"Is the boy still asleep?"

She poured a cup of coffee. Tucker recognized the mug as the one he had bought for her while still in grade school. The red heart was all but worn off the face.

"Annie says that he's a real good sleeper—whatever that means."

His mother added cream and sugar and stirred slowly, the clinking a comforting sound from Tucker's childhood. "He seems like such a polite boy."

"He has his moments, Annie says. But I think he's a good little guy."

His mother sat at the table and set her cup down carefully. Tucker saw her eyes dart over to the wall by the desk.

"Why didn't you mention that Annie had made that? The gift you gave me at Christmas," she said, her words almost pleading.

"I don't know. I guess I didn't think about it. Since you hadn't met Annie and all." He scrutinized his mother's face. He didn't remember the web of lines about her eyes and on her throat. "Does it make a difference?"

She shrugged. It was unlike his mother to shrug.

"I don't know," she said slowly. "I guess I feel like I know her now. I can't tell you how many times I just sit and stare at it. There's something. . .something very knowing about all of it. That's not the right word, but you know what I mean."

Tucker simply nodded.

Both then heard a creaking of wooden steps. Neither of them saw the boy, but Chance's small voice came from the top of the basement steps. "Can I get up now? My mom said I have to be real, real polite and ask for things."

Tucker's mother, for a brief instant, looked like she was about to cry. She hurried to the steps, took the young boy by the hand, and led him over to the table.

"Of course you can come up, Chance. You're our guest. But there is one very important thing you need to tell me."

Chance remained somber and serious.

"You need to tell me what you might like for breakfast. Pancakes? Bacon? Eggs? Oatmeal? Waffles?"

He grinned. "Yes."

"Yes?"

"I like all those things."

Tucker laughed and made the decision for him. "My mother makes great pancakes and bacon, Chance. How would that be?"

"Yes, please," the boy said firmly. "And maybe. . .well, I don't know if I should ask or wait to be asked. . . ."

"What?" Tucker's mother said and placed her hand on the young boy's shoulder.

"Maybe chocolate milk? I like chocolate milk, too."

"Of course," Tucker's mother replied. And when she stepped toward the refrigerator to begin to prepare the meal, Tucker thought he actually saw the hint of a smile.

"You sleep okay?" Tucker asked.

"I did. I got scared once, but then I saw you across the room and knew everything was okay. I went back to sleep. It's different than my room at home."

Tucker's father came into the kitchen already dressed for work. He hung his blue blazer on the back of his chair. Then he switched on the radio—to WCCO—and adjusted the volume. He checked his watch. He had seldom missed the morning farm report. Although he wasn't a farmer, he dealt with farmers and millers and grain elevators and always knew the latest market conditions.

Tucker listened as he glanced over the local paper. He heard the swishing and fluffing of the fork in the pancake batter, the sizzle of the butter on the griddle pan, the hiss of the first pancake, the scratching of the spatula. They were potent sounds from his childhood, sounds he hadn't really heard in years. Perhaps it was because his mother wasn't that big on cooking breakfast that he remembered the few times she had. Chance silently watched the muted images dance on the television screen. Tucker didn't think Annie let Chance watch television at breakfast, so he didn't offer to turn it up.

Tucker's father didn't say a word to anyone else until he had addressed the young boy. "Chance, how would you like to come with me this morning? I have to do a walk-through at the grain elevator in town—insurance reviews and all that. But you could watch as they tip big trucks to unload them. There may even be a railcar or two and an engine. I bet I could talk the engineer into letting you climb aboard. Would you like that?"

Chance paused—his forkful of pancakes, dripping with syrup—halfway to his mouth. "Could I really? A real train? Honest and true? I'd have to ask my mom. . . ."

"Ask your mom what?" Annie said as she entered the compact kitchen. She, too, was dressed and, from her expression, was slightly embarrassed for being the last one to rise.

"Mom," Chance chimed, still chewing on a mouthful of pancakes, "Tucker's dad asked if I could go with him to an elevator with trucks and trains and stuff. Can I go? Can I?"

Tucker saw a perplexed look flash across her face. "It would be fine, Annie. My dad does these walk-throughs every now and again. A grain elevator is a pretty cool place."

"You're sure he won't be in the way?" Annie asked.

Tucker's father smiled to reassure her. "He'll be fine. I took Tucker once when he was small—although I don't remember you being as excited as Chance here."

Tucker could only shrug in his defense, having no memory at all of any such visit.

Tucker didn't give his mother a chance to invite herself to the activities he had planned for himself and Annie that morning. After breakfast, he announced that he was giving Annie a tour of the town with a stop at Pioneer Village, a collection of log homes and old buildings on the eastern edge of the fairgrounds.

The collection of pioneer structures had been a source of town pride for as long as Tucker could remember. It had started off with the church, built before the Civil War and deconsecrated when the congregation built a newer brick structure closer to town sometime at the turn of the century. A schoolhouse was built nearby, and both buildings were used as school and offices until the beginning of World War II. After the war, civic backers and promoters gathered up other old buildings in the county, dismantled them, then rebuilt each one on the site of the now-abandoned school. Now there were more than twenty buildings and barns and sheds, some filled with antiques, some empty, but all part of the grand pioneer theme.

The village was quiet that morning. *Too early in the school year for field trips,* Tucker thought. He and Annie might indeed be the only visitors. A hedge of clouds appeared and softened the sunlight. The temperature remained warm. The scent of burning leaves and plowed fields twined in the air. Tucker led Annie along the worn paths from building to building, providing what historical comment he could remember. They peered in windows and stared up at the fancy millwork on some homes, the rough-hewn wood on others.

"Do you want to sit down for a while?" Tucker asked. "There's a bench over here on the side of the old livery barn."

Annie nodded. When they reached the bench, she gathered her skirt under her legs and sat down. "This is so nice," she said wistfully. "We'll have to bring Chance back here."

Tucker sat next to her. "Maybe. But I remember being his age, and all of this would have been boring to me then. Now it fascinates me—the perseverance of the pioneers, the skills that they needed, the hard choices they made—but I think most of that would be lost on Chance."

Annie closed her eyes as the sun peeked through the clouds. "Maybe you're right."

All Tucker could hear was the faint whisper of the breeze. There was no traffic at this far end of the fairgrounds. He listened hard and could only hear the faint chugs and workings of a tractor.

Tucker's gaze moved over to Annie. Her eyes were still shut. He wanted to take her hand in his. He wanted to slip his arm around her shoulders and draw her close. But he chose not to. Instead he began to speak. "Annie," he said softly, "about last night. . ."

"Yes," she replied.

"I guess I want to apologize. I was much too forward."

"No, I was," she answered. "It's just that we were both tired and maybe a little giddy from the long drive and the walk and all."

"Yes, that's it," he added. "It all sort of snowballed. It wasn't planned."

"I know," she said as she turned to him.

She waited and then both spoke at the same.

"I think I'm too old—"

"I think I'm too young—"

Both stopped, surprised, and their eyes met.

And then both spoke at the same time again.

"No, you're wrong about that—"

"You're not at all—"

Annie broke their gaze, turned away toward the steeple on the old unused church, and laughed. Tucker began to laugh, as well.

Then he moved so he was facing her. "You have Chance and your art and your business," he said quietly. "You don't need another worry right now."

Annie pivoted on the bench and faced him. The morning sun lit up her hair like a halo. "And you have the church to worry about. That's probably enough on your plate right now."

As she turned her head slightly, the sun illuminated her face and the whisper of lines about her eyes that deepened when she laughed. He gazed into her eyes with a knowing and caring look. He examined her lips, with their tiny creases at the corners, the result of hours and years of smiling.

"We do have enough choices to keep us busy, don't we?" he said.

Annie nodded and cast her eyes downward.

There were a thousand other things that Tucker wanted to say. He wanted to tell her about his childhood and what he wanted out of life and how wonderful a little boy he thought Chance was. He wanted to tell her how absolutely happy he was that she'd agreed to come here with him and was sitting with him, the autumn sun on their faces. He wanted her to know that, at this particular moment, he was more at peace with the world than he had ever been in his life. And it was not just a happenstance of the right time or the right place or the right person, but a delirious concoction of all three that turned his heart giddy with an enchanted intoxication.

He debated for a single instant—debated as to what he should do about this whirl of newly understood awareness.

And then he decided.

Annie's gaze was fixed on her hands. He memorized her nose and her forehead and the shape of her hands and the gentle coming and going of her breath.

He heard a flutter of wings as a gathering of starlings cawed across the sky.

He had spent enough time waiting and not choosing. He had spent enough time making choices by not making a choice. It was time, he decided, to be direct. To make a personal choice for himself—without considering how his mother would react, or his father or his teachers or his friends or the church.

It was time for Tucker alone to decide on what was important to Tucker.

He reached over with his hand and lifted Annie's chin with gentle fingertips. She turned it to him, offering no more than a petal of resistance. She let him gaze into her eyes. Tucker couldn't be certain as to how long he looked. But after a time, he let himself draw nearer to her. Nearer and nearer until she turned her head and he turned his and they met in a deliberate and tender kiss. He could almost feel the air as her eyelids fluttered open and shut.

He felt her arms move slowly around him, as his did the same to her. Then she broke the kiss and embraced him, tighter than he had ever been embraced before, holding him with a gentle fierceness, with hardly a breath coming between them. When they finally broke apart, he bent to her and kissed her once again, chaste and soft, for only a heartbeat.

He knew that to talk might spoil that moment. So instead he stood, took her hand in his, and walked north through the Pioneer Village to a stand of oak trees on a small rise. From there the town was spread out below them, covered in gold and crimson, lit by the fall sun, alive and vibrating with beauty.

He kept her hand in his as they stood together. She placed her free hand on his forearm and leaned into his side, her head resting against his shoulder.

He hoped she was thinking the same thing he was thinking— that this was the most perfect day in his entire life. He wanted nothing more than to stand where he stood, with Annie by his side, until the world ceased revolving.

❦

The following Sunday, Tucker's mother and father stood at the curb and continued their farewells. Tucker had loaded the car earlier in the day, packed up the cooler with fresh sandwiches and ice placed in Ziploc bags.

Tucker couldn't remember such a public display from his parents who had, up until this departure, always made their goodbyes in the foyer of the house and waved from the front window. Perhaps it was the introduction of Chance that called for different measures of farewell. Tucker's mother knelt to the young boy's level and hugged him tightly, making him promise that he would return soon. Tucker was doubly surprised when his mother gave Annie an unexpected embrace and offered her thanks again for the visit and the unfolding.

Tucker's father, even less demonstrative than his mother, gave a firm handshake to Chance and a brief, uncomfortable embrace to Annie.

The visit had gone well—Tucker was certain of that—but not as well as the farewells indicated.

Chance had been captivated at the grain elevator and had gotten the opportunity to sit in an actual diesel locomotive and to blow the whistle. He had watched the operators tilt an entire semi full of corn and dump its load into an underground pit. When they all met for lunch, Chance would not stop talking about his adventures. Annie and Tucker had simply remained silent and marveled at Chance's torrent of words.

The five of them had gone to visit the farm of a friend in

Medford, and Chance got to see cows and chickens close-up. The lumbering bulk of the cows intimidated him, but he enjoyed feeding the chickens and watching them scramble about in a feathery rush.

The night before the three of them were to return to Chicago, Tucker's father had treated them to a fancy meal at a nice restaurant—at least the most fancy meal Tucker had ever eaten in Steele County.

Today, as Tucker pulled away from the curb, Chance knelt in the backseat and waved until Tucker's parents and the house faded from view.

"Buckle up, Chance," Annie said.

"Then you buckle up, too," he said back to his mother as he slipped the metal parts together. Annie had slipped closer to Tucker on the front seat and reluctantly scooted toward the door to latch her belt. She smiled at Tucker and mouthed a silent, *I'm sorry.*

Chance piped up, "What? What did you say?"

Annie's cheeks flushed. "I didn't say anything."

"I saw your mouth move. You said something," he replied.

Annie folded her hands in her lap and turned halfway in her seat. "I just whispered to Tucker to drive safely. We have a long drive ahead of us."

Tucker could see Chance's eyes in the rearview mirror and knew that Chance hadn't bought his mother's explanation.

By the time they reached the outskirts of Rochester, less than an hour into the drive, Chance had slumped down against the door. Annie turned around in her seat and used her coat as a pillow for him, snuggling him into a comfortable position. When she was done, she turned back toward the front.

Tucker grinned as Annie scooted much closer to him than when they had started the trip.

"You're not going to wreck the car, are you?" she asked. "There doesn't seem to be a seat belt in the middle position here. I checked."

"I won't crash," he answered. "Just don't make any sudden moves, okay?"

He let his right hand fall to the opening on the seat between them, palm up. She placed her hand inside his, and he tucked her fingers in his. She leaned her head against his shoulder.

"This has been a wonderful few days," Annie said.

"It has been," Tucker replied. "Maybe some of the best days of my life."

"Me, too."

She picked up his hand and turned it and brought the back of his hand to her face. She brushed it against her cheek, then kissed it gently.

He inhaled. "That may constitute a sudden move in Minnesota."

"Sorry," she said. "I couldn't help it."

She nestled his hand between them on the seat, and they drove on in silence into the brightening day.

On the way to Chicago, Illinois

Chance continued to snooze through much of Wisconsin. He had had a very full week, and the activity had caught up to him.

"I have to stop for gas in a bit," Tucker said. "Maybe lunch, too."

Annie nodded.

"What are you thinking?" he said quietly, not wanting to wake Chance. They had not talked much since leaving Owatonna, yet Tucker had not felt uncomfortable in their silence.

"Are we dating now?" Annie asked.

Tucker swallowed once. "I think so. Do you want to be dating?"

Annie looked down at their intertwined hands. "I think so."

"Do you know what this means?" Tucker asked.

"I think so," Annie replied. "It means you pass mushy notes to me in fifth-period biology class, right?"

"Only I can't get caught. Another detention and I'm off the track team."

Annie giggled.

"But you do know what it means," Tucker said again, this time more seriously.

"I do. It's been awhile, but I think I remember some of the rules," she said softly.

"Me, too."

"I have to think about Chance, too," Annie continued. "I don't want to do anything to hurt him."

"Like dating a man who isn't serious," Tucker said.

Annie turned to him. Tucker knew he couldn't stop the car and look back, but he did turn his face to her for a second or two.

"I don't want Chance hurt. I don't think you will. I don't think you're that sort of man."

Tucker didn't respond.

"You're not that sort of man, are you?" she asked again.

"No. I'm not."

"Then we're both serious about this?"

"Yes, I'm serious," Tucker replied.

Several miles passed in silence. They both heard Chance stir slightly.

"Are you scared, Annie?"

"No. Yes. Maybe. A little. Not about you. Maybe about me. The differences."

Tucker nodded, then squeezed her hand. "Me, too."

A few more miles passed.

"Me, too," he said again.

Eighteen

Chicago, Illinois

TUCKER PRESSED HIS FACE against the front window overlooking the street. He could tell immediately who was leaning on the bell.

"Mrs. Alvarez," he said with great cheer after he hurried down the steps.

She did not greet him with the same cheer. "We need to talk, *Pastor* Abbott," she said firmly, her emphasis sharp and hard on the word *pastor.*

"Shall I make coffee? Do you want cookies?" Tucker said, hoping to lighten the mood.

"Neither. It is only talk that I want."

They took the steps slowly and in silence. When Mrs. Alvarez finally made it into his kitchen, she lowered herself on a chair and took a deep breath. "I changed my mind. Make the coffee," she commanded. "It will give me a chance to catch my breath. And while you're doing that, find a cookie, as well."

Tucker hurried to the tasks and, within a few minutes, had hot coffee and a plate of chocolate-chip cookies placed in front of his guest.

She took a sip, then picked up a cookie. "You know why I am here, do you not?" she asked, gesturing at Tucker.

Tucker knew but did not say. Instead he offered a vague gesture.

"I talked to Annie," Mrs. Alvarez said. "She is a good girl. She says that I am like a mother to her. She does not hold secrets back from me."

Tucker leaned against the stove and waited. He hoped the burner was off but didn't want to make any sudden moves.

"Last night, I come to the Laundromat not to wash but to visit. I am curious as to how her trip went to your hometown and your parents. I want to know if my little man Chance got to see a real farm and cows."

Tucker did not move. He wanted to take a drink from his coffee cup. He wanted to sit down at the table. But he knew either gesture might be seen as a lack of paying attention on his part, so he remained still.

"Annie tells me how wonderful the town is. She tells me that your parents are nice. She tells me Chance visited a farm and rode a horse and a tractor. I am very pleased. Chance deserves so much, and Annie does not have deep pockets."

Tucker moved to sit down. Mrs. Alvarez glared at him for a second, but he pulled a chair out and sat as properly as he could.

"Annie tells me she had a wonderful time. I look at her, hard, and I see something in her eyes. Something that she holds back from me. That is not like my Annie. Annie tells me everything."

Mrs. Alvarez paused and chewed on a cookie. Tucker was sure she was trying her best to remain stern. "I see something there—something bright and sparkling. I tell Annie that she must tell me everything."

Tucker found himself offering small, almost secret nods, to keep the story flowing. He dared not speak yet.

"She blushes, Pastor Abbott. Annie *blushes*. When you are older, like Annie, and you blush, that tells a story all by itself. Blushing? What does Annie have to blush about, I ask myself."

Tucker held his breath. He had known that the trip would be the point of some discussion. But he'd hoped it would not unfold in this particular way.

"I ask Annie. I say, 'Why are you blushing?' "

Tucker waited. He didn't know what Annie would say. After their brief discussion in the car, Chance had woken up and had chattered on about his experiences for most of the rest of the trip. By the time they had reached Chicago, he had barely finished retelling his experiences of riding on the tractor with Tucker's cousin.

Tucker and Annie had exchanged silent looks as they'd unloaded the car. Tucker had hauled Annie's bags up the stairs. Chance had insisted on hefting his own. They'd had, perhaps, a half minute alone on the steps, hidden in the dimness.

"I'm nervous," she had said, taking his hand and squeezing it.

"Me, too," Tucker had said.

And then they had leaned toward each other and enjoyed a fleeting hug and an even more fleeting kiss. Chance had galumphed down the steps, offering them both an odd, disjointed stare, as if he somehow knew he had interrupted something private.

And since then, for the past two days, neither Tucker nor Annie could find a private moment together.

So Tucker was interested, very interested, in how Annie described what had happened between them.

"Do you know what she says?" Mrs. Alvarez asked, snapping Tucker back to the present.

"No," Tucker replied.

"She says that you two. . ."

Tucker exhaled, willing the words to come.

"That you two are," Mrs. Alvarez continued, *"together.* That you kissed her several times in Minnesota. At night and in the middle of the day in broad daylight in a park, and once after your parents went to bed, in your living room."

Tucker inhaled.

"Is that true?" Mrs. Alvarez asked.

Tucker nodded. "Yes."

Mrs. Alvarez shook her head. "I warned you," she said, her gaze piercing. "Did I not say that Annie is too old?"

"You did. But it doesn't matter to either of us."

Tucker could have sworn he saw the faint beginnings of a smile on the old woman's face.

"You will promise me now—promise me again—that you will never *ever* hurt Annie or Chance."

"I promise, Mrs. Alvarez. I promise."

The old woman stared at Tucker for what seemed like several minutes, as if analyzing his eyes, his face, and his demeanor, judging and evaluating the truthfulness of his words and his promise.

After a long stretch, she did indeed smile. And then she grabbed Tucker's cheek and tweaked it hard.

Tucker knew for a certainty that this time would result in a bruise.

With her words as honed as a butcher's knife, she said, "You keep your promise, Pastor Abbott, or I will be God's instrument." She paused and patted his now-throbbing cheek. "Do you understand?" she asked with a smile but with words of ice.

"I understand," Tucker replied with as much solemnity as the occasion warranted.

⁓≈⁓

Tucker took the front steps of the church two at a time, hurried along by a chilly autumn rain. He shook off his coat in the foyer. The lights in the main office were on, and the scent of brewing coffee was as strong as the drink itself.

He laid his coat and briefcase on the hall table and stepped into the bright lights. Pearl was sitting at her desk, a coffee mug in front of her, her arms crossed, her lips pressed together.

"Good morning, Pearl," he called out as he walked to the coffee urn.

Pearl did not respond.

He stood in front of her desk as had been his custom for the last months. "Are we going to have a busy day?"

It was his standard question.

She did not speak.

"Pearl?" Tucker asked, worried briefly that something may be wrong. When he examined her face, he realized that something *was* indeed wrong.

"What did I tell you?" she barked, not loud but firm.

Tucker had heard that voice before—from his mother when he was young and from a few very strict teachers in elementary school.

Hoping this had nothing to do with Annie and himself, Tucker managed a smile. "About what?"

Pearl shook her head like a mother who has just found her child in obvious and deliberate disobedience. "Tucker Abbott, you know very well what I mean."

He decided to let the game play itself out. "No. I don't."

Pearl appeared as if she wanted to stand, but instead of rising, she simply tensed. "You and Annie. Does that name ring a bell? Or shall I ask Mrs. Alvarez about it?"

Pearl didn't sound angry or upset but weary.

"You know Mrs. Alvarez?" Tucker asked.

"All my life, Tucker."

He blinked several times.

"You didn't know that, did you, Tucker?"

Tucker shook his head and quickly rehearsed a dozen different responses to Pearl. He wondered if he could get away with being flippant, or perhaps he should be very, very serious. In the end he simply stood there.

"I thought we had an agreement. That Annie is a very nice person but that she is too old for you. She's probably fifteen years older than you."

"Just ten and a few days," he shot back. "We compared drivers' licenses."

Pearl stood up and came around her desk. For an instant Tucker wondered if he should prepare to be slapped. Instead Pearl placed her hand on his forearm.

"Tucker, do you know what is going to happen if you keep this up? Don't you like preaching at this church?"

Tucker wished he could put down his coffee mug. He felt at loose ends holding it. He couldn't gesture as he wanted since he'd filled the cup to the rim and didn't want to add spilling coffee on the floor to his list of errors.

"You are. . .*involved*, right?" Pearl said, as if the word *involved* left a bitter taste on her tongue.

"Yes. Annie and I are seeing each other."

"Since your trip to Owatonna?"

"Yes. Sort of. Maybe. I think I knew I wanted to before we

left. Wanted it without admitting it."

She looked down and shook her head—much the same gesture as Mrs. Alvarez had made a week earlier. But Tucker was certain Pearl wasn't about to pinch his cheek.

"Tucker, is this serious?"

Confused, he stared at her. He knew how he felt about Annie, but he simply couldn't understand other people's reactions to his new status. "I think it is. I don't know exactly. I mean, how early in a relationship do you know that it's serious?"

Pearl squeezed his arm hard. "She has a little boy. That's how you know it's serious. It's not a situation you can play with. You have to know right away."

"Then it's serious," he said quietly and walked out into the dark hall and toward his office.

⊷∾⊶

Tucker pressed the buzzer.

From the steps above, he heard a whooping and the sound of what might be a herd of cattle stampeding down the wooden steps.

"Tucker's here!" Chance shrieked, opened the door, and leapt into the air. Tucker had prepared himself. That was Chance's standard greeting. Tucker embraced him in a fierce bear hug, growling and carrying him back up the stairs.

Annie stood at the landing, a worn dish towel in her hands. "Chance," she called out, more good-natured than angry, "how many times do I have to tell you? Be polite. Life is not a wrestling match."

"Annie, it's okay," Tucker said, laughing. "Once I get him to the top, I'm going to wrestle him down to the floor."

Chance responded by a renewed chorus of shrieks and growls and laughs. Annie stood aside as Tucker carried her son inside and tossed him gently onto the couch.

"Dinner is almost ready," she said. "Now listen. Both of you!"

Tucker and Chance looked up.

"No breaking anything. Promise?"

They both promised, and as soon as Annie walked into the kitchen, Chance leapt at Tucker and latched his arms around Tucker's neck. For the next ten minutes, they tussled about the living room, both taking great pains to avoid collisions with the furniture. The previous evening, Tucker had backed into a small table and knocked a brass picture frame to the floor. The frame was fine, but the glass had shattered, with great drama, into a thousand pieces all over the living room.

So this night their wrestling stayed more sedate. Even before Annie called Chance to wash up, man and boy were sitting side by side on the sofa, talking over their respective days.

"I hope you like soup, Tucker," Annie said. "It's one of Chance's favorite meals. When I asked you to dinner again, I realized that I didn't have much else in the house."

"Soup is great," he said, pulling in his chair.

"Soup is good food," Chance chimed in, wiping his hands on his shirt.

The aroma of the soup and freshly made bread wafted through the dining room like a pleasant, intoxicating fog. Tucker ate slowly, watching Annie, listening to Chance, enjoying every morsel and tidbit of conversation.

Chance finished first. "May I be excused?"

Annie said he could, and Chance carried his plate and spoon out into the kitchen.

"May I watch television?" he asked.

Annie tilted her head at her son. "What show?"

"Just cartoons."

"Good cartoons or bad cartoons?"

"Good ones, Mom," he replied.

Tucker wondered if Annie saw the slight roll of his eyes. He was sure she had but chose to ignore the gesture.

"Go ahead. Not loud. Bedtime in thirty minutes."

"Okay," he said, and his departure left the room silent. A few seconds later, cheerful animation hissed and chattered from the front room.

Tucker smiled at Annie. He peered around as if he was about to be observed, then took her hand and squeezed it. "I love being here with you—both of you."

She nodded. "Can you stay until Chance goes to bed?"

"Sure," Tucker replied quickly. Then he saw her concerned expression. "Any reason?"

Annie looked at him—not sad, not happy. "We need to talk. I need to talk to you. Okay?"

He nodded, then stood to help clear the table. This time he washed and stacked the dishes in the wire rack on the drainboard. He was as comfortable doing this small task as he had ever been in his life. Working in Annie's kitchen was simple, yet profound. . . and filled with meaning. He hummed as he worked.

Later, as he finished the last glass, carefully wiping it dry and clean of all fingerprints, he felt Annie's arms encircle his waist from behind. He let her hold him for a minute, then turned and faced her.

"You want to talk? You sounded so serious."

She took him by the hand and led him into the front room. "Chance is asleep already. Playing hard with you like that before dinner just tires him out. He sleeps better when you have dinner with us."

"I'm like medicine, right?"

Annie smiled. "Good medicine."

Tucker looked about the room. Annie had turned the lights low. The dining room lights were off. More light came into the room from the street below than from the two lamps she'd turned on. They both sat on the couch.

Annie squirmed, then asked, "Tucker, are you sure about this?"

"About what? Nightfall? Dinner? This couch?"

"Tucker, I'm serious. About you and me. About us. About Chance and me."

"I am, Annie," he said, facing her. "I said so at the very beginning."

She brought her hand to her throat. "I heard that Pearl talked to you today."

Tucker sighed. "Are there no secrets anywhere? I thought that this only happened in a small town."

Annie touched his hand. "She called me. She told me what you had talked about. She's concerned for both of us."

Tucker's chest tightened in anger. "She has no business in what we do. Neither does Mrs. Alvarez. I know they both mean well, but this is between us and not them."

"I know, I know," Annie said, soothing and calming. "But they are concerned." Then Annie stared directly into Tucker's eyes. "Pearl said that the elders will no doubt bring the subject up."

"It's no business of theirs, either," Tucker replied, his words louder and sharper than he'd anticipated.

Annie put her fingertips on his lips. "I know it isn't, Tucker. I know." Her lips began to tremble.

He embraced her tenderly, cradling her in his arms. "Don't worry, Annie. It will be all right. It really will be."

But, deep inside, he wondered if it really would be.

Tucker figured he'd dodged the bullet. The elders didn't once mention Annie's name during their next meeting. Instead they focused on the search process.

Stan Gleason, one of the elders, happened to be on the committee that had rewritten the church constitution nearly fifteen years earlier.

"The search committee is willing to commit to maybe a year's worth of weekly meetings."

Tucker had expressed surprise. "A year? Seems like a long time."

"Maybe," Stan said. "But we talked to other churches who said if you hurry it, you'll make a mistake. We don't want to make any mistakes."

Tucker watched the other elders nod in agreement.

"It will be awhile until you have to get a resume printed, Pastor Abbott. Not until after the first of the year. Nothing happens in November or December. Now, Tucker, you know that the committee has ultimate say in who they talk to, but we all think that they'll talk to you first. But we can't tell them to. They might want a few candidates at one time, I don't know. Last time we had two to pick from, and one was Pastor Yount."

Tucker relaxed some. There would be no decisions or even the start of a decision until at least January.

The weather grew colder and the skies lost their blue, replaced by iron gray clouds. As much as Tucker thought he was influenced by the weather, he welcomed the chill. When he and Annie and Chance gathered around the kitchen table to play silly board games, there could be no guilt over not enjoying the outdoors.

Tucker had been careful. He and Annie "dated" perhaps twice a week and hardly ever ventured into public. Babysitters were hard to come by even in the church youth group. There were few, if any, teenagers who needed money badly enough to resort to babysitting. Tucker thought that Mrs. Alvarez might be a sitter candidate, but Annie merely arched her eyebrows in response.

"She's in her seventies, Tucker. Chance can be a handful, you know."

So they cooked meals, popped popcorn, rented videos, read, did art or wrote, and acted as peaceful as an old married couple—content with small events, happy to be in the same room, not requiring any fancy dinners or shows or nightlife to keep them joyous together.

Chance still went to bed at an early hour, so Tucker and Annie had their private time, as well. They would sit on the sofa and watch old movies, holding hands and eating Garrett's Caramel Corn out of the bag. Some nights saw them at opposite ends of the couch: Tucker with an open book on his lap, Annie fussing with her latest unfolding. And some nights found them in the dark, cuddling, holding each other close. Tucker was careful not to let his emotions run too fast, though it became more and more of a struggle as the days drew on. He knew Annie felt the same frustrations.

And yet everything in their relationship was wonderful.

Tucker could not have scripted a better relationship, had he been given the chance. He loved being with Annie, loved her laugh and her smile and her tender kisses. He loved being with Chance, his passionate embraces, his from-the-stomach laugh, his fierce play. Even from that first moment when Tucker said he was falling in love with Annie, he continued to know that Annie was the right choice for his life. He had never known that love could be as all-encompassing and total as his love for Annie and Chance had become.

Annie dried her hands on the towel and slipped it over the handle to the stove. She wondered if every woman draped her dish towels there. It was a grilled-cheese and tomato-soup meal, so the cleanup had been simple. She had shooed Tucker and Chance out of the kitchen and told them to go play—but warned once again about roughhousing. Two nights ago they had managed to knock over a large, stable upholstered chair. Annie had been so grateful that no one lived beneath them and that the rumble of the washers and dryers covered their noises. At least Annie hoped they did.

She snapped off the light and walked into the dining room. She could see Tucker and Chance, seated side by side on the sofa, their faces lit by the blue flickering of the television. She heard the cartoon music. She saw Chance giggle and Tucker smile, then watched as Tucker tickled her son on his side. Chance laughed louder, and Tucker pressed on his assault with both hands. Soon her son was quivering with laughter. He reached up and hugged Tucker's neck.

Annie put her hand on her mouth. She felt like crying from

the beauty and the simplicity of the scene before her. She remembered her earlier prayer, asking God to send a man into Chance's life so he could see love and respect and joy modeled in the life of a man.

And Annie began to cry silently, wiping the tears quickly from her cheeks, as she realized that God had indeed answered her prayers.

Nineteen

THREE SUNDAYS AFTER THE New Year's service, Tucker stood in front of the church, bowed his head, and offered a closing prayer. He thought, as he began to pray, that you could tell a lot about how the pastor viewed the service by the length of his closing prayer.

If it was long and expansive, filled with flowers and flourishes, then the pastor had had a good day and wanted it to continue just a bit longer. If all the pastor did was issue a blessing and a dismissal, it had not been such a good day.

Tucker went on and on this Sunday, rolling and building in his prayer, making it almost a mini-sermon. When he was done, he lifted his head, then his arms, and called out, "Go in peace." He had never used that form of dismissal before, but it felt right today.

Then he hurried down the center aisle before it filled and positioned himself at the rear door, as had been his habit since Pastor Yount died. Tucker liked to get immediate feedback, although it could be dangerous.

"I liked the music today. The worship team is really great."

"I couldn't hear anything after all that loud jungle music. And it's too cold in here. You're going to get a note from me on this."

"I like the lyrics on the overhead. I got a cousin who sells projection units. Call me if you want to get a good deal on a used one."

"Pastor Abbott, the music was so loud my ears are ringing. I almost walked out. I'll have a headache for the rest of the day now."

"Finally we had some music written in this century. Keep it up."

"When are we going to sing my favorite hymns again?"

"We're not ever going to sing those old hymns again, are we?"

"I liked what you said in your sermon. About time you got around to telling those people how to behave."

"Pastor Abbott, you'll have to show me where you got that application from that verse. I'll call you Monday. Oh, no, wait. You pastors still take Monday off, right?"

"Pastor Abbott, I love what is happening to this church. For the first time, I'm excited about worshipping again."

"Are you ever going to wear a vestment? I like my preachers in a robe."

"Are you coming for dinner?"

The last comment came whispered from Chance Hamilton. Chance and Annie were among the last to leave the sanctuary that morning. Tucker had bent to take his handshake. Chance was wearing a tie, askew around his neck; and his shirt, per usual, had completely escaped his trousers. There was a red stain on his chest—must have had red juice for their snack in children's church.

"Chance," Annie reminded him, "you're not to be offering invitations. That's Mommy's job, not yours."

"So can he come? Please?"

Annie glanced at her son, then at Tucker. "If he would like to. It's only chili today."

"Yeah! Chili! I love chili!" Chance crowed.

"Sure," Tucker said quietly. "About one?"

Annie smiled, nodded, took her son's hand, and led him out the doors and into the chilly air.

Tucker took a deep breath. There were still a few people milling about in the sanctuary. There always was. Today's parting comments were as mixed in style and tone as they had ever been. Tucker was happier on those Sundays when the positives edged out the negatives. That was not a frequent occurrence. Some Sundays, the confusing and perplexed comments edged out everything else, causing Tucker to wonder if he had preached in a different language.

Tucker knew he couldn't please every person in the congregation. But he did have an obligation to listen to each person with as much respect as he could, even when they were not respectful to him or the church. Such slights came with the territory, Tucker told himself. Yet knowing they were part of the job didn't necessarily lessen their impact.

He walked to his office, still the small office in the hall with the single window. Unlocking the door, he went in and snapped on the light. He couldn't help but notice the single sheet of notebook paper on his desk. He picked it up, read it, and sighed deeply.

Pastor Abbott,
> *Could you meet a few of us for coffee tonight?*
At Mason's Coffee Shop—about seven?

> > > > *Stan Gleason*

Stan was not the senior elder, but he was one of the more vocal elders. Tucker liked him up to a point but thought he could be edgy and rough on occasion, with little regard for people's feelings.

Tucker folded the paper and slipped it into his shirt pocket, making a series of mental notes not to forget the note or the time or place it indicated.

Chance and Tucker sat by the television silently, side by side, staring at the flickering images. Annie was in the kitchen. Tucker could smell chili and. . . He sniffed again. Corn bread, if he wasn't mistaken.

If Chance had been in the room alone, he might very well have tried to find some replay of wrestling and turned the sound way down low so his mother would not hear. But with Tucker at his side, he wouldn't try any illegal moves. Instead of wrestling, the pair of them watched a sporting event called the "Extreme Challenge," a combination of skateboarding and biking. With every complex and potentially limb-sacrificing and dangerous maneuver, the riders twisting and contorting in a hysterical fashion, Chance would look over at Tucker and say, "Oh, I can do that one. That's really easy."

Tucker knew that Chance could barely ride a bike, but he played along. "Did it take you long to learn? You only got your bike last summer."

"Naw. I started doing it right away. You have to be good, though. I'm good."

Annie called them into dinner. Tucker had been right. There was corn bread on the table, a full plate of grated cheddar cheese, and a smaller plate of freshly chopped onions.

"Sunday dinners don't get much better than this." Tucker breathed in the delicious aromas.

"Yeah! Chili!" Chance added, rubbing his hands together as if he had not eaten in days.

At the end of the meal, Tucker was unable to reconstruct much of the dialogue between the three of them. Chance went on and on about some sort of animated cartoon hero that Tucker couldn't even pronounce, let alone remember, and gave a very detailed explanation of his powers and weaknesses. When Chance paused for a breath, Annie and Tucker discussed the service that morning and how Tucker got the feeling that his meeting tonight with "a few of" the elders was going to focus on him taking the church too far too fast into the uncharted waters of contemporary worship.

"I don't think so, Tucker," Annie said as they cleared the table. "Everyone I looked at was smiling and pretty much participating in the service. Even Mr. Wallace was clapping his hands. He had a big grin on his face."

"Really? I didn't notice."

"If the elders ask you to tone it down, will you? So many people have been waiting a long time to see these sorts of changes happen."

Tucker took up his station at the sink, dish towel in hand. "I don't know. They *are* in charge of the church, not me. If I don't think they understand what we're trying to do, then I will defend my changes."

"But would you change it back to the way it was with Pastor Yount if they asked?" Annie repeated.

Tucker shrugged. "I don't know. They say you have to pick the hills on which you're willing to die. I'm not sure about this one. Maybe. It's important to me, that's for sure. I want people to celebrate when they're in church—not act as if they are at a funeral."

All of a sudden, Annie cocked her head. Tucker heard it, too.

It was the braying voice of an announcer at a wrestling match. Then the voice dimmed.

Annie offered a wry smile. "I think my little man in there is attempting to watch something that he shouldn't."

Tucker took a step toward the living room. "Do you want me to change it back? Tell him he can't watch it?"

Annie hesitated. Tucker could almost see her weighing her options. Tucker thought she might want him to, in order to be absolved of the disciplining just once. But then Tucker watched her eyes, watched her gaze seek out his. Tucker was not Chance's father.

"No," she finally said. "Thank you, though. This is something I have to handle."

Tucker watched her walk toward the living room. He was both relieved and sad, a little bit sad. He wondered what he would have done had Annie allowed him to go.

Annie claimed she had work to do on a few of her incomplete unfoldings. Christmas had been good for her art, and she had promised several galleries replacements for the pieces that had sold.

"I should go back to my place and work on a few things, as well," Tucker said with some reluctance. He had hoped that Annie would ask him to come back and do his work on her dining room table. But he also knew that if he came, they would most likely not get anything done on their respective projects.

Annie glanced at Chance before she ushered Tucker out onto the landing of the stairs. She slipped her arms around his waist, and he encircled his around her. Once again he marveled at how comfortable she felt in his arms.

"When will we see each other again?" Annie gazed up into his eyes. "I already miss you."

"Maybe Tuesday evening? I have some of the youth group leadership coming over tomorrow night. Sort of a mentoring session."

Annie lay her head against Tucker's chest. "Tucker," she said softly, "what do you tell people about us?"

"I tell them the truth."

"The truth?"

They hadn't been on this particular road before. But Tucker was sure that Annie wasn't simply leading him on to trick him into saying something he wasn't ready to say. If he'd thought that was the case, he would have pulled back. He knew she just wanted to know what he saw as the truth.

"The truth?" Tucker repeated. "The truth is, Annie Hamilton, that you are the most wonderful woman I have ever known. When I am with you, I feel at home, warm, at peace."

He put his hand under her chin and lifted her face to his. He bent down and brought his lips to hers in the gentlest of kisses. "And the truth is, Annie, I'm in love with you."

"Me, too, Tucker. Me, too."

And with those words, Tucker felt an unspeakable lightness in his heart, as if it were now fully unfolded for the first time, embracing Annie and understanding what love really meant.

Tucker fussed around his apartment that afternoon, accomplishing very little. He changed clothes for the third time that day. The suit he wore in the morning was only appropriate for Sunday morning activities. The sweatshirt and jeans he wore to Annie's could be seen as a bit too casual, even for a lazy Sunday afternoon. Instead he ironed a pair of khaki trousers and pulled on a more expensive, sweaterlike sweatshirt. He hoped he didn't have to explain his clothing options.

Mason's was only a short distance away. Tucker didn't want to arrive early, as if he were nervous, which he was. Nor did he want to arrive too late, as if he didn't care at all, which was not the truth.

He cared about the church and his position. After so many months, he was just hitting his stride. He was surprised at how deeply he cared about this place and these people. As he walked toward the coffee shop, he thought about how important the church had become in his life. The church, as well as Annie, occupied much of his thoughts. He was pouring himself into this ministry and felt good about it—about how he was impacting the lives of others, how he was making a real difference in the life of the church.

He grabbed the door handle of the coffee shop and prayed that the elders wouldn't be too upset over the music. Of all that he had done, he was most happy that the music was now lively, worshipful, and seemed to speak to more of the congregation than ever before.

Stan Gleason stood by a table in the back. He waved to Tucker. "Back here," he called.

Tucker hoped they hadn't been waiting on him long.

"Sorry I'm late," Tucker explained as he sat down. "This was farther than I thought."

"No problem at all," said Herb Miller, an architect. "We just arrived, as well."

In addition to Stan and Herb, there were Kenny Wolbert and Gary Harris.

"Pull up a chair," Stan instructed. "You want a coffee? A latte? Some squirrelly drink with fruit and nuts? You name it. My treat."

Tucker actually considered what his drink selection might mean. Instead of ordering his usual medium latte with an extra shot of espresso, he decided on the safe choice of a coffee with cream.

"So, Pastor Abbott, lots of music this morning," Stan began as he pulled up his chair, passing Tucker's coffee to him. "It was really different."

Tucker tried to read the man's face. Stan was not the most poker-faced of the elders. If he disliked something, he generally made it easy to tell. He would wince or grimace or even stick out his tongue in mock disgust. But Tucker saw a smile on the man's face this evening—and that almost threw him. He was expecting something else, indeed.

"I know it was a little loud," Tucker began, "but the fellows are working hard at getting the balance just right. They tell me the sanctuary is an acoustical nightmare with lots of sound bouncing off hard surfaces."

"It sounded great to me. I told Pastor Yount a hundred times to try some new music once in a while. I think we ought to do it all the time."

Looking around, Tucker saw that each of the four men nodded, some more enthusiastically than others. So it seemed all agreed that the new sound was acceptable.

If it isn't the music, Tucker thought, *then what is it?*

Stan folded his hands in front of him and looked at Tucker. None of the others spoke; all cast furtive glances toward Stan.

Tucker remained quiet.

"Pastor Abbott, we didn't come to talk about the music."

Tucker waited.

"We came to talk about you. . .you and Annie Hamilton."

Tucker swallowed a gulp of coffee. "Oh" was his initial response.

And as he peered around the table, the only elder with eyes not partially or totally averted was Stan Gleason. And even Stan didn't appear totally comfortable.

Tucker put his coffee cup down. "Oh."

Twenty

None of the elders spoke for a minute. A couple of customers walked toward a table farther in the back. Stan watched them pass.

"We want to talk to you about Annie," Stan said again, as if he was making sure everyone knew the subject of tonight's meeting. "We need to talk about it."

Tucker's shoulders stiffened. "What about Annie?" he asked, keeping his words as even as he could, yet knowing he failed at keeping his voice from turning edgy.

Stan opened his hands and laid them flat on the table. "Tucker, all of us like you. We really like you."

"Thanks," Tucker replied.

"And we all like what you're doing with the services and all. The music may be louder than I would pick, and a lot newer, but my kids are excited about it. They actually want to come to church. I don't have to threaten them anymore. I like that a lot. You know how hard it's been with Stan Jr."

It wasn't the first time Tucker had been made aware of the strong feelings of Stan's children. His eighteen-year-old son, now sporting pink-tinged hair, had actually shown up at the youth group meeting last week and contributed, smiling. Tucker saw that as a huge step in the young man's spiritual journey.

"Really, Tucker, you're going great guns," Gary added. "I've talked to elders at other churches, and they say that when they lost a pastor—not just by them dying off, but quitting or retiring or whatever—the church really takes a big hit. That hasn't happened here. And that's a real good thing."

Tucker enjoyed the compliments, the first true assessment from the elders he had received.

"Well, truth be told," Stan continued, "you're the number one candidate for the position right now. You've been the number one candidate since the very beginning. All of us thought you were a sharp young fellow when you first came, and we think the same now."

"Thank you," Tucker said. He was trying not to anticipate what Stan was going to say next, trying not to develop his rebuttal to that imagined stance.

Kenny spoke up for the first time. "And we all like Annie, as well. We think she's 'good people.' Raising that child as her own. She's not a rich woman. We know that. And being a single parent is a big responsibility. We give her a lot of credit, Tucker, a whole lot of credit. And we love what she does for the pregnancy center."

"We do like her a lot," Herb added. "This has nothing to do with who she is and how she got that way. We're not here to judge at all. That's been her business, and we want to keep it that way."

"Her business?" Tucker asked.

Stan ignored the question. "You are seeing her, aren't you,

Tucker?" he asked. He didn't sound angry but stated the question as a matter of fact.

"Seeing?" Tucker asked. He knew what they meant, but he was delaying his response by a few seconds.

"Tucker, you know what we mean. I'm sure you do," Kenny replied.

"Dating. Becoming involved. Seeing each other. . .like in a relationship," Stan said, calmly clarifying his question.

They all waited for Tucker's response.

"Yes," Tucker said, not debating his reply. "Annie and I are seeing each other."

Stan looked at his fellow elders, then took a breath—a deep breath. He exhaled slowly, as if trying to compose his thoughts. "Tucker, you're our number one man for the job—our number one candidate. You know that."

"Yes," Tucker replied.

Stan looked at each elder again, then focused on Tucker. "But if you continue to see Annie, then I'm sure that the committee won't be able to recommend you to the congregation for a vote. They just won't be able to do it, no matter how much all of us like you and no matter how good a job you're doing."

Tucker tensed. Somehow he'd guessed that particular statement was going to be uttered by one of the elders as soon as he heard Stan mention Annie's name in public.

Stan opened his hands, almost in supplication. "Tucker, you have to believe us that it is not because of who Annie is or anything we think she has done. She *is* good people. I like her a lot. But the two of you? That's a whole other issue."

Kenny had been staring at the floor. He looked up. "Tucker, think of this: How would it look? What message will all of this send, especially to our young people? They are already pretty confused."

Tucker turned his body toward Kenny. "I think it would send the message that we are a church that understands grace."

Stan shook his head. "Well, maybe there is that take on the situation. Maybe a few people will feel that way. Maybe some of the younger people who have been coming to church. But not the old-timers. You know, the ones who are set in their ways. The age difference is just too big an issue for them. And I don't have to tell you where the bulk of the tithes come from. The old-timers, that's where."

Tucker turned back, trying his utmost to hold his anger from growing. "So it's about money?"

Gary spoke up. "No, it's not a money thing, although that may be an aspect of it. We just think that. . .with the age difference and all. . .that it's something that people are going to have a really hard time understanding."

"Age thing?" Tucker said softly.

Herb wiped his palm over his mouth. "Tucker, you're not blind or stupid. Annie is, what, fifteen years older than you?"

"It's ten years. That's all. Ten years."

"Well, that's a good many years. Plus with her having a child on her own and all."

Tucker almost snapped his reply but instead took a breath. Then he said more calmly, "The child was left in her care. She didn't give birth to an illegitimate child."

Stan spread his hands. "We know that, Tucker. But other people don't. They just see an older woman, not married, with a child. What would you think?"

"If she wasn't so much older, Tucker," Gary said, "there might be a chance. But being older *and* having a child that's not her own. . . . If you want to be a senior pastor, you have to consider these things."

"But. . ." Tucker was so angry inside now that it was hard to come back with a cogent and calm response.

"If you were forty, Tucker," Stan said, "and you were dating a young woman who was only twenty-five or so and who maybe was still in college—do you think people would smile and say that's fine?"

"Pastor Abbott," Herb said, "we don't want to do anything to hurt the church. We don't want to. And I know you don't want to. Things like this can split a church. It can. I have friends who say church fights have broken out over smaller things than this. We don't want that to happen."

Stan put his hand on Tucker's shoulder. "We love this church, Tucker. We know you do, too. We know you don't want to do anything that will hurt the people in this church."

Herb stood. "You have to think about this, Tucker. You really have to think about what you're doing here. Okay?"

Chance sat on the couch. Annie bustled about the dining room, cleaning and straightening.

"Is Tucker coming for dinner?" he called out.

"No, honey, we just had dinner, remember?"

"Oh, yeah," Chance replied. "I forgot."

Annie swept off the table with a dishcloth and gathered the crumbs in her hand. She dusted them together over the sink.

"Do we have dessert?" Chance shouted from the front room. "I don't think we had dessert, did we?"

Annie put her palms against the counter. She thoroughly disliked Chance shouting at her from two rooms away and had told him so often. "If you want something, find me rather than just shouting," she had said repeatedly.

"Do we have dessert?" Chance shouted again.

Annie took a deep breath and waited, hoping her instructions would come to his mind.

"Do we have dessert, Mom?" came the louder and higher-pitched scream.

She resisted the urge to run in there and clamp her hand over his mouth. She had learned that, with Chance, anger begot anger. But it took every ounce of her being to resist the impulse. It was times such as these that she so desired a break in the pressures of raising a child on her own. She so wanted someone else to discipline Chance—even once, at home—so the scoldings and reprimands and teaching didn't always have to come from her mouth.

She stepped into the doorway and glared at Chance. He responded with an uncomprehending look of incredulity.

"Well," he said after a bit, "do we have dessert?"

Annie closed her eyes and tried not to laugh—that bitter, angry laugh—in frustration.

"We always have dessert when Tucker is here," Chance claimed.

She took another deep breath. She tossed the dish towel onto the table, forgetting that she was carrying it with her, wringing it tight.

She could see that Chance was about to make some angry remark, but he saw the look on her face and remained cautiously silent instead.

"How come Tucker isn't here?" he asked.

She sat next to her son on the couch. She studied him for a long time before she answered, before she could answer. "Tucker won't be here every night, Chance. He has his own place, his own apartment."

Chance appeared as if he understood. "But it's just down the street. I like it when he's here."

Annie put her arm around her son. She didn't squeeze him tight like she wanted to do, because Chance was already trying to shrug off some of those hugs. She knew he loved the hugs, but she also knew he was already staking out some masculine territory that she knew so little about. One minute he would cuddle and coo in her arms, and the next he would stomp about the apartment, growling and barking and pushing aside any hint of affection from her.

"I like it, too," Annie admitted. "He's fun to be around, isn't he?"

Chance nodded and focused on the television. A Japanese animated cartoon was playing—one of several that Annie had seen and couldn't begin to comprehend. If asked, Chance would provide a detailed commentary on every facet of the show and the characters. Annie knew better than to ask.

Chance blinked and stared out the window. Annie knew that meant he was serious about something.

"Will Tucker ever be my daddy?"

The thought, the question, came so suddenly and so without warning that Annie was breathless. "I don't know, Chance," she whispered. "Why are you asking about this? Did somebody say something about it?"

Chance knew the words *marriage* and *babies* and *husband and wife,* but Annie was sure they were only words to him. He had no idea of their implications.

"No. Nobody said anything. But I don't have a daddy. Tucker likes to wrestle, and daddies like to wrestle with their little boys, right?"

"They do, Chance. They do," Annie replied, her throat tight.

"Well, I like to wrestle with him. And he lets me win sometimes. I like that."

Annie drew her son a bit tighter, and he allowed her to do so. "You like Tucker?"

"I do. He's nice. You laugh more when he's here. That's nice, too."

Annie thought for a minute. "I guess I do laugh more. Tucker can be so funny."

"Yeah, I like it when he tells stories about when he was a little boy."

Annie turned to face Chance and placed her hands on his shoulders. "Do you want Tucker to be your daddy?"

Chance looked back at his mother and chewed his bottom lip, just as Annie did when faced with a complex question. "Sure. And I think he wants to be my daddy, too."

His answer was simple, direct, and unequivocal. Annie's heart swelled at his childlike assurance.

"How do you know that, Chance?"

He shrugged. "I dunno. I just know. Like I can tell what he's thinking without him saying the words. You can just tell, Mom. You can just tell."

Annie chewed on her lip for a second. "Mommy is older than Tucker."

Chance shrugged again. "Is that bad?"

Annie shook her head. "No. But some people might think so."

Chance furrowed his brow. "But you say that we shouldn't care what people say if we do what Jesus wants. Does Jesus think it's bad?"

Annie inhaled deeply. "I don't think so, Chance. I think He just wants people to love each other—especially mommies and daddies."

Annie pulled Chance closer again and held him. He rested his head on her shoulder.

In a small voice he whispered, "Will you give Tucker my room?"

Annie smiled and kissed the top of his head. "No, Chance. Your room will always be your room."

She felt him sigh. "I guess it's okay, then."

⟨∞⟩

After he left Mason's Coffee Shop, Tucker didn't know where to go. He imagined that if this had been a movie, he would have marched into some tavern somewhere, tossed back a dozen whiskeys, throwing the last glass at the mirror behind the bar.

But he wouldn't do that. He had tasted whiskey once, at a party in college, and was so disturbed by the taste that he'd stopped at the twenty-four-hour pharmacy for some medicinal-tasting mouthwash to rid himself of its acrid coating.

Besides being a pastor, Tucker was not a man given to fits of anger. Instead he walked. Emotions—anger, hurt, dismay, bitterness—swept over him, changing like the skin on a chameleon faced with a dangerous enemy.

After a while, he found himself staring into an all-night donut shop. He didn't really like donuts, but the whiteness of the lights and the clean expanse of white countertop lured him inside.

A very petite woman—Indian, Tucker guessed—stood behind the counter.

"May I help you?"

The wall of donuts intimidated him. He could only shrug in helplessness. Then he pointed. "Two of those chocolate ones—the rectangles."

The woman looked at the wall of donuts and back to Tucker. Then she gently touched one tray of round chocolate donuts with a hopeful, quizzical look in her eyes.

"No, not those, the ones on top," Tucker said, realizing that it really didn't matter at all what he ate. In fact, he was not sure he was going to eat any of them. He was simply renting space at the counter for a few minutes.

The woman pointed again, this time to the right tray.

"Yes, two of those," he said, holding up two fingers.

"Coffee? You want coffee, too?"

Tucker opened his palms. "Sure. Cream, sugar."

Might as well go the whole way, he thought to himself. He took the cup and the crinkly bag of donuts to the counter and sat on a stool, facing the street. He unwrapped one of the donuts and took a bite without tasting it, having to remind himself to chew and swallow.

After a few minutes, both donuts were gone. But Tucker had no recollection of eating them.

"More coffee, sir?"

Tucker looked down. His cup was empty. "Sure."

As he stirred the creamer into his cup, his thoughts clarified. Everything that the elders said, everything that Pearl said, his mother, Mrs. Alvarez, Annie, Elizabeth, the waitress from Ev's— all mixed and swirled together. But in truth, all led to the same single question.

Do I choose Annie, or do I choose the church?

Tucker tapped the spoon on the side of the cup.

Those are the two choices I have—Annie and Chance or the pulpit.

He sipped at the coffee.

And after a moment, the answer came to him with such sudden clarity that he thought it might be audible, not only to him but to the lady behind the donut counter. He turned around and eyed her, but she stood impassively, staring out the front door to the street beyond. If she had heard anything, she hid her surprise well.

Tucker took a dollar out of his pocket, left it by the coffee cup, stood, and walked out of the door, into the dark street.

He knew what he had to do. He simply didn't want to do it.

Twenty-one

TUCKER DIDN'T CONSULT HIS WATCH, BUT he knew it was late. City traffic took on a different pace after midnight; it became more deliberate. He stood in the pink glow of the WASH-DRY-FOLD neon sign hanging in the front window of the Laundromat.

He glanced up at the windows in the dark front room. If a lamp had remained on, it meant Annie was awake. She was too frugal to waste electricity lighting an unoccupied room. Tucker took a deep breath and clamped his eyes shut. He tried to compose a quick prayer, a "God-please-help-me-now" sort of prayer, but found the words elusive, even for an abbreviated supplication.

He imagined Annie sitting there, alone on the couch in the dark. He saw her face, her hair, her lips, her hands.

He almost pressed the buzzer but did not.

Tucker didn't want to wait. There could be nothing to gain in hesitating until tomorrow. He wanted her to hear the news tonight. He worried that she might find out secondhand, through Pearl or some other well-meaning friend. He owed her that much, at least a face-to-face meeting, for certain.

But it would have to wait until tomorrow. He stepped back from her doorway and trudged toward his apartment. He saw a light snap on in the alcove of the duplex across the street. He stopped. It was the duplex where Mrs. Alvarez lived. The door opened and Mrs. Alvarez trundled outside, holding a tied plastic bag in her hand. She hurried down the steps and toward the alley and the garbage bin in the back.

Tucker hurried across the street.

"Pastor Abbott," she said as she stepped into the light, "you are out very late for a man of God."

Tucker nodded, then said softly, "Can we talk, Mrs. Alvarez?"

Tucker knew she could probably see the deep concern etched on his face. Her motherly instincts took over.

"You come in and talk to me. You can always talk to me."

"Your church elders meet on Sunday night?"

Tucker shook his head. "It wasn't a real meeting," he explained. "Not an official one, I mean. This was personal. Personal matters."

Mrs. Alvarez nodded imperceptibly.

"They are concerned," he said. "They know that Annie and I are seeing each other."

Mrs. Alvarez did not move.

"We haven't tried to keep it a secret." It was an obvious statement, small and nervous as a mouse. "They reminded me that I'm their number one candidate for the senior pastor position. They reminded me that everyone likes me at church and that if things go as they have been, I could almost expect to be offered the position."

The older woman listened intently.

"They asked me if I liked what I was doing—being the shepherd of this flock. I have had my doubts, but in the last few months, I've learned that I've never appreciated something so much in my life. I am growing to love being a pastor and serving God this way."

As he spoke, Mrs. Alvarez said nothing. He tried to figure out what she was thinking, but her eyes gave away nothing.

"I am beginning to think of myself as a pastor."

Tucker had stared at his hands as he spoke, wanting his words to be right and well placed.

"And you cannot be their pastor if you are with Annie?" Mrs. Alvarez replied.

"I don't think so," Tucker replied, his words flat, emotionless.

"What do you love more—this church or Annie?"

She was right, Tucker knew. It wasn't a choice between God and Annie. The response to that decision would be painful but easy. Tucker wasn't deciding on God. But to face a choice between a church and a woman? A church was simply a collection of God's people. It was not God.

Tucker opened his hands. "I don't know. Mrs. Alvarez, the elders told me what they thought about me, about me and Annie, about me and the church, and that it was inappropriate for Annie and me to be together—and all I could think of was how bleak and empty my life would be without her. But I also thought of how bleak my life would be without this church."

Tucker was on the verge of tears. Explaining to Mrs. Alvarez was like explaining a deep hurt to a grandmother.

"This is not an easy question, Pastor Abbott. In our church, such questions do not arise. Perhaps that is simpler."

"Mrs. Alvarez, I believe it's too late for me to consider that sort of change."

She smiled. "Pastor Abbott, I am in great concern for you. I love Annie like a daughter, and I have seen over the past months that she has blossomed. She smiles and is happy. Little Chance loves you, Pastor Abbott. Only a blind man would not see his face light up when you are together."

"I know. That makes this all so difficult."

Mrs. Alvarez placed her hand over Tucker's and squeezed. "Is there no other church in which you may serve God?"

"There are other churches," Tucker admitted. "But I love this church. I cannot see how I can leave it."

"You will know the right answer, Pastor Abbott. I am sure that the Father of us all will tell you what you must do. I am sure He will provide comfort for whatever pain that decision brings."

Tucker felt shaky. "Thank you, Mrs. Alvarez. I'm so thankful that you are my neighbor and that I know you."

She reached up and grabbed Tucker's neck, pulling him close. He expected the usual tweak and resulting bruise. Instead she kissed him loudly on the cheek.

"You are a good boy, Pastor Abbott. You will make the right decision. God will see to it that you make the right decision."

He stood to leave.

"You do have that confidence, don't you, Pastor Abbott?"

"I do," he replied, hoping his words convinced them both.

That night Tucker tossed in bed, unable for a long time to find sleep to free him from his troubles and to knit up his concerns.

When he awoke, the sunlight was streaming into his room. He sat up, disoriented. He never woke late, never after sunrise. He looked wildly about, a frantic churning in his stomach.

"Good grief—it's nearly eight," he said to himself, running his hand through his hair. He jumped up and was ready within ten minutes. He could get coffee and a roll on the way to church.

He had to see Annie this morning. Hurrying down his steps, he raced to her door and pressed the bell. There was no response. He pressed again. Nothing.

He leaned over and squinted in the window of the Laundromat. There was a man in the office. He hurried over. It was Carl Zietz.

"Howdy, Pastor Abbott," Carl said with great cheer. "You about to do your laundry this early?"

"No," Tucker replied. "I'm looking for Annie. Do you know where she is? I rang the bell and no one answered."

Carl scratched at his salt-and-pepper beard. "She's not here."

Tucker waited. Finally he was forced to ask, "Do you know where she went?"

Carl slowly shook his head. "Nope. She asked me last week if I could watch over things this Monday, and she didn't give me a why. Just asked if I could. And I could."

Tucker pushed his hair back and racked his brain, trying to recall if she had said anything at all about today.

School? Relatives? Galleries?

"When will she be back? Did she say when she'll return?"

Carl nodded. "She's picking Chance up at school and said she would be back at five."

Tucker thanked the old man and hurried out.

Now I have all day to obsess about what to tell her.

"You are prepared for the congregational meeting tonight, aren't you?" Pearl said calmly.

Tucker blanched. He was certain he did it better than his mother ever did. "Tonight? No. No, no. It's next week."

Pearl appeared more perturbed than normal. "Tucker, when do you decide to listen to people on the platform? Or do you just listen for your own voice?"

"I always listen."

Pearl sighed most unhappily. "Herb Miller was on the platform two weeks ago, right after New Year's. He said that, owing to a couple of elders heading out on cruises and seminars or something like that, the annual meeting that was supposed to be held the first week in February was being moved to tonight. It's been in the bulletin all month. Or perhaps you no longer read the bulletin since you no longer put it together."

Tucker had not done the bulletin in months, passing the job on to a very enthusiastic design student at Northwestern.

"I read it," he said, defending himself. "I must have overlooked that part, that's all."

Pearl offered a smug smile. "So you haven't done anything, have you?"

Tucker was about to defend himself again, then thought better of it.

"No," he admitted.

Pearl tapped her fingers on the desk. "Do you want to know what you have to do?"

Tucker looked blank, not being able to recall if the elders gave him any instructions about the meeting.

"You don't have to do anything, Tucker," she said with gloating humor. "It's a business meeting. They argue over spending forty dollars for a new fan for three hours; then everyone votes yes on the budget and goes home. They've done the same thing for the last four years. I don't see why this year should be any different."

Tucker exhaled with relief. "Does the pastor have to say or do anything?"

Pearl tilted her head. "Pastor Yount always opened and closed the meeting with prayer. I imagine you could handle that without too much preparation, right?"

"I think I could," Tucker said, relaxing.

"And Pastor Yount was always keen on speaking for five minutes at the beginning of the meeting. Saying hello, saying that we had a great year, thanks for coming, that sort of thing—then he just turned it over to the head elder and sat back."

"I think I could handle that."

As he turned to walk away, Pearl added, almost as an aside, "And there is a report due from the pastoral search committee. That might be of interest to you."

Tucker's stomach lurched. "How long do they have on the agenda?"

Pearl consulted the paper on her desk. "It says here 'five minutes.'"

Tucker relaxed again. How many fireworks could happen in five minutes?

"What do you mean she said eight o'clock?" Tucker said sharply into the phone. "This morning you said she would return at five."

If Carl was offended, it wasn't obvious in his slow, measured response. "Well, Pastor Abbott, she called no more than five minutes ago and said she was running very late and asked if I could deposit the day's money in the bank around the corner, then lock up the office and leave everything else open. She says she's done that before. I said I was uncomfortable with that and I would stay until seven thirty. That's when the business meeting starts. She said she would try and be back by then. If not, I was to make the deposit, lock the office, and she would be back shortly."

Tucker did not want all that information. He just needed to talk to Annie. "Did she say where she was?"

There was silence for a few more seconds; then Carl replied, "Well, no, she didn't. I didn't quite think to ask. Was that wrong, Pastor Abbott?"

Tucker sighed. "No, Carl. That's okay. But if she calls again, let her know that I really need to talk to her. Have her call me the second she calls, okay?"

"Will do, Pastor Abbott. You can count on me."

Tucker had hung up before the man had finished his sentence.

Herb Miller called the meeting to order, then turned to Tucker. Tucker stood on cue and delivered a short prayer, as well as a three-and-a-half-minute welcome to the hundred or so members who had braved the cold weather to attend.

Tucker had prepared his remarks to sound as casual as he could make them. He offered a small joke, a couple of statistics, and a call to face the future with joy and confidence.

He thought it stirring—especially since he had prepared the words on such short notice. Tucker always found it harder to be brief than expansive.

The meeting quickly headed to budget matters. Webster Avenue was not a rich church; nor did it have anything in the way of a comfortable endowment. Yet it almost always made budget, Stan had reminded the members; and this year, facing no major repairs or renovations, allowed the elders to expand the missions budget for the first time in five years.

From the back, from an older man Tucker did not recognize, came a series of pointed comments and questions on the amount of money budgeted for heating and cooling for the next year. Tucker smiled, remembering Pearl's remark about the fan.

The debate over finances did indeed take up the greater part of an hour and a half.

Tucker sat off to the side and tried not to form opinions on those who offered odd comments, hardly ever germane to the original argument.

It was nearing nine thirty when Stan stood up and presented the budget to a vote. Paper ballots were passed about, and nearly thirty more minutes passed as they were counted.

"Budget passed by 82 percent of the vote," Stan called out with some pride. "A sight better than the 57 percent of last year. Good job to all who participated."

He bent to confer with two elders sitting in the front row.

"We have a short report from the pastoral search committee," Stan announced. "Mary, would you like to speak for the committee and give the report?"

Mary nearly jumped to the podium. Her nervousness was obvious. She fussed with papers in a manila folder, taking several minutes to sort them out, rustling them loudly into the microphone. She apologized several times for the confusion.

Tucker heard Stan remark, "And she's the calm one on the committee."

Finally Mary smoothed out her paper jam and tapped at the microphone. "Is this on?" She gazed out over the crowd, spotted Tucker on the side, and smiled broadly.

She began by outlining what had occupied their time over the last several months—the survey, the demographic research, the job description, the interviews with staff and volunteers. She bent close to her notes, then leaned away, as if adjusting her eyes.

"Now you all know that we do our work independent of everyone else. Not even the elders know what we are doing. I mean, we let them know what we're doing, but they don't know all about it."

She offered a very nervous laugh, and a few in the audience joined her. "I'm sure you know what I mean."

She shuffled for another paper, then held it aloft with a smile, as if the congregation had been rooting for her to find it. "This is what I am looking for. I thought I left it at home."

She smoothed the handwritten note on the pulpit, then began to read:

> *I know that this may not be the prescribed process, but none of us on the committee made much sense over the process that is described in the constitution. We all think that attorneys wrote it just to confuse us—and, well, they did. So we didn't pay attention to what it said about the details. We decided that we would not do multiple candidates. Last time this happened, there were several pastors to consider. Even though we got Pastor Yount out of the deal, we didn't like that idea. So we began to think, "Who would be a logical first candidate? Who would be a good person to consider as a replacement for Pastor Yount?" And we didn't have to go very far. Our first candidate that we want the church to*

*consider—and there'll be an official timetable published in
our next bulletin—is none other than Pastor Tucker Abbott.*

Tucker was sure his heart came close to stopping. No one
expected this sort of announcement. He looked over at the elders
and saw that all of them wore the same shocked expressions.

Then he turned to the congregation. Many, if not all of them,
were smiling or nodding in agreement. He glanced at Mary, her
hands clutching the side of the pulpit.

"So, Pastor Abbott, what do you think?" Mary asked.

So much for a five-minute report avoiding fireworks, was the
first thought to jump into his mind. *What do I do? Do I say thank
you? Do I ask them to wait?*

And then, as if unfolding in slow motion, came an image so
sharp and clear that Tucker was certain the others in the room
could see it, as well.

Tucker pictured himself in thirty years, stepping out of a run-
down cottage by the side of a Wisconsin lake, with an arthritic
dog at his side, the scent of old fish and decaying leaves strong on
the air. Tucker, in this vision, looked about and saw no one, no
one at his side, no one in his life, no one except the dog and the
wind and his hollow, bitter memories of what might have been.

Tucker shook his head to clear the thoughts. He wasn't completely successful. But he stood anyhow. He turned to face the
congregation. "I'm. . .I'm so appreciative of this honor," he said,
his words hoarse. "Thank you. I love this church. I love the people in this church. I love your mission and your service to God."

Tucker stared down at his knuckles. He clenched the pew in
front of him. His knuckles turned white from the pressure. "But. . ."

He looked at Stan, who stood for a brief moment, then sat,
confused.

He looked at Mary, shuffling through papers, holding a pen as if to note Tucker's positive response.

He looked over the crowd, searching for Annie. She was not there.

"But. . .I cannot be a candidate for your senior pastor. I'm sorry. I'm so sorry."

He hardly heard the throb that coursed through the crowd after a silent thirty seconds.

Twenty-Two

"WHAT DO YOU MEAN YOU TOLD them that you can't be a candidate?"

"I told them the truth."

Annie stood in the doorway to Tucker's apartment. She was wearing old sweatpants and still had her bedroom slippers on. Her hair was pulled back into a wild ponytail. It was obvious that she had just heard the news.

"What do you mean you told them the truth?" she all but shouted.

Tucker had been awake most of the night. He hadn't gotten home until well after midnight. After he had declined the invitation, the business meeting floundered as small groups of members formed, broke apart, and re-formed into a loud buzzing of whispered conversations. Tucker had given only the barest of reasons for his turning down the church's consideration. He mentioned his involvement with Annie, a single woman ten years his senior, with a child, and the board's displeasure with that involvement.

None of Tucker's brief remarks could have been interpreted as bitter or angry but merely a restatement of the facts.

The small meetings and conversations escalated. Tucker left soon after making his declination, announcing his leaving to the elders, explaining that he was sure that the church had much talking to do and that his presence might be a hindrance to their unfettered discussion.

And after he left, he walked, first to the lake, then past the zoo, then home.

"Who told you, Annie?" Tucker asked.

Annie stood there, hands on her hips, angry. "Pearl called five minutes ago. I can't believe it, Tucker. We should have talked about this. I had no idea what our relationship might mean to your career."

Tucker took a deep breath. "Annie, all the while the elders were telling me about what they thought about me, about you and me, about me and the church—all the while they were saying that, I was only thinking about you. While they were saying that it was inappropriate for you and I to be together, all I could think of was how bleak and empty my life would be without you. All I could think of was trying to serve the Lord with a broken heart—and not a good broken heart, Annie. But a heart broken of bitterness and regret and a life wasted by being afraid. That's not the choice God gives us, Annie. He tells us to be brave and to seek after His heart. I am doing that. And I found you. He led me here. He led me to you and to Chance. The choice He gave me is not whether or not I will serve Him—I already know the answer to that question—but whether I will let love into my heart."

He moved closer to Annie and took her hands in his. Her hands trembled like an electric motor that had lost its center and was now wobbling and distracted. He pulled her closer to him.

"Annie, I told you all of that because what the elders said and what I had to do doesn't matter. I will serve God. And I will be with you. It is up to God to tell me that I can or cannot serve Him as senior pastor of this particular church. God will let me serve if He sees fit. If not, He will let me move on."

Annie sniffed again. Her voice was as slight as a breath. "But, Tucker, I can't ask you to give up so much. I can't."

"Annie, don't you see? If I give you up, I give up everything. God is not asking that question. I don't have to make that choice."

Annie looked away, out the window, toward the lake. "Tucker, I'm so much older. Maybe. . .maybe they are giving you godly advice. Maybe they're right."

Tucker's hands tightened around Annie's. "No. Maybe they mean well. Maybe the advice is well considered. But they do not know my heart. *I* didn't know my own heart for the longest time. I don't want to do the 'right' thing at the expense of what my heart longs for. I want to be married to you, Annie. There's nothing in the whole world that I want more. Nothing at all. I don't want to wake up in ten years, in twenty years, and realize that I have never followed my heart. I want to be married to you."

Annie's gaze was piercing. "Are you sure?"

"I've never been more sure of anything, ever."

Tears welled up in her eyes again, but now they were tears of joy, not sadness.

"You haven't answered me, Annie. Will you marry me?"

She didn't hesitate but whispered, "Yes," then embraced Tucker fiercely.

For that moment, as they stood together, the world disappeared.

Tucker could not recall being more content. The city all but grew silent as he held Annie in his arms. She remained still, her arms about him.

"Annie, you did say yes, didn't you?" Tucker asked.

She nodded against his chest. "I did."

"Are you sure?"

She looked up and took his hands in hers. "I am."

"Completely sure?"

"Tucker, are you trying to get me to change my answer?"

"No."

"That's good. I said yes because I love you. And because Chance loves you. I saw that in his eyes the first time you came for dinner. I didn't ask him about it. I didn't talk to anyone else about it. But I saw it. He saw a father when he saw you."

"Really?" Tucker asked.

"Really."

Annie squeezed his hands in hers. "And the age difference doesn't matter to you?"

"No. It doesn't. Besides, women live longer than men anyhow. It means we both die at the same time."

Annie scowled, then laughed. "Always the romantic, aren't you?"

"You know, Annie, after meeting with the elders on Sunday, I found myself, hours later, sitting in a donut shop over on Clyborne, debating what I had to do. I think I knew what my answer had to be from the very first moment the choice was presented to me—but I'm prone to being overanalytical. After hours of silent debate, I heard your name spoken aloud. I turned around, thinking it might have been the waitress, but I was alone. It was your name that was called out. I don't know if that was God's voice, but I am sure of you and Chance and how much I love you both."

Annie hugged him hard.

"When do we tell Chance?" Tucker asked.

Annie answered quickly. "We tell him now."

A few minutes later, Tucker stood by Chance's bed. Annie sat next to her son and gentled him awake. "Chance, we have something to tell you."

"What?" he replied, rubbing the sleep from his eyes.

Annie smoothed the hair off his forehead, and Chance moved his head to the side.

"I like it messy," he mumbled.

"Okay," Annie replied. "Chance, honey, you like Tucker, don't you?"

"Sure."

"Remember you asked once if he could stay here?"

"Uh-huh," he replied.

"Well, sweetie," Annie said as she took her son's hands in hers, "Tucker asked me if I wanted to be married to him. That would make him your daddy."

Chance's expression did not change. "What did you tell him?"

"I said yes, Chance. Are you okay with that?"

Chance almost nodded, then turned to face Tucker. "Mom says you can't have my bedroom."

Tucker tried his best not to smile. "That's okay with me, Chance. You can keep your room."

Chance extended his small hand. "You have to shake on it."

Tucker grasped his hand, and Chance pumped enthusiastically. "Deal?" Tucker asked.

"Deal," Chance replied, then turned to his mother. "Okay, Mom. It's okay with me."

Annie bent and gave him a quick kiss on the forehead. "Now

you go back to sleep, okay?"

"Okay."

They slipped out into the living room. It was barely past dawn. Annie looked at Tucker. "Now I guess. . .I guess. . .all we have to do is decide when." She hugged him again.

"And you have to call your parents," she added softly.

Tucker waited a moment, then replied, "Annie. . .could you call them?"

He fully expected Annie to punch his arm as her answer.

Tucker's phone was ringing as he walked back into his kitchen. It was Pearl.

"The elders want you at church this morning. At eight."

"I'll be there," he said, then added, "Pearl, I'm sorry for all of this. I really am."

Pearl's reply was unexpected. "You have nothing to be sorry about, Tucker. The elders were dead wrong in asking you to turn away from love. Dead wrong."

Tucker showered, shaved, and tried to get his thoughts in order. He vowed not to change his stance, regardless.

The elders were all seated in the unoccupied senior pastor's office. They nodded or murmured a quiet hello or good morning to Tucker as he took the empty seat at the far end of the table.

Stan spoke first, as was most often the case. "Pastor Abbott, we need to get a few cards on the table here."

Tucker faced him without comment.

"Last night. . .well, none of us knew what the search committee was planning to do. That was pretty obvious. Especially after our discussion at Mason's on Sunday. We were as surprised as you were. And none of us thought they would make that announcement in that public setting. I'm sure they had their reasons, but in light of everything, I'm sure they wish they could take it back."

Herb interrupted. "It's not that they made the wrong choice here, Pastor Abbott. They really do like you and want you to be a candidate. It's just that they picked the wrong venue for making it public."

Tucker nodded. "I understand. And I have to apologize, as well. To say I was surprised is an understatement. I hadn't considered it at all. I would have remained silent last night, but they were definitely waiting for me to give them a yes or a high sign or some positive response—and I just couldn't give them that. And to wait and tell them later would have meant all sorts of further problems. Maybe I should have waited, but that's water under the bridge now."

A soft chorus of agreement followed.

Stan spoke again. "We need to know if what you said last night is your final decision, Pastor Abbott."

"It is," Tucker said. "If the choice is between Annie and being considered for the senior pastor position of this church, I am choosing Annie. I will always serve God, but I will follow my heart when it comes to Annie."

There were fewer murmurs.

"Gentlemen," Tucker continued, "you will have to do what you think best for this church. I understand your mission. I understand that some choices are harder than others. This decision is hard—for all of us. I will understand if being with Annie will prevent me from serving this church. I truly will. There will be no hard feelings, and I will not try and dissuade people from acting as they feel God would have them act. When I assumed the role of associate pastor, I accepted the leadership of this church. And you men are my leaders. What you decide, I will abide. You have my solemn word on that."

Stan nodded. "That is what we wanted to hear, Pastor Abbott."

Tucker stood and excused himself from their meeting. "I know that you have many things to discuss, and that discussion would be better served if I am not in attendance."

He walked out, shut the door behind him, and walked past Pearl. She didn't say a word, yet Tucker saw the redness in her eyes and figured it had to come from crying.

Tucker tapped at the office window of the Laundromat. Annie looked up from the desk; and when she saw him, her eyes crinkled and her face lit up with a smile. He stepped inside and hugged her.

"You haven't changed your mind in the last couple of hours, have you?" he asked.

"No. And I will never change my mind, no matter how many times you ask."

They held each other for a long time.

"Was it a hard meeting?"

"No," he replied. "I left early to let them talk. Afterward, they asked me to stay on and preach, at least for two more months. I said yes. I didn't ask what they had decided to do long-term."

"Are you okay with that, Tucker?" Annie asked as she sat back down.

"I am," he replied. "I keep hearing what my old pastor told me that day on the lake. He said he thought that I was a special man and that he could see God's calling on my life. He said that he knew God had something special in store for me."

"I agree with him," Annie said. "You are special."

Tucker looked out over the washers and dryers. "But what he said next—that's what I remember most. He said everything in life for a Christian is a calling. He said I could serve God anywhere. He said that it doesn't have to be in a church."

Tucker stood at the pulpit. The church was as crowded as it had ever been. He was sure that some people just came to see if Tucker would mention what happened at the meeting. They were the kind of people who relished fireworks and the turmoil.

He was just as sure he would do nothing to feed that desire for turmoil and destruction. But he also knew that he had to address the issue.

"Friends," he said as he ended his sermon, "most of you know what transpired last Monday. I was asked to be a candidate for the position of senior pastor and I declined.

"Someone said this was just like when the Duke of Windsor abdicated the throne for Wallace Simpson, the woman he loved. But I realized that most of you—save for you history buffs out there—have no idea who Wallace Simpson was." He paused and smiled at the congregation. "Yes, Wallace is a woman, and, no, she is not a character on *The Simpsons*."

A light dusting of genuine laughter fell among the audience.

"I have asked Annie Hamilton to marry me. I am following my heart. I can do nothing else. I will serve God where He places me—that will never change. For those I have hurt or disappointed, I humbly apologize.

"God does not look at our afflictions, but our hearts. We are all broken vessels. That's how the light gets into us and shines from us. I love Annie. I love her son, Chance. I love all of you.

"This is the hardest choice I have ever made. Being with Annie is a choice that my heart and my head agree upon. The time at Webster Avenue Church is so dear to me, like a jewel worn by my heart. I love you all."

This time Tucker did not stand in the doorway after the service. Instead he hurried to his office and closed the door. He was not hiding but wanted to avoid making anyone feel uncomfortable. He could preach and do administrative work for a few months, and by then the embarrassment would fade.

Midway through the following week, Pearl stepped into his office. She seldom visited. She sat and crossed her legs. "Tucker, I don't know what the elders will do."

Tucker grinned. "That makes two of us." Then he added, "Do about what?"

Pearl leaned forward in a conspiratorial way. "About the phone calls and messages. People are saying, 'Who cares about a few years' difference in ages?' and 'Where in the Bible does it say that a man has to be a certain number of years older than his wife?' and 'We love Pastor Abbott—losing him would be a mistake.'"

Tucker waited. He was pleased that people liked him, but he abhorred starting any divisions within the body.

Pearl looked up hopefully at Tucker. "If they ask the elders, if they ask you, if they change their minds. . .will you stay?"

"I don't know, Pearl," he said thoughtfully. "After all that's been said. . ."

Pearl looked away as if she might cry. Tucker was sure she didn't want him to see that side of her.

Twenty-three

THE FIRST GREENING OF SPRING
lightened the air, filling the city with a hint of birth and of new
life. Tucker paced back and forth in the hall outside the sanctuary of the Webster Avenue Church. He was wearing a tuxedo, a
choice he had not wanted. But he had made the mistake when
talking to Chance, saying that "a man gets married in a tuxedo."
Chance had taken it to heart and would not rest until Tucker was
measured for a very nice—but very subdued—tuxedo.

Chance insisted that he would have one, too, so they rented a
second very small tuxedo.

Annie and Tucker had not invited that many guests. They
realized that to invite even a few chosen church people would
open the floodgates, and scores and scores would want to know
why they could not attend, as well.

Mrs. Alvarez and the widow ladies from the neighborhood
attended. Pearl was there. Tucker's roommate from seminary had
come, along with his wife, all the way from California. An uncle,

an aunt, a few close friends, and the pastor from the Presbyterian church nearby came to officiate.

Annie sent an invitation to her father, and he had sent a check with a note saying he would be out of town that weekend. If Annie was disappointed, she did not show it.

Tucker had phoned his parents with the news within days of their decision. Both his mother and father initially sounded pleased, but the conversation grew strained. A few days before the wedding, Tucker's father called. He said that Tucker's mother had come down with a very bad cold that might cause them to miss the ceremony.

Tucker graciously accepted their excuse.

The organist began playing. It was Tucker's cue to head to the front side door, where he and his roommate from seminary would enter and wait for Annie.

Just as Tucker was about to head around to the side entrance, the front door swung open. Outlined in the bright spring sunshine stood his mother and father. She was both anguished and relieved.

"It's not over, is it?" she cried.

Tucker could not have been more surprised. "No, Mom. We haven't started yet."

"Oh, thank the Lord. I am so sorry, Tucker. I was confused and I wasn't going to come because. . .oh, I don't know. Because I didn't think you were doing the right thing. I was hurt. I wanted to take it out on you. I came to my senses this morning, and Nathan drove like a madman to get here on time; then we got lost in the city, and. . .well, I'm just so happy that we're here. I get to see my baby get married."

Tucker embraced his mother. His father patted Tucker on the shoulder.

"We don't have much time. The organist has already started. I have to go."

His mother held his face in her hands, staring at the man's face that not so long ago was a child's. She lifted up on tiptoe and lovingly kissed his cheek. "I love you, Tucker," she said. "And I know I will love Annie and Chance, too."

Tucker, with tears in his eyes, hurried to the front office, where Chance was waiting.

"Let's go," Tucker said.

"Okay. . .Dad," Chance replied.

The word caught in Tucker's heart, a barb of delicious and overwhelming pleasure.

Tucker knew he would never be able to recall exactly what happened that day, his wedding day. He remembered Annie coming up the center aisle—a vision in white and pearls—with Chance. Tucker remembered his face hurting from smiling so much.

The Presbyterian pastor delivered his sermon, but Tucker had been so captured by the glow about Annie that he scarcely heard a single word. Not until the pastor said, "You may now kiss your bride," did Tucker become fully cognizant. He bent to Annie and kissed her gently, holding her in his arms. He only barely heard the applause.

"The time has come for us to celebrate," the pastor said. "I now present to you, for the first time, Tucker and Annie Abbott, husband and wife."

Applause greeted them again, and Chance joined his mother and new father in a hug. The family and friends in attendance applauded and cheered.

"What God has joined together," the pastor said solemnly, "let no man put asunder."

Tucker bent to his wife and whispered in her ear, "No man ever will, Annie. I will love you and Chance for the rest of my days."

And the small gathering of family and friends spilled off the platform and down the aisle and into the rest of Tucker, Annie, and Chance's lives.

ABOUT THE AUTHORS

Jim and Terri Kraus have been writing together for nearly a decade and have produced two fiction series: *Treasures of the Carribean* and *The Circle of Destiny*. They live in the Chicago area with their son, Elliot, and Petey the Cat. They love to travel as a family. . .except for Petey the Cat.

Terri worked as an interior designer for twenty years before becoming a mom. Besides writing, she is the women's ministries coordinator at their church, hosts a monthly book club, quilts, plays piano, and is studying Italian.

Jim is a senior vice president at Tyndale House Publishers. He loves riding his most recent toy—a black Vespa motor scooter. He teaches Sunday school, loves every kind of music, and finds the best time to plot out a new book is during his long nighttime walks.

You may write to Jim and Terri in care of Author Relations, Barbour Publishing, P.O. Box 719, Uhrichsville, Ohio 44683.

OTHER BOOKS BY JIM AND TERRI KRAUS

The Unfolding
The Choosing
   MacKenzie Street Series

The Price
The Treasure
The Promise
The Quest
   The Circle of Destiny Series

Pirates of the Heart
Passages of Gold
Journey to the Crimson Sea
   Treasures of the Caribbean Series

His Father Saw Him Coming by Jim Kraus
The Silence by Jim Kraus

ALSO AVAILABLE IN

ALSO AVAILABLE IN

Barbour Fiction

The Unfolding
by Jim and Terri Kraus

Annie Hamilton doesn't expect her life to change dramatically when she opens her modest home to a rootless and pregnant neighbor. But when the young woman abandons her newborn son, Annie summons her courage and decides to raise the baby as her own. All is well—until the day the birth mother returns to claim her child. Distraught, Annie searches for answers—and finds them in the most unlikely places. Can this path of darkness be the way that God unfolds his plan for her? This deeply moving story will open readers' eyes to the power of redeeming love—and the power of faith.

304 pages / 1-58660-859-2